Ouida

Frescoes etc.

dramatic sketches

Ouida

Frescoes etc.
dramatic sketches

ISBN/EAN: 9783337383404

Printed in Europe, USA, Canada, Australia, Japan

Cover: Foto ©Andreas Hilbeck / pixelio.de

More available books at **www.hansebooks.com**

ETC.

Dramatic Sketches

BY

OUIDA

A NEW EDITION

London

CHATTO & WINDUS, PICCADILLY

1885

CONTENTS.

FRESCOES

FRESCOES.

The Countess of Charterys, Milton Ernest, Berks, England, to the Hon. Henry Hollys, English Embassy, Rome, Italy (by telegram):—

'June 16, 1881.—Send me somebody to paint the ballroom.'

———

Mr. Hollys to Lady Charterys (ditto):—

'Be more explicit. Fresco, oils, gouache, panels, wood, satin, plaster?'

———

Lady Charterys to Mr. Hollys (ditto):—

'Fresco. But be quick about it. The P. and P. are coming.'

———

Mr. Hollys to Lady Charterys (writes):—

'My dear Esmée,—It is of no kind of use telegraphing; the thing can't be done like that. Surely even you, my dear, might know enough about art to be aware that you can't have a room painted in fresco as easily as you can put up a French wall-paper. Your ball-room is as big as the Colonnas' here. It will take a long time, and it will cost you a great deal if you have a true artist, and you can't employ a mere copyist ; I give even you credit for wishing for something original. When do you expect the P. and P.? I know the very man for your work, but I am not at all sure he would come, and you must understand that the time required would be considerable. Yours ever,' &c.

Lady Charterys (telegraphs):—

'Send the man. H.R.H. has not fixed visit.'

Mr. Hollys (writes):—

' My dear Cousin,—Allow me to observe that a man is not a packet of cigars to be sent by the parcels post. I told you that I was not sure the person I had in my eye would consent to take your work in hand. I have sounded him since then. I think he is not unwilling. He has true feeling, indeed absolute genius, but nobody knows him. In these Italian studios a man who is out of the common run may languish all his life undis-covered. Conventionality always gets to the front in these miserable and most vulgar days. You must understand that if he come over, your expenses will be very great: do you mind that? But I never knew you "mind that" yet; more's the pity. And another thing occurs to me, will it be quite proper? He is if not a young, well, not an old man, and exceedingly good-looking. I have my doubts about the proprieties of the thing; and whatever you do wrong they blame me for, you know that. I am, as ever, yours,' &c.

Lady Charterys (telegraphs):—

'Send him. Give him anything you like. Propriety? Tabby is always here.'

Mr. Hollys (writes):—

'My dear Esmée,—Owing to the fact that, in a hitherto incomplete state of civilisation, telegrams are unable to accomplish either punctuation or notes of interrogation, they remain slightly and regrettably incoherent. Besides which, they are very expensive. You disdain this, but I don't. You are a very rich woman, my dear Esmée. I am a very poor man. I am shocked at you calling your most illustrious and reverend grandmother, Tabby; but it is, I suppose, an incurably bad habit; you have so many equally bad, equally incurable. It is a hideous social responsibility to be your trustee, and I am always at a total loss to imagine why I was selected for the extreme but perilous honour. Thank God, you are of age! To revert to your ballroom. Why I have selected this artist—by the way, his name is Renzo—is because I have seen a little out-of-the-way mountain church high above Subiaco that he has decorated for the sheer love of art; the village which holds the church is his birthplace, his *paese*. The frescoes (as you say in your English jargon) of that little place are a marvel. If you knew anything of art I could descant on them for twenty sheets; but as you do not, it would be waste of time. Suffice it, representing the life of S. Julian Ospitador, they recall Botticelli by their colouring, and Michael Angelo by their vigour and anatomy. You will say, I am no niggard in praise; no, I am not, when I am pleased, which is, you will admit, sufficiently rare. I have since visited Renzo's studio in the Via Magutta, and there seen things of a most admirable fancy and delicacy in design, which, joined to the fact that he prefers fresco to any other medium, has suggested to me that he is the person most adapted to make your ballroom worthy of the rest of Milton Ernest. You yourself, I believe, are wedded to Paris upholstery, and are actually inclined to turn your grand old house into a copy of the last new hotel in the Avenue de Villiers with a picturesque jumble inside it of *turqueries* and *pochades*. Do not mistake me; I adore Japan and Turkey in their place, and I can stand a few " *impressionistes* "; but they are none of them in their place in a Tudor mansion which has its own old oak and elm furniture; nor do the contents of a Teheran bazaar look well emptied out in a hall that possesses panels carved by Grinling Gibbons. To return once more to Renzo. I need not say that one would hardly ask him to decorate a ballroom, even yours, if he were a famous artist; as it is, he is quite unknown, and poor in the actual unromantic sense of that unpleasant word. At first he would not hear of it, and appeared inclined to be angered and offended; but little by little I soothed him down, and persuaded him that it would be a very delightful thing to decorate a ballroom fifty feet long with the Decamerone or the Orlando stories, absolutely at his own fancy and pleasure. I have assured him he shall have his own apartments, and be undisturbed. He leaves by the steamer from Civita Vecchia to-morrow, and, I suppose, will be at Milton Ernest some time next week. I hope you will be tolerably civil to him, for the man is a gentleman. As for paying him, he insists that you shall give him what you please when the work is finished, as they used to do in the palaces and monasteries to Sodoma or Domenichino. This may be Italian astuteness, for when people say "what you please," they expect you to give them three times what they would have the impudence to ask. Or it may be pride; it strikes me that Messer Renzo has this mark of race, though in his mountain village they said he was the nameless son of a poor girl who died and left him to be brought up by the parish-priest. But this does not concern you. You, with your peculiar views of art, will scarcely consider him higher than your groom, not to be named beside your tailor. You take tea with your tailor, don't you? One word more. Be sure you interfere as little as your nature will permit you to do with the designs and decisions of the Roman artist I send you. He will know what he is about, and you won't. Remember that in fresco no one can tell the effect till the colouring is seen as a whole. I believe it was Sir Joshua Reynolds who said that what is unfinished should never be shown to children or simpletons. You are neither the one nor the other; but—you are opinionated and capricious. Let the dash represent the very biggest of big big D's if by so doing it can impress this fact upon you with anything like the force that is to be desired.

'P.S.—I imagine Renzo is coming by sea, because he hadn't money enough to come by land ; and he would not take any payment in advance, though it will be simply justice for you to repay eventually all his expenses. Take care your plaster is sound.'

Lady Charterys (telegraphs) :—

'All right. How you do prose ! Street has seen to the plaster. Thanks very much.'

*Leonis Renzo, Milton Ernest, Berks, England, to the
Reverend Don Eccellino Ferraris, Florinella-sopra-
Subiaco, per Roma, Regno d'Italia :—*

'Reverend and dear Father, —It rains so much this
day that I can do nothing on the walls, so I consecrate
my leisure morning to you   The country of England
appears to me to possess the peculiarity of looking very
green and very wet, also of having houses at every yard :
it has a terribly over-furnished look, and a disagreeable
quantity of chimneys; the chimneys are very tall,
belonging to furnaces or factories; the houses are very
low.   London looks provincial and commonplace after
Rome, and you fancy you will knock the roofs off
with your hat.   The atmosphere of the great city
appears of the thickness of polenta : you feel inclined
to cut it with a spoon.   However, I did not stay in
London, but came on straightway to Berkshire, after
going to the National Gallery for an hour, where they
have some very valuable pictures which ought never to
have left our shores.

'Berkshire is, it appears, the name of a province
It is very pretty and wooded, and reminds me of parts
of Umbria, only here there are no mountains to lend
majesty to the repose ; and the sky is a woolly-looking,
low-hanging, pallid sky, in lieu of our glorious arch of
radiant light.   At a little village station, there were
waiting for me a vehicle on very high wheels, and a

most admirably made horse. It seems the station exists on purpose for this house of Milton Ernest. A couple of miles of wooded lane brought me to the park-gates; it was now evening. I was shown at once to my rooms, and a bath had been made ready, and they served me dinner. I saw and heard of nobody but a servant, who appeared to have the special office of waiting on me, and who happily knew a little French. In the morning I was shown the ballroom by a grave and stately functionary, and told that her ladyship would receive me at noon in the library. So she did. I had figured to myself a person of middle age, but she is evidently quite young. She made me a little frigid nod of her head, and asked if I had all I wanted; and without waiting for an answer, inquired how Mr. Hollys was, who is, it seems, a cousin and sort of guardian of hers; and, equally without waiting for reply, said that I had better begin at once, as she was in a hurry about it; and she hoped I would make it Corot-like and pretty, and drape the figures, because people were so silly. Then she nodded again, and I understood that the interview was over.

'Pardon my incoherent gossip. I am more skilled with brushes than with pens, as you know; but you forgive all blunders and errors of your godson. This is a very grand and gloomy place; I admire it, but it oppresses me ; its terraces are too sombre under their heavy cedar and elm boughs, its fine hall is too dark with all its armour and its oak, yet I would not alter it; it is all in character and unison with the deep green of the landscape, and the grey tones of the atmosphere. What is not in character with it is its mistress. Figure to yourself a very lovely woman, very whimsical, very frivolous, very disdainful, always dressed in the extreme of the *mode*, even when she has a breakfast gown on; she is young, but she darkens her eyes, I suspect her of even tingeing her hair, and she is altogether absolutely artificial. She is not married, as I supposed her to be from her title; she inherited the title, it appears, from her mother, who, on the death of the late Earl Charterys, took it, she being his sister, in default of male heirs. This can be done, it seems, with some English titles; with some it cannot. The result here has been to invest a foolish and mindless woman with an enormous property and an immense power, of which she is as indifferent as a child would be of a jewelled reliquary. You must not suppose from this that I have seen much of her, but she is one of whom it is easy to take a diagnosis at a glance.

'The house is full of gay people. It seems that the season of London is just at its close. All these gay people tormented me endlessly the first few days; it was impossible to work, and their suggestions drove me mad; I told Lady Charterys at once that if I were not allowed to lock the ballroom doors I would pack up my colour-box and go back to Italy without even sketching the cartoons. She assented with a very bad grace, and I am now at peace. I have nothing otherwise to complain of; I have my rooms to myself, and they bring me things to eat, very good things, and French wines, and on the whole treat me much as if I were a prisoner of state. I perceive, however, that the servants have a natural contempt for me; I am on a level in their minds with the glazier who comes to mend the ballroom windows. It does not matter.

'This ballroom is by the way a fine room inside, grandly proportioned, with a domed ceiling.

'I have been greatly disappointed not to find, as I hoped to find, wet plaster; in a newly-built room one might reasonably expect to have it so. But instead I find the walls prepared in the usual modern manner; that is, dry, and slightly granulated. I did not conceal my dislike for this process, and told the lady straightway that she could not possibly look for any luminosity or transparency in fresco upon walls cemented by this method, and that she might as well have had large panels done in oil. She did not appear to care. I imagine she only has these walls painted in fresco because somebody has told her it is *chic*.

'Architecturally the ballroom is a frightful mistake; it has been built out by Lady Charterys within the last year; and it suits an old Tudor hall as well as a huge gilded glass vase, made yesterday at Baccarat, would suit a Cellini mounting. However, though incongruous, its proportions are fine; and happily, without, it is hidden from view by heavy plantations, so that it does not mar the general site of the hall, and will no doubt be a great gain to the gaiety-loving châtelaine when she fills her house as it is filled at this moment. There was only a long and narrow gallery to dance in before this erection.

'The house itself is fine, though it seems low after our palaces. The lackeys in it are legion, and the quantity of flowers is extraordinary. The picture-gallery here does not contain much that is old. They are proud of their Venetian Masters, but most of these are obviously copies: I offended a very stately old dame, who is here, by saying so ; she is grandmother to my patroness; the mother, that is, of her father, who is dead. The name of this terrible lady is Cairnwrath of Oswestry; I copy this appalling title from one of her cards. If I be on a level with the glaziers in the eyes of the household, I am on a level with the upholsterer in the eyes of this terrible old dowager, whose regard is enough to change one into stone.

'The greyness of the light troubles me ; it con-fuses me ; they say it is always like this. I confess I was happier painting in your holy little church, my beloved Father ; I think I should not have come here at all, if I had made any money during the winter and spring ; but I was absolutely *a secco*, and hunger was very near. A good skipper I knew offered me a free passage from Civita Vecchia to the port of London, and I sold a little bronze figure I had to obtain enough to come on from the coast here and buy the necessary colours. In this house, of course, I want no money:

it is well, as I have none. Perhaps the servants smell out that. They are always very like rats who know where the grain lies.

'I salute you, beloved and reverend Father. I am now going out in the park: everything is very wet and dark, but it all smells very sweetly, and the deer are beautiful creatures; I am never tired of watching their graceful postures, of studying their elegant groups. To think that a woman should own them who never looks at them!'

———

Lady Charterys, Milton Ernest, to Mr. Hollys,
Rome:—

'Your Renzo is here, and seems to me to do nothing except stand and stare at huge sketches of grey paper, making lines on them now and then with a bit of chalk. He has turned me out of the ballroom, insisted on being allowed to lock the doors and work by himself; I am sure he only smokes and sleeps. He would be intolerable if he were not so handsome. He is wonderfully handsome! I remember a picture of Cæsar Borgia just like him.'

———

Mr. Hollys, Rome, to Lady Charterys, Milton
Ernest:—

'There are three portraits of the famous Cesare, each one utterly unlike the other two; which do you mean? I see no resemblance to any. I told you he must be let alone; no man can do anything worth doing if he has a lot of frivolous people pestering him at his elbows. Of course he has to think out his cartoons. You can't alter a line once done in fresco. If you make a mistake, there it is for ever, in a fine and complete allegory of life. You fine ladies understand neither tempera nor trouble.'

Lady Charterys, Milton Ernest, to Mr. Hollys, Rome :—

'I mean Columbus, not the Borgia man; we have a portrait of Columbus in the gallery. Your "friend" is an interesting person and speaks exquisite French. It seems he studied for years in Paris: I suppose his method is all right, but he is awfully slow about it. If the P. and P. do come, I shall have fluted satin put up *pro tem.* He told us yesterday all about his own life; he was quite a poor lad, no shoes and stockings, running wild on the hills and living on chestnuts. It seems the priest brought him up, but I don't see how the priest, who is quite a poor old man—though a noble, he says —gave him that grand air he has got. I asked him to dinner, and he said he had no evening clothes, and I suggested his getting them; and he made me quite a scene, but very grandly, not a bit violently, something like Chastelard, you know. Have all the Italians that

sort of manner ? Does it come of their having been
Romans once ? You know what I mean ; the *civis
Romanus*, isn't it ?   I mean what Lord Palmerston and
dear Lord Beaconsfield used to make every Englishman
look like abroad.'

*Mr. Hollys, Rome, to Lady Charterys, Milton
Ernest :—*

'There are few Italians who are pure Romans; a
great number are Latins, a great number Greeks, quantities Jews, and some by descent Lydians, and otherwise
Oriental.   It seems to me ominous that you find
Renzo so interesting, that you are even induced to cast
a backward, if wandering, glance over the field of
history.   Chastelard seems to me, too, an allusion
fraught with untold tragedies.   I shall be truly sorry if
I have sent this unfortunate man into peril, for he has
the soul of a great artist in him.   I ought to have
known that Diane Chasseresse will not spare even a
dog, when she has for the moment no lions.'

*Lady Charterys, Milton Ernest, to Mr. Hollys,
Rome :—*

'Was Diana such a muff that she shot her *dog* ?   I
thought nobody but cockneys and volunteers ever did
that.   As for there being nobody else, there are in the

house at this moment, Bertie Prendergast, Lord Colchester, Colonel Royallieu, the Comte de Surennes, and
Dickie Haward, and Vic. will be here in a week.'

---

*Mr. Hollys, Rome, to Lady Charterys, Milton
Ernest:—*

'You know very well what I mean, and I wish you
would marry Vic. and have done with it; he would suit
you down to the ground, and he wouldn't let you make
victims of poor painters. *Are* you getting flirting with
my Roman ? Don't.'

---

*Lady Charterys, Milton Ernest, to Mr. Hollys,
Rome :—*

'Does one flirt with a Trastevere beggar because he
looks picturesque on the steps? Do have more sense
and decency.'

---

*Mr. Hollys, Rome, to Lady Charterys, Milton
Ernest :—*

'Your reply is in bad style, and is besides only an
équivoque. Can't you go away on a round of visits
and leave the frescoes to be painted in peace ?'

*Leonis Renzo, Milton Ernest, to Don Eccellino
Ferraris, Florinella-sopra-Subiaco :—*

'It gives me pleasure that my tedious scrawls en-
liven your solitude, dearest and best friend, to whom I
owe the eternal debt of that knowledge, which, if it be
not power, is at least compensation and consolation. I
enclose you a sketch of this house, and another of my
patroness. Patroness is not a pretty word, but since it
is the one that describes the actual position—*lasciam-
molo star!*

'This sketch of her does not, I must confess, do her
full justice. She is handsomer than a few lines of red
chalk can describe. She has the wondrous blush-rose
skin of the best English beauty. I did not think it
could be natural; she would be a perfectly beautiful
woman if her mouth were not so contemptuous; and
her eyes have a dissatisfied, impatient expression: it is
the look of a cynic, not of a young Venus. I presume
she has had the misfortune to want nothing all her life,
which is almost as bad as wanting everything. I told
her that in Italy, if I had a few coppers to buy me some
bread and fruit, and enough colours to paint with, I was
quite content with my *déjeuner de soleil.* She yawned
a little, and said she had been a whole winter in Italy:
she did not care about it: she had liked the riding on
the Campagna. She supposed when people could paint,
it must amuse them very much, for she knew Leighton

and Millais, and they never seemed to be bored anywhere; but she did not see how it could be amusing to
do it, though it looked pretty when it was done. She
said she knew women went in for art, it was all the
rage just now; but she did not go in for it herself;
they only made dowdies of themselves; your *couturière*
knows what you ought to put on much better than you
do. Though others had come up, she still thought
Worth better than any of them; when you had a
costume of his, and a bonnet of Mrs. Brown's, you were
sure to be all right. Then she opened her large, contemptuous eyes, and seemed surprised that I did not
reply! I never even heard of Mrs. Brown!

'It is plain that she thinks me a barbarian, and I
confess I think her one—only occupied like a true
savage with her beads and feathers! the whole domain
of art, and fancy, and meditation closed to her; her
whole horizon bounded by a blank vast wall of egotism
and inanity!

'The manners of the English ladies do not strike me
as at all distinguished; they want grace; they have an
unpleasant, ill-bred manner of staring; they are very
eager to secure the attention of their men; all this I
observe when they come into the ballroom, for they
quite forget I am there. They are very fashionable, no
doubt—I know enough of Paris to know that—but they
are exaggerated in all they say and do; they have not
the charm of the Parisienne nor the grace of our own
women; not even the grace of one of our peasant girls,

drawing water at Arricia, or carrying seaweed at Amalfi.

'*À propos* of peasant girls, I have chosen the pastorals of Theocritus for the frescoes. They will offer beautiful scenes. Miladi asked me on the second day how long it would take to complete them. I said, a year at least; perhaps two years. She was astonished and angry, and said, in return, that she wanted it finished by the autumn. I thereon told her very simply that she did not seem to me to require an artist, she should summon a decorator; there were plenty in London and Paris. She seemed still more astonished, and went away. I wrote a little note requesting permission to leave. She wrote me another little note begging me to go on with my labours, and take two years if necessary; the Prince and Princess had postponed their visit. I did not know what princes she meant, but I consented to stay. I would not deny that I am glad to stay. The work interests me, and after years of privation, and solitude, and struggle with adverse fortune, there is a repose in the mere freedom from taking thought for the morrow, which is welcome. I can give myself up absolutely to my creations; I have no need to think how the studio rent can be paid, or whether I shall have *soldi* enough for a cup of coffee in the morning. What I have envied to rich people has always been their independence.

'One night, quite late, she sent me a verbal invitation to dine with her and her guests, and the formidable grandmamma. I did not think the method of invitation courteous : I sent back a verbal message that I was occupied. Next day she sent word that she wished to see me. I could do no less than wait upon her. She was in her own room, a pretty little niche of Saxe china and Louis XVI. lacquered white wood. She put out her hand for the first time, and seemed surprised that I bowed over it, only touching the tips of the fingers. "Why would you not come to us last night ? " she said abruptly : she has always that abrupt manner, they all have it, and yet, despite it, they never appear to be in earnest. I answered her that I had been occupied, and added that I did not know it was English etiquette to invite people by word of mouth, through a servant. She coloured a little at that. " Oh ! I beg your pardon ; I did not mean anything rude," she said in her quick fashion; " I thought you might be bored, all alone. We are all horribly bored, though I have my people in relays ; only eight days each set of them. Well, will you dine to-night, now *I* ask you ? " What could I say ? I said the truth, that I had no evening clothes, no *bout de toilette* of any kind. It might be a humiliating confession, but it did not seem so to me. She looked astonished : " But why don't you telegraph for your things ? " she asked. " Surely your man could send you all you want from Rome." I laughed outright. " Miladi," I said to her, " I possess no servant in Rome, and no fine clothes in Rome or elsewhere. I supposed that Signor Hollys would have told you I am a man so poor that I might very possibly have died of sheer hunger if you had not summoned me for this commission of your ballroom." She grew now quite pale; I saw then that she does not paint her face; the blush-rose colour is natural. "I am very sorry," she murmured, quite as if the fault was hers; "but why shouldn't I—why shouldn't you—you can have any quantity of money that you like." "Pardon me, miladi," I said to her—and I suppose I looked angry—"I want for nothing here; I merely told you the truth, because unless I had given you the true reason I should have seemed callous to your courtesy. But you cannot buy clothes for me as you do for all those powdered gentlemen in your antechambers. When the frescoes are finished, you can pay for them what you and your friends think is just. If you do not like them, you will give me nothing; I shall always remain your debtor for a year of happy labour, and of immunity from the little daily burdens and cares which accompany poverty." She said not a word, and I bowed very low and left the room, going out of it backwards.

'I confess that I felt I had had the best of the argument, the *beau rôle* of the interview; which, for a man who is in the ridiculous position of being without an evening coat, is not a small triumph. It seemed to me that miladi had never before conceived the possibility of any one existing without a valet and a suit of dress-clothes. There is one thing quite certain, she from this moment cannot confuse me with the *fournisseur*; the *fournisseur*, whether of Bond Street, the Boulevards, or the Graben, would never be without the correct conventional garments of broadcloth. For me a white serge jacket in summer, and an old brown velvet one in winter, is enough,— if they would only be so good as to wear for ever!'

Lady Hermione Latrobe, Milton Ernest, Berks, to her Sister, Lady Dorothy Latrobe, The Cloisters, by Chesterfield, Derbyshire:—

' My dear Doll,—There is quite too lovely a creature here, a Roman; Esmée has got him over to do the ballroom. You never saw anything so handsome; he is like a picture. And to think we were in Rome all winter, and never saw him! He is entirely *farouche*, and by so much the more fetching. He locks himself up in the ballroom, he is doing frescoes there; and if we happen to meet him in the woods or anywhere he bows and runs away. He seems to think us a set of wild animals. I got Esmée to send for him the other evening, but he wouldn't show. It is too tiresome. Tabby says we all are too ready to treat him as if he were a gentleman; but I assure you he looks like one, and artists nowadays go everywhere and actors too, and at the Duke's, last week, there were two of them, and all they thought about was mussel-dredging down in the bay. It's dull down here, on account of Tabby, she's such a grim old cat ; but Esmée's awfully sweet and precious, and I wish you'd come ; and Henry Hollys, I think, is coming, and he is always good fun, though he scolds. Last night, as the Roman wouldn't come to us, Esmée had five-o'clock tea taken into the ballroom ; he couldn't run away, and he was *charming* ; told us such delicious Italian stories, and sang such lovely Italian songs, just, you know, as we heard them sing going by in the moonlight in Naples, four or five of them, with their guitars, don't you remember ? And then he sketched us all, and gave us the sketches ; and I wished he had wanted to keep mine, but I dare say he can do me from memory. I thought Italians were always *so* courteous, but he isn't one bit : he says awfully rude things, and Esmée got quite angry, but he has a pretty way of saying them too. He seemed glad when we went away, and I heard him lock the door again while we were still in the corridor. He is to be here a whole year; all by himself in the winter; but winter's a long way off; Esmée will go to Cannes, and means to have the " Glaucus " to cruise about in. If she asks me to go with her, I shall.

' Your affectionate

' Hermie.'

*Leonis Renzo, Milton Ernest, to Don Eccellino
Ferraris, Florinella-sopra-Subiaco :—*

'The days go on the same with me, my honoured
and dear friend. My work progresses as well as the
uncertainty of the weather will permit; I have contented myself with six of the cartoons necessary, the
remaining twelve are still in a vague, incomplete state.
When I shut my eyes I see our little village, its oak
and chestnut woods, its crags of grey marble and red
porphyry, its strips of maize, and narrow ledges of
pumpkins, and beans that need such coaxing to grow
up on high upon the rocks; I see the bright, brown
buxom maidens with their breasts heaving under their
linen bodices, and the earthen jar balanced on their
heads; and my heart with my thoughts flies back to
you all, and I would that I were sitting with you in
your little porch, under the great pine-trees, with the
night coming on, so violet, so silvery, so clear and
bright, with the glow-worms shining like little stars
under the cabbage and pumpkin leaves. If I had only
enough to live on, without being a charge to you, never
would I have been thoughtless enough to leave our
sweet, silent Sabine hills.

'I find the luxury of this place grow oppressive to
me : these endless carpets, that muffle every sound;
these endless servants, who anticipate every simplest
wish or act ; these interminable meals, which need the

appetite of Gargantua; this perpetual panorama of idle people, who are always changing, and yet look to me always the same—for there is such a likeness and sameness in fashion!—of all these I grow sick and impatient. One may lock oneself up alone as one will, there is no escaping the influence of the atmosphere of a house. A house has its moral atmosphere as a city has. Then, the climate has a great heaviness in it. I feel only half awake; I am not myself without the full sunlight. And these eternal clouds are not grand as our tempest clouds are; broken through with shafts of light, hurled by the wind, piled one on another in masses like mountain crests, taking at evening on them, when the storm is spent, a pomp of colour, a glory unutterable. No; they are more like great dusky feather-beds; indeed, I hear they are called woolpacks by the country people; they merely present a monotonous, uninteresting expanse of vapour; and as for a sunset, I have not seen one since I saw Civita Vecchia fade away in the evening glow. You will say I have nostalgia! Of course I have; but that does not prevent me from appreciating the rich and pastoral calm of this country, the strength, and courage, and good-humour of the people, the cleanliness of their homes, and the excellence of their agriculture. If we could transplant some of these qualities into Italy, in especial the cleanliness, we should truly have a paradise. I am ungrateful to murmur at my exile, for I have that greatest of all blessings, work that is sympathetic and delightful to me.

' After a few attempts at suggestion and interference on the part of my employer, which I rejected more peremptorily than was perhaps polite or politic, she has left me entirely to my own choice of theme and treatment. I imagine her cousin has written to her that I am an intractable. I have been here three months now: all this time there has been a constant succession of visitors; but these of course do not affect my own life; I have no more to do with them than if I were in the moon. They have, or rather she has, however, made a custom of coming into the ballroom for their six o'clock tea, whenever they are in the house at that hour, and there have been several rainy afternoons. I cannot be churlish; she is distinctly in her own right. Hearing that I am something of a musician she has had an Erard placed in the big bare room for my use; I cannot of course refuse to play to her when she comes. Indeed, I confess these afternoon hours break the monotony of my days, and I find myself stupidly disappointed when they are all out riding or driving, or playing their lawn-tennis, which is a boisterous, meaningless game, that I do not admire, when I chance to cross their court, as I walk in the gardens. She has ceased to complain of the frescoes being slowly executed; I think she begins to take interest in seeing the blank plaster bloom like the rose.

' I have had some charming fair children out of the village as models; but they are *only* fair, they have no soul in their round blue eyes, and I could only model their little healthy bodies, and well-fed white limbs: their faces said nothing. Now, Italian children have the whole Inferno and Paradiso in their wonderful eyes: why is it? They have no soul *in* them, or at least they will sell any they have for a copper centime to buy salt fish or a tomato. But the look is there, and it is not here; is it because we have to much tragedy in our blood, in our soil? Or is it because the Italian mothers still croon strophes of Tasso and Metastasio over the sleeping babies? The English mothers certainly do not sing snatches of Shakespeare or Herrick over the cradles of these pretty, flaxen, pink-cheeked creatures.

'I have been translating Tasso, impromptu, into French, to miladi and her ladies; it seems poor stuff in Gallic dress, yet something of its spirit and sweetness seems to reach them. As I read to them by one of the great windows of what they call my prison-house, with the green lawns and huge cedars outside, and these lovely women around me, I must look like a story-teller of the Decamerone, and I believe that the grim dowager-grandmother disapproves me. She has no power, however, to make the rod of her displeasure felt, for miladi is her own mistress, and, having passed her majority, owes obedience to none. I imagine she was spoilt all her life. She expects impossibilities, and can be both insolent and capricious. Yet I think her nature is good, though so incrusted with the habit of the world that the actual heart in her can seldom beat as it might do.

'There is here, at this moment, a certain Duke of Kingslynn, who is one of her multitude of distant cousins, and with whom it is desired by her world in general that she should marry herself. He is a good-natured, amiable young man, whom she calls Vic., and torments incessantly; he has a certain simple dignity which makes him look manly when she teases him, but he is not her equal in intelligence, and if she take him it will only be because she wishes to be Duchess of Kingslynn, and they will both be extremely sorry for the step all their lives long, even if nothing worse ensue. I wish I could set her before you with any sort of distinctness. I enclose another sketch of her; I made it last evening. She had been riding, and got down at the foot of what they call the yew terrace, and I was standing there, as the terrace is just outside the ballroom. She took off the little melon-hat she wore, and leaned against the balustrade, and talked a little while; the redness of sunset was shining beyond the heavy bows of the yews; it touched her hair with its warmth and made her eyes look quite soft. I shall make a large picture from the sketch when all this is over, and I am back in Florinella, and ask myself if it be not a dream that ever I painted frescoes in England. I dare say she will have married 'Vic.' by that time, and have begun to break his heart and spoil his temper.

'She and those she calls her house party came to the ballroom last afternoon. I cannot always lock out the mistress of it, and was forced to open the door, with

some reluctance I confess. There was a quantity of
people, male and female. They talked English, of
which of course I understood nothing; I wished I had
had an Italian with me to have been able to return them
their bad manners in kind. Bad manners seem to me
the *rôle* of these English patricians. I threw my cigar
away when they entered, but the men, and one or two
of the women, smoked the whole time. They had tea
brought them, and the men drank the most horrible
compound produced by mixing together brandy and a
kind of soda-water, and the women ate an incredible
quantity of all kinds of hot cakes, sweet cakes, candied
fruits, chocolates, and sugared dainties, and I knew that
their dinner-bell would ring at eight! I wonder that
they do not all die of indigestion.

'When they at last remembered my existence, they
spoke to me in French. Then I confess a silly
demon of vanity entered into me. I perceived they
thought me of no more account than one of my lay
figures; and I said to myself, " Leonis Renzo, at the
Grecco and in Paris they have always said you could
talk : try now, and see if you cannot make these soda-
water drinkers look stupid." So I did try. French
seemed to them all the same thing as English, except
to a very dull being called Lord Colchester, who has a
glass screwed in his eye. I exerted myself to entertain
them, and succeeded; soon I had the pleasure to see
that the cake eaters paid no more attention to the soda-
water drinkers; I told them stories; I sang them

songs, for I had my old lute in the room; I played them a concerto of Schubert and some of the "Mose in Egitto." Then I permitted myself to satirise them, and the only drawback to this diversion was that they were too stupid to be easily stung. Only miladi—my patroness—got angry, and defended her order and their ways of life, which I confess appear to me to be of a silliness and a selfishness that are degrading in view of the immense interests that the world contains. *Basta!* I had my turn and used it. They stayed till their dressing-bell rung, and they no more regarded me as a lay figure. Just before they left me, I spoke at some length, in Latin, to a man whom they call Bertie, who appears a scholar and a good critic of art. He looked surprised, but he answered me in the same tongue. Miladi called out, "Oh! you must not speak Latin, you know we don't know it." "Miladi," I said to her, "you know it as well as I know your English." At that she was a little conscience-stricken and ashamed. "A very good lesson, neatly given," said this gentleman, whom they call Bertie, to me.

'I hope they will not take the habit of having their tea here; it is not good to get angry, and it deprives me of the sunset hours' light, and there is so little light in this country at the best of times. Dear and reverend Father in God, I salute you lovingly.'

*Mr. Hollys, Rome, to Lady Charterys, Milton
Ernest:—*

'I should be only too delighted to come over, as
you so kindly propose; but there is not a ghost of a
chance of my getting away till September, and I shall
hardly get ten days then. You know I am left in
charge, and the dear chief won't be back from his
stag-hunting till November. It is awfully hot and
fearfully dull. I make a *scappata* to the villas of
friends, and sleep very often up at Frascati or Tivoli,
or down at Palo at Odescalchi's place; but one can't
get out of the leaden weight of the intolerable heat,
unless one goes fairly off up into the mountains, and I
can't leave the Chancellerie long enough to do that:
there are complications, and the Chambers may re-
assemble any moment. By the way, you have not
mentioned either Renzo or the frescoes for ages: this
strikes me as much more ominous than if you indited
me reams in his praise. Have you already wholly
destroyed him? Has he taken an over-dose of chloral
in despair, and been interred under the yews of Milton
Ernest? If you do not answer me, I shall write and
ask your grandmother. I shall have the truth from
her.'

Lady Charterys, Milton Ernest, to Mr. Hollys,
Rome:—

'You will have the truth, my dear Harry, from me,
though your absurdity scarcely deserves it. Your *envoi*
is perfectly well, and the walls are getting covered, in
outline he calls it, for the most part; but it looks very
well and will have a very good effect. The music-
gallery he proposes to do in *graffiti*, whatever that may
be; but I have obeyed you to the letter, and never
interfered with him. He is left entirely to his own
devices; he thinks lawn-tennis ungraceful and senseless,
so he can't be asked even to join in that. Now and
then, once a week perhaps, we visit the ballroom; and
then he sings a little, or plays, or reads some Italian
poem very nicely. He really does sing very well; I
wonder he didn't go on the stage like Capoul. Vic. has
taken quite a fancy to him, which is droll enough, for
they can't say more than six words to each other; you
know Vic.'s Eton French, which ought to be so good,
but isn't, and only just lets him understand naughty
operettas, and order supper at Bignon's. Nobody knew
he could ride; but the other day, just as all the horses
came round, Souchong (you remember her?) got loose
and tore away; he was down in the home wood as
Souchong dashed through it, and he actually stopped
her, mounted her, and, after she had torn away with
him, literally over bush and briar, for three miles, got

her well in hand, and brought her in as quiet as a lamb, just when we all supposed she had broken her back in a ditch.'

————

Mr. Hollys (on a post-card) :—

'Charming lady's hack, Souchong, but who was the hero ?   Surely you knew Vic. could ride ?'

————

Lady Charterys (on a post-card) :—

'Who was to suppose an Italian could ride ?   I thought they were like Frenchmen.'

————

Mr. Hollys (on a post-card) :—

'Forgive my stupidity, I stand corrected.   Correct, in return, your narrow insular prejudices.   Italians can ride ; but they won't, as a rule, feed their horses. As for Frenchmen—ever been to the Chantilly hunt or seen 'em go after boars in Ardennes ?   It is very generous of Vic. to like the *dompteur* of Souchong.'

————

Lady Charterys (on a post-card) :—

'I am afraid the heat makes you dream strange things.   Souchong isn't the least bit *domptée*, and is quite as ready to bite her groom and kick her loose-box into splinters as ever she was.'

Mr. Hollys (on a post-card) :—

'Only one word more: Do you mean to go to Cowes as usual?—*or—not*?'

Lady Charterys (on a post-card) :—

'Why on earth do you underline such a simple inquiry?—No; I do not; because the "Glaucus" is being recoppered, and I want her in the winter.'

Mr. Hollys (on a post-card) :—

'Thanks: I could have predicted the answer. In winter will you want the "Glaucus" cabin done in *graffito*? I have just seen the man I *ought* to have sent you for the ballroom: he is sixty-eight, decorated, diploma'd, a "professore," an "alunno" of a thousand artistic societies, and an ass; but if the frescoes would have suffered, at least their designer would not, and I am quite sure he would not have translated Tasso or done Mazeppa on Souchong. But one is always wise too late.'

Lady Charterys (on a post-card) :—

'I have sent a paragraph to the society papers to inform the world of the distressing fact that the Hon. H. Hollys, so well known, &c., &c., &c., has gone mad in consequence of a severe sunstroke incurred in the discharge of his diplomatic duties in Rome.'

Mr. Hollys, Rome, to the Duke of Kingslynn, Milton Ernest :—

'Dear Vic.,—You know you have my very best wishes, but what can I do? I never had much influence over her, and at a distance I have none. If I wrote to her urging your desires she would probably be utterly set against you : women are "kittle cattle," and she more "kittle" than most. I am quite sure she has great regard for you, and I don't think anybody would be as good a husband for her as yourself, setting altogether aside the tremendous advantages that have made you the hope of Belgravia ever since you left the Eton Eight. You will acquit me of any such snobbish meaning. It is your loyalty of nature, your honesty of purpose, your knowledge of her character, and your own sweet and patient temper, which would make of you so good a companion of her life. But if you feel she doesn't care for you, do not give her the chance of

making you wretched. Esmée is a woman who if she
loved a man might be made anything of by him; but
if she have only for you a good-natured, indifferent,
friendly regard, then—then, my dear Vic.—cut your
heart out with a knife now, rather than spoil all your
glorious future by wedding yourself to eternal disappointment, carking jealousy, and perfectly useless
devotion. I have said my say, and you must do as you
please. I wish you would tell me one thing: Have I
done any harm by sending Renzo over to Milton
Ernest? I thought she might bother him in his
painting, but it never occurred to me that she would
notice the man any more than she does the doctor or
the curate. To be sure, I underrated the attraction of
a perfectly regular profile and eyes of onyx.'

*The Duke of Kingslynn, Milton Ernest, to
Mr. Hollys, Rome :—*

'No; I don't think there's anything of that sort
with the Italian fellow. He seems wrapped up in his
painting. I like him myself; though he is tremendously good-looking, he is neither a fool nor a flirt. He
seems an awfully proud beggar, and keeps out of our
way as much as he can. I think he is down on his
luck; I suppose you know all about him. I should
hope she'd as soon think of the groom. I mean to try,
despite all you say, though I dare say you are right.

She doesn't care much for me, but then if she don't care for anybody else we shall get along. I can't put it in good language, nor look at her as the Italian fellow does when he reads 'em Tasso, but I would do anything in the world for her, and I don't believe there's another woman in the world like her. If she's got any faults I don't see 'em; she may treat me like dirty boots if she like, I shall love her as long as I live.'

Mr. Hollys, Rome, to the Duke of Kingslynn, Milton Ernest :—

'The true thing, my dear Vic., but women never care for it, and they do treat it like dirty boots; and I'm afraid they prefer to be treated like dirty boots themselves—odd taste, but they are made so. I have heard much of the acute vision of love; but love has always seemed to me to be as blind as ten thousand bats, and yours is no exception in cecity. However, God bless you, dear lad ; go in and win if you can.'

The Duke of Kingslynn, Milton Ernest, to Mr. Hollys, Rome (telegraphs) :—

' I've had my innings and I've made the duck's egg. She won't hear of it for a minute. I shall go and pot elephants. I am now off. Write me at London.'

Mr. Hollys, Rome, to the Duke of Kingslynn, Guards Club, London (telegraphs):—

'So awfully sorry. Don't go to Africa; you don't want knife-handles. Go to Benderrick or Glenlochrie, and I will try and run over to you for a week up there.'

———

The Duke of Kingslynn, Guards Club, London, to Mr. Hollys, Rome (telegraphs):—

'Very well. Young birds very strong this year. It's no more the Roman than it's the stable boy. You are a good fellow, for you don't say "I told you so." Come to Glenlochrie.'

———

Leonis Renzo, Milton Ernest, to Don Eccellino Ferraris, Florinella-sopra-Subiaco (writes):—

'I have received yours with delight and gratitude, dear Father. I am concerned poor Tessa's son has drawn a bad number; conscription is hard on men, but harder still on women. All the news of Florinella is charming to me; when I read your lines I hear the cicala boom, the maize stalks rustle, the *chiu* hoot; I smell the wild honeysuckle hedges, and the lemon flowers, and the dewy summer dawns; when I go into the conservatories here I think I am walking in the

Italian fields at sunrise in mid-June! Miladi is almost alone in the house now; her guests are gone, with the exception of a pretty child called the Lady Hermione, and of course the stately grandmamma. The young Duke has been refused by miladi, so the head-gardener tells me; he talks French well, and I have won his heart by suggesting to him your simple cure for his vines, which are afflicted in their hot-houses with what we call *criptommia.* It is certain the young Duke is gone. He behaved like a true gentleman to me; but he would never have suited miladi, who laughed at him, and plagued him, and plainly thought him a simpleton, which I do not think he was, though he had that awkward manner and clipped bald speech which seems to characterise these young Englishmen of rank so far as I can judge by what I have seen in this house.

'Miladi and the young Hermione still come and have their tea in the ballroom, and they are beginning really to understand something of Tasso. Miladi has a beautiful mezzo-soprano voice, but I do not like the way she has been taught to sing: it is too florid and not sufficiently accurate. She lets me correct her with great good humour, and I teach her to use my old mandoline. These lessons, however, will not last much longer, for she is going away on a round of visits to grand houses; she says there is nothing so tiresome. It seems it is the shooting season in Scotland already, and she is going there first, and she says the men are all out after game the whole day, and

stupid as sheep or as stones from fatigue all the evening.
These very great people seem to me to create for themselves a very vast number of tiresome duties. They all
hate what they are doing, and yet they all continue to
do it. If I were one of them I should surprise them
by leading my own life.

'Could you post to me that large sketch book full
of my illustrations to the Morgante Maggiore which I
did when I was quite a youth? Miladi would like to
see it. She has been much amused with the poem,
which of course I put into decent dress for presentation
to a lady. I have been telling her how our peasantry
still make dramas of these old poems, and play them
on our hills with no scenery save nature's. She is not
hard to interest when her fancy is taken; she has mind,
too, only it is frittered away. I confess I am touched
by the change there has come in her since she repented
of wounding me about the dress-clothes. She is full
of delicacy and courtesy. She cannot altogether alter
the certain *brusquerie* of her manner which seems
natural to her, but she tempers it. She does not in
any way resent home truths that I venture to tell her,
and she seems now to be mortified at her own ignorance of artistic and intellectual matters, whereas at
first she was proud of it. Her education has evidently
been much neglected, though she tells me that from
four years old to seventeen she was in the hands of
governesses of all nations, and crammed with all manner
of science she calls rubbish. At seventeen she went

into the world, and all her studies were over. That is five years ago.

'She listens with great pleasure whenever I speak of you and tell her of your vast attainments, your infinite goodness, and of the home that you have made so dear to me in that little hermitage-like house of yours with dear old Marta to scold me if I let the chickens get amongst the flower-beds or the thrushes steal the olives. When shall I see the dear little whitewashed presbytery again?

'I am now painting Hylas drawn down into the water by the nymphs. I have no fit model for Hylas; I must go to my memory of the slender-limbed brown lads plunging in our hill streams for fish. To give the night too, the beautiful night that mariners love, I must go also to my home memories. The moon seems to me always to dwindle when she rises here. The stars, when they are visible, which is but two nights out of five, seem pale and small. Oh, to see once more Venus burning with her translucent light above the dark brows of Soracte or the snows of the Leonessa!'

Don Eccellino Ferraris, Florinella-sopra-Subiaco, to Leonis Renzo, Milton Ernest:—

'I have despatched the book as you desire, my beloved son. I sent it down to Subiaco by Ammaro, so that I trust it will reach you by the post thence in

safety. It delights me that so far away our humble
dwelling and our little hamlet still keep a hold upon
your heartstrings. Nowhere, my dear son, will you
have warmer welcome than here; whenever again your
steps shall bring you up our narrow mountain path, you
will bring joy with you. Marta grows very old; but
not too old, she bids me say, to love you. May I, your
oldest friend, presume on one word of caution? You
take a natural interest in your English hostess. Be
heedful that it grow not too strong an interest. My
mind misgives me when you tell one of those music
lessons, those readings of our poets. No doubt you are
of as great an interest to this great lady ; but since she
is a great lady and you are a man as proud as poor,
there can be little to be hoped for from this intimacy,
and surely its enjoyment is one fraught with peril.
Forgive me if I hint this, and attribute my timidity to
that which is always timorous—a great affection. God
be with you !'

*Leonis Renzo, Milton Ernest, to Don Eccellino
Ferraris, Florinella-sopra-Subiaco :—*

' Dear and reverend Father,—Be not afraid; I have
a triple armour of poverty, art, and pride, however mis-
placed pride may be in one born as I was. She is
lovely; and interests me, I admit, if by mere force of
contrast betwixt the obvious faults of her character and
its potential powers for good. Her intense but uncon-

scious selfishness and her possible greatness of nature, were higher emotions ever to touch her, make a psychological study quite out of the common. This sounds very abstract and didactic; but it is this contrast which interests me, nothing more. However, even this will soon cease to be near me. She leaves here as I told you: it is doubtful whether she returns at all before going to the Riviera for winter.

'It seems they go on from one house to another until a whole autumn can be passed in this series of *viavai*. It appears to me that they are always as much *en scène* as if they were on the stage itself. It is an endless round of dressing, dining, trifling, talking; as I have come to understand it through the photography of her conversation, it seems to me the most vapid existence possible, but she assures me it has its excitements. She says that when once you are *dans le train* you could never lead any other kind of life. I am grateful that I shall never have the chance to be *dans le train* myself!

'Be easy on the score of my danger; I have a triple armour, I say, in my poverty, in my pride, in my art. Long ago I loved the woman in Paris that I told you of one summer night sitting in your little ·porch with the great golden round moon coming up through purple clouds over the eastern mountains. She died, and, what was worse, was worthless. Love-madness and I have parted company for evermore; and I shall be lonely as any hermit in this great house all through the windy English autumn and the darksome English winter. If only there be light enough to paint by, I shall be content.

'I am now painting the Burial of Daphnis. I have no models amongst these burly husbandmen and rheumatic labourers, but I have memories—so many memories—of lithe, light limbs, of brown leaping forms, of ox-drawn harvest-wains, of rythmic dances under the arching olive boughs, of naked figures supple as river reeds, drawing water with the pole as in the days of Daphnis; in so much we are so little changed in Italy since the years of Theocritus. Ah, dear and best friend, be sure of this, my heart is too much with Italy to wander elsewhere in any folly. Besides, be also sure that if I have grown higher in miladi's estimation than the *fournisseur*, I am no more than a secretary or a teacher in her eyes, at best a Rizzio to whom this haughtier queen would hardly drop a glove or give pity with a look. But I want neither glove nor pity; I shall be quite content if, when she shall see her ballroom finished, she shall smile—and bid me go. *A rivederci*, beloved and true friend!'

Mr. Hollys, Glenlochrie, Argyllshire, to the Countess of Charterys, Milton Ernest (telegraphs):—

'Why don't you come to Drumdries? They are all furious, and I shall not see you at all, for I am only away for two weeks.'

*Lady Charterys, Milton Ernest, to Mr. Hollys,
Glenlochrie (writes) :—*

'I'm too sorry, dear Harry, not to see *you*, but I really can't stand Drumdries. When I accepted to come I could not tell that poor Kingslynn would be close by on his own moor. I thought he was going to kill elephants in Africa or India. I should be quite afraid to stir a step outside the gates there for fear of meeting him; he bores me so unutterably. I know as well as you do that he is a dear, good little boy; he never does anything naughty except when he's in Paris, where it is conceded to all British virtue to go about in slippers; but I can't marry him, even to be one of the dozen Duchesses of Great Britain and Ireland, which all my friends are unanimous in declaring is the only thing worth living for in this world. I am quite content as I am. Yes, I am going on a lot of visits very soon, but not just yet. I have Hermione here; she is rather taken with one of our neighbours, John Herbert of Wardell; he is only just come home from endless travels, and if they like one another there would be nothing for anybody to say against it, for though they are only baronets, the Wardell family counts back ages before that.'

Mr. Hollys, Glenlochrie, to Lady Charterys, Milton Ernest :—

'That is it, is it? Hermione and Jack Herbert, and you and——, a pretty *partie carrée!* Well, there's nothing to say, as you justly observe, against *Herbert.*'

———

Mr. Hollys, Glenlochrie, to the Dowager Lady Cairn wrath of Othwestry, Milton Ernest :—

'Dear Aunt,—Pray pardon me, but can't you make Esmée keep her engagements and go to other houses if she won't come to Drumdries? It begins to look very odd. If she won't go out, get a lot of people down. For heaven's sake break up the thing somehow. I would come myself, but must be back in Rome in sixty hours.'

———

Dowager Lady Cairnwrath of Othwestry, Milton Ernest, to Mr. Hollys, Glenlochrie :—

'My dear Henry,—No one can be so painfully sensitive as myself to the lamentable imprudences (I might almost employ a stronger word) of my granddaughter, Lady Charterys. But I can do nothing ; she is entirely independent, and you know of old her headstrong self-will. She does not go to Cowes ; she does not go to any of her friends' houses ; I confess with humiliation that I believe she remains at home because she finds a most lamentable attraction in the society of the Roman artist whom you deemed proper to send here. There is of course no absolute indiscretion committed; even Esmée has sufficient respect for my presence to make that impossible. But there are very great irregularities, a most reprehensible degree of intimacy. She actually asked this person to dine with us; he had good sense and feeling enough to refuse; but this will indicate to you the footing on which she treats him. He teaches her Italian and corrects her singing; you know to what this sort of thing is invariably a prelude. Of course you could not imagine that Esmée could so far forget herself as to make a companion of a young man sent to paint her ballroom, but it is very unfortunate that you could not find some one at least middle-aged and less good-looking than this person is. The whole matter is painful to me, and scandalous to a degree which I cannot describe. I am entirely at a loss what to do. Were it any one else I should at once leave a house in which I have ceased to have any influence, but I cannot of course be the first to ruin my granddaughter's reputation by such a step. I foresaw that some miserable complication would ensue from this ridiculous idea of having an Italian over to paint the ballroom; if it had been put in the hands of good decorators they would have done all that was needed, and Esmée would not have entered it until the walls were completed. You may be sure that I

have exhausted all possible arguments in the endeavour
to persuade her of the great and irreparable injury
which will fall on her by her familiarity with a foreigner of whom even you admit you know nothing,
except that he painted the altar of a Roman Catholic
church in some village. But I regret to say that I
produced no impression; at first she laughed and said
there was no harm in learning Italian; at the end of
my repeated counsels she hinted to me bluntly that
Milton Ernest was hers and that the manor-house at
Staines was mine; of course she meant to suggest that
I should go there! Cannot you and Lord Llandudno,
as her trustees, interfere?

'P.S. It is impossible to ask people down when
Esmée would not speak to them if they came; and she
would not if they were asked in despite of her.'

---

*Mr. Hollys, Rome, to the Dowager Lady Cairnwrath,
Milton Ernest :—*

'Dear Aunt,—I am quite too sorry and can't forgive
myself for being such an ass. But as Esmée has never
before spent three months out of the twelve at Milton,
how on earth could I tell this mischief would come on?
I am afraid Lord Llandudno and I have no jurisdiction
except over the property. We have no right to dictate
to her about asking a painter to dinner. In point of
fact, we both ask painters to dinner ourselves. You

think painters are sweeps, but indeed the world has changed its mind about these things ; I think she might ask him to dinner, but I am quite with you in thinking that for her to flirt with him is a hideous enormity. Besides, it is rough on the poor wretch himself, since nothing can come of it, for when she's tired of Tasso and the mandoline she'll forget he exists in twenty-four hours, and expect him to take five hundred pounds for his frescoes and be grateful. I don't fancy you need worry yourself seriously, though I can entirely understand how annoying it all is to you, and I wish to heaven I had never found out Renzo's studio. It was hard enough to find, for it was up a hundred and ninety-five stairs, precipitous and pitch dark, and it had a pumpkin tied to a string for a knocker.'

Dowager Lady Cairnwrath of Oihwestry, Milton Ernest, to Mr. Hollys, Rome.

' I am unhappily aware, my dear Henry, that your world now-a-days thinks all social distinctions unnecessary and all serious considerations pedantry. At the same time, if Lord Llandudno do ask painters to dinner he would be the last man to allow one of his daughters to marry one of them, and I now solemnly warn you that I consider it quite possible that my granddaughter Esmée might in her madness and furious obstinacy throw herself away on this man. It is time, I think you will allow, for a *conseil de famille* on this most terrible dilemma.'

———

Mr. Hollys, Rome, to Dowager Lady Cairnwrath
of Othwestry, Milton Ernest :—

'But there are no *conseils de famille* in England. What on earth shall we do?'

———

Dowager Lady Cairnwrath of Othwestry, to
Mr. Hollys (telegraphs) : - -

'Cannot you get his Ministers in Rome to order him home? What use are extradition treaties?'

———

Mr. Hollys to Dowager Lady Cairnwrath of
Othwestry (telegraphs) :—

'But if he have done nothing wrong how can we demand his extradition? I am at my wits' end. I'll write to Llandudno. I am sure he will run down to Milton.'

———

Dowager Lady Cairnwrath of Othwestry to
Mr. Hollys (telegraphs) :—

'I shall be happy to see Lord Llandudno, and I imagine Lady Charterys can scarcely turn her back on her own trustee.   But be so good as to remember that it was *not* Lord Llandudno who sent this person here.'

---

*Lord Llandudno, Milton Ernest, to Hon. H. Hollys,
Rome :—*

' Dear Harry,—I came down here as you asked me; I made a pretext out of the Monmouthshire leases. On my life I don't see what I can do.   I think Tabby's fears have run away with her judgment.   If Esmée is sweet on your Roman friend, she conceals it remarkably well.   I like the man myself: he is a gentleman, and he has out-and-out talent.   He will make a superb thing of the ballroom: his designs are worthy a Parthenon.   It seems the fellow reads Italian with her, and is correcting her style of singing and showing her the tricks of the mandoline, and all this goes on at tea-time in the ballroom ; she lets him be quite quiet till five o'clock.   I told Lady Cairnwrath (*who raves*) that I thought we did better to leave Esmée alone ; she is not a baby, and she gets her back up very soon, and really to suggest to her that she can't be decently civil to a person, who is doing things for her worthy of Domenichino, without compromising herself, or meaning to make a fool of herself about him, seems to me to be going very near the wind ; I never do favour saying things to women that a man would knock you down for if you tried 'em on with him.   Interference, I always believe, is the very hind-hoof of the devil.   She is not the sort of woman for imprudences: it will be much more like her to amuse herself with the fellow while the novelty lasts, and then write him a cheque and forget his existence. She's as proud as blazes, and never would let herself down. It was a mistake having him in the house perhaps: he might have lived in the village; but I don't think it matters. If she don't move before, she'll go to Cannes. I wish with you that she'd take poor Vic., but I can't see a chance of it. Little Hermie Latrobe is here and going on with Herbert of Wardell till all's blue. Tabby will have it that your friend's an adventurer, a schemer, all the rest of it, and that he has all kinds of dark conspiracies to compromise Esmée and drive her up in a corner to marry him. But all this is moonshine. The man strikes me as a thorough gentleman. He hangs back whenever Esmée wants him to come out of his painting-room. They talk French, and I am not A 1 at French, but as far as I can make out they quarrel a good deal. Hermione knows all they say, but she's a sly little mouse when she chooses. At all events, I'm quite sure interference wouldn't do any good; if you try to ride Esmée with a gag-bit she flings you a cropper at once; just like my daughters.—Truly yours, dear Hollys,   LLANDUDNO.

'P.S. Tabby's always for the gag-bit! What a time the defunct C. of O. must have had of it, and how glad he must be of those eternal shades, where the bothered are at rest! *But if she join him when she dies?!!!!*'

Mr. Hollys to Lord Llandudno:-

'Dear Llandudno,– So many thanks! you relieve my mind tremendously. The venerable C. of O. always foresees a conflagration of the universe whenever anybody strikes a match, especially if it's struck on the *wrong box.* Renzo is a gentleman, I am sure; there's such old patrician blood in so many of those fellows even when they're not very sure where they come from originally. I quite agree with you about riding with a light hand. Pray forgive a scrawl; I have to write a report on the quantities of jute and other similar articles used in this country during each year, which really and truly is only consular work. Nobody at F O. in the least wants to know this, and nobody will ever read the report; it will be safely pigeonholed for fifty years and then be burnt, still unread; but duty is duty, even when the thermometer is at 45 R. in the shade, and it is the twentieth day of August which finds your wretched friend in the Urbs—Eternal City it is no more: it is all going; pounded into dust under tramway cars and the modern builder's hods of stucco. We are in an age in which nothing is sacred. I expect they will get chopping at the palm of Augustus. Ever yours,' &c.

Leonis Renzo, Milton Ernest, to Don Eccellino Ferraris, Florinella-sopra-Subiaco :—

'Best beloved Father and Friend,—Your kindly fears for my peace may be at rest. Miladi is gone; they say she will not return till the spring. A week or two ago, there arrived on a visit here an English lord, with a name I cannot remember, and could not spell if I did. He was one of her *tutori*; only now that she is of age to be her own mistress, his powers of jurisdiction only extend to her property. In England it appears the property is always the first care. It is so fenced up and tied about in favour of people unborn that nobody ever seems thoroughly to enjoy it: but I am by no means sure that this self-denial is not the cause of the nation's great prosperity and solidarity.

'I think she is sorry to go. She seems interested in the studies that I have persuaded her to take up; she is beginning to understand what good singing is; I suppose her professors were too intent in making them agreeable to a young Countess with two hundred thousand pounds a year, to make themselves *disagree-able* by insisting on accuracy and moderation in the use of natural powers. She is certainly regretful to go; she said as much frankly to me last night. But it seems she has neglected many engagements, and these unhappy great people are the slaves of their own world; it reminds me of Frankenstein! The lord with the strange Welsh name did not, I think, approve of her intimacy with me. He was a very light-hearted, pleasant, easy person, but he had quick eyes and a great deal of tact under that peculiar rough *nonchalance* which is so common to English gentlemen ; they wear it like a sort of loose overcoat, under which they conceal everything. I do not know whether it was by persuasion or ridicule that he induced her to make these visits which she had promised to make in the coming month, but directly or indirectly he induced her to do so ; a week after he left, she went away ; her grandmother is gone also.

'This great place seems very silent and lonely. Nothing can exceed her kindness in the orders she has given for my comfort. I am to ride or drive any horse I please, and the household is to obey all my commands. I imagine the servants do not like this at all. I am half afraid they accredit me with the delightful profession of a spy! My friend the head gardener alone is content ; he is very fond of me because I love flowers and understand something of them, as all artists are bound to do. So here I am alone, with the exception of this legion of servants who seem to me to do nothing but eat, yawn, and dress. The place grows on me for all that, and were there only fewer rainy days, there would be little of which to complain. The grandeur of the yews and cedars, of the huge oaks and of the long avenues of lime-trees is always solemn, quieting, and beautiful. When the day grows too dark to paint more, I go out in the park; in the home woods, as they are called. Some of the deer are growing to know me, and one doe has become so friendly she comes to meet me. They say she is old; but she is a pretty creature with a silver collar round her throat, placed there by the last earl, whose pet she was. Her name is on it, Nerina—the name, you will remember, of my poor mother. It is like finding an old friend in this strange land. I hear this earl, whose name was Alured, was much in Italy, and had what the people here call foreign tastes. I believe he was not at all a good man, and there are odd tales of him; so my ally the gardener-in-chief tells me; this gardener, by the way, has a charming house in the village; keeps a pony carriage, and has an income that would make a Venetian or Florentine gentleman rich! This gossiping will only interest you as enabling you to figure to yourself my daily life here. I confess I miss the presence of miladi: it would be strange to do otherwise; but I am solitary without being dull: I am never dull where I have my fancy free and can go at will into the open air. It is true the air here is not always inviting.

'I am becoming afraid, I candidly own, of getting too used to this life of *lusso*. I have always seen bare floors, bare walls where I had not scrawled over them, the simplest furniture, the simplest food, a dish of soup, bread and fruit, a little flask of *nostrale* wine making all my banquet; but now—so soon does one learn bad habits!—now it seems quite natural to find my bath filled for me, my clothes brushed and ready, my wants all anticipated, a table spread thrice a day for me alone, with eggshell china and Queen Anne plate, and all sorts of dainties and French wines, while two powdered giants move around me as noiselessly as if they were mice. It all seems so natural, and I am humiliated to feel that I shall miss it all when I go back to the old life of privation. And I used to think myself not so long ago a philosopher, a poet, content with the food of the spirit and scorning the comforts of the flesh. I am half afraid that, like many other wiseacres, I only scorned what I was ignorant of! To be sure, in our climate it is easier to be reconciled to a crust and a handful of plums than it would be here, and a bare floor does not seem so amiss when it has our sunbeams shining down on it, and a trail of a wild vine straying across it. Still—it is ill to lie in Capua when one knows that on the morrow one must go away to toil and uncertainty and the hunger of hope deferred. No; believe me it is not, as you will suppose, regret for a woman that makes me feel that it will be a heavy trial to leave this place. It is considerations much grosser, much baser, much lower that weigh on me. I am neither so stoical nor so spiritual as I thought, but I am, as ever, your devoted and grateful,' &c., &c.

*The Lady Charterys, Acornby, Salop, to Signore
Leonis Renzo, Milton Ernest, Berks :—*

'Comment va la peinture? Ecrivez-moi ici et
donnez-moi de vos nouvelles.'

———

Leonis Renzo to the R. P. Vicario, &c., &c. :—

'I have something to tell you, which excites and
oppresses me, yet when you hear it you may think it is
nothing. I must premise this by saying that miladi,
when she left, gave me the keys of the library, and free
permission to look over, and employ as I chose, all the
works on art, and all the old engravings and drawings,
of which there are many. The family has not been a
studious one as a rule, but it appears that the late Earl,
the Alured to whom her mother succeeded, was a col-
lector, a *dilettante*, a *virtuoso* (the terms are not entirely synonymous), and almost all these collections that
concern art were made by him. I demurred to having
the keys of these cabinets left with me, but miladi so
insisted, and seemed so bent upon giving me this mark
of her trust in my good faith, that I could not without
churlishness refuse, though I would willingly have been
without so great a responsibility, and I believe Mr.
Landon, the magnificent major-domo, was extremely
offended. However, I thought I could not reject so
kind a sign of confidence, and there is an amount of
congenial work to be done in this room on those rainy

days of which there are so many. The drawings (really valuable old masters) are all in confusion both as to dates and manners, the miniatures and medals are similarly pell-mell, and a fine collection of old proof-engravings, chiefly Italian, are in as much disorder as though they were mere cuttings from illustrated newspapers. I lock up the library when I am not at work there, which makes the dignified Mr. Landon regard me as his mortal foe. Now amongst all this chaos, of which almost every component part has a distinct artistic value, there are sketches by the late Earl Alured, who died some thirty years ago or more. They are sketches of considerable power and spirit; if he had not been a great gentleman, he might very likely have been a famous painter. Amongst these sketches, which are chiefly of figures and faces, there is one in red crayon of a Roman girl, and this girl has the features that I so well remember as those of my mother. There is nothing written under it; but in another portfolio I found three other drawings, all of the same face, and one a full-length figure bearing on her head a water-jar; you will say this may be the merest coincidence and accident of resemblance, the national type; no more. It may be so. On the other hand, is it impossible that this man was her lover? Will you, my best friend, be so infinitely good as to write me word any details that you can remember or collect of her? Was the nationality of my father ever known? Pray reply to me fully and at once.'

Don Eccellino Ferraris, Florinella-sopra-Subiaco, to Leonis Renzo, Milton Ernest :—

' I reply instantly, my dear son, to your letter which Ammara brings me from Subiaco this afternoon. But I know no more than I have already and repeatedly told you : that your mother was known all her life to the people of these hills; that she was the daughter of Evaristo Renzo the *buttero* : that a foreigner was about here some weeks who was supposed to be an artist : that Nerina Renzo went away with him and was absent for a year, in which year Renzo the *buttero* was killed by a bull he was lassoing : that on her return she said no word of where she had been : inherited just enough to live on from Renzo the *buttero,* and in a few months' time gave birth to a son—yourself—whom I myself baptised and registered under the names of Leonis Renzo. I gave you Leonis as the name to which my little church here is dedicated, and Renzo as that of your grandfather. Your mother lived till you were seven years old, and when she died she was only twenty-five years of age. She never, in the confessional or out of it, told me a syllable as to her history during the year she had been absent, or as to the name, country, or rank of the man who begot you. Though she was a most lovely creature in person, and quite sane in many ways, I never believed that she was quite in possession of her mental faculties after your birth. Some great

grief which she had had, and the shock of hearing of
her father's death, which was told her abruptly and
with all its horrible details by a shepherd whom she
met on her way here, had, I think, unhinged her mind
without destroying it. However this might be, it was
impossible to extract a word from her as to your paren-
tage. I have always concluded that she was deserted
in some capricious and sudden manner by her lover,
who very possibly might not even know that she was
gravida. It is not improbable that he was a noble.
The few people here who remember him all say he was
un' vero signore. But they would say that of any one
who spent a little money. This is all that I know, my
beloved son, who has been truly a son of the spirit to
me. If I knew more, under the seal of the confessional,
I would not hesitate to reveal it to you; but your
mother either never wholly trusted me, or loved her
seducer too well to speak of him. She erred in that;
but it is my belief, as I have said, that her mind was
always clouded after her return. She adored you, and
perhaps would have left some truth for you to hear, if she
had lived till you were older, or if she had had any foreboding of her early and sudden death from heart-disease.
It is strange that you should have found any picture
which is like her in that English house so far away.
But you will forgive me if I suggest, my beloved Leonis,
that the childish memory, even of a mother's face,
cannot be entirely trusted; and the purely classic type
of face which she had, and which you have, is by no

means rare in our country, especially in remote places where the blood has been kept pure and unchanged since the days of Æneas.'

———

The Lady Charterys, Acornby, Salop, to Mr. Hollys, Rome (telegraphs) :—

'The D. of K. has arrived here, so I go to the Adrian Vansittarts to-morrow. What good do you suppose can come of this intolerable annoyance? Make him understand that no one can bully me into anything. I shall have a big party at Milton for pheasants. Come.'

———

Mr. Hollys, Rome, to Lady Charterys, Acornby, Salop :—

' All I shall see of pheasants will be quails : I reply *more hibernico.* Do you mean you are going back next month? I thought you never *could* be at Milton in autumn because it was so damp?'

———

The Lady Charterys, Redleaf, Devon, to Mr. Hollys, Rome :—

'It is damp in a damp autumn. This is a dry one. I shall soon be home.'

*Mr. Hollys, Rome, to Lady Charterys, Redleaf,
Devon :—*

‘ Perversity, thy name is woman ! ’

* * *

The Lady Charterys to Mr. Hollys :—

‘ Not an original remark.   Was it worth paying a
post-card to say *that?*   Why I should not invite my
own friends, to my own house, to slay my own pheasants,
is, I confess, wholly beyond my own comprehension
Perhaps you will explain a little ? ’

* * *

*Mr. Hollys, Rome, to Lady Charterys, Lifford,
Hants :—*

‘ In my trade we never explain.   A discreet roundabout is all we venture on ; I have given a hint, I dare
no more.’

* * *

*The Lady Charterys, Lifford, Hants, to
Mr. Hollys, Rome :—*

‘ Hints and innuendoes are first cousins.   Neither
are remarkable for courage ; and I confess I am never
disposed to be at the trouble to take their masks off.
If you like to come to Milton, do: I shall be most

happy to see you. If you don't, stay; and eat your
quails rolled up in vine-leaves, and spare me moral
saws and stale apophthegms, and inappropriate counsels
that don't dare show their faces.'

* * *

Mr. Hollys to the Lady Charterys, Montolieu Abbey,
near Winchester :—

'You are unkind, and are you quite grateful? The
ballroom would never have been painted if it hadn't
been for me. You would have had a *fournisseur* and
you *wouldn't* have discovered a " dry autumn." By-
the-bye, the Meteorological Report states the rainfall
in England this September to average 2·52 inches!'

* * *

Leonis Renzo, Milton Ernest, to Don Eccellino
Ferraris, Florinella-sopra-Subiaco, &c., &c. :—

'She has returned, bringing a great number of gay
and great personages with her; she is very sweet and
thoughtful in her manner to me, but it seems to me as
if I were millions of leagues farther off from her, since
the possibility which haunts me that I may be the
bastard of her uncle: it overwhelms me with shame.
There are coming here some English Princes, and the
ballroom and all my outlined frescoes are being covered
temporarily with primrose-hued satin, so that I am

driven from my labours; and she has proposed to me that I shall take her portrait, and send it to the Salon or the Academy next year. I cannot refuse. So every morning she gives me a sitting in the library, of which she allows me to make a temporary studio; she would not take back the keys of it. I admit that it is a trying thing for me to do, with this suspicion upon me, which is indeed to my mind almost a certainty, that the Earl Alured, to whom she succeeded, was the faithless lover of my mother. I have ventured to speak of him to her, when we have been alone in these sittings, but she knows very little about him. She was not born when he died suddenly, being thrown from his horse; she has always been told he was an eccentric, wayward, capricious man: she said, with a little laugh, that capriciousness was in the blood of the family. The Lady Cairnwrath has returned with her; and alas! conceives it her duty to be almost always present in the library during the time that I am painting this portrait; they regard me as a wild beast, seeking to devour this lamb with the golden fleece! The portrait will be beautiful and grand; I have dealt with it in the Venetian way: she wears a wonderful dress of dead-gold brocade, with scarlet touches in it here and there, and holds a large fan, black and gold, and is just looking over her shoulder with a little smile; her great Leonsburg dog Berwick is beside her; he is grey, and tones down the intense mass of gold and scarlet. But the face! there is the miracle and glory of it. She is much more beautiful than I first thought her, and her expression is changed; deepened and softened both. This week the sittings are interrupted by the presence of the English Prince and Princess. The house is all *sotto sopra* on account of them. Stupendous efforts are made for their entertainment, and the English Prince, with seven other gentlemen, slew fifteen hundred pheasants in a day, which is considered admirable. I am always glad to think that I never in my life slew anything. I have seen many other better ways of proving one's address, if one needs to do so. There was a grand ball last night, in the room that I am temporarily turned out of: I keep away from it all, of course. I even proposed to her to go wholly out of the house during the time, but she would not hear of it; and the other afternoon she showed the Prince and Princess what I have done of her portrait, and sent for me and presented me to them both, and they said gracious things, which I am conscious were not overstrained, for I know my force in my own art. One of the gentlemen of the suite told me later that the Princess would command me to paint her portrait. I answered him, perhaps wrongly, that I was no portrait painter. Miladi scolded me very prettily, for being *bourru* and proud at the wrong moment. " When they are delighted with you, what is there to offend you even if they are princes? " So she remonstrated, and had reason in her remonstrance, and perhaps I was thankless; I suppose it is these people who represent the

goddess Fortune nowadays. The royal guests remained
here but three days, during which, I am told, they were
well pleased.   They sent for me again before their
departure, and again expressed themselves with much
grace and kindness. The greater part of the other
guests also went away; to-day and to-morrow she will
sit to me again. I fear that the civility towards me
of the royal persons did not gratify my formidable
enemy the Lady Cairnwrath. But what does it all
matter! Soon they will leave me alone again. The
long winter will pass, and the spring will probably find
the ballroom and the portrait alike finished, and then
I, too, shall go away, and she will not hear, see, or
remember me any more. There is one thing quite
certain : I will not take her money for either of the
works. Perhaps fame may come to me through her;
and for that I shall be grateful. Yet I do not care
for fame of any kind : I care only for art. I should
be glad to have moderate wealth, enough to spend my
life as I like, after my own manner, and in the pursuit
of my own dreams. I must seem to prose to you intoler-
ably, but it is a relief to me, for there is no one here
in whom I can confide my thoughts. To miladi I dare
not ; to the others I could not ; and you have been my
confessor since the hour of my first sin! . . .'

Lord Llandudno, Milton Ernest, Berks, to Hon. H. Hollys, British Embassy, Rome:—

'Dear Hollys,—It was no use. She *would* come back, and she asked a whole tribe of people, and then to top it the P. and P. suddenly fixed their arrival for the end of the month, so there was no more to be said, and all my ingenuity in having succeeded in persuading Esmée into these visits was bootless. She made the painter begin her portrait, and, whatever else she means, she's getting plenty of good work out of him. The fellow is amazingly handsome; he reminds me of somebody, but I can't remember of whom. Esmée certainly puts him to the fore a good deal; she talked about him so to the P and P. that she made her point and was allowed to present him to them. But this may all be done only to rile Tabby. There is no knowing with a woman like Esmée what she's really up to; she knows the world down to the ground, and if she makes a move she's a purpose in it; but yet again she's a weathercock. The Italian adores her, that's plain to be seen; when we were last here, he'd the whip hand of her; now, she's the pull over him. I suppose it's only her fun, but it will be rough on the poor devil. I don't see what we can any of us do. Esmée isn't a chicken. If you'd sent the diploma'd and decorated ass that you spoke of, there would have been none of this bother. She *says* she's going to

Cannes next month, and has ordered the " Glaucus " to refit and get in Mediterranean trim. She can hardly take the painter on board with her. The C. of O. informs me that you and I are responsible for all this scandal. You, I know, are; but I don't see where I come in; by the way, in case we're obliged to have more to do with this man, can't you learn really something about him ? '

Mr. Hollys, Rome, to Lord Llandudno, Milton Ernest :—

'Dear Llanny,—There is nothing to learn; he never concealed where he came from ; he's the natural son of a woman of Fontanella, and his grandfather was a *buttero*—that is, please your ignorance, a wild-cattle-keeper. The priest of Fontanella—who has a history too, for he is a noble and took the vow of poverty and entered the Church in consequence of the tragic death of a mistress—loves him, but has nothing to do with him : as to that all the folk of Florinella are agreed. The priest educated him and maintained him afterwards at the University of Rome, where he took high honours. He then studied art (living very miserably, I suspect) in Paris and Munich, and then spent his life between his studio (a garret) in Rome and the priest's little house up in the hills at Florinella, where he painted those frescoes in the little church which led to my most unfortunate acquaintance with him. That is all that is to be known. He is now thirty-three years of age. You will see it is all quite creditable, more creditable perhaps than yours or mine; but, as society is constituted, Esmée must no more look at him than if he were a forger or a hangman. I suppose we are all humbugs, but *telle est la vie.* If you are at your (very clever) wits' ends on the spot, what am I a thousand miles off? What I should most fear would be an irreparable breach between Esmée and the C. of O., and the adoption as *chaperon* of some frisky matron like her friend Mrs. Alsager, who will let her do just as she likes and get compromised in a hideous fashion. My chief hope lies in Renzo himself; I think he is a man of honour. I think if he sees mischief ahead he will go away out of it.'

Lord Llandudno, Milton Ernest, to Hon. H. Hollys, Rome :—

' I have never believed in Joseph; especially would Joseph be an impossibility when a beautiful young woman offered herself *en tout bien tout honneur.* Don't be alarmed; she's not at that point yet, perhaps never will be. As yet she is only having her portrait taken, and I bet it will beat "La bella di Tiziano." The C. of O. presides at the sittings, looking like Duty on a rock staring at Danger, or something of that sort. The Alsager *is* going on the " Glaucus," and that may

mean any amount of mischief. Vic. was at my house
the other day, looking very blue, poor boy. He won't
take his punishing without whimpering. How could
that marriage miss fire? You and I should have had
nothing to do except to sign our names to the most
perfect settlements the world ever saw. To think, too,
how the properties dovetail into one another! It is
flouting Providence, but she has done the same thing
twenty times a year ever since she left her school-
room.'

----

*Mr. Hollys, Rome, to Lord Llandudno, Milton
Ernest (telegraphs) :—*

'Do you mean to say you think the affair with R.
serious?'

Lord Llandudno to Mr. Hollys (writes):—

'It looks like it. She put me off the scent last
time, but now I begin to think the C. of O. not altogether so wrong. However, it may be all caprice. She
is, after all, only having her portrait taken; why should
we interfere? I tried to say something this morning,
and she looked me in the face with the coolest little
smile and just said: "It is so much nicer than a
photograph that people can sell whether one lets them
or not." Just as if she couldn't have Carolus Duran or
Baudry to take her portrait! Just as if she hadn't

been painted half a score of times before now ' I do believe he has a great influence over her; she has left off using the kolb to her eyes; she wears her hair in loose soft masses instead of crimping and frizzing her fringe; she has taken to quite simple sorts of gowns with old-fashioned gold girdles and gypsires as her only ornament. "I suppose that's æsthetic?" I said to Hermione, and Hermie regarded me with scorn: "How can you be so silly? It's Renzo. She sent some of his sketches over to Worth with orders. Esmée never did care a bit about the æsthetes, but she likes to please him, don't you know?" I did know, and I groaned, and I know the man ought to go away, but on my life I don't see why he should throw it all up merely to oblige us. Besides, he is honestly in love with her; he is the only person in the house perhaps who does not know it, but he is so. As she is perfectly charming and enchantingly considerate towards him, why should he turn his back on all that?'

Mr. Hollys to Lord Llandudno:—

'You know as well as I do that men who are poor *do* turn their backs on all that when they are gentlemen, and I think he is a gentleman; but I grant the temptation is terrible if he really can see he has any influence over her. I confess the whole thing seems so incredible to me that it is like a nightmare. What

does she mean to do ? She never can mean to marry
him. He hasn't a *soldo*, and not even a name !'

———

Lord Llandudno to Mr. Hollys :—

'I certainly don't dare hint to her that she does,
but I think her quite capable of it. She would love to
do it if only for the pleasure of braving the C. of O. and
quarrelling with all the rest of us. She is her own
mistress, you know. No hope of the Lord Chancellor
here. Frankly I want to be out of it, so I'm going to
shoot bears and steinbock with Hohenlohe in Styria. I
think if she's left quite alone she'll see the folly of the
thing. The sense of opposition keeps her obstinate;
not, mind you, that there's anything definite yet.
They're only still at this eternal portrait. The portrait will be grand ; he handles the dead gold and the
scarlet with amazing skill ; you certainly knew what
you were about and picked out a man who could paint.
Hermione and Jack Herbert have come to terms;
they'll be married some time after Christmas. Everybody quite pleased all round. " *That* would spoil it to
me," said Esmée the other day. I declare I quite
believed her. She likes a chopping sea and a stiff
wind when she's out. If she do lose her head about
the Roman it will only be out of " contrariness." '

Leonis Renzo, Milton Ernest, to Don Eccellino Ferraris, Florinella-sopra-Subiaco :—

'Dearest Friend and Reverend Father,—You are quite right; the suspicion which has come into my mind concerning the Earl Alured poisons the peace and pleasure I had found in my pursuits here. It may be altogether fanciful and unfounded, but the mere shadow of it is enough to darken my path; especially when I am in her presence the thought is oppressive and of an almost unbearable humiliation. If I could speak of him I could ask her permission to seek through any papers he may have left for more evidence, more confirmation, but this it is impossible to do; I could never bring my lips to frame a hint of it. After all, too, I should most likely see nothing more. The mere pastime of an English nobleman with an Italian girl would leave no impression on the life and memory of such a man as he, even if he loved her, as the name on the doe's collar would suggest. These great gentlemen break so many of these poor butterflies upon the wheel in a summer's day.

'The portrait grows; they say it is like the style of Cabanel, which incenses me; Cabanel is a great master, but I hope I am not borrowing from him or any one; I paint what I see as I feel it, and if I have any master at all, I go farther back than Cabanel, and straightway to the Venice of the Cinque Cento. Miladi is all that is sweetest and most kind ; nay, she is too good to me ; it offends all her own people, that I can see. When the portrait is done she will go away at once on a vessel of her own southward, and the long, cold, blank English winter faces me; well, if only there will be light enough I shall occupy myself. I rise at daybreak to go on with the Theocritian frescoes; I cannot bear her to suppose that I purposely delay my work for sake of the ease of my life here. If the weather serve I mean to finish them by next Easter. She does not, I believe, return until then, as she goes from the Riviera straight to her house in London, without coming here after her winter in the South. She asked me a little abruptly this morning if I would not like to go to Rome for the winter ; she said I was not to think for a moment that I was bound to finish the ballroom until it was quite convenient to me ; if my habits or my health needed a warmer air in winter—then she stopped and looked at me and I did not altogether understand her, but I felt my face grow hot, for I knew that I had no money to return to Rome ; I spent all I had in coming here and in the purchase of the colours ; and certainly I would die sooner than tell her that. When I hear all these people talk of going here, going there, of flying this way and that, like so many happy birds, I understand that to be poor is to be a bird without wings, like that poor hopeless, ugly apteryx which is the laughing-stock of naturalists and the cruel jest of nature.

•   •   •   •   •   •

'The lord who is a sort of *tutore* came to me just now when I was alone and commenced conversation. He does not speak French very well, but I could fairly understand him. He said some hard things of miladi. He ended by hinting to me that she was "*coquette et fine mouche.*" I said to him that I did not think that concerned me; and that it was not for me, who received many benefits from her, to listen to blame of her. This confused him a little. He got up, said quickly, "*Eh bien, je m'en lave les mains!*" and then added that he was himself going away into Styria. He seemed to wish me to give him some assurance, but I did not see that any was needed. They seem to attach much more importance to me than I can possibly claim. Is she a coquette? I do not think so. And if she be, what is that to me? I am only a man who paints her portrait and her ballroom. And I may be something she would think yet lower than the sweeper who clears her terrace of its leaves!

.   .   .   .

'This morning whilst it was still very early she entered the ballroom when I was beginning my work. She has risen early the last week or two; I have seen her, and once or twice met her in the gardens soon after sunrise. "Why do you work so hard?" she asked me when she had looked at what I was doing. "Why are you in such haste to have finished the thing? Are you tired of England, of Milton?" I told her that I thought common honesty needed that the work should be done with as little waste of time as it could. "And when it is done," she said in her abrupt fashion that yet is graceful too, " will you go away and have no regret for us ? " I felt myself grow pale, for I knew that I should suffer,—much,—but I answered her that if in the end she considered the work well done I should have no regrets : none ; I should have only great gratitude. " Gratitude ! " She repeated the word with some anger. She looked very beautiful. She had a white woollen gown on with black fur all round it, and she had a quantity of red autumn roses in her hand. " It is we who owe you gratitude," she said warmly. " It is I who owe you gratitude ; you give my house beautiful fancies and images, and you have made me think, you have made me feel ; you have made me conscious of the emptiness and the egotism of my life." I said nothing—what could I say—to *her* ? " I think you are far too proud," she said after a little pause, " and yet you have so far too much humility. Do you mean to say you will like to remain here all alone all the cold, dreary, lonely winter ? You will be miserable. You have no idea how cold it is, how unutterably dull ! " I told her I did not think that it would be colder than my fireless garret had been in Paris or was even in Rome, when the tramontana blew ; and I said that I should not be miserable, because her memory—and her portrait— would remain with me. Perhaps it was wrong to say even so much. But it did not offend her. She smiled

and gave me one of her roses, and ordered me to come
to breakfast with her. I hesitated very much, but she
insisted so that I could not refuse. I breakfasted with
her and the little Lady Hermione before any one else
staying in the house was up, and we laughed and
chattered and were merry and happy, and the smell of
the sweet wet grass and the late roses came through
the windows which we could leave open a little, for it
is here what we call St. Martin's summer. Well, it is
much to have these beautiful hours to remember, even
if afterwards one goes out into endless hunger and
darkness for evermore!

'But, looking back on it all, here, as I write alone,
the thought comes to me which seems in itself almost
madness. Is it possible that she would—that she
does—love me? What must I do? Counsel me.'

---

*Don Eccellino Ferraris, Florinella-sopra-Subiaco,
to Leonis Renzo, Milton Ernest, &c., &c. :—*

'My beloved Son,—It is not for me to counsel you
at such a distance from you as I am, and having so
long and altogether abandoned the great world. But
your nature is noble, your pride is great, greater perhaps because some would deny your right to it; act
therefore as both these bid you. That this lady is
drawn towards you I can well believe, that you care for
her more than you know I have long felt; but I confess

I see nothing but suffering in store for you through this passion. If you wish to leave the place and the country, command me; you know my purse, meagre as it is, is always open to you, and here you may find, as I have done, peace at least of conscience, if pains of memory pursue you even to these heights.'

Leonis Renzo to Don Eccellino Ferraris, &c., &c. :—

' You are, as ever, good beyond my merits. If she leave here, I will stay on and complete the work. If she remain, you are right—I must go. Peace will be no more mine wherever my steps may turn.'

The Countess of Charterys to Mr. Thomas, Yacht 'Glaucus,' Cowes Harbour :—

'Take her round to Marseilles and there wait telegram from me.'

Leonis Renzo, Milton Ernest, to Don Eccellino Ferraris, Florinella-sopra-Subiaco, &c., &c. :—

' She is gone. I suppose some pressure was brought to bear on her, or perhaps she wished to escape from a position that became an embarrassment. I do not know; I think she has some love for me; but I hear always the voice of that old lord saying, "*Elle est coquette et fine mouche.*" Yet I wrong her; I am base to want more than she has given me—the utmost sweetness and delicacy and consideration to the last; so much more than I should have been warranted in expecting! The evening before she left she came to take farewell of me when I was at work on her portrait, which is all but finished; a few touches to the drapery and to the dog alone are needed. She said to me, " If it be very cold indeed you had better go to Rome, or will you come out to us at Cannes and make another picture of me amongst the palms?" Her voice was very low and kind. It cost me very much to look at her calmly and say as I did say simply, No. I think she understood that it was no discourtesy. She said nothing else. She gave me her hand. There were tears in her beautiful eyes. Mine were dim. You were right. There is pain, great pain, for both of us, but hers will soon pass, rich, happy, adored. surrounded, amused with a thousand distractions as she is and will be; but mine—— No doubt what she feels for me is mere interest, mere compassion, rather than the divine pity of Desdemona; perhaps she has respect for me, too, because I have never flattered her. But it is impossible that she seriously loves me. If she did, she is far removed from me as though mountains were between us. If I could accept her were she to offer it, how she would despise me then and for ever !

'I have my first taste of an English winter to-day.

It is bitterly cold, and rains, and hails, and snows. It is impossible to paint. I continue my work in the library; I have seen many cases and drawers full of drawings, manuscripts, and engravings, still to examine and arrange. It is a noble room, and the great fire lit at either end fills it full of mellow colour. I could be quite happy here if—if—if! I have sent to my friend Vico in Rome to dispose of the pictures there are in my studio if he can, even if he get but twenty francs a piece, and send me the money; I can leave here if she return, as it is her choice to do sometimes at a day's notice. She wrote me a most kind and pretty note this morning. It cost me much to answer with a few formal lines, but she would despise me if I let myself do more. She has reached Cannes a fortnight ago. She describes her villa with its orange woods and gardens and its walls of many-coloured marble, and the little harbour all to itself, with such deep water that her yacht can anchor there. She asks me to go out and see it, and paint it all: she puts aside my refusal as if it had never been uttered. Do you think she would be so cruel as to play with me so far? Yet I am a fool and thankless. No doubt she only means it in innocent kindness and never dreams that I shall distort it so.'

Mr. Hollys, Villa Gloriette, Cannes, to Lord Llandudno, St. Gowan's, Merioneth :—

'Dear Llanny,—I have run over here for two days to see the object of our mutual anxiety. Vic. is near too by my advice : he's got his old tub in the Villefranche bay ; I think she is looking worried ; she says very little to me. I asked her about Renzo, and she said very coolly that he was in England at work on the frescoes, and hang me if I could muster up cheek enough to say any more. She has a way of looking at you that shuts you up at once. I pleaded Vic.'s cause ; but I suppose very badly, for she only looked bored, and said it was a pity to bring boys out anywhere near that horrid Monte Carlo. She had been there herself and couldn't see why people cared to go, but they did, and I had far better send Vic. home. I objected that an English Duke aged four-and-twenty, who was in the Life Guards, was not to be treated like a child in the nursery. She looked more bored, and asked me the name of a horrid cactus that looks like a tennis racquet covered with bristles. I don't know its name ; I don't know why such a creature should have a name at all. I am out of temper. I candidly confess it. I am very fond of Esmée, and I don't like being treated as if I were somebody seen at the gaming tables or the railway station for the first time to-day. I don't like Mrs. Alsager either, who is staying with her and does her no good. When I tried to get something out of Mrs. A. as to Renzo, the woman only laughed and said she thought he was coming here! The C. of O. is in bed with a chill. She sends me little pencil notes three or four times a day—agonising, frigid, terrible little effusions. She evidently considers I could marry Esmée to Vic. out of hand if I did my duty. She has fever from the sun, rheumatism from the mistral, smells typhus in the rosebuds beneath her windows, and cholera in the mignonette; is invisible, impotent, and still terrible, restricts her diet to Liebig and her receptions to the English clergyman ; if Renzo come to Cannes, she will, she declares to me, be carried out of her bed in a *chaise à porteurs* to die. On the whole the atmosphere is depressing despite a buoyant barometer, a gay thermometer, and a sea and a sun for ever smiling. I don't see what I can do. As I said before, if Esmée mean it she'll do it, and my only hope is in the man himself; I don't believe he will come to Cannes, and I do believe he is too great an artist to be a blackguard. I go back to Rome to-night and am thankful. I feel like a fool when I look at Esmée and tell myself that I don't dare to ask her a point-blank question. But you didn't dare either ! Sincerely yours, H. H.

'P.S. Vic. lost a hundred thousand francs yesterday over there, and he would go back this morning first train. Lelah Dé is at the Hôtel de Paris, and I am very greatly afraid she'll get hold of him,'

Leonis Renzo, Milton Ernest, to Don Eccellino Ferraris, Florinella-sopra-Subiaco :—

' You were wiser than I, dear old friend. I see in an English journal which I can just spell out that the young Duke is at Cannes also. Will she end in doing what all her friends wish? It must take so much courage, so much constancy, in a woman to resist the pressure of her world; and she is courageous but not constant. At least I should say so. I may do her injustice; I did her much in the first day I knew her. The days go by drearily, and are very cold and dark ! I am glad when the night comes, and the lamps are lit, and the big dog and I are alone after dinner in this library which has become almost a home to me. The head-keeper asked me yesterday if I would not go out shooting. I could see that no words could have measured the might of his scorn when he had heard that nothing would induce me to kill any bird or beast that lives. The entire household thinks me a harmless lunatic, but they begin to like me.

' I work sedulously at the fresco when the light permits ; I ride sometimes ; I read a good deal. There are thousands of Latin and of French books, and some few Italian ones. Her portrait stands on a large easel at the north end of the library. Both the dog Berwick and I look at it, and regret,—in our divers ways. I am sure that he knows it is hers.

' It was Natale yesterday : a great deal was given away in her name by the stewards to all the poor for many miles around, but the people looked to me sullen. Perhaps they feel that she does not care a straw about them or know A from B amongst them. It is a pity. She might so easily make herself beloved.

' At the end of my solitary dinner they brought me the national pudding, a gorgeous, indigestible globe ; I thought it very nasty ; Berwick approved and ate it. To-day there is a violent snowstorm. The whole country is white, the yews look very grand against the snow. I have been out and seen the deer fed : Nerina nibbled at her turnips from my hand. It is intensely cold. I pity the peasantry. The stewards give away a great deal of coal and clothing.

' She has sent me another little letter ; she says she is sitting amongst geraniums in full flower on the edge of a marble wall overlooking a blue sea with the thermometer at 20° Réaumur in the sun. She asks me if I sometimes do not envy that ? I envy the flowers that are near her—yes—but I answer her merely, and that is the truth too, that I am growing enamoured of these keen winds, this white landscape, these sombre woods, these dusky oak-panelled chambers with their warm fires and their painted oriels. Perhaps I grow so fond of them because I know that in a little while I shall leave them for ever, and my place will know me no more.

'I have made a discovery which overwhelms me so that I can scarcely see the paper on which I write to you. I have discovered documents that make me believe I was the legitimate son of the Earl Alured; at least so it seems to me, beyond any possibility of error. This is how I found them. Forgive me if I be incoherent. In arranging the drawings, etchings, &c., I had the permission of miladi to open all drawers, cabinets, and cases; she gave me an old and very imperfect manuscript catalogue to help me. In one corner of the library there is a secrétaire of fine Louis XV. work. It was full of old letters, old cards, old sketches; I did not like to touch these, though she had expressly told me to look anywhere I chose. As I was about to close the doors of the bureau I suppose I must have accidentally touched some unseen spring, for a panel turned and a secret drawer shot out: in the drawer was a packet of letters, a curl of dark hair, and a folded paper. I lifted the paper to re-shut the little drawer and then saw that it was a record of their marriage in the church of S. Helena in Rome. I copy it below; you see there is no reasonable doubt of it. I will write you more to-morrow. I feel stunned and the room goes round with me. If I am not the sport of a delirious dream—oh God, if my mother were living!

  .   .   .   .   .   .

'My letter was too late for the post last night. I add all I know. I send you copies of the letters that were tied up with my mother's hair. They are her letters—*cara anima*!—Italian, ill-writ, over-fond ; telling so little and yet saying all. I see the whole story in these piteous letters. He married her privately, and was ashamed of her, and she was left in obscurity and he went into the world, and then came jealousy and misunderstanding and rage and doubt on her side, and anger and indifference on his ; and there must have been some Iago near to suggest to her the doubt that her marriage had been only a farce, and so she ran away blindly, madly, to her own old home and found her father dead. There are only her letters. There is nothing to tell us what Lord Charterys thought or did. I imagine he was a heartless man who found his liberty welcome and did not seek her and so never knew of me. I dare say he was ashamed of his folly in wedding a peasant girl from the Sabine hills. One cannot tell. That is all a blank. But the records of the marriage are clear. The date is thirty-four years ago. I am his lawful son. I am her cousin.

•   •   •   •   •   •

' Two days have passed since I wrote you. I am somewhat calmer. A deep gladness has succeeded the madness of my first amazement. The shadow is gone off my life. I am any man's equal now. I do not know whether these things would content the law ; they content me ! How strange the hand of fate that led me here ! My poor mother ! how plainly one sees her story in those letters! The passion, and pain, and jealousy, and doubt, and all the pitiful weakness and ignorance are so sacred to me. They did not touch him, I suppose they only irritated him. Some men are made so. When they are thus, women only break their hearts on them like frail ships on a rock. He must have been cruel to her. I cannot forgive him. But what I think of more than of her or of him, heaven pardon me, is Esmée; I may call her so now. I shall stand in her place; she will hate me. After being the recipient of her goodness and her trustfulness, I shall despoil her of her kingdom if ever I make this known. It is I who am Lord Charterys! She will hate me. . . . I have been out in the great dusky woods. It is very cold and the wind is high, but it did me good; it cooled the fever in me. I feel as if I had done her some treasonable wrong. This is childish, I know, but I cannot help myself. If she had not trusted me with these library keys I should never have known my own rights.

    .   .   .   .   .   .

'To-day my friend in Rome sent me word no one would buy the sketches, but he sold a little marble that I had, which is said to be of Mino di Fiesole, for thirty napoleons, which he sends me. I will go up to London and get the address of a great lawyer from our consul there, and take the lawyer's opinion on the facts. I shall give him no names, so there will be nothing risked. I have spoken of the Earl Alured with the

land-steward, who knew him well. He describes him
as a wayward, inconstant, and unstable man. He was
thrown by his horse shying near these very gates and
died instantly on the road. Perhaps had he lived he
might have sought my mother out in after years. I
will try to think so.

•   •   •   •   •   •

'I have been to London and seen a famous man of
law. I showed him copies of all the documents without
any names to them, and, after careful examination, he
gave it as his opinion that the marriage was quite legal
(as a merely religious marriage was so at that period in
Italy, and this Earl was of our own religion, as the
whole race was in old days), and that the proofs were sufficient to give the son, by such a marriage, title to inherit,
provided the son was distinctly proved to have been born
at the date I described. That, we know, is easily done.
The lawyer said there would be, no doubt, long litiga-
tion: the other side would contest; marriages in Italy
before the Independence were irregular, and often secret,
and so subject to suspicion; the case would go up to
the House of Lords; it would be long, but there could
be no doubt, he thought, of the ultimate result if the
facts and the papers were as I stated to him. I thanked
him and came back here.

'When the great gates were thrown open in the
twilight I felt that I came home. It was very odd to
know that I was the owner, the master here; an English

earl—I! Then as I sat before the hearth with her
dog's head on my knee, other thoughts came over me.
The lawyer had said *the other side would contest.* The
cold sentence had gone to my heart like a knife. She
and I should be enemies! There would be nothing for
either of us to be ashamed of in the facts that would be
made public, yet it would be hateful, we should be foes.
The lawyer, indeed, suggested that perhaps the present
owner of the property and name might yield without
law if convinced of the justice and veracity of the claim.
Yes: she would yield at once, my beautiful proud
cousin! She would go out of my house, and leave me
master here, and never see my face again! What should
I have profited?—and there is a meanness and a treason
about it, too; but for her condescension to me, her
trust in me, I could never have known this. I could
never even have guessed that my poor mother had
wronged herself by her hasty flight and unhappy suspicions, and that I had been born in wedlock. It seems
treacherous, unworthy, to use the results to dispossess
her of her heritage. This is what torments me; I can
see no way by which I can come by my own without
injury and pain to her.

'There is more still to remember: as I say, when
once she knows that I am the Earl Alured's legitimate
heir she will wait for no decision of the court; she will
scorn to defend herself by any legal quibble or flaw that
may present itself; she will give up everything and—
hate me for ever. Or, even if she be so generous as not

to hate me as an usurper, she could never, she would never, forgive the man who took advantage of a search which she permitted to him, of a sojourn to which she invited him, and whilst he stayed beneath her roof used his leisure to undermine her claims—claims that the law and the world have allowed her all her life. Even if she believed all these papers to be genuine (and she might even not believe that), she would despise the person who brought them forward against her. This is my torture, my perplexity. So well I love her that to be recognised as the Earl of Charterys by all England will avail me nothing if I lose her smiles. Though my honour be cleared, and my pride is now a permissible thing, I am more miserable than I was before I opened that secrétaire. I see no way by which I can make good my title and yet retain her favour. If I show her these papers I must seem her foe for ever; I may even seem a traitor too! I would sooner remain Leonis Renzo whom she respects and whom—perhaps—she loves. Counsel me, dear and reverend friend.'

The Don Eccellino Ferraris, Florinella-sopra-Subiaco, to Leonis Renzo, Milton Ernest :—

'I dare not advise you, my son, in a matter of such lifelong moment. Your whole future hangs on your decision. I see the difficulty that fronts you. You love your cousin better than name, or place, or power. I do not say that you are wrong. You hesitate to alienate her from you by an effort to secure the recognition of your just rights; I understand your hesitation; even if it did not make her your enemy, it would be at least a barrier (insurmountable to a proud woman) to any confession on her part of affection. She would never submit to the appearance in your eyes and the world that such a confession at such a time would present. On the other hand, your cousin may not be worthy such high devotion, such extraordinary sacrifice. You will remember that when you saw her first she seemed to you insolent, capricious, artificial, a mere creature of the world and of its follies. Are you sure that your colder estimate was not the juster? The fascination she now has for you may blind you to the truth. If this be so, you may lose a career of happiness and usefulness, a life of peace and dignity, the possession of a noble name, for a woman too idle and shallow to appreciate such a sacrifice if she knew of it; and she will never know of it or suspect it. All your suffering, all your loss, will be borne mutely and be unrecognised. I do not dare to sway your decision either way. All I say is, think long, and do nothing on impulse. There is no need of haste. You are expected to remain where you are until your work is finished. It will be time to decide when she returns. The generosity you contemplate is almost superhuman, but I believe you are capable of it and would not even regret it if you knew her worthy it. If!——you will

have had my other letter in which I answered the marvellous intelligence you gave me ; alas ! that your poor
mother had not courage enough to confide the truth to
me ! My poor Leonis ! when I think of your many
years of privation and unrecognised genius, my heart
bleeds for you ! I pray heaven that these tidings of
great joy come not too late.'

------

*Leonis Renzo, Milton Ernest, to Don Eccellino
Ferraris, Florinella-sopra-Subiaco.*

'The days are gloomy and seem very long. I feel
in a strange confusion and agitation; your kind calm
letter does not lessen my trouble, for you put so clearly
before me the truth that "either way I must repine."
If I claim my inheritance she is surely lost to me for
evermore; and if I bury the secret in my own heart,
how can I ever approach her ?—I, who shall still seem
to every one a mere adventurer, a mere beggar, and
who would be scorned even by herself if I so far forgot
the dignity of poverty as to say a syllable of supplica-
tion to one so far removed from me. Either way it
seems there is no chance for me to be able to approach
her with any hope of becoming more to her than I am
now. You say truly there is no haste. I have locked
the papers up in a little iron box, and, unless I choose,
no eyes, save mine and yours, will ever look on them.
Does it seem to you so very quixotic that I can think

of the possibility of going on all my life long with this secret untold, this great birthright unclaimed? Do you not know I would do anything to see her eyes smile at me? and the smile would never come there if she knew it—never, never more. It seems strange as I move about here to realise that it is all mine, actually mine!—when I have never had anything of my own except a box of colours and a hired garret with a cast or a bust here and there.

'I sit doing nothing all the long evenings with the dog at my feet, and it seems to me that I can never take it all, since for me to take it she must lose it. And she was so thoughtful of me, so considerate, so delicate, so kind—shall I repay her by robbing her? I work on when the light lets me at the frescoes; these at least I wish to do me honour. The other day I laughed outright when the major-domo spoke with some little insolence about them; it seemed so ridiculous. If he had only guessed who I was, how he would have cringed and kissed the dust! To think I have the right to sweep all this *valetaille* out of the house! But it is not the power or the possession of this birthright of mine that makes the temptation; it is the leisure, it is the repose, it is the ability to pass all my life in the pursuit of the ideal, to surround myself with all that is beautiful and spiritual—but then, without her, even with all that my life would be only a " home without music," a " ruche sans abeilles.' What can I do? I sit and muse hour after hour, night after night, and am

no nearer to any determination. I look at her portrait,
and the thought that I could ever despoil that glorious
creature seems to me almost a crime. I have not
heard from her again. If she should marry the young
Duke———. No, I do not think she will do that.

    ·   ·   ·   ·   ·   ·

'The winter is long, long, long. It is now the
26th of February ; in Rome how the land laughs, how
the flowers spring, how the blood dances in one's veins
so near to March ! Here all is snow and wind, or fog
and sleet, and the poor deer look shivering and sad
under the leafless trees amongst the black frosted
bracken.

'The house-steward has just brought me a telegraphic
message he has had from her. It is sent from Paris
and merely says, " We come home to-morrow." To-
morrow ! Like that ' Without a word of preparation.
He says it is the way " my lady " always does. My
God! what shall I say to her ? How shall I receive
her ? I know not whether I am most overjoyed or
most wretched. If only I knew what I should most
wisely, most rightly, do ! And to think that it is all
not hers but mine—that she is in truth my guest! She
has been away four months. For some time she has
not written to me. I may have become no more to her
than the nameless painter of her frescoes. If so—well,
I will never take up my rights. It would be too much
like vengeance. If she seem to care at all—well, then

I will go away, send her portrait to the Salon, perhaps conquer a name in the world great enough to make it not too impossible for me to say to her " I love you." No : I will not take away her little kingdom from her; I have a wider kingdom—Art. She trusted me. She shall not have cause to repent it.

    •   •   •   •   •   •

' The " to-morrow " is now "to-day." I could sleep not at all. It is now noon; she may be here at any moment. I scrawl this with a crayon in the ballroom. There is still snow, but the sun is shining. They have sent her Russian sledge to meet her with the three Russian horses. Berwick is gone of his own accord with the sledge. He would never leave me before. It seems he knows. How shall I meet her? What shall I say? I feel as if I were false to her. It is absurd, but I cannot resist the feeling. I hear a noise of sleigh-bells, of voices, of great doors opening and shutting, of dogs barking : then all is still again—she is come.

' It is nearly four o'clock and almost dark. I scarcely see to scrawl this to you by the light of the fire. The frescoes are not one-half finished ; this vexes me much ; but the weather has been so utterly against all work. Her friends will tell her I have purposely delayed. I suppose I shall not see her till to-morrow. The man who especially waits on me has been in with wood, and says that Lady Cairnwrath has returned with her : no one else ; but that many people are expected

in a week from this. By that time I shall be gone.
She must get the frescoes finished as she can. . .
They have brought me word that her ladyship sent me
her compliments and wished to see me in the library;
she is taking her tea there after the journey. Will I
go at once? I cannot refuse. She has not forgotten.
I tremble at the thought of seeing her, though I long
so greatly to do so. I feel as if she would read all my
secrets in my face. I love her so well and yet I cannot
say a word! Pray for me, dear Father. When next I
shall write I shall be in Rome. Rome is the Mater
Dolorosa, the Mother of Consolation.

    .   .   .   .   .   .

'This was not posted last night. I open it to add
that no one under heaven was ever so greatly blessed as
I. Even now as I sit in the clear morning light, in
my own chamber, I cannot believe in my own paradise;
I cannot believe that, having wrestled so long, the
angel blesses me at last! When the servant brought
me her message in the ballroom, I got up and walked
through the house, and felt like a drunken man as I
moved. To see her in the library! It seemed to me
as if the very walls would speak to her, as if the French
secrétaire would find a voice! I was like one in a
dream. I found myself still as in a dream; standing
before her in the familiar room. It was dusk, for which
I was thankful, the long dusk of these grey English
days. There was a gleam of low light from the windows

which look west, and the full warm glow of the great fire. It shone on the silver tea-tray and samovar, on the white bear-skin by the hearth, on her as she stood there. She looked very pale and a little tired; she had what they call a tea-gown on, a thing all soft old lace and gleaming trailing satin : a thing which most becomes her, I think, of all she wears. She put her hand out to me and I bent low over it. I said nothing; I could say nothing. She, too, seemed more silent than her wont. She murmured in a hurry, indistinctly, all sorts of little phrases: there was fever at Cannes, her grandmother was unwell, she had been so bored, it was only London emptied out by the Mediterranean, she hated the mixture of scorching sun and icy wind, she liked a fast gallop over a wet Berkshire road much better : I remember all these sentences now; at the time I do not think I heard them. I was gazing at her, and thinking how I loved her, and of how I must go out of her presence and away from her in silence. I could see no other way. All this while I never spoke a word.

'She came closer to me in the half glow from the firelight and the lingering daylight ; and we stood quite near together on the hearth. I still could not speak ; I kissed again the hand she again held out to me ; I kept thinking if she knew—if she knew !— Perhaps I looked strangely, for her eyes had a startled glance in them. She said at last, in her old, pretty, quick fashion, " Well, have you not a word to say? Are you displeased that I am home again? What have

you done on the walls? Have you been very dull?"
I could not have uttered a word to save my life or hers;
I could only gaze at her, and I saw she grew very red;
rosy-red, like the hothouse camellia she had at her
breast. "Why would you not come to Cannes?" she
said, without looking at me. "I wanted you; could
you not understand?" I said nothing; I could hear
my heart beat as if it would break my breast, but I
said nothing. Then she touched my hand with hers.
"Why will you be so proud?" I heard her ask in quite
a whisper. "You do like me a little, why don't you
tell me so? I do not care what any of them think : I
only care for you. We might be so happy, if you would
not be so proud!" Then I fell at her feet and kissed
them. Later that night I told her all the truth. I
showed her all the papers; she does not mind. What
is hers is mine, what is mine is hers. The world can
think what it likes. If it deem her the most generous
of all living women, it will only be right for once!'

---

*The Lady Charterys, Milton Ernest, to Don Eccellino
Ferraris, Florinella-sopra-Subiaco :—*

'I love you already! You must come to us at
Easter. He means to buy that deserted palace above
Florinella, and make it beautiful, so that we may often
visit you. He says Bramante built it, and that you
have often regretted to see it forsaken.'

The Lady Cairnwrath of Othwestry to Lord Llandudno, White's Club, London :—

'A great scandal has been most mercifully and providentially averted. Lord Charterys—for this gentleman is indisputably Lord Charterys; I see a strong resemblance in his features to poor Alured's—behaves in the most admirable manner; he will not hear of the truth being made public. He says the world may think him the debtor of his wife if it please. It does not really matter, because of course, either way, the first son she has will bear the same title, and ultimately inherit. I am very thankful the publicity is avoided; and I reflect with pleasure that I never allowed the obscure name and place of the unknown painter to prevent my recognition of him as a high-bred gentleman. You will remember that I always said he had *l'air noble.* It will certainly be difficult, as you observe, to make society comprehend why we consent to such an apparently unequal, indeed improbable, union; but when it is known that we all approve, no one will venture on an adverse comment; every one will be aware that I should never give my countenance to what was either unwise or incorrect. Besides, I do not see why, in a private sort of manner, the facts should not be made known. If you think proper you can tell one or two of your friends in the window at White's, quite confidentially; it will soon be all over the town, and it will perhaps be better than to allow people to suppose a mésalliance possible *to us.* Esmée has been a great and sore anxiety to me for many years. I am thankful that my responsibility will pass at last into other hands. She is quite *extraordinarily* in love with him, and obedient to him. I should never have supposed she could so change through the mere influence of a senti-ment.'

Leonis Renzo, Milton Ernest, to Don Eccellino Ferraris, Florinella-sopra-Subiaco :—

'You must come for Easter, and leave your sanctuary on the hills for once, to give us your benediction, my first and my holiest friend!'

Mr. Hollys, Rome, to the Lady Charterys, Milton Ernest :—

'I am thoroughly bewildered. But I heartily congratulate you both. I feel, as our beloved Transatlantics say, "a little mixed." When will the frescoes get finished? I suppose you forgive me?'

The Lady Charterys, Milton Ernest, to Mr. Hollys, Rome :—

'Yes: I forgive you even the rude nonsense you wrote. I shall always call him Renzo. We shall remain here all the summer, and he *will* finish the frescoes!'

AT CAMALDOLI

A SKETCH

DRAMATIS PERSONÆ.

DUCA DI BASTIA.	THE COMTESSE DE RIOM.
MARCHESE DELLA ROCCALDA.	MADAME DE SAINTANGE.
MR. WYNNE-ELLIS.	MRS. VANSCHELDT.
PADRE FRANCESCO.	

AT CAMALDOLI.

Scene: *The Hotel in the Monastery.*

In the Pharmacy.

Comtesse de Riom. It makes one long to be ill, to have an excuse to come here.

Duca di Bastia. I need no excuse ; I buy liqueurs.

Comtesse de Riom. Did you ever see such exquisite old blue pots ? All pure Savona. I have offered my soul for one of them, but the monks are obdurate.

Duca di Bastia. Do not tempt them. Selling is the modern curse of Italy. It is a comfort to find that monastery walls can exclude the temptation ; they too often do not, and our angels are sold to shiver in the fogs of London and the snows of Berlin.

Comtesse de Riom. Does not one get back into pure *quattro cento* here ? Romeo's apothecary must have had just such conserve pots and sweet-water jars as these.

Duca di Bastia. You would like my old palace at Squillace, madame ; it has such quantities of such old pottery as this, all as dusty as the soul can desire.

Comtesse de Riom. I should delight in dusting them.

Duca di Bastia. How happy you would make me! I should envy the cobwebs.

Comtesse de Riom. What! when I should destroy the cobwebs?

Duca di Bastia. It would be better to be destroyed than to be unnoticed.

Comtesse de Riom. That is according to taste.

Mrs. Vanscheldt. How do you do, Duke? Whatever are *you* doing at Camaldoli?

Duca di Bastia. If it were not impolite to reply to one question by another, I should ask what do you— the idol of Paris, the queen of Aix, the *reine gaillarde* of London?

Mrs. Vanscheldt. All that is very pretty, but behind my back I dare say you call me that horrid American; don't get off by a *faux fuyant;* what makes you bury yourself in this pinewood?

Duca di Bastia. My adoration of Americans.

Mrs. Vanscheldt. Don't expect me to believe that, when you might have married Elise Hicks last winter, with the biggest fortune that ever came out of Arkansas lumber. (*To* Madame de Riom.) He might indeed, and she was a very pretty girl too, and—my!—her pearls!

Comtesse de Riom. The Duke was ungrateful.

Duca di Bastia. As ungrateful as the monks who won't sell their pots. My prejudices and theirs have probably the same roots.

Mrs. Vanscheldt. But why do you come to Camaldoli—*you*? Can you live without a Club?

Duca di Bastia. I find Camaldoli charming; a most admirably healthy air, perfect quiet; pinewoods which are so good for the lungs, and, as Madame de Riom remarks, divine pharmacy pots to keep alive in one the love of the fine arts. What can one ask more? Perhaps the cookery leaves something to be desired, but that is just the amount of mortification which one ought to be willing to endure in a monastery.

Mrs. Vanscheldt. All the same you must be bored to death, *mon cher.* Shall we get up a little baccara to-night?

Duca di Bastia (hesitates). Madame de Riom does not approve.

Mrs. Vanscheldt. What! is the Countess to be the keeper of all our consciences? Then we shall be as dull as a Boston Sunday, for she sets her face dead against all fun.

Comtesse de Riom. You think me a Puritan! Indeed I am no such thing, but I detest all kinds of play; I have seen so much suffering caused by it.

Mrs. Vanscheldt (aside). Now she will preach like a young Dominican friar.

Comtesse de Riom. No; I never preach; play if you like, but if you must play, why do you come to Camaldoli?

Mrs. Vanscheldt. I come to wait for Mr. Vanscheldt, who is in the course of crossing the ocean, and because, as the Duke wisely observes, the odours of the pine-woods are so good for the lungs; my lungs are seriously affected, only nobody ever will believe it.

Duca di Bastia. Nobody will believe that mine are.

Mrs. Vanscheldt. I am sure we have both done our best that they should be. Did *you* come for your lungs, too, Countess?

Comtesse de Riom. No; I came for quiet. But it seems that the world sends its echoes even up amongst these saintly hills, and you have brought as many *fourgons* as if you had come to Monaco in January. I have brought nothing but serge.

Mrs. Vanscheldt. Serge smothered in Mechlin, however. So much depends on what one *can* wear. You are such an elegant creature that you may put on sacking and you will look just as well. If I'm not dressed up to my eyes, I'm a dowdy, a fright—nobody'd look at me—the very birds would peck at me. I wouldn't put on those plain tailor-made suits that you can wear if it were to save my life.

Duca di Bastia. There is Saxe china *pimpante* and charming, and there are marble Venuses, white, serene, superb. One may admire both.

Mrs. Vanscheldt. Very prettily said, Duke. But I know you don't admire me; you told a friend of mine that I was like a doll out of the Palais Royal.

Duca di Bastia. That friend must have thoroughly understood the mission of friendship. If I could hope that such a friend were of the masculine gender——

Mrs. Vanscheldt. You would quarrel with him about a cigar or a newspaper, and hack him about afterwards with a sabre: I know your ways. Why will Italians always fight with sabres? It is very barbarous.

Duca di Bastia. It is not pretty. The rapier is much more elegant and the pistol much quicker. But every nation has its prejudices; the sabre is ours.

Mrs. Vanscheldt. It ought not to be so; it is not sufficiently graceful. The rapier is more like what your national weapon should be. The rapier is amongst swords what the mandoline is amongst instruments.

Duca di Bastia (bows). Henceforth I will fight with the rapier.

Comtesse de Riom. I hope you will not fight at all; it is very barbarous.

Duca di Bastia. It is a little, but it is wholesome. If that friend whom Madame Vanscheldt spoke of——

Mrs. Vanscheldt. It was a she!

Duca di Bastia. Ah! I might have supposed so. Some one who has envied your toilettes, or whose receptions I have neglected. Malice is always so busy one wonders there are two people left on speaking terms with each other.

Padre Francesco (approaching). Our mountain roses are very simple things, but if their Excellencies would deign to accept them?

Comtesse de Riom. Oh, mon Révérend! how exquisite! How can I thank you enough? Monsieur de Bastia, say something pretty to him for me.

Mrs. Vanscheldt. Poor old man ! And we order ten thousand for a ball, and never look at them.

Comtesse de Riom. How very kind ! What sweet roses ! I must really learn Italian to be able to talk to these delightful old people.

Duca di Bastia. Let me have the honour to teach you, madame.

Mrs. Vanscheldt. When Italians teach a pretty woman their language, they always begin with Dante. They get to the *galeotto fu il libro e chi lo scrisse*, and there they stop. The lesson never advances.

Comtesse de Riom. We will begin with Silvio Pellico

Duca di Bastia. We will begin with what you like, provided we end in Alcina's Gardens.

Comtesse de Riom. Alcina's Gardens ? That is in Ariosto.

Duca di Bastia. It is in Ariosto. But Ariosto found it in Love. It is still there.

> [*The Comtesse de Riom colours and plays with her roses.*

Mrs. Vanscheldt (smiling). Did Ariosto ever come here—for his lungs—I wonder ? Do these dear old male goodies sell cigarettes, do you know ?

Duca di Bastia. I fear they are not yet at that height of civilisation. They sell liqueurs into which I believe oil and honey enter in equal proportions. Here is one with a title fit for an ode of Meleager's or Ovid's, the *Lagrime d' abete.* What can be more poetic ?

Mrs. Vanscheldt. I'll taste. It won't beat Delmonico's pick-me-ups.

Duca di Bastia. Alas! what can the old world——

Mrs. Vanscheldt. Don't be hypocritical. You despise us utterly from the height of all your twelve centuries of nobility. Tell us all about your twelve centuries; it is very interesting. I don't go back myself farther than my own father.

Duca di Bastia. You are laughing at me; that is very unkind.

Mrs. Vanscheldt. Honour bright I'm not. I think it must be perfectly delightful to have an ancestry that is just a *cours de l'histoire* in itself. There were Bastias in the time of Constantine, weren't there? Tell us all about it. We are in a mood to be educated. Is it true you were kings of Corsica once upon a time?

Duca di Bastia. Pray spare me. I will send you the volume B. of Ingherami; I shall so at least not *see* you yawn.

Mrs. Vanscheldt. I shouldn't yawn; I think your Italian genealogies as delightful as wonder-stories and as interesting as a lecture of Caro's. What shall we do with ourselves to-day? If you won't read us Ingherami——

Duca di Bastia. I will read you the ' Decamerone ' under the pines yonder.

Mrs. Vanscheldt. Oh, but isn't that very shocking?

Duca di Bastia. I will take care not to shock you. It will be Madame de Riom's first lesson in Italian. I assure you we are very little altered since the days of Boccaccio. The middle classes are changed, but I think our class and the *popolo* are both very much what we were in the *medio evo.* Here and there we have put electric bells in our villas, and bought a threshing machine for our fields, but even that is rare, and would have been better let alone. Life in Italy is still a picture and an idyl, our old walled gardens and our *loggie* still hear the lute.

Mrs. Vanscheldt. Let us go under the pines then, *et va pour* Boccaccio!

Comtesse de Riom. If the Duke do not translate it, I shall understand nothing.

Duca di Bastia. I will translate it, and will remember the Boston susceptibilities of Madame Vanscheldt.

Mrs. Vanscheldt. My Boston susceptibilities have had a good airing on the boulevards; that produces a wonderful change in them. The starch comes out with quite astonishing rapidity when once one has eat a beefsteak at Bignon's.

Mr. Wynne-Ellis. You would not let anyone else say that, Mrs. Vanscheldt.

Mrs. Vanscheldt. Why, of course not. One laughs at one's country and one abuses one's husband, but one don't let anybody else do either.

Duca di Bastia. Happy country! Thrice happy husband!

Mrs. Vanscheldt. Don't you be impudent.

Duca di Bastia. Impudent! I only sigh for a felicity that cannot be mine.

Mrs. Vanscheldt. You might have married Elise Hicks.

Duca di Bastia. No one has any right to say that I could. Mdlle. Hicks is about to marry a Prince Galitzin; there are three hundred and thirty-five Princes Galitzin. I do not know whether he is at the top of the list or the bottom.

Mrs. Vanscheldt. I believe you are regretting Elise. Well, let us get to Boccaccio. All *I* know about him is that stupid little operetta. I ought to have been learned, coming from the 'hub of the universe,' but I'm not.

Duca di Bastia. You are so many things so much more delightful. Boccaccio would have adored you, especially when you wear that red cloak.

Mrs. Vanscheldt. Adoration that depends on the colour of a cloak won't kill one with over-devotion, and I don't think you are as respectful as you might be, Duke.

Duca di Bastia. Respectful! I am neither twenty nor sixty. Need a man be respectful to ladies between those ages?

Madame de Saintange. Not if he wish to please.

Mrs. Vanscheldt. How shocked Mr. Ellis looks. Englishmen are always respectful; I believe they remain so even when they talk to a ballet-girl.

Duca di Bastia. They are born *en froc et cravate blanche.* At the risk of shocking Monsieur Ellis again, I will tell you a story. It happened to me myself.

Perhaps you will say it is too like *Toto chez Tata* to be true, nevertheless——

Mrs. Vanscheldt. I think we'll pass over it, Duke, for Mr. Ellis is blushing in anticipation. I'm half afraid to trust you with Boccaccio——

Duca di Bastia. I assure you I will be penetrated with respect, though I agree with Madame de Saintange that it is an unlovely quality. You shall have a 'Decamerone' that might be read in Boston on a Sunday; can I say more?

Mrs. Vanscheldt. I am afraid you have said a little too much. However, we will go under the pines and hear your worst.

Duca di Bastia. There are listeners for whose ears the type of the 'Decamerone' would change of its own accord into the type of the 'Imitatione Christi.'

Mrs. Vanscheldt. You are speaking to me, but you are looking at Madame de Riom. She might perform that miracle in printer's type, I certainly shall not. Well, let us go. These old men are wanting to be alone with their stills and herbs and flowers. What delicious old fellows they are—in their white flannel gowns and their broad flapping straw hats. What a pretty world it must have been when everybody dressed picturesquely!

Duca di Bastia. And when monks were as many in the land as song-sparrows in the trees. Nothing 'comes' better, as artists say, in the Tuscan landscape than two of these white-frocked figures going up a grass path under the olives, or passing along a sunny road through the vine-shadows; and if the bells are ringing within hearing at the time the thing is perfect.

Mr. Wynne-Ellis. It is only a trivial and profane mind which can consider the monastic order—the curse of so many centuries—as the mere ornament of a decorative scene.

Duca di Bastia. Ah, dear Mr. Ellis, I am so sorry, but I am always trivial; I am profane too; yet, so near Alvernia, do you think we should speak ill of a community that held S. Francesco? Trivial as my mind is, I do not feel inclined to do that. I dare say there are many monks great rogues, but still, when I see a monk I take off my hat to him, for if he be nothing or even worse than nothing in himself, he represents so much in the past that was holier than anything we shall ever see again.

Mrs. Vanscheldt. That is a pretty feeling, and I shall not let Mr. Ellis dispute it with you. You have kept the soul of the Quattro Centisti, though you have eaten, like me, the *bisque* of Bignon. But we shall never have Boccaccio read at this rate, and the sun will be going down if we don't make haste into the woods.

In the Woods.

Marchese della Roccalda. Caro mio, you have read remarkably well. To make Boccaccio decent and yet diverting is a task that might daunt any man; but where failure was almost certain you have achieved success.

Mr. Wynne-Ellis. The Duke did not wholly avoid some questionable suggestions, but in the main, for an impromptu translation, it has been well done.

Mrs. Vanscheldt. Dear Mr. Ellis, to the pure all things are nasty; that's Scripture, and it's such a pity I'm a naughty woman, and I can't for the life of me see what was left that was objectionable.

Mr. Wynne-Ellis. There were suggestions——

Mrs. Vanscheldt. Oh, only suggestions! Well, you know, I must be very obtuse, I really didn't notice them. Perhaps a course of the *petits théâtres* has hardened my conscience and my tympanum.

Comtesse de Riom. How beautifully you have read, or, rather, improvised, Monsieur de Bastia! you have given us a great pleasure. All that marvellous life of old Florence seemed to live again.

Duca di Bastia. I am happy, indeed, to have your praise. As I said before, we are not so very much changed at heart or even in manners since those days. It is easy to reproduce them in fancy. It requires no talent—only memory.

Comtesse de Riom. Perhaps genius is only memory; I have heard it said.

Duca di Bastia. Oh, do not give such a great word to my slight efforts. I am a very idle son of the soil, with a trick of rhyming and of improvising in which any one of our mountain peasants would excel ten times better than I.

Marchese della Roccabla. We might be holding one of those Courts of Love of which Italy saw so many in Boccaccio's days. Those big dusky pines, those lovely ladies, Bastia's lute, the Countess's great peacock fan — it might be all up at Urbino in Bembo's time, or at Ferrara in Lucrezia's.

Duca di Bastia. The lovely ladies certainly made heaven of Urbino and Ferrara then, as they do now of Camaldoli; but the pinewoods you would have been puzzled to find in either place.

Marchese della Roccabla. You are hypercritical.

Duca di Bastia. Nature created me so. When De Musset made an *Andalouse* in *Barcelone,* he spoilt his poem for me.

Comtesse de Riom. The mistake does not prevent the poem thrilling like the song of a nightingale and the thrust of a dagger.

Duca di Bastia. No; it has the passion of a lifetime and the moonlit nights of a whole summer of love in it. After all, his city is not Barcelona only, but anywhere where heaven is found upon a human breast.

Mr. Wynne-Ellis. What frightful waste of talent Alfred de Musset's is! Perhaps if he had never met George Sand——

Duca di Bastia. Waste? I would sooner have written *Rolla* than have cut the Suez Canal. If he had never met George Sand—if Tasso had never met Leonora—if Dante had never known Beatrice—if Abelard had never met Héloïse—Comtesse, love is not an accident, it is a destiny.

Comtesse de Riom (with a smile). You are very fond of talking about love. Is that Italian?

Duca di Bastia. We never talk about anything else. Love has a much larger share in our lives than in those of your northern men; there never was but one northern who understood us, and that was Henri Boyle.

Mrs. Vanscheldt. Didn't he say that all men are tyros in the art of love beside the Italian?

Duca di Bastia (with emphasis). Because with us it is an art, exacting and imperious as an art, which absorbs our heart and soul, our passions, our entire being; an art which we think is worthy to occupy our lifetime.

Mrs. Vanscheldt. Ah, yes, just like a painter! His art is one and indivisible, it is only his subjects that change; he can't help painting a mill one day, and a tree the next, and a horse the next, and so on; it is always art. So with you, it is sometimes grey eyes, sometimes blue eyes, sometimes brown eyes, but it is always love.

Duca di Bastia. Did you learn all this, Madame, at Boston on a Sunday?

Mrs. Vanscheldt. No, it is the result of my observations since I came East. In our great country, sir-*ee*, there's such an uncommon deal of marriage that love gets kind o' hustled. Men and women too, down our way, walk out so much together that they just lose flavour for each other, and feel like two tame 'possums sitting on a gumtree. Now don't say I can't talk Yankeese!

Mr. Wynne-Ellis. Do you really think, Mrs. Vanscheldt, that marriage is unappreciated in the States?

Mrs. Vanscheldt. Heavens, no; it's too much appreciated. There's such a lot of it, it's like eating oysters by the sack. If it was a little harder to do, and a little harder to undo, perhaps Americans would learn to make love. As it is, they can't, no more than they can say a clear monosyllable. You never met an American who didn't split the monosyllables, did you?

Mr. Wynne-Ellis. I have observed what you mean. It is very extraordinary. Perhaps climatic influences on the trachea——

Mrs. Vanscheldt. I dare say. (*Aside*) Is it climatic influences that produce the genus bore?

Marchese della Roccalda. How happy Madame Vanscheldt would make me if she would only say one monosyllable to me : '*tu*'!

Mrs. Vanscheldt. I'm more likely to say in my own vernacular, '*goose*'!

Marchese della Roccalda. That is what you call ' chaff;' we do not possess the equivalent in our language. It is not even precisely the same thing as the Gallic *badinage.*

Mrs. Vanscheldt. No; it ain't half so delicate, and it don't want any wit.

Duca di Bastia. We have something like it in Pulci and his compeers, and in our peasants, too, on a market day, or when they are in a merry mood anywhere. Comtesse, shall we go for a little walk before the sun sets? This brook that comes tumbling down amongst us seems to promise all sorts of delightful recompense to the adventurous.

[*They saunter away together.*

Mr. Wynne-Ellis (to Mrs. VANSCHELDT). Is that *the* Madame de Riom—the very rich one?

Mrs. Vanscheldt. Yes, I think so. A charming woman, so Bastia seems to say.

Mr. Wynne-Ellis. Belgian, I believe?

Mrs. Vanscheldt. Yes, they are big people in Belgium; as big as they can be in that mouse of a country.

Marchese della Roccalda. Madame de Riom would remind us that the mouse has had the spirit of a lion ere now; and that it has come nearer to ourselves in art than any other country on the map of the world. Are not the De Rioms Brabant nobility?

Mrs. Vanscheldt. I believe so; they are immensely rich. This one is the widow of Henri de Riom; she is uncommonly handsome.

Marchese della Roccalda. We might think so, perhaps, if Madame Vanscheldt were not by.

Mrs. Vanscheldt. Now, my dear Marchese, what rubbish! I haven't a feature in my face! I've a little *minois chiffonnée* crumpled up like a rag ball, with two sparks for eyes, and that's all. But you are so used here to regular profiles that you don't appreciate them; they are *toujours perdrix*; you like a little ugly mobile gutta-percha face better, because it's new.

Marchese della Roccalda. The mobile face is the only one of which one never tires.

Mrs. Vanscheldt. See if you'd say so if we were shut up opposite each other through a cold spell in Ottawa, or the sickly season down Florida way.

Marchese della Roccalda. I am convinced that the thermometer would always stand permanently for me at 20° R. under those circumstances, and its sister instrument at ' set fair.'

Mrs. Vanscheldt. It's set fair with Bastia.

Marchese della Roccalda. It's only the red dawn that precedes the stormy day. It is quite evident he means to marry her!

Mrs. Vanscheldt. Why don't they have *chaises à porteurs* here? Who can climb who eats six times a day? Besides, the human's not meant for a climbing animal. He has no hooks to his toes. We'll sit still, and wait till they come back.

Marchese della Roccalda (casting himself at her ject). Paradise!

Mrs. Vanscheldt (looking about her). I only do hope there are no snakes. When you've seen a hooded come wriggling along, you don't love them any more, however fond you may be of the study of natural history.

Marchese della Roccalda. We have no snakes in Tuscany, only harmless chains of green and gold, that hang head foremost from the boughs, and look at us.

Mrs. Vanscheldt. You must have adders, anyway. They're a universal institution, like marriage.

Marchese della Roccalda. When you say these things I cease for one moment to envy M. Vanscheldt. All the rest of my life is consumed in envy of him.

Mrs. Vanscheldt. Well, that aren't too civil, seeing there's no living man sees less of me! Here's a peasant; how miserable she looks! *Perche piange?* What does she say? Does she talk High Dutch?

Marchese della Roccalda. Mountain Italian; equally unintelligible. Her husband's in prison because he dared to plant a cabbage or two on a bit of forest land, that is, of government land.

Mrs. Vanscheldt. Poor soul! tell her to go and ask my maid to give her twenty francs. Guess you worry your poor too much, drives 'em all our side. Seems to me if the man 'd stole his cabbages you couldn't have done more to him. Is it true your hill people eat grass?

Marchese della Roccalda. *Saggina,* a sort of seeding grass; yes, they do, *poverini!*

Mrs. Vanscheldt. Here we grumble if the fish don't come up every day, and if the truffles run short now and then! Marquis, there's enough buckwheat on God's earth for every man to have his handful. How is it we've become so right on wicked that we stuff while they starve? It's not in nature.

Marchese della Roccalda. Oh, yes, pardon me, it is in nature. Look at monkeys.

Higher in the Woods.

Duca di Bastia. Will you not believe me? Did the devotion of a whole winter prove nothing? What can I do to induce you to take pity on me?

Comtesse de Riom. Dear Duca, you are well known to be a most desperate flirt. No woman in her senses ever takes your pretty speeches seriously.

Duca di Bastia. Every man is a flirt until he oves sincerely. I have been most serious. It is now seven months since I saw you first; it was at a novena at St. Peter's; you were all in black. The next night I saw you at the Apollo; you wore a marvellous crimson dress, and you had some great red lilies.

Comtesse de Riom. *Red* lilies! To be sure; they dye even the poor flowers nowadays. What a pity it is! Red is the only colour that tells in a theatre; it is the colour of crowds. To impress the multitude soldiers should only wear red; when they are grey they have no moral effect.

Duca di Bastia. In red, or in grey, or in black, you 'awe me through my eyes.' Why will you not believe it?

Comtesse de Riom. You are always saying those

pretty things to women ; you may even mean them at the moment, but——

Duca di Bastia. Do you think that a little thing would make me bury myself under these monastic pines ?

Comtesse de Riom. I thought it was for your lungs ?

Duca di Bastia. You never thought any such thing. When you left Rome at Easter, you said you should come to this religious solitude, and there-fore——

Comtesse de Riom. This religious solitude is pro-faned by the click of Mrs. Vanscheldt's roulette ball, and resembles the big world as a lizard resembles a crocodile. Where can one go nowadays that one is not pursued by the cigarette smoke of 'society'?

Duca di Bastia. You cannot, because society goes where you go.

Comtesse de Riom. Oh dear no! I am a very insignificant person. If you really wish to know, I have come to Camaldoli because it is—cheap!

Duca di Bastia. You are pleased to jest.

Comtesse de Riom. I was never more serious. I am much more serious than you were just now. My dear Duke, do not let us beat about the bush. You think I am the widow of Henri di Riom, who was very rich. I am the widow of Otto, the younger brother, who had only a younger brother's portion, and ran through that in two years.

Duca di Bastia. But—but—surely——

Comtesse de Riom. You mean that I look as if I had a hundred thousand francs a year to spend on my gowns? That is the way of all of us in our world. We had a very pleasant winter in Rome. I should be sorry if it were to leave the slightest cloud of painful remembrance with you. (*He is silent. She looks at him and smiles.*)

Comtesse de Riom. I am so often supposed to be my sister-in-law, Marthe de Riom, Henri's widow. She never leaves her château, and never spends a sou that she can help, just because she has millions. I have fancied once or twice that you were misled into thinking me the owner of these millions. Oh, I do not bear you the slightest grudge. Why should I bear you any? It has been all my own fault for letting Worth dress me too well. Really I have next to no money at all. My own people are poor noblesse, and, Otto once dead, the de Rioms have nothing to do with me. Madame de Saintange lives with me *par respect des convenances*, but she pays everything for herself. Now that I have been quite frank with you my conscience is clear. I know marriage in Italy is only a question of *chiffres*. 'I have so much: how much have you?' That is all that your Hymen inquires. Love you keep between the leaves of Boccaccio; or—where was it you said that Ariosto found it?

Duca di Bastia (very pale). Madame——

Comtesse de Riom. How white you look? Do not

be afraid; I do not mean to hold you to your pretty speeches. If I did you could justly retort that they are only for Alcina's Garden. I understand it all quite well; you have a great name and a delightful wit, but you are very poor; you see in me a woman who does not displease your taste, and in whom, by a fatality of misunderstanding, you believe you meet one who has the riches and the estates that you are obliged to seek in marriage. As soon as you speak seriously to me I tell you the facts as they are. I am quite poor too; horribly poor, for a woman who likes luxury, and must go to courts and embassies. Our toilettes mean nothing except that we spend all we do possess on them. I have some fine old jewels; they are all. I had a tiny *dot*, which is what I have to live on now. I married poor Otto when I was sixteen; I cared very little about him. I was in love with love, as girls are. The man was but a peg on which to hang a dream-coat of many colours. He gambled, and died very early. I am five-and-twenty years old, and I feel a hundred. Don't waste your time thinking about me. Go away from the monastic solitude and enjoy yourself. There is nothing more to be said. I am not what you believed me. You will put me out of your head from this moment, and take nothing worse away from Camaldoli than a bottle of the *lagrime d' abete.* You will shed no tears of your own.

Duca di Bastia (bitterly). Nor can I hope for any from you!

Comtesse de Riom. Oh, that would be really too much to expect. Remember how many women, to be Duchessa di Bastia—and your title is so old that it is really attractive—would have only let you find out the truth so late that you could scarcely in honour have drawn back ; or, if you had drawn back, my brother Louis, who is always enchanted to kill anybody, would have tried the sabre encounter with you which Madame Vanscheldt thinks so ugly. I might have done you a very great deal of harm, and I refrain from doing you any. You cannot reasonably expect me to weep for you as well, can you ?

Duca di Bastia. You have never deigned to believe in what I expressed.

Comtesse de Riom. Yes, I have done in a measure. I see that I am agreeable to your taste, that you approve of me, that you find pleasure in talking to me. Those things are never assumed, or, when they are, one at once detects the assumption ; but then you saw me painted on a golden background, like the Quattro-centesti Saints. When you realise that I am that much-to-be pitied creation of modern life, a well-born woman, accustomed to all kinds of self-indulgence and elegances, with a certain rank to keep up, and a mere pittance to do it on, which all goes to the pockets of the Paris tailors, you will view me with quite different eyes. Take away the golden ground, the saint is no saint, but a mere commonplace woman, with no nimbus at all. (*He is silent.*)

Comtesse de Riom. Haven't you even one compliment left with which to contradict me? You look terribly shocked, considering that there is no real harm done. If you keep your own counsel no one will be the wiser. They all know that the Duca di Bastia is a great flirt. They will not be surprised that you grew tired of flirting with anybody as grave as I am. Really, the wonder is that you have been so constant for six months, and that you have endured Camaldoli for six days, even with the support of the liqueurs.

Duca di Bastia. You are very mirthful. I suppose I ought to rejoice that I amuse you.

Comtesse de Riom. It is very amusing that you should have taken me for Madame Marthe. She is everything that I am not; small, dark, prim, very religious, full of economies. Because she could spend half a million of francs with Worth any year, she has all the year round a camelot gown that costs fifty centimes. I do not know why she saves so much; she has no children, and her money would go, if she died, to some distant relations. To be sure she may marry; why don't you go and marry her? She is not handsome certainly, but there is no doubt about *her* fortune; she has *rentes, actions, valeurs* of all kinds in all the banks of Belgium and in the banks of France too. I will give you a letter of introduction to her. The château is near Malines, it is called Quincampoix; it is all *pignons et tourelles*, with stonework like old Flanders lace; it is really worth seeing. It has fine woods too, and in

Henri and Otto's time the shooting was good. You might revive its glories; there is a peculiar breed of hounds very famous there. Well, you are not excited? I should have thought you would have been already half-way down the hill.

Duca di Bastia (bitterly). It is evident, madame, that you deem the offer of my hand a diverting comedy. It is true my hand is empty!

Comtesse de Riom. Here is Madame Vanscheldt, who has tired of sitting still. To her all life is a comedy. What a delightful temperament that is! It is a perpetual amulet against ennui.

Mrs. Vanscheldt (to Mr. WYNNE-ELLIS). How glum that gay Duca looks! You bet she's refused him. I didn't think she would. But to be sure she's all the dollars. I don't think he's a rich man himself; if he were driven to say what he lives on——

Mr. Wynne-Ellis. The Italian nobles are impoverished by the inordinate taxation, and the Duca di Bastia inherited embarrassed estates; his way of life is not calculated to disentangle his difficulties.

Mrs. Vanscheldt. Well, his way of life would be smooth for ever if Madame de Riom would say yes, but he don't look as if she had said yes. Suppose she thinks he's after her money.

Madame de Saintange (overhearing, with a smile). Margot is not suspicious.

Mrs. Vanscheldt. She mayn't be, but when one's got a pot of money one can't help feeling like a sugar cask in a street. Do tell me now, you who are her intimate friend, will she marry him?

Madame de Saintange. I am not in her confidence.

Mrs. Vanscheldt. Then you may be sure she won't, for if she had meant to do it she couldn't have helped telling you.

Madame de Saintange. You think we always boast of our good actions?

In the COMTESSE DE RIOM'S *room.*

Madame de Saintange. What have you done to the Duca di Bastia? He did not dine to-night.

Comtesse de Riom. He is probably gone to take the train at Arezzo. My dear friend, he mistook me for Madame Marthe.

Madame de Saintange. What do you mean?

Comtesse de Riom. Precisely what I say. He took me to be the widow of Henri, whose millions would have been very serviceable to him. So many people have always confused me with Marthe. What can I do? I cannot wear a placard on the back of my gown proclaiming that I am the widow of Otto who left me *sans le sou*?

Madame de Saintange. Did the Duke ask you if you were Marthe?

Comtesse de Riom. Of course not; he took it for granted. He asked me to marry him; I replied that he was under an illusion, that I was not Marthe, and had not millions, that I had in fact scarcely enough to pay for my gowns.

Madame de Saintange. I do not think you were called on to explain that unasked.

Comtesse de Riom. Oh-h-h!

Madame de Saintange. I do not really. He is certainly in love with you, even if he did make that error; that was all you had to do with; you should have accepted him, since you like him; the rest would have revealed itself in time.

Comtesse de Riom. When in honour he could not have drawn back! Philosophers are right; women have no conscience.

Madame de Saintange. If he had inquired point blank if you were Marthe, you must have answered that you were not, but as no doubt he only made love to you——

Comtesse de Riom. Because he imagined that I possessed a large fortune which would have restored his own. Certainly, I admit that he—he—perhaps likes me really a little, one can never tell; Italians are such exquisite actors that they cheat themselves into belief in their own fictions, but he would never have allowed himself to say so if he had not been misled by some impression (current in Rome, I know not how) that I was the rich Comtesse de Riom. All I had to do was to undeceive him; the rest will come of itself. When he is fairly away from Camaldoli he will forget that there exists an extravagant woman who has gowns and old jewels that nobody ought to have under half a million of francs a year. He has been near a great danger. Whenever he remembers it, if he do remember it, he will feel a little catch of his breath, as a man does when he recalls how he has been once within a moment of an avalanche's falling or within an inch of a runaway express-train.

> [*She turns away; she laughs a little; the tears are in her eyes.*

Madame de Saintange. Chère Margot! if he have escaped an avalanche you have not altogether escaped a slight that wounds you. I am certain you care for this abominable man; though you are so generous and so lenient towards him, you suffer something, much more than he merits to have suffered for him.

Comtesse de Riom. Pray do not make him such a hero, or raise me into a martyr; we are two very useless *gens du monde*, who if we had had Marthe's million might perhaps have gone through life in very fair amity together, but as we have not, shall be quite content to go our several ways apart. He will marry some heiress, and I—I dare say I shall marry, too, some rich old man, some day when Worth's account has more zeros to it than usual. What is there to regret? I don't know Italian, and I have had Boccaccio charmingly translated to me; that is a solid gain.

Madame de Saintange. Your jests do not deceive

me. You care very much for the Duca di Bastia; he is the only man who has ever had power to interest you. You will never marry for a fortune, because you have refused so many alliances already which would have tempted you if you had been to be bought. This Italian Duke is poor, but Italian poverty is graceful. It lies on a marble step in the sun and smiles; it is not appalling. And as it is—you are really unhappy.

Comtesse de Riom. One is always unhappy when one's vanity has been wounded. My reason of course accepts the fact that in view of one's not being Marthe, a man can do only his best to forget one as soon as may be; but at the same time one cannot be proud of that, and I have always liked to be proud.

Madame de Saintange. Oh, why did you tell him?

Comtesse de Riom. For shame, Pauline! You would have done the same had you been in my place. Do not belie yourself; we are weak creatures perhaps, but we are not quite base.

Madame de Saintange. But you care for him!

Comtesse de Riom. Perhaps I could have done. There! it is not worth while to think of any possibilities of that sort. I will sell my jewels which so fatally lead people to imagine that I must be a rich woman. When you are poor you have no business to wear diamonds; there ought to be sumptuary laws about it. Do you know, when I am a few years older I think I shall go into one of those delightful Flemish Béguinages of ours; I have often thought them charming; their cloisters, their stone courts, their little quiet gardens, their beautiful ironwork gates. One would have a grey flannel gown; one would not want Worth's advice about that. I wonder what it would feel like; all the world shut out and nothing left but recollection. They look peaceful enough, these women; so do these old men here. Do they really grow contented? Is it best after all for human life to become a stone that is never turned, and feels neither the sun nor the rain? [*Her maid enters with a bouquet:* Madame la Comtesse, M. le Duc —— *She takes the flowers; her hand trembles.*] The Duca di Bastia!

Madame de Saintange.   The Duca di Bastia? He has not gone to Arezzo?

Comtesse de Riom.   These flowers did not grow at Camaldoli! He must have ordered them whilst he was still under the impression that he knew the Comtesse Marthe! They have evidently come from Florence.

Madame de Saintange. Wherever they came from, surely, since he has sent them now——

Comtesse de Riom.   Do not suggest such an idea to me; I am convinced it is wholly groundless.

Madame de Saintange.   Well, flowers have been the messengers of love ever since the world began, in the days of Lilith.

Comtesse de Riom.   In the days of Lilith the

world was very easy to live in; in ours it is very difficult, especially if you are *dans le train* and have a certain dignity of name to keep up, and little with which to do so. The Duke and I are both in that position; his bouquet comes to say adieu, an amicable adieu; that is all.

Madame de Saintange. They are nearly all orchids. Do orchids mean farewell or separation?

Comtesse de Riom. I think orchids mean nothing; they come from the West, Lilith did not know them.

Madame de Saintange. You are very perverse.

Comtesse de Riom. People always find us most so when we are most reasonable.

Madame de Saintange. Will you not come down-stairs? They will miss you, and will notice that your absence coincides with Bastia's.

Comtesse de Riom. I have a headache, and I do not care to hear people screaming at Poker, or see them growing greedy at Roulette.

Madame de Saintange. We can go out of doors.

Comtesse de Riom. Do you go; I will come later.

Madame de Saintange. Why will you not admit that you care for him?

Comtesse de Riom. I will admit if you like that my vanity has been wounded, also that the Duca di Bastia is a charming companion. But I am not a *pensionnaire* to weep for a lost lover, and I perfectly understand that, though he might adore me, he would be obliged to put me out of his thoughts. The thing for which I reproach myself is that I did not take some means to let him know earlier that I was as poor as he is. There was nothing to tell him in Rome, when one stays at an embassy and goes everywhere, that one is as poor as a church mouse.

Madame de Saintange. I do not see why you should so reproach yourself. If he had inquired he would have learned.

Comtesse de Riom. I am sure he would never have asked. He is too true a gentleman to speak to other persons of any woman that he regarded with any sort of friendship.

Madame de Saintange. You think very well of him.

Comtesse de Riom. I think he is a gentleman.

Madame de Saintange. Well, considering he comes from the Byzantine emperors, he ought at least to be that.

Comtesse de Riom. It does not follow. I have known a descendant of great kings take the change for a franc from a cabman after a *course.*

Madame de Saintange. Well, that is better than squandering the money of a nation.

Comtesse de Riom. Perhaps; but as there are some vices that are generous, so there are some virtues that are mean.

Madame de Saintange. It is very mean, though it may be very prudent, to adore a woman under the impression that she has millions, and to desert her because the millions are not there.

Comtesse de Riom. My dear friend, you speak as if I were Hetty Sorrel or Manon Lescaut! The Duca di Bastia owes no sort of allegiance to me.

Madame de Saintange. He has been your shadow for six months.

Comtesse de Riom. He has wasted six months then. He has hurt no one by doing that except himself. Do you not think we have talked enough about him? Pray go down; I will follow. It is ten o'clock; Poker must be now at its height. There is a pretty Jewess who lets herself be plundered that she may get spoken to.

Madame de Saintange. Very un-Semitic.

Comtesse de Riom. Not so very; look what *la grande Juiverie* wastes on entertaining the fashionable Christians in all the capitals of the world. 'Rob me, but visit me,' they say to society. Pray do go down, my dear. If I be not too lazy I will come.

Madame de Saintange. Lazy! you are unhappy. What a pity it all is! I will leave you if you really wish it.

> [*She goes; the* COMTESSE DE RIOM *takes up the bouquet and looks at it with a sigh.*

Comtesse de Riom. Why did he send it? What is the use?

In the Refectory.

Mrs. Vanscheldt. Is the Duke really gone? What a pity! Let us sign a *supplica* to Madame de

Riom, to ask her to recall him. There is nobody half
so delightful.

Marchese della Roccalda. You make me feel
homicidal towards my oldest friend. I can only hope
that if I were also absent you would praise me as
amiably.

Mrs. Vanscheldt. You must deserve it first. Has
she really refused him ? Do tell us.

Marchese della Roccalda. I cannot imagine Bastia
enduring that degradation ; but everything is possible
at the hands of woman. But do we really know that
he offered himself ? Our lively imaginations have built
up a romance on the simple fact that we found them
alone under some pine-trees, and thought he looked
more serious than usual.

Mrs. Vanscheldt. And he disappears, he don't even
come to dinner ; she keeps her own room, her maid is
seen carrying a magnificent bouquet, and her bosom
friend Madame de Saintange is as cross as two sticks in
the salon.

Marchese della Roccalda. Which would argue
that if Madame de Riom have been cruel she has at
least felt remorse.

Mr. Wynne-Ellis (enters with an open letter). I
have some curious intelligence, dear Mrs. Vanscheldt,
which I am sure will interest you. I had an impression—a mere impression—that the charming lady we
have with us here was not the rich Madame de Riom ;
that she was, in fact, the widow of the younger

brother, who was a great gamester and died very early I wrote to a friend of mine in Brussels, and I find my impression was correct; my impressions are usually correct. So I think we may conclude that the departure of the Duca di Bastia is—well—let us say, a prudential piece of diplomacy. Perhaps he had a friend in Brussels too!

Mrs. Vanscheldt. Dear me, Mr. Ellis, how kind of you! Have you any friend in New York, too, that you've written to about me? I do assure you our pile's sound. We made it about five years ago, sending tinned clams to Europe. Nobody 'd thought of tinning clams till we did. (*Aside to* ROCCALDA) He'll go and tell that in London and Paris.

Marchese della Roccalda. Do you mean, Mr. Ellis, that this beautiful Madame de Riom, who has the jewels of an empress, is *sans le sou?*

Mr. Wynne-Ellis. Well, as the world looks at such things, she is. She had a slender dower (her people were the Comtes d'Evian of Brabant, very poor people); that is all she has now to live on, and I imagine her gowns——

Marchese della Roccalda. Then Bastia must have learned it somehow or other in time?

Mrs. Vanscheldt. Probably she told him. My dear Marchese, a woman born a d'Evian, who wedded a de Riom, isn't an adventuress to marry a man on false pretences!

Mr. Wynne-Ellis. Any way he has evidently

thought prudence the better part of valour, and has retreated in time.

Mrs. Vanscheldt. Then he is a white-livered cur! When he has been *faisant la cour* the whole winter and spring, when he is as much in love as if he were eighteen!——

Marchese della Roccalda. What can he do? He has hardly anything of his own. A very picturesque, utterly unprofitable, estate in Calabria drags on him like a cannon-ball, because he will not sell and cannot afford to improve it. He is like us all; he is a man of the world, with all the ways of the world, and the extravagance of it. She is the same. They may be lovers if they like; it is impossible they should marry. How can we all have taken for granted that she was the rich *veuve* de Riom! There is a rich one?

Mr. Wynne-Ellis. Oh yes, there is a rich one. Monsieur de Bastia should go and see her. I believe she never leaves a château of hers called Quincampoix, but she is worth millions; an ugly little woman, but he need not look at her; with his lamentable principles his wife will naturally be the woman he looks at least.

Mrs. Vanscheldt. Well, I'm sorry. Madame de Riom hasn't been particularly civil to me, and she has a chill sort of manner with her, but she is wonderfully handsome and I like her, and I wish she'd got the millions, and I think Folko di Bastia isn't much of a man for running away like that. We should call it real mean our side.

Mr. Wynne-Ellis. He has certainly gone.

Marchese della Roccalda. What else could he do?

Mrs. Vanscheldt. Well, he don't reward the woman much if she were honourable enough to tell him herself. I wonder if she did, or if he found it out. Madame de Saintange looked as black as thunder last night. Well, men are poor creatures.

In the Monks' garden the next morning.

Comtesse de Riom. What a charm there is in old monastic gardens; in all Italian gardens indeed! In the datura growing with the black cabbage, in the clematis climbing beside the beanstalks; it is all so rough and simple and entangled and luxuriant, and yet it might all have sprung up because the feet of a nymph had passed by! I think I should like to be one of these song-sparrows, flying all day amongst these green silences. Ah, Padre Francesco! What beautiful roses again! You are always so kind. *Mi rincresce di non capire*—I have learned that one phrase of regret.

Padre Francesco. *La Signora Contessa deve imparare la nostra lingua toscana; è bella sulle belle labbra.*

Comtesse de Riom (to herself). How I wish I could talk to him! I would ask him the secret of his content. They always say it is the privilege of philosophers, but surely it is rather the privilege of ignorance. It must be easier to be content in Italy than elsewhere. There is art in the air, and there is joy in the light. If one could only live without that silly great world which is so little, which is always making us spend so much more than we ought, and squander our time in follies that we despise, and put away our gowns unworn because we have been out in them three times. Oh, the intolerable nonsense of it all! And yet it is like any other habit, it becomes a chain; we wear the chain till it grows into a very part of us. If one were quite happy, I think one could be content with very little wealth and nothing of the world, but then nobody is happy; the world is of such use to us just because it makes us forget that. I would go to Scheveningen or Blankenberghe now to get out of myself, only all the people here would be sure to say that I went away because he had gone.

Duca di Bastia *enters the garden; he bows in silence.*

Comtesse de Riom (*in surprise, with a forced smile*). Are you here still, Monsieur de Bastia? I thought you went to Florence last night. Do you want that note of introduction to my sister-in-law? I will go indoors and write it.

Duca di Bastia. Pardon me; did you receive my bouquet?

Comtesse de Riom. Some gorgeous orchids?—yes. You had ordered them for Marthe, I am sure. However, they were not wasted on me, for I am very fond of flowers, and I painted one of them on a china plate as soon as the sun was up; one gets such good habits in the country.

Duca di Bastia. Did it tell you nothing?

Comtesse de Riom. I thought it told me that you had gone to Florence, but it seems I was mistaken since you are still here. My sister-in-law——

Duca di Bastia. Madame, your sister-in-law is, I am sure, everything that is most estimable in woman, but I confess that she does not interest me; let us leave her in peace at Quincampoix. I have come here to speak of a person much less worthy, but who does interest me much more—myself. You were very cruel to me yesterday——

Comtesse de Riom. On the contrary, I was most kind. I saved you from the consequences of your own unconsidered impulses, and from the results of a mistake which might have been to you most disastrous, had you been taken at your word.

Duca di Bastia. You were very cruel. You gave me a *douche d'eau froide* that it still ices my blood to remember. Now I will not pretend to be better than I am. I did, I confess, understand in Rome that you were that Comtesse de Riom who possesses one of the largest fortunes in Belgium and is——

Comtesse de Riom (with irritation). My sister-in-law! I know. I saw your error, and rectified it as soon as I saw it. There is no more to be said. You owe me no apologies.

Duca di Bastia. Pray listen ! I am one of those unhappy people who have a great rank and yet are very poor. There are many like me in Italy. Fortune is not indifferent to me; no man in my position could declare honestly that it was so. But you were in error when you said that marriage with us was only a *question de chiffres.* We are not so base as that. I sent you my orchids that they might tell you so. They seem to have spoken in vain, and yet what I meant them to say is very simple. It is this—I love you!

Comtesse de Riom. Why do you repeat it? It is of no use. I thought you understood yesterday that I am no richer than yourself. You certainly appeared startled out of all illusion.

Duca di Bastia (impatiently). Cannot you forgive me a few moments of disappointment and astonishment? I am aware that it was unromantic to show either. I ought to have been so indifferent to all save yourself that I should have been scarcely sensible of what you told me. But you did not tell it mercifully. You threw your facts and your sarcasms pell-mell in my face with so rude a hand that I was stunned by them for the instant. You attributed mercenary motives to me so unhesitatingly, and made such a jest of my declaration, that you unmanned me; I was disconcerted and defenceless. *La nuit porte conseil.* I went over the hills to Alvernia; though I am no saint, there is a sort of holy influence in such a place— it soothes one at the least. I do not know whether you will laugh again, or again despise me, but I came back to say to you, if you would not be afraid of the future I should not. I could get an embassy, they have often offered me one; or we could lead an idyllic life all by ourselves on my old estates in Calabria—it is so Greek there still! We should be poor certainly, for I have very little, but if you were not afraid——

Comtesse de Riom (growing pale). My dear Duke! you are dreaming. You have been asleep at Alvernia and had visions. You would not say these things if you were really awake.

Duca di Bastia. I am entirely awake, and was never in my life more serious. You should believe me, for I do not attempt to disguise the truth from you. I thought you a rich woman, but do not raise that mistake into a crime. I love you; I love you for your beauty, for your grace, for your charm, for your frankness—for your very faults; I love you with the love that makes a man willing to give his life. We are both *gens du monde,* as you said, but I think we are both something more. Let us try and make a fate for ourselves which shall laugh at the world, or let us conquer the world together, which you prefer.

Comtesse de Riom (with emotion). You had better go to Quincampoix! It would be wiser.

Duca di Bastia. I might have been wise in that way very often, and I have always refused to be so. When they told me you had millions I should never have looked at you if I had not seen in you what I could love. I have nothing on earth save an old name, an empty palace, and a few square miles of classic soil that is as Greek still as any idyl of Theocritus; they are all I have, but I offer them to you. Will you take them, or will you ridicule them?

Comtesse de Riom (*in a low voice*). If ever you repent, do not reproach me! I have been unhappy— yes, I do not mind confessing it all now, but—I fear we are going to be very unwise!

Duca di Bastia (*kisses her hand*). There is only one wisdom on earth; it is to love.

Comtesse de Riom. Take care! you will shock Padre Francesco!

Mrs. Vanscheldt (*enters*). What! are you come back, Duke? I thought you were gone for ever and ever? Will you read us some more tales of Boccaccio?

Duca di Bastia. I feel more inclined for Petrarca to-day. But I will read anything you like, even all you ladies' fortunes if you desire me.

Mrs. Vanscheldt (*with a smile*). I guess you have already told Madame de Riom's!

AFTERNOON

A COMEDY

Cloth of gold, do not despise
To match thyself with cloth of frieze

AFTERNOON.

SCENE I.

The long arbutus alley in the grounds of the Villa Ludovisi in Rome.

Present : L'ESTRANGE *and* IPSWICH.

L'Estrange. Not to *feel* the Ludovisi Juno! What an utter Philistine you are!

Ipswich. Well, it's a big stone head. If you hadn't told me, I should have thought it was some severe mother-in-law of some dead Caius or Valerius.

L'Estrange. How right Matthew Arnold is! What absolute, shameless, besotted blockheads English Philistines are!

Ipswich. One can't be a pillar of light like you, and adore marble dolls and pictures as brown as a cocoa-nut.

L'Estrange. Can a ' pillar ' ' adore '? Confine yourself to Pall Mall jargon. You are only intelligible then.

Ipswich. But I say now, tell me, what *do* you æsthetes see in that big bust?

L'Estrange. What is the use of telling you? It is the purest ideal of womanhood that we possess.

Ipswich (murmurs). I prefer Jeanne Granier!

L'Estrange. It is the symbol of chastity, dignity, maternity, sovereignty. It is divine. It should be set in the centre of St. Peter's, and have the church dedicated to its worship. Almost I become a Comtist before that glorious incarnation of woman! If you had any mind or soul, you would feel so too : as you are a mere lump of flesh, clothed by Poole, you can never understand it, let it be explained to you how it may.

Ipswich. A lump of flesh! *I!* When I've won the Grand Military three times running!

L'Estrange (with scorn). A steeplechase is your limit and conception of the divine!

Ipswich. Oh, I say, it's not to be sneezed at; and you ride hard enough yourself sometimes at home.

L'Estrange. To ride is one thing; to tear over hurdles in a monkey's silk jacket, with all the scum of the betting ring cursing you as you break your beast's back in a ditch, is another. Who is that coming yonder? She knows you.

Ipswich. That is the Princess Sanfriano—such a jolly little cat!

L'Estrange. Surely not Italian?

Ipswich. Canadian. Awfully nice. She don't get on with her husband; but, herself, she runs pretty straight as yet. She'd no end of money; which the cad married her for, of course.

Princess (coming close to them). Lord Ipswich! Are you actually ' doing Rome' like Cook's cherubs?

Ipswich. Princess, will you allow one of my oldest friends to have the honour? [*Introduces them.*

Princess (to L'ESTRANGE). Have you been long in Rome? I don't remember to have met you, and we all meet fifty times a week somewhere.

L'Estrange. I came last night only; but I always shun society in Rome.

Princess. Good gracious! Why?

Ipswich. He thinks it profanity here—money changers in Temple, you know; that sort of feeling.

Princess. I see. Well, he will commit his first blasphemy at my house to-morrow. Mind you bring him.

L'Estrange (murmurs sulkily). Too kind— charmed.

Princess (continues). And as reward you shall see my beautiful and famous friend, Madame Glyon. She never goes out, so you can't see her anywhere else.

L'Estrange (interested). Not the artist?

Princess. Certainly, the artist. But prepare yourself; she is as lovely as she is clever. You have seen the things she can do?

L'Estrange (with a little shudder). The things! Certainly, Princess. I never miss the *Salon,* and the grand landscapes of Madame Glyon are one of the few spiritual and yet perfectly faithful works that the age has afforded us.

Ipswich. He praises something modern at last! Rome will fall! Do you know, Princess, he has been boring me all the morning about the big head in there; it appears to me to have a 'front' like my landlady in Duke Street, and wear the severity of countenance suitable to a Dame at Eton.

Princess. The Ludovisi Juno? Ah! I can't see much in it; but Madame Glyon raves about it.

L'Estrange. If you will allow me, I will go and rave again also at the goddess's shrine, for I find I left a volume of Winckelmann in the gallery.

Princess. Is that *the* L'Estrange?

Ipswich. What do you mean?

Princess. I mean the one who was such a brute to his wife.

Ipswich. Brute! Nonsense, my dear Princess; he made a horrible mistake, tried to remedy it, and failed.

Princess. He *killed her!*

　　　　　　　　　　　[Ipswich *laughs out loud.*

Princess (very severely). Oh! we know very well men never kill with neglect, or ill-temper, or insult! I say he *killed* her; killed her as much as if he had danced on her in Lancashire clogs, or put arsenic in her sherry. Why, he used to write notes to her about the wrong way she held her teacup!

Ipswich. Well, why not? He married a little peasant.

Princess. She was a gardener's daughter; Tennyson has sanctified that.

Ipswich. She was a gardener's daughter, and he saw her first hoeing potatoes.

Princess. Pineapples!

Ipswich. Potatoes! Princess, excuse me, but people don't hoe pineapples, and *she—was—hoeing* !

Princess. Very well, if she were? She didn't brain him with her hoe! *She* didn't ask him to marry her.

Ipswich. That was his Quixotic chivalry. He has repented it ever since.

Princess Do you mean to say he has redeeming grace enough in him to feel remorse?

Ipswich. Oh, remorse! Come, I say! That is rather strong.

Princess. He ought to be haunted to his dying day. The Lords ought to have impeached him and hanged him in Palace Yard.

Ipswich. Dear Princess, be reasonable! What did he do? You can't have heard the right story. He married the French peasant when she was fifteen—beautiful as a dream, that I grant, but ignorant! . . . Oh, Lord, you don't believe me, I see ; but I assure you she tried her gloves on her feet, and asked the servants to warm her first ice!

Princess (severely). Not reasons to divorce a woman.

Ipswich. Divorce! Who talked of divorce? He bore it all like an angel.

Princess. While he was in love. Exactly. Then in six months' time all the blunders and the innocence that had seemed to him so divine, grew stupid, ugly, unendurable!—I know,—and she was sacrificed to the petty shame of a capricious and arrogant young man who knew nothing of any passion save the basest and most fleeting form of it.

Ipswich. Not at all—nothing of the kind. Of course he began to see that he had done a thing that put him in a hole; that it was out of the question to take her about in London at all; of course he remembered his position.

Princess. Position! The one god of the Englishman!

Ipswich. Then there was his mother—wild.

Princess. I can imagine the British matron under such circumstances! Poor Claire!

Ipswich. How did you know her name?

Princess. I was at the convent he sent her to— the beast! I was a good deal younger than she (we always *say* that, you know), and I was struck by her beauty, by her despair, by her history—as any child would be.

Ipswich. And she really did—kill—herself?

Princess. He really did kill her, if you want to speak the truth. They could do nothing with her, naturally; she was sunk in apathy and misery;

nothing roused her; and when she drowned herself, he was as much her murderer as though he had killed her with his own rifle.

Ipswich. My dear Princess! How could he ever foresee it?

Princess. If he had had two grains of sense, a pin's point of a heart, he would have *known* it? Can you worship a woman for six months and make her mistress of all you possess, and then turn her off to be a schoolgirl in a convent?

Ipswich (doggedly). I don't see what else he could do. Of course in two years' time or so he would have taken her back. I don't see how he could have stood the chaff of London if he had gone on living with a Touraine peasant girl who didn't know the common A B C of manners, and——

Princess (passionately). You will excuse me, Lord Ipswich, but *I* prefer the veriest Don Juan of them all to such a cold-hearted, paltry-spirited truckler to conventionalities. I say I prefer Mephistopheles himself! I can tell by the look of him that this wretch never cared a straw. He is as cold as a Canadian winter, and as self-engrossed as——

Ipswich. Well, you know it's eleven years ago. A fellow can't wear crape on his hat all his life.

Princess. Lord Ipswich, I hate you. Go and ask if my carriage is at the gate. I see my friend at the end of the alley, and I want to speak to her alone.

Ipswich. Why, she's living in your own house.

Surely you'll let me stop, and send that boy sweeping yonder for your carriage?

Princess.   How should that boy know my carriage? Go directly, or never venture to bow to me again.

Ipswich.   Dread and unjust lady, I fly!

Princess.   How glad I am to be rid of him!   All this distance off, I can tell she has something to say to me, and this morning it can only be—Well, my dearest dear!   You look pale.

MME. GLYON *enters : she looks grave, a little agitated; she seats herself on a stone bench beside the* PRINCESS. *For a moment she does not speak.*

The Princess (eagerly and anxiously).   You have seen that man?

MME. GLYON *gives sign of acquiescence; then, in a low voice, says:*

You knew he was in Rome?

Princess. No—no—no!   Good heavens! as if I would not have told you!   But when did you see him? how? where?   He was talking here with Ipswich a moment since.

Mme. Glyon.   He was entering the sculpture gallery as I came out.   [*Her voice is faint and grave.*

Princess.   And you said nothing happened?

Mme. Glyon.   What should happen?

Princess.   Much.   If I were you!

Mme. Glyon (smiling slightly).   You and I are very unlike, my dear.   I have seen him often in the streets in Paris, and even in the *Salon* before one of my own pictures; it is nothing new; nothing to wonder at; only—only——

Princess (striking her sunshade into the earth). Only—scoundrels have the power to torture good women when they have lost all title even to be remembered by them.

Mme. Glyon (dreamily). I do not think he has a grey hair yet; and I, how many?

Princess (with scorn). I dare say he *dyes*!

Mme. Glyon (indignantly). Ridiculous! He never cared in the least how he looked, and he is not a *ci-devant* beau of sixty.

[*Her voice gives way and she bursts into tears.*

Princess (sympathetic and yet angry). Oh, my darling, I know how you feel; and yet, how *can* you feel anything? You must be a very much more forgiving woman than I! I should hate him, loathe him, abhor him! I should tear his eyes out of his head—I should make him scenes wherever I met him, so that he would grow afraid of his very shadow!

Mme. Glyon (with an effort). Like the deserted mistress of the stereotyped boulevard novel! I am quite sure you would do nothing of the kind, Laura.

Princess. I *should!* Or probably I should have shot him long ago.

Mme. Glyon. *Quel mélodrame!* You are very violent to-day.

Princess. Because that idiot Ipswich has been having the impudence to defend him.

Mme. Glyon. You spoke of me?

Princess. We spoke of L'Estrange's marriage and of his conduct to his wife. Ipswich is his friend. He made lame excuses. It has left me rabid for the day. I tell you, my dear, I have not your divine forgiveness!

Mme. Glyon (with coldness). Who told you I forgave? Not I.

Princess. Your conduct! Patient Grizel was never gentler.

Mme. Glyon. You do not read character very well, Laura. You have been the best of friends to me, my love, but I think you have always taken me on trust. You have never understood what I felt or why I acted.

Princess. Oh no; you are like the Ludovisi Juno to me. I gaze; I try to admire; I am dumb; I fail to comprehend. I cannot appreciate the Colossal.

Mme. Glyon (with a tired smile). Am I colossal? I am as unconscious as the Juno herself.

Princess. Colossal! You are supernatural! Now, if you had torn his coat off his back in that gallery, you would have been human and akin to one.

Mme. Glyon (sternly). Do not talk in that fashion, Laura. It is quite unworthy of you, and you do not mean it.

Princess. I do.

Mme. Glyon. At all events, spare me the expression of your sentiments when they take that colour.

Meanwhile, do something else for me. You are intimate with Lord Ipswich. Learn from him if—if—his friend stays long at Rome. Because if he do, I will return to Paris and come to you some other time.

Princess (*rapidly*). I know he is going away directly—Asia Minor, I think. (*Aside.* I never dare tell her I have asked him for to-morrow night!) But, if you have passed him so often in Paris, it can't hurt you so very much to pass him in Rome!

Mme. Glyon (*in a low tone*). It hurts me always.

Princess (*kisses her hand with effusion*). Oh, my dear Claire, forgive me! I am a wretch, and, of course, I am quite incapable of understanding you. What does the proverb say? Fools, you know, always rush in where anybody else would be afraid to tread.

Enter IPSWICH.

Ipswich. Ten thousand pardons if I've seemed ages, but your people were right down at the end of Via S. Basilio.

Princess. Thanks. I must be off. I've got the Japanese Legation to breakfast, and it's one o'clock now.

Ipswich. Let me go to the gates with you. (*Aside to the* PRINCESS) Is that your great artist? What a beautiful creature?

Princess. You shouldn't say so to me, as she is the precise opposite of everything I am! But she *is* very handsome. I can't introduce you, for she won't know strangers, and she hates Englishmen.

> [*Exit from the alley;* MME. GLYON *a little behind the* PRINCESS *and* IPSWICH.

SCENE II.

Drawing-room, Palazzo Sanfriano.

Present: The PRINCESS, MME. GLYON, LADY COWES, MARCHESA ZANZINI, IPSWICH, *various minor personages. It is six o'clock. Tea on a guéridon.*

Lady Cowes (whispering to MARCHESA ZANZINI*).* Such a dear creature, the Princess; but she always *does* know such queer people!

Marchesa. Who you mean? La Glyon? Oh, but an artist, you know—that excuse everything!

Lady Cowes. In a studio, perhaps. Not in a drawing-room.

Marchesa (laughing). Ah, you dear ˉEnglish! You are always so ironed—I mean, so starched! For me, I care for my own house; but I care not who I meet other people's.

Lady Cowes. But the Princess introduces her!

Marchesa. What if she do? The new woman must call first. You not return her card. That very simple. Everything stop there.

Lady Cowes. But the Princess would never forgive it!

Marchesa (stolidly). Pooh! What matter what a little *bastarda* American like or no like?

Lady Cowes (shocked). Oh, *dearest* Marchesa! Indeed, indeed, the poor Princess was not—was not what you say. She was *nobody*, indeed; but I am sure her parents were quite respectable, and very rich. Indeed, my son, when he was fishing in Canada, *dined* with them!

Marchesa (shaking with laughing). Ah, ha! and the dinner is the sacrament of respectability; is it not so? But I mean not what you think. *Bastardo* with us, that mean, what you call it, mongrel—not born —*née de rien*—how you say it?

Lady Cowes (still shocked). Yes, yes; I see quite so; you speak English so beautifully, Marchesa! Ah, dear Lady St. Asaph is over there.

[*Rises and goes to that end of room*

Marchesa (to IPSWICH). Come here and recount me of the stipple-chase. You won, they tell me; is that so?

Ipswich. Yes; after a fashion. I rode an awful screw.

Marchesa. Screw? There is corkscrew; there is screw to a steamship; there is screw that you put into wood; how you can ride a screw? Tell me.

Princess (passing by). Marchesa, he will call you a purist.

Marchesa. Ah, my dear, as you are here, tell me, who is your friend, La Glyon?

M

Princess (colours a little). She is Madame Glyon. Surely you have heard of her?

Marchesa. My child! She is one of those of whom one hears fifty thousand things every five minutes, but perhaps none of them may be very true things. That is why I ask you (because Lady Cow do ask me) who was she, whence come she, who was M. Glyon—or, it maybe, who *is* he?

Princess. She is a widow. Forgive me, there are people coming in.

　　　　　　　　　　[Escapes to receive new comers.

Marchesa. She not care to talk about her. That is ill. I will ask Carlino.

Ipswich. Who is he?

Marchesa. Sanfriano. Carlino!

Sanfriano. Marchesa?

Marchesa. Who is La Glyon, your wife's friend? I spik English because *queste gente* they not spik Italian.

Ipswich. I'm afraid *we* haven't often such good manners in return!

Marchesa. Pooh! We not come to you for *manners*; we come to you for *morals*! Carlino, answer me, who is La Glyon?

Sanfriano. On my honour, I do not know. She was at the same convent with Laura in Paris. They are great friends.

Marchesa. And who was Monsieur Glyon?

Sanfriano That I cannot tell you. A scoundrel,

I believe, who married her when she was very young.
You know, of course, that she is a great artist?

Marchesa.   You never ask the Principessa more?

Sanfriano.   I never ask the Principessa anything;
quite content if she return the compliment.   There is
the Californian beauty.   Look at her.   Is she not
adorable?   Fresh as a daisy; white as a lily!

[*He goes to greet the Californian beauty.*

Marchesa.   There is something bad about La Glyon.
I shall not send her a card to my ball.

Lady St. Asaph.   How do, Marchesa?   How are
your sweet little grandchildren?   They were quite the
stars of the babies' ball at our embassy.   Do tell me—
(*drops her voice*)—you know everything   Lady Cowes
has been making me quite uncomfortable about that
Frenchwoman over there, who is staying with the
Princess.   She says she is—well, you know, not at all
what one likes to meet where one visits.   Is it true?

Marchesa.   I shall not send her card for my ball;
Sanfriano think not well of her; her husband, he dis-
appear; not a soul know who she was.

Lady St. Asaph.   But it is intolerable of the
Principessa!   I am grieved I brought my girls

Marchesa (*grimly*).   She will not eat dem.   She
only get all the men round her.

Lady St. Asaph.   Perhaps she is *separated*!

Marchesa.   Dat is very likely.   Why not?

Lady St. Asaph.   But it is horrible, scandalous!
Couldn't one speak to the French ambassador?

L'Estrange (to Princess*).*   Dear Principessa, will
you not do for me the kindness that you denied me the
other night?

Princess (nervously).   Madame Glyon never makes
new acquaintances.

L'Estrange.   But she and I should have so many
themes of talk in common, and honestly, I admire her
pure and wonderful genius so greatly.

Princess (pettishly).   Oh, she is bored to death
with people praising her genius.

L'Estrange.   Undiscerning praise, perhaps.   Nothing more wearisome; but——

Ipswich.   But this Ruskin of the drawing-room,
this St. James Street prophet, this æsthetic of æsthe-
tics, who sees no excellence out of Lionardo, will give
her a very different thing to vulgar compliment.

L'Estrange (coldly).   Certainly; I should presume
to offer her sympathy.

> [*At that moment* Mme. Glyon, *who is at the tea-
> table, has the lace at her wrist caught by the
> spirit-flame of the silver kettle; her sleeve takes
> fire.* L'Estrange *is quicker than any one: he
> extinguishes the burning lace with his handker-
> chief, and is slightly burnt in the palms of his
> hands.* Mme. Glyon *says nothing, but sits
> down and grows very pale.   Buzz of excite-
> ment from others round them.*

L'Estrange (smiling).   Indeed, I am not hurt.
The skin scorched—nothing more.   Madame Glyon,

fate has been kinder to me than the Princess. I have implored in vain a presentation to you. Will you not allow the kettle to be my sponsor? If you will not, I assure you that I will pour vitriol on my fingers and declare that I am crippled for life by saving you!

Mme. Glyon (bows coldly). I have to thank you for great presence of mind. I fear you are hurt yourself.

L'Estrange. Would that I were! But, at all events, let the kettle's misdemeanour allow me to introduce myself, and—will you not at least give me a cup of tea?

Mme. Glyon (she pours him out a cupful as she speaks). As you please.

[*He seats himself at the table.*

Lady Cowes (to LADY ST. ASAPH). Is it not extraordinary, my dear Anne, how women of *that* kind of character always attract men?

Lady St. Asaph. Because they lay themselves out for it!

Marchesa Zanzini (aside to IPSWICH). Ah, ha! And what do your girls do at your lawn-tennis? I not wish to know La Glyon, but I am quite sure she never jump about in jersey with perspiring man in shirt!

Lady Cowes (to LADY ST. ASAPH). How anxious the little Princess looks because Lord L'Estrange has got attracted by that woman! But *why* does she have her here? Is it because—(*mysteriously*)—because the Prince *compels* her to be civil, do you think?

Lady St. Asaph (also mysteriously). It can hardly

be that. You know he would not be *allowed* by the Duchess Danta ;—she holds him *so* close.

Lady Cowes. Then, what *can* it be ? She was at the same convent as the Princess. Is it possible she knows of any school-girl imprudence, and *therefore* has to be propitiated ?

Marchesa Zanzini. Suppose that it only just is that they do like each other ?

Lady St. Asaph (with a sour smile). I don't think that's possible ! Why, when they are together she actually *kills* the little Princess, overtops her, washes her out ! No ; there *must* be a reason for the friendship. We will hope that it is a good one.

Marchesa (with a chuckle). And pray that it is a wicked one, eh ? Oh, look not so scandalised. Good reasons, they give other folk no diversions ! I cannot endure them myself.

Lady Cowes. You are cynical, Marchesa ?

Marchesa. Ah no ! It is not me who have ever the spleen !

Lady Cowes. To be sure—of course ; your lovely sun, no fog, no east wind ; who *could* be ill-natured in Italy ?

Marchesa. To be certain, nobody, unless they bring with them their ill-nature in the train, as they do bring their umbrellas, and their sponges, and their— how you call it— portable baths ?

Ipswich (aside, laughing). How merciless you are, Marchesa !

Marchesa (aside). Ah! that Miladi Cow, she make me impatient. It is just that she want Milord L'Estrange for her daughter Luisa. La Glyon, she is nobody; I not know her myself; but she *is* handsome, and to men she is cold. See! she leave L'Estrange now and go and talk to that old Monsignore instead. Your friend, he look gloom—how you say it?—glum? He not like to be *planté-là* alone with the teacups!

Ipswich (with surprise). She does seem uncivil to him.

Marchesa (with sarcastic smile). You Englishmen, you so spoiled by your own women, you think any woman who not throw herself at your head uncivil. Your women are forwards, and that is always bad. It spoil men.

Ipswich (with a sigh). Well, they do butter us, and come after us, too much at home, that's true. You can't get away from 'em anywhere.

Marchesa (grimly). Poor creature! You honey; they flies. Now here, it is *we* are the honey. That is prettier.

Ipswich. *Much* prettier, and a long shot better fun.

Marchesa. Long shot! You speak strange English, you young men. Well, I go; it is seven o'clock. I dine your embassy. You dine too? *A rivederci.*

[*A general rising; people go out one by one.* L'ESTRANGE *approaches the* PRINCESS *to say adieu.*

L'Estrange. Madame, your friend is too cruel; she scarcely deigns to speak to me.

Princess (sharply). I am sure you must have done so much cruelty yourself, and endured so little from others, that the change is the best thing possible for you!

L'Estrange (a little coldly). Certainly Madame Glyon is a great artist and I am only a poor dilettante; still, I cannot see what I can have done to offend her, and ——

Ipswich. You have been *snubbed?* How delicious! I could kiss the carpet where Madame Glyon's feet have just passed! It is the very thing you have wanted all your life long, only it comes too late!

L'Estrange. Really, Ipswich, you have a good deal of the Margate 'Arry about you. You have all the wit of a cheap-tripper. Princess, you are so exquisitely kind yourself that I feel confident you will soften the heart of your friend towards one of the most sincere admirers of her genius, and, if I may add it without offence—of herself.

Princess (giving him her hand in farewell). I think I shall do nothing of the sort. To be 'out in the cold' a little must be excellent discipline for you who have been brought up in a hothouse amidst parasites all your life.

L'Estrange. A frost more often kills than cures, madame.

Ipswich. Princess! You *will* promise me the cotillon to-night? Pray——

Princess. I will tell you, after the last waltz.

[*They take leave of her and exeunt.*

Princess (left alone). Marco, go and beg Madame Glyon to be so good as to come to me a moment.

[*Servant exit.*

Princess (aloud). Good heavens! What wretches men are! If she were his wife now, he would be finding every fault in her that a human creature could have, and be for ever writing notes to her about convention‑alities, and breaches of precedence at her last dinner-party! Just because she seems something new, un-common, indifferent, incomprehensible, the base weak monster is piqued and almost in love! They are all alike—all alike! If I were but somebody else's wife, Sanfriano would be mad about me, and ruin himself in five minutes to satisfy my caprice or my curiosity. Because I *am* his wife, he never even sees what sort of gown I've got on; and if he is obliged to spend an hour with me, he goes to sleep! And yet I am ten, fifteen, twenty million times prettier than that yellow, lean, black-browed Danta woman! (MME. GLYON *enters.*) Ah, dearest Claire, how good of you to come down again; but there are heaps of time before dinner, and I did so want to tell you—you have made that man in love with you.

Mme. Glyon. Laura! If you were any one else——

Princess. Than myself, you would leave my house before dinner! But I am myself, dear, and privileged to say anything. Don't look so stern, and so reproachful. If you choose, in a fortnight's time he will be as much in love with you as—as——

Mme. Glyon. As he was with a gardener's daughter in Touraine!

Princess. Oh Claire! you are the proudest woman in the world.

Mme. Glyon. No, I am the humblest, or should be, for I have been the most humbled.

Princess. But now, if you took your revenge?

Mme. Glyon. Revenge? A ghastly word, not one I like or use.

Princess. It was a religion here in Rome, and should be yours. Oh, my dear, I know we are not in the days of daggers, and that if we were, you would not use one; but I mean a vengeance innocent enough, but just. Make this man love you, and then, when he will suffer tortures in your rejection, tortures of passion, tortures of pride, then—avenge with one word 'No' the gardener's daughter of Touraine. You will? You will?

Mme. Glyon. Laura! you talk as if life were a game of tennis, or a struggle between two gamesters— nothing more. You never understand——

Princess. I never understand life as *you* see and read it. To accept outrage and neglect, to condemn yourself to solitude and sterility; to let the destroyer

of it pass off unpunished, and have society like a gilded
ball at his foot, to kick or play with—this is what you
think honour and dignity and duty. Well, to me it is
a folly, nothing more; a grand, idiotic, sublime, and
most useless tomfoolery. There!

Mme. Glyon. My dear, we see things with such
different eyes. I said so the other day. I grieve that
I listened to you, and stayed here against my better
judgment; but who could foresee the little accident
that gave him opportunity and leave to speak to
me?

Princess. And he admires you beyond everything;
your pictures he thinks perfection; yourself——

Mme. Glyon (with heat and pain). Oh, spare me,
for heaven's sake, more evidence that no ray of recollection dawns on the utter night of his absolute forget-
fulness. His admiration—*his!* A dog would have
more recognition, more instinct, more remembrance.

Princess (surprised). But you always dreaded any
recognition?

Mme. Glyon (losing her calmness). Who has said
that our granted wishes are our curses? Do not mistake me; I know that any suspicion on his part would
lead to misery for him and for myself, and were
there any chance of it, I would put seas and deserts
between him and me. Yet—ah, my dear, women are
weak! when he looks at me as on a stranger, when he
speaks to me with the compliment of society, it is hard
to bear.

Princess. But, dearest, do be reasonable. To him you have been dead so long: there is your memorial marble in his chapel. What can you expect him to——

Mme. Glyon. I know, I know! I said the same thing myself the other day in the Ludovisi gardens. Yet one might have thought—when I spoke—some accent, some tone might have touched some chord in his heart.

Princess. He has none! He never had any. Would he have done what he did——

Mme. Glyon. What he did was done from pride. He was ashamed of me; he was mortified before his world by my ignorance and my errors. Perhaps I should have understood that, but I was so young. You cannot give a child of fifteen all the most exquisite joys of love and life for a year's time, and then drive her away from all the happiness you have taught her and consign her to the dreary tedium of a convent life without making her mad or worse! I loved him—you know how I loved him! Could he widow me at sixteen and think I should be patient? And then to know how he had wearied of me, how he blushed for me, because I knew not all the little laws of his own world; how every day had been a greater shame and bitterness of regret to him until he thrust me out of sight and memory under the sophist's pretext that I had received no education and should gain it best amongst the women of my own religion! Oh God! the torture of

it, the martyrdom, the death in life! And you think
to please me and console me because you tell me that
he admires my pictures and my face!

Princess. Claire! you frighten me. Pray don't be
angry. I only thought, I only meant, if I were you I
should revenge myself. You are famous, you are beautiful, you are independent; I would make him die of
love for me, and die in vain! He has no heart, but he
has passions. I would wring his very soul!

Mme. Glyon. You would do nothing of the kind
if you had loved him once. Nor would there be
decency or dignity in any such poor revenge as that.
Besides—what a romance you weave because he scorched
his hand! He only sought me because he is a connoisseur, and therefore artists are the poor moths he puts
under his microscope.

Princess. But you must feel proud of having
achieved such a position for yourself.

Mme. Glyon. I can be proud of nothing. A man
loved me, and wearied of me. That is humiliation
enough to crush the pride of an empress into dust.

Princess. You should not be humiliated at all.
You are greater than he. You should scorn him.

Mme. Glyon (with her teeth set). Perhaps I do.
But that cannot take the sting from the wound. Yes,
it was cruel, and so contemptible! He was a man of
the world; he knew its codes, its exactions, its false
estimates; he knew also that a peasant child, taken
from field and orchard, who had only learned the Credo

and the alphabet, could not by any miracle comprehend the ways and the demands, the rigour and the mockery of a patrician society. He should have sent me to the convent first, and waited for marriage until I was more fit for his people and his sphere. Indeed—indeed— had he said even to me, when he did send me from him, 'Do this for love of me, my child,' I would, I think, have borne the exile and the shame of it. But he grew colder and colder, more silent every day; he was too courteous to say to me all he felt, but in his eyes I read the daily humiliation that I was to him, and when he wrote to me—*wrote to me!*—that he was going on an Indian tour, and would be away two years, and those two years he wished me to pass at the convent learning, as he phrased it, the ordinary rules and graces of society; what girl of my age then could have en- dured such agony? And I—I adored the very dust he trod, I would kiss the heads of the dogs he had laid his hand on! To him, no doubt, it was but one of many episodes; an idyl lived out and found insipid. No doubt I was ignorant, and for him my ignorance was fatigue and shame; but to me he and his love were all my life, and I could not tell why what he had earlier praised as pure and fresh and unconventional should have later lost all charm for him—I could not tell— hush! There is the Prince!

Prince (entering). Care mie! are you not going to dress to-night? We dine in ten minutes, Laura, and then there will be two hours wanted for you to get into your ball costume, and we must be punctual, since the Queen goes.

Princess. Oh! the Court never gets anywhere till eleven. You always fidget so! and you are always late yourself. My maid always gets me into my clothes in fifteen minutes by the clock. *I* do not paint my skin.

Prince. There is so very little to put on you when it is question of a ball! Two inches of corsage and a little wreath for a sleeve. It might be done in *five* minutes!

Princess. *My* gowns are always decent. The Duchess Danta's exhibition of her vertebræ——

Mme. Glyon (pushing her gently to the door). My dear! what is the use of that? It prevents nothing, and embitters everything.

Prince (angrily). Madame Glyon, you see! She prick, prick, prick me every hour like that, and then she do wonder that I like better other women!

Mme. Glyon. My dear Prince, what pricks you is your conscience. You know you do neglect Laura sadly,

Prince (opening his eyes widely). I leave her alone. She has her own way. I only want her to do the same by me. *Ma quando sono gelose le donne!*——

Mme. Glyon (smiling). No wife is wise. But I shall be late for dinner. [*Exit.*

Prince (to himself). *That* is a woman I could have got on with; not that I care about her. Antonio! *un bicchierrino di Vermouth.*

[*Exit towards dining-room.*

Scene III.

Studio of Aldred Dorian. Tapestried Walls, Paintings, Marbles, Bronzes, Carved Chairs, Artistic Litter.

Present: Dorian *and* Mme. Glyon.

Dorian (turning dissatisfied from one of his easels). You are a greater artist than I.

Mme. Glyon. Oh! *pas de phrases!* You are a Titian, and paint physiognomy for posterity; I am but a poor limner of windmills, corn-fields, and little brooks that wash the linen.

Dorian. You portray the face of Nature. It is the higher art. The sunset is nobler than a rosy cheek.

Mme. Glyon. I can only paint a rosy apple.

Dorian. Who would dare say that of you? You are as true, as grave, and as lofty as Millet.

Mme. Glyon (smiling). You must be a very great man to say that of a woman—if you mean it.

Dorian. I always mean what I say, and to you I could not use an empty flattery if my lips could frame one (*he pauses, hesitating*). Madame—Claire—you are greater in the art we love than I am, far greater, but I can own it with frankness and without jealousy, because—because—cannot you divine why?

Mme. Glyon. Because you have a noble nature, and also too great a distrust of yourself.

Dorian. No! It is because I love you.

Mme. Glyon (staring at him with wide-opened eyes). Love me? *Me?* Are you mad, Dorian?

Dorian. Mad? No; if I be, it is a lunacy that many share. Have you never guessed, never seen? I should not dare to speak, only our common love for our common art gives me some courage. I am rich, for an artist; forgive me if I say so vulgar a thing, but I mean that I have the power to make your life a happy one, one of leisure to study, and aspire to the highest heights, which those who must needs work for bread can never do. I love you, I adore you—I adore you in the double form of woman and muse. If you would not scorn me—you have showed me some esteem, some friendship—if you would be my wife——

Mme. Glyon (stupefied). *Your* wife? Yours? You forget yourself strangely. Do not make me regret the confidence I have felt in a comrade, in a fellow-worker!

Dorian (with some anger). Madame! how do I forget myself in offering to you an honest name, an honourable love? I worship you, I believe in you, I kneel at your feet. What wrong is there? I do not seek to know your past; I do not, I will not, ask you of your marriage; the man is dead. I would forget he ever lived.

Mme. Glyon. Pray cease! I cannot hear you. I shall never marry—again. I must ask your pardon for my hasty words. You do me much honour. I will endeavour to be grateful.

Dorian. I want no gratitude. I want your love, your beauty, your genius, your grand and tranquil nature ; I want *you.*

Mme. Glyon. Mr. Dorian, you will compel me to leave your studio.

Dorian (seizing her hands). You will never listen ! You will never cease to care for that dead man who they all say was but a brute to you !

Mme. Glyon. I can but say what I have said. I shall never marry. I shall never love—again.

> [DORIAN *releases her hand, and, without a word, leaves his studio hurriedly by one door as there enter from another the* PRINCESS SANFRIANO, *the* DUCA DI MONTELUPO, *and* L'ESTRANGE.

Princess. Have we kept you waiting too long, Claire ? But I know that you and Dorian can always talk together twelve hours at a stretch. But, goodness ! where *is* Dorian ? You told him we were coming ?

Mme. Glyon (with a little embarrassment). He went out a little while ago. No doubt he thought we were old friends enough to be content with his works without himself. You know they are the best part of every artist !

Princess (looks at her quickly). I shall wait till he comes back. I shall get his tea, and the dear little Persian cups and the apostle spoons, and the *niello* tray, and the Roman *maritozzi*, and his negro will bring us his *samovâr*. (*Rings; a black servant appears.*) Bring the urn, Eblis; you see we are old friends; I know your name.

> [*She busies herself getting the Persian cups off an old oaken 'cabinet.'* MONTELUPO *engrossed in helping her.*]

L'Estrange (*to* MME. GLYON). It is strange of Dorian. I saw him an hour ago, and told him we were to meet you here and see his treasures. *Entre nous*, I think himself a much finer creation than his works. I care nothing for his pictures, but he is a rather noble fellow. You seem to know him well?

Mme. Glyon. I have seen him often in Paris. I think he is a great artist, but his manner perhaps is hard and his colour too thin to do his fine conceptions justice.

L'Estrange. He cannot be named by you.

Mme. Glyon. Oh, why compare a pastoral and an epic?

L'Estrange. True! Besides, there is nothing except Turner's with which one could compare all that you give us.

Mme. Glyon. You cannot be serious. You abhor modern art. Why except from your censure what a woman does?

L'Estrange. One must except Rosa Bonheur and Mme. Glyon. Would you tell me—do not think it barren or impertinent curiosity, all these questions are of such vital interest—would you tell me where you studied, and under whom ?

Mme. Glyon. Chiefly in the open air and from Nature.

L'Estrange. Ah, how right! It is the indoor work, the copying, the slavery to *technique*, the hot-stove atmosphere, the gas-lit colouring that are the curses of modern painters. Then—may I ask again—although you live in Paris, it was not there that you studied chiefly ?

Mme. Glyon. No.

L'Estrange. Madame, I see you think me a rude Englishman, full of graceless and rough inquisitiveness. But, believe me, it is my entire sympathy with your marvellous works which makes me long to learn under what influences they were inspired.

Mme. Glyon. That is only the language of compliment.

LEstrange. On my honour, no !

Mme. Glyon. Lord L'Estrange, when a man speaks to a woman, his word of honour is a very elastic thing !

L'Estrange. I do not see why you should disbelieve me.

Mme. Glyon. Oh ! perhaps you mean it now.

L'Estrange. Now? Why, now ? If I find an infinite charm of the finest feeling finely rendered in your works, my judgment is at least mature, and not likely to be capricious. Alas ! I am young no longer.

Mme. Glyon. Caprice is not a thing especially of youth.

L'Estrange (impatient). On what grounds do you think me capricious?

Mme. Glyon. You have the reputation of it.

L'Estrange. I do not think reputation is just to me, then. My taste never varies. One must be faithful in art, or be indifferent to it.

Mme. Glyon. To art! I meant to persons!

Princess (bringing a cup of tea, MONTELUPO *following with cakes).* Here, Claire! I always thought Dorian's studio one of the nicest places in Rome when he was in it; now he is out of it, it is the *very* nicest.

L'Estrange (handing tea to MME. GLYON*).* Poor Dorian! And you are eating his excellent *maritozzi,* Princess, and have no more gratitude than that? (*He notices* MME. GLYON'S *left hand.*) She has no ring on; did Glyon never live except in fiction? (*aside*).

[*He seats himself again on low chair beside her.*

L'Estrange. Now that your charming friend is gone to flirt with Montelupo once again over the samovâr, let me implore you, tell me something of yourself.

Mme. Glyon. Artists have no biographies, and their memoirs are written on their canvases.

L'Estrange. Nay, who has not made a pilgrimage to Urbino for Raffaele's sake? I would make a pilgrimage to *your* Urbino.

Mme. Glyon.   What if it landed you in a cabin ?

L'Estrange.   Then the cabin would be as sacred as a temple.

Mme. Glyon.   Lord L'Estrange, you are an admirable flatterer.

L'Estrange (angrily).   I never flatter! Flattery is as vulgar as abuse. But I must not weary you by asking for what you will not tell me.

Mme. Glyon (impatiently).   There is nothing to tell. I was a happy child. I was not a happy woman. Accident taught me to find solace and strength in art. There is the end.

L'Estrange (smiling).   Your history must be far from its end! But what fate, what creature, could be vile enough and blind enough to cause you sorrow ?

Mme. Glyon (curtly).   My husband.

L'Estrange.   He must have been a brute, indeed, and a madman too !

Mme. Glyon.   Neither. He was but an egotist, and changeable.

L'Estrange.   Changeable ! When *you* were given to him as his ' fixed star ' ? Good heavens ! That the baseness of a low-natured man should have the power to wound the great soul of such a woman as you are !

Mme. Glyon.   His was not a low nature ; nor was he base. I had the misfortune to be his wife—that was all ! Come, we must look at Dorian's work for

the Academy and the *Salon,* or we shall not be able
to excuse ourselves for stealing his tea and his
maritozzi.

> [*She rises and turns one of the easels towards a
> better light.*

Princess (aside to Mme. Glyon). What was he
saying to you?

Mme. Glyon. Pretty phrases—the small change
of society. Go and talk to him. If you are so
engrossed by the little Duke, the club will be told to-
night of the good fortune of Azzelino Montelupo.

Princess (pettishly). It would serve Carlino right.
But then, to be sure, Carlino would not care.

Mme. Glyon. I think he would care, and take his
sabre out of its scabbard. Duca, I want to see some
wondrous missals that no one is allowed to see at the
Vatican. You have two uncles Cardinals. Can you
get me permission?

> [*She keeps* Montelupo *with her, strolling from
> easel to easel.*

Princess (to L'Estrange). Do you care for Dorian's
things?

L'Estrange. Dear Princess, why will you always
call pictures 'things'?

Princess. Because I am of the great uneducated.
I don't care the least for any picture. I only like
Claire's because they are Claire's.

L'Estrange. Affection *versus* comprehension. It
is a very old question which is worth the more. I see

you can be a good friend, Princess—that is even rarer than true appreciation of art.

Princess. I thought nobody in creation understood art except yourself and Mr. Ruskin. It is no merit in *me* to be a good friend to *her.* She is the noblest woman upon earth.

L'Estrange (with unusual warmth). Of that I am quite sure, though I have had the honour only to know Madame Glyon ten short days.

Princess. You admire her?

L'Estrange. Who could fail to do so?

Princess. I don't think that's an answer. It is an *équivoque.*

L'Estrange. Then let me say it unequivocally, she is altogether my ideal of a perfect woman; her personal beauty just gives the softening touch that strength and genius in her sex are too often without; she is, in a word, all that I most admire. But I perceive she will not let me say so.

Princess. She distrusts all praise.

L'Estrange. Surely she is no cynic?

Princess. No. But she was badly treated, wickedly treated; and you know when one is so, it warps all one's belief in anything. I know that.

L'Estrange. Oh, Princess, you never can have known anything like neglect!

Princess (sentimentally). Ah, none can guess what a woman suffers in silence! You think because I chatter like a parrot——

L'Estrange (irrelevantly). Princess, you really believe that Madame Glyon has been embittered by her marriage?

Princess. I never said she was *bitter*. She could not be. She has too sweet a temper. But you know—you know—he was such a wretch.

L'Estrange. Is it possible? to such a woman? Who was he? what was he?

Princess. Oh, he was—he was nothing at all. A gentleman, you know; but that don't make any difference. They are the worst, I think.

L'Estrange. How terribly you are *portée* against us! But do tell me more about him—what did he do?

Princess. I am afraid I can't talk about her if she don't talk about herself. She wouldn't like it; she would never forgive me. Claire is very sensitive.

L'Estrange. And Madame Sanfriano is very loyal. You are friends of long standing?

Princess. We were at the same school.

L'Estrange. And what was her maiden name?

Princess. I—I really forget. I always called her all sorts of pet names. Why are you so interested in all this? Is it purely artistic, æsthetic—what is the word?

L'Estrange. It seems to me simply natural that, meeting so beautiful and famous a person, one should feel a desire to know all her history, all her influences —all, in a word, that has united to make her what she is,

Princess. Yes? Well, I don't think I should trouble about who she was. She is *herself* the cleverest, the bravest, the best of living creatures. By-the-bye, do you know, I am quite certain that Dorian's disappearance *means* something. He has been in love with her for years, and I do believe that, just as we came in, he had told her so.

L'Estrange. Would she marry again?

Princess. She says no; but of course she would if she cared for anybody. She never does; that is the worst of it.

L'Estrange. She is wedded to her liberty and solitude? Dorian is a fine fellow, but very inferior to her. I should not think that she would stoop to him.

Princess. I suppose she didn't, as he disappeared; but I don't know about the inferiority. He is very eminent, and he is so good—so good!

L'Estrange. Princess! whenever were daughters of Eve won by goodness?

Princess. But she isn't a daughter of Eve at all. She is utterly above all *our* follies.

L'Estrange. And above ours too. Perhaps that was her fault in her husband's eyes. It would humiliate some men.

Princess. Would it you?

L'Estrange. Surely not. I think one should always feel before one's wife a certain reverence, a certain shame at one's own memories.

Princess. I will tell Carlino! It is very pretty

and chivalrous sounding ; but you know as well as I do, Lord L'Estrange, that nobody ever *does* feel that. Once married, you only see your wife's faults—her freckles, if she have any—her foibles, her follies ; if her feet are large, it is of them you think ; and if she have exquisite feet, but a large nose, then it is only the nose you see.

L'Estrange.   Princess, that is not love.

Princess.   It is as much love as there is.   What is love ?   A dizziness, a syncope, a dash of cold water, an unpleasant awakening, and as we wake, we throw the cold water over everybody else.

L'Estrange.   Who is cynical now ?

Mme. Glyon.   Laura, it is growing late ; we shall have no time for the Pincio.

Princess.   And you never will miss a sunset from the Hill.   Now, it never occurs to *me* to look at the sky.   I think you artists get a great deal more enjoyment than we do, and you get it out of nothing.

L'Estrange (softly, looking at Mme. Glyon*).*   The eyes that see !—yes, they are the most precious gift of heaven.

Princess.   Come, we will take you and Montelupo both up there ; he and I will talk, and you and she shall look.

Mme. Glyon.   Laura, I have forgotten that I promised to be with the Countess Dantzic at the Molinara by six o'clock ; I must for once renounce the evening red and gold behind St. Peter's.

Princess (aside to Mme. Glyon). Oh dear, that is because I asked him to drive with us! How could I help it? I brought him.

Mme. Glyon (in the same tone). You could have helped bringing him.

L'Estrange (coldly eyeing Mme. Glyon). Dear Princess, you are always too kind, but I fear I must renounce the pleasure. I dine with a Prince of the Church to-night who has the bad taste always to begin his admirable soups at sunset.

Princess. Well, I shall not take *you,* Azzelino, all alone behind my horses. You would be so flattered you would be insufferable till Lent. You can walk somewhere like Lord L'Estrange; I will go in my solitude and stare at the sky, till I manage to see something in it. Did you say the Molinara, Claire?

Mme. Glyon. Yes, my old Düsseldorf friend is there; you can call and take me up after your drive.

Princess. What a fuss we are all making! People talk less nowadays of going over to New Zealand or the North Pole! Cross? (*to* Montelupo, *who had murmured in her ear*). Yes; I am cross. I generally am, and these *maritozzi* are very indigestible.

L'Estrange. If you would excuse my escort down the stairs, I think I will leave a line for Dorian.

Princess. Pray do, and tell him I am the culprit as regards the *maritozzi*—I always own my sins.

   [*They leave the studio :* L'Estrange *remains. He throws himself into a large gilt leather chair, and lights a cigar.*

L'Estrange. Why does that woman shun me? It is quite unmistakable that she does. Her eyes are frank and pure, yet one could swear she had a secret she was ashamed of; it might be low birth, but that is impossible. She has *race* in every line, in every movement. Something there must be, because even the little chattering fool of a Sanfriano keeps her own counsel. If ever I saw a noble woman, she is one; and yet—she wears no rings, she will not say who this dead man was, nor where they lived, nor where he died; perhaps she was deceived—perhaps Dorian would know. He has been a friend of hers in Paris, and there is a freemasonry between artists. I will write and ask him, and somebody must make excuse for this litter of teacups and apostle spoons.

Enter DORIAN; *he is pale and grave; he pushes back the tapestry from a secret door.* *Seeing* L'ESTRANGE, *he pauses, disconcerted.*

Dorian. I thought you were all gone.

L'Estrange. Most hospitable of celebrities! You are too complimentary (*then he looks hard at* DORIAN *and ceases to smile*). Why, Dorian, what has happened? Have you been near us all this time?

Dorian (*pointing to the door by which he entered*). Yes, I was at home. I heard a little that you said: not much. I heard you say how greatly I am inferior to her. You were right; I had said the same to her myself this afternoon.

L'Estrange.   My dear Dorian——

Dorian.   Do not deny it.   I know a lie, even a kind one, chokes you as it chokes me.   We Englishmen have not a flexible trachea for falsehood.   It is often awkward for us.

L'Estrange.   But what ails you?   Why did you shut yourself away from us?

Dorian.   Because the little parrot of a Princess said aright; the only woman I have ever wished to make my wife had, five minutes earlier, rejected me. You were quite correct in thinking that she would not stoop to me.

L'Estrange.   Dorian!   I spoke idly.   I never meant——

Dorian.   You spoke as you thought; why not? She is greater than I am.   Love might bridge that, if it were there ; but it is not—on her side.

L'Estrange.   You must—pardon me the question —but you must know her history, since you would give her your name?

Dorian.   I have no idea of her history.   I am confident it must be a blameless one, when I look at her.

L'Estrange.   And you know nothing?

Dorian.   Nothing.   Her life in Paris is austere and untainted by a breath of calumny.   That I do know.   But beyond that nothing.   Do you think I would insult her with a doubt?

L'Estrange.   But in your wife?

Dorian. She will no more be my wife than will the marble Ariadne of the Capitol. But I would make her my wife without a single question that would seem also a suspicion.

L'Estrange. That is very noble, but——

Dorian. You would say the same if you loved her.

L'Estrange. I think not. 'The world is with me,' and I share its judgments—if you will, its prejudices.

Dorian. Yes; once you committed for the world's sake the most selfish sin of your life.

L'Estrange. What?

Dorian. I mean the exile of that poor child you married.

L'Estrange (annoyed and slightly embarrassed). Why rake among the ashes of dead years? I acted naturally, I think; how could I tell she would so take it to heart——

Dorian. As to destroy herself. I suppose you could not. I never saw her, and cannot judge; but between two people there is always one who sacrifices, one who is sacrificed.

L'Estrange. And you really, in all truth, know nothing of the past of this singular woman to whom you would trust your peace, your honour?

Dorian. Absolutely nothing.

L'Estrange. Not even who was Glyon?

Dorian. No.

L'Estrange. It is incomprehensible. Then——

Dorian. When you married that hapless peasant child, did you hesitate because——

L'Estrange. That was utterly different. She *was* a child, I knew the absolute innocence and childishness of her life, and all her short and simple past. No suspicion could rest on her.

Dorian. And if you say that any suspicion lies on Claire Glyon, I will never admit you in these doors again.

L'Estrange (touched). My dear fellow, you are very generous; you are like a knight of old. I am ready to believe in her.

Dorian. Then why insult her in her absence?

L'Estrange. I never thought of insult. I was only desirous to know the key to her coldness, her apparent loneliness, her silence as to her past.

Dorian (coldly). I cannot help to satisfy your curiosity.

L'Estrange. It is not curiosity alone. But if we argue in this manner we shall end in a quarrel, and that would be beneath both you and me. Besides, I am due at Cardinal Roxano's. Good-night, my friend; I will not wish you consoled, for consolation is only the harvest of feebleness, and you are strong.

[*Presses* Dorian's *hand, and leaves the studio.*

Dorian (to himself). Or the harvest of selfishness. He thinks of her already! To think of her is to love her.

Scene IV.

Salons in Palazzo Sanfriano.

Present: the Princess, Mme. Glyon, L'Estrange, Ipswich, Marchesa Zanzini. *A Bric-à-brac seller is showing ivories, carvings, stuffs, and a triptych.*

L'Estrange (giving him back an ivory nestkè). Mr. Brown, this is no more Japanese than I am. Don't you know that the Japanese take ten years of their lives to carve a ladybird on a rose-leaf? This is Dutch work, and very coarse work even for Dutch. Have you never learned the A B C of your commerce, Mr. Brown?

Princess. You shouldn't be so hard on the poor creature. He admits he is obliged to keep a heap of rubbish to satisfy the Americans.

L'Estrange. Satisfaction is the antithesis of my emotions in surveying his treasures. May I ask why you have this mountain of fraud in your presence?

Princess. Why, surely I told you. I am going to wear a Venetian page's dress at the Malatesta ball, and I wanted an old Italian dagger, and he brought me one. *This* is genuine?

L'Estrange. Have you bought it?

Princess. Certainly. Oh, good gracious! isn't it right?

L'Estrange.   Perhaps it is not worth while telling you, and yet you *must not* be seen with it.   It is German work; it was made at Berlin last week.   Even were it old, it would be of no use to you.   You want a Venetian poniard or stiletto; this is copied from a French *miséricorde* of the Valois time.

Princess.   Oh dear! and I have given five hundred francs for it!

L'Estrange.   It is worth fifteen francs.   Send the impostor away, and when you buy things, do ask some-one who knows.   It is ignorance that allows these people to flood the world with anachronisms and counterfeits.

Princess.   Well, I confess if a thing's pretty I don't mind much who made it.   Now I shall have to roam all over the place looking for a poniard.   You have been very cruel.   Nobody would have noticed——

L'Estrange.   I will get you what you ought to have, if it be in Rome; and if not, I will telegraph home.   I have a collection of daggers, and there are some of the *Cinque-cento* amongst them.

Princess.   Too charming of you.   Of what haven't you a collection at home?

L'Estrange.   Not of Dutch *nestkès.*

Marchesa.   I have got at home the *daga* with which Cesare Borgia had my forefather killed, after a banquet, on Quattro Capi bridge, one nice dark night. When they took him home, it was between his shoulder-blades: he dead.   If you like, Princess, I will lend it you with pleasure.   It is the right epoch.

Princess. Oh, dear Marchesa, you are so kind. But, if it murdered a man, it would be unpleasant to wear it.

Marchesa. Pooh! They must all have murdered many mens if they are real daggers. How you look! And you think nothing of staring at the stipplechess out at Albano when young Stanhope he kill himself.

Ipswich. But that was *fair*, Marchesa. Stanhope pitched on his head: who could help it?

Marchesa. Ah, your distinctions are too subtle for my simplicity. You think nothing of killing if it done in sport; me, I think more excuse for it when it done in passion. But I go to see their comedietta at Barberini. You come with me, my dear; you improve my English; your own is so choice.

Ipswich. I come! But, hang it, Marchesa, one can't talk like old Johnson.

Marchesa. Why not? We talk like Dante.

Ipswich. You see, one can't be chaffed.

Marchesa. Chaff? that means to teaze, to insult, to jeer, to grin. No; we not do that to one another. Where is there wit in rudeness?

[Exeunt MARCHESA and IPSWICH.

[PRINCE *takes the tradesman apart to look at his stuffs;* L'ESTRANGE *approaches* MME. GLYON.

L'Estrange. You were sketching in the Cimontanara this morning? You go often?

Mme. Glyon. Yes; it is beautiful there, looking out to the San Giovanni gate.

L'Estrange. Can one come?

Mme. Glyon. No; you must be a friend of the owner. I believe there is one day in the week when anybody may go.

L'Estrange. I certainly do not covet that one day in the week. Mme. Glyon, you are very frigid always, but I want you to thaw to me enough to tell me why last week in Dorian's atelier you told me you had heard I was capricious? What common friend have we who so thoroughly carries out the modern theories of friendship as to malign me thus?

Mme. Glyon (hesitates). I know no friend of yours. I am not in the world.

L'Estrange. Then, if it were your own fancy only, what made you think so?

Mme. Glyon (lifts her head and looks at him coldly). The story of your marriage is common property. I have heard it like everyone else. If you find me too intrusive on your private life, do not blame me —vous l'avez voulu.

L'Estrange (is silent a moment and annoyed). Yes; certainly that very old, old story of a folly is common property. But I should not have supposed that anyone had remembered so mere an episode, and one so long ago.

Mme. Glyon. An episode! I heard it was a tragedy.

L'Estrange. Who can have talked to you about it? Ipswich?

Mme. Glyon. Oh no! I heard it—once—very long ago, as you say.

L'Estrange. A stupidity in one's life is never pardoned. A thousand crimes are easily enough forgotten and forgiven. So it is this silly tale that has prejudiced you against me? I dare say you actually believe me a modern edition of Bluebeard?

Mme. Glyon. It does not seem to me the sort of past that one would expect a man to jest at. I do not presume to judge you; but, as I say, the tale gave me an impression of both caprice and cruelty.

L'Estrange (angrily). I have neither in my character. That I can declare with a clear conscience. I have no illusions about myself, nor do I claim any especial superiority of temper; but this I can say honestly, I am incapable of cruelty to any living creature. I am even that miracle, an Englishman who hates a gun!

Mme. Glyon. I did not say you shot your wife.

L'Estrange (with a little laugh). Madame, I am your debtor that you acquit me even of that much! My wife—well, yes—she was my wife, certainly; but, good heavens! if I could tell you how impossible it seems to me that such a passage can ever have occurred in *my* life! I feel convinced that I must have read it in some novel, seen it on some stage, and had a nightmare, dreaming the history was mine.

Mme. Glyon.   I suppose it was all so very long ago
—you have forgotten?

L'Estrange.   No; it is not the sort of episode that
one forgets.

Mme. Glyon.   You are very fond of the word
'episode.'

L'Estrange.   It seems to me to describe correctly
the short period in my life of which we are now talking.   It was an episode; it was not more—it was an
episode of unutterable folly, infatuation, disillusion,
pain, and repentance.

Mme. Glyon.   Repentance?   It seems to sit lightly
on you.

L'Estrange.   I mean repentance of a foolish and
hasty action which made me very absurd in the world's
eyes, and caused an amount of comment, misrepre-
sentation, and interference on the world's part such
as I am the last man upon earth to endure with
tolerance.

Mme. Glyon.   I beg your pardon.   I fancied you
meant repentance for your injury of a girl's life.

L'Estrange.   Madame!   That is really too pre-
posterous.   What injury could I do the poor child?   I
injured myself, if you will!

Mme. Glyon.   I thought you married her?   That
is what I always heard.

L'Estrange.   Well, I married her!   Where is the
injury there?   I could have done no more for a duke's
daughter, for a crown princess.   It is that which was

my intolerable idiocy! my absolute madness! Looking
back, I cannot conceive——

Mme. Glyon. Is it so very long ago?

L'Estrange. Ten years, eleven, twelve—it is not
the length of time, it is the strange delusions which
possessed me, which make it seem impossible to me I
ever was the man laughed at by all Europe for present-
ing at an English Drawing-room a French peasant's
daughter.

Mme. Glyon. Did this peasant do anything very
strange at the Drawing-room?

L'Estrange. Strange? No; not that I remember
She was shy and stupid, of course, like a little sheep;
but I think my mother hustled her through without
accident; only when the Queen spoke to her she
answered—I suppose from sheer force of habit—'*Merci,
ma bonne dame!*'

Mme. Glyon (*with a cold smile*). You should have
sent her to Tower Hill for treason.

L'Estrange. You are pleased to laugh; I can assure
you it is no laughing matter to have such a joke as that
against the woman who bears your name running like
wildfire through all the clubs of London.

Mme. Glyon. Position seems to bring with it
strange pusillanimity. Were I a man, I should not
be a coward.

L'Estrange. A coward! It is no question of
cowardice. It is the sense of being made ridiculous.

Mme. Glyon. Pray, what is that but cowardice?

I hardly see what there was to be so very ashamed of.
Your wife was a little peasant—everyone knew that. It
was not wonderful in so strange a scene, so bewildering
a crowd as a royal reception must have seemed to her,
that words which she no doubt had been taught by her
own people to say as the most perfect phrase of courtesy,
came to her tongue before the Queen. Lord L'Estrange,
I am a Frenchwoman, and not of the highest classes
myself. You will pardon me if my sympathies are
rather with your wife than with yourself. If the poor
little simple '*Merci, ma bonne dame!*' was all your
wrongs, I think——

L'Estrange. Wrongs! What wrongs can an innocent and harmless child do one? She never wronged
me, but she did worse. At every turn she irritated me,
annoyed me, confused me before my friends, made me
look like a fool—as the vulgar phrase runs. She was
as lovely as the morning, but as ignorant as the little
swine she had been used to drive to find the truffles.
At every moment of intercourse I was met by that blank
wall of absolute ignorance; she understood nothing that
I said or that I alluded to; my dog comprehended better
the topics of the day. She made grotesque mistakes in
everyday etiquettes that were as simple as A B C. The
women laughed at her and laughed at me, till I was
beside myself. When I tried to teach her or correct
her, she cried out that I had ceased to love her, and
sobbed for hours. I wrote her little notes as to the
things she ought to know or do, and she thought those

more cruel than spoken words. What was I to do? I
did what seemed to me most simple and best for both;
I arranged a tour in India for myself and sent her to a
convent at Paris to be educated. The issue was terrible; but I have never seen that I did anything so
very cruel. I repeat I thought that she would be wise,
and learn the sort of learning without which a woman
is a laughing-stock for society, and—and—well, you
know she took it in another light, poor creature!
and——

Mme. Glyon. She died. It was very stupid.

L'Estrange (angrily). You are very unjust to me.
I meant neither to injure nor desert her. It was impossible that I could imagine so simple an arrangement
for her welfare would be taken to heart in so tragic a
manner. I was neither faithless nor heartless. It
seems to me that I only did a most natural thing in
placing her where she could learn and unlearn, and
where she could be made able to hold her own in the
world we lived in.

Mme. Glyon. Oh, no doubt it was very natural.
I believe most egotism is so.

L'Estrange. How was it egotism? It was for the
poor child's own good.

Mme. Glyon. Oh, of course; only it seems that
she was too stupid to appreciate it. You know women
are foolish; they expect love to endure : they are ready
to sacrifice themselves, and so fancy men will do the
same. They are tragic, as you say, and take things

au grand sérieux. Of course your wife ought to have appreciated your excellent intentions, and understood your susceptibilities, which she was so perpetually and unconsciously outraging. She should have had no such false sentiment as her own pride and her own affections. I quite see from your point of view that she must have been irritating and wearisome—most irritating, most wearisome. But why would you marry her?

L'Estrange. She was very beautiful, and I—I have said I was foolish to an incomprehensible degree, and I had at the time all sorts of romantic notions as to my wife being unspotted by the world, and moulded to my hand, and all that kind of thing. It is twelve years ago. Looking back at it, I cannot now understand how I came to commit such an unutterable insanity.

Mme. Glyon. All your pity is evidently for yourself. And yet—she *did* die, did she not?

L'Estrange (with pain). Yes, she died. Poor little fool! Who could ever foresee——

Mme. Glyon. You should be very grateful to her now. You never could have made anything of her from your point of view. She would never have been a *grande dame*; and only think now how tired and sick you would be of her! She would be worse than a sham *nestkè* carved in Amsterdam!

L'Estrange (gloomily). You are pleased to make a jest of it. It is not one to me. She was full of promise; her mind was delicate and lofty; her natural grace was great: with culture——

Mme. Glyon. Oh no, believe me, she would always have said '*Merci, ma bonne dame!*' somehow or other, or its equivalent, and disgraced you.

L'Estrange. She disgraces me now, I see, in your eyes! You evidently believe that I behaved abominably and cruelly to her, while in truth I had no other thought but to make her fit——

Mme. Glyon. For you and your exalted station!

L'Estrange. Madame! I am not a cad!

Mme. Glyon. No; you are an accomplished gentleman and a man of the world; but for those very reasons you only considered yourself. And since you have brought on this conversation of your own will, will you not confess now, that in your shame of her, and your want of courage in supporting her and the world's laughter, there was an element of—of—do not murder me!—of snobbishness?

[L'ESTRANGE *grows red and rises in silence.*
MME. GLYON *pours herself some tea.*

The Princess (approaching). How very angry you look, Lord L'Estrange! What has my friend been saying to you?

L'Estrange. That which is the one unpardonable sin, Princess—a truth! Your dagger shall be here as quickly as a telegram can summon it; and, for heaven's sake, have nothing more to do with *bric-à-brac* Brown. Mesdames, I must leave you. There is a terrible dinner for the Grand Duke to-night that I shall be late for—a man-dinner of all horror!

    [*He shakes hands with the* PRINCESS; *bows to* MME. GLYON, *and goes out.*

    Princess (*to* MME. GLYON). What *did* you say to him?

    Mme. Glyon (*rising and putting down her cup*). He would speak of his marriage. I tried to avoid it, but he would continue the subject. Then I told him home-truths that stung him. Oh, my dear, that ever I should have worshipped the ground such a man trod on! He is worse even than I thought! so poor a spirit, so miserable and petty a pride! He owns he separated himself from—from his wife, because she offended his taste in conventional things and got him ridiculed before conventional society. He cited, as though it were some treason, some great crime, that one poor little fault of '*Merci, ma bonne dame!*' to the Queen of England. It is cowardly; it is contemptible; it is vile!

    Princess. But, my dear, you knew all this.

    Mme. Glyon. I knew it in a measure. I knew that he sent me to the convent because I did not content him. But who would have thought that after twelve long years these miserable little mistakes would live in his memory as gigantic sins? Who would have dreamt that when he thinks her dead—dead—the creature he once loved—he would have no remembrance left but for her sins of omission and commission against the trumpery bye-laws of a worthless world?

Princess. Oh, dear Claire! It is always so. A glove that does not fit her rankles in a man's mind against a woman when he has forgotten all about her lie, her treachery, or her meanness. They would sooner, if they could, take you into the Divorce Court because you freckle, than because you have spent a fortnight at Monte Carlo with someone else. That is a man all over. Talk of our love of trifles! Why, it is nothing to theirs. If we have London shoes on instead of Paris ones, they know it!

Mme. Glyon. Yes; the fools do, the *gommeux* do; but he is neither. He has intellect, character, and high culture; he had a heart, too—once; and he seemed the very soul of chivalry. And yet, so has the world eaten into him, so has the false code of society bound him to it, that he justifies his conduct—justifies it!—because I, only three months from my vineyards and my cabbage-field, taken to that bewildering dazzling crowd of the Queen's Drawing-room, frightened by his mother, who awed and hated me, forgot the lesson I had learned by heart, and when I came before the throne, and the kind voice of the royal lady said kind words to me, I stammered out the old phrase of my babyhood, '*Merci, ma bonne dame!*' Yes, I had been taught to say that when I was a little child, if any gentlewoman gave me sweetmeats or centimes, and I disgraced him with it there, and all the London clubs laughed at him! And to this day, though twelve long years have passed, it is terrible to him, and unpardonable still. What do you call that? I call it petty pride, poltroonery, snobbism—the sign of a trivial nature, and of a poor base mind!

Princess. Did I not always say his must be?

Mme. Glyon. But his was nct! I repeat, he had a noble character, and a fine intelligence. He was spoilt by the world's adulation, perhaps, and by a foolish and arrogant mother; but he had a noble and generous nature—at that time. Who could have thought he would have forgotten all our love, all our joy, all our beautiful and happy hours, and merely remembered a few social blunders that made the clubs laugh? I think he does not even recollect he ever loved me! He only speaks of his marriage as an unimaginable idiocy—an incomprehensible madness!

   [*Servant announces* Milord L'Estrange.

L'Estrange (returning). A thousand pardons, Princess, but I forgot to ask you the *precise* epoch of your Venetian costume? What year are you?

   [Mme. Glyon *leaves the room. The* Princess *is a little confused.*

Princess. The year? Oh, I don't know. About the sixteenth century will do, won't it?

L'Estrange (smiling). ' About a century ' is rather a wide margin. No; you must take a year, and be scrupulous in adhering to it; you know, Italians are always most exact in these matters.

Princess. Ah, yes, because they have all their ancestors' things hung up in their wardrobes. But I haven't any ancestors, nor any things, and you are going to lend me yours.

L'Estrange. I should be too delighted if I could give you my ancestors, Princess. Unhappily Sanfriano has been before me and has given you his! Well, does the time of Giorgione suit you? We will fix it so. That will give you range enough, and charming costumes; but Sanfriano must know as much as I.

Princess. Oh, if I were anybody else, he would be all day in the studios getting me sketches! He is busy on the Duchessa Danta's costume. She goes as a sorceress; I offered him a black cat for her. Don't go away this moment, Lord L'Estrange. I want to know why you and Claire were quarrelling.

L'Estrange. Is her name Claire?

Princess. Yes; what of it? It is a common name in France. Why were you quarrelling?

L'Estrange. I assure you——

Princess. Oh, it is no use. Claire looked contemptuous, and you looked angry. What was it about?

L'Estrange. I have the misfortune never to please Madame Glyon. She dislikes me.

Princess. I am not sure of that. But Claire is a very proud woman, and she is always very strong in taking other women's parts, and you know—don't you know?—I suppose I ought not to say it, but there is that story of your marriage, and that goes against you. Tell it how you may, you look so heartless, so inconstant, so capricious. I ought to beg your pardon——

L'Estrange. Pray do nothing of the kind. Madame Glyon herself has explained at full length her views upon that subject. She has heard a few outlines of the affair, and this skeleton she has clothed with all the riches of her imagination and her sympathies; very much to my prejudice. She said very rude things to me; but I am bound in honour to admit that some of them were very true ones; although her exaggerated compassion of my—my victim—renders her singularly unjust to me.

Princess. It is not at all like Claire's usually delicate taste to begin personalities.

L'Estrange. Oh, the fault was altogether mine. I worried her till she spoke. I was punished as I deserved to be. We cannot complain of receiving what we ask for, and I asked her to speak without compliment or reticence—and—she did so.

Princess. She offended you?

L'Estrange. She offended me. We are very poor creatures, and are as thorny as porcupines the moment anyone stings our pride. What most especially annoyed me was that she should not for a moment consent to look at the facts from my point of view.

Princess. She would probably do so if you were not present. That is just like Claire.

L'Estrange. I am sure she would not. She has made up her indictment against me as coldly and accurately as she would do a problem in mathematics. But I will confess to you, Princess, that the moment I had left your house I felt ashamed of my anger. Her defence, after all, of another woman was noble ; most women always side with me, praise me, and tell me I did quite right ; most women always go without examination against the woman in any story. And what vexes me, I will confess also, is that in answering her I must have looked a very sorry creature. All the arguments I put forward, though true ones, were selfish and shallow. She told me I was a snob——

Princess. Oh—h—h—h!!!!

L'Estrange. And honestly, she had cause to say so. I did lack courage—moral courage ; and although it is not so easy as she deems it for a man to bear his marriage being made the joke of the town, yet I can fancy that to her my defence seemed trivial, mean, and vulgar ; and lowered me in her estimation. She says she is of the people herself; is that so ?

Princess. I believe she—was—not anybody, in your sense of the word.

L'Estrange. But she is so perfect a gentlewoman.

Princess. Yes; she certainly is. And *so* clever !

L'Estrange (abruptly). What was Glyon ?

Princess. I—I really don't know.

L'Estrange. But he is really dead ?

Princess. Oh, yes ; he does not exist, thank goodness !

L'Estrange. Was he a brute to her ?

Princess. I think her husband was—not very good.

L'Estrange.   That would account for it, then.

Princess.   Would account for what?

L'Estrange.   For her violent partisanship of that poor young girl—my wife of a year—for whose tragic death I was not to blame; upon my word I was not. If I had had any foreboding or conception of the manner in which my departure affected her, I would not for worlds have left her, even though every hour of our life together had its thorns.   I wish you would persuade your friend of this.   I must have seemed to her unmanly, and a mere selfish, cowardly knave; and I do not like so grand an artist, and so noble a woman, to have so poor an opinion of me.   Will you be my friend, Princess?

Princess.   Lord L'Estrange!   You are very charming when you are natural.

L'Estrange.   Natural?   Heaven and earth!   You do not mean that I am ever a *poseur*?

Princess.   Just a little sometimes.   Don't be. How horrified you look!

L'Estrange.   Well, to be called a snob and a *poseur* in one day——

Princess.   *Is* hard for a leader of art and fashion, and a son of the Crusaders!   I will be your friend with Claire.   But she is terribly obstinate, and in a sort of way she is terribly democratic too.   If you were a painter *sans le sou* she would be more easily disposed to be amiable to you.

L'Estrange.   You make me wish for news that my

old abbey is gutted and the Bank of England is bank-rupt.

Princess. Are you as serious as that?

L'Estrange. Quite. And I commend myself to your merciful hands, Princess.

Princess. Do you go to Keudell's to-night?

L'Estrange. I will if you will promise me the cotillon. [*Exit.*

Princess (goes to the door of the inner room). Claire! Come back one moment. He is gone.

Mme. Glyon enters. I am tired. Do not keep me long.

Princess. You are not tired, you are unhappy. Oh, my dear Claire, I am sure he is so fond of you still!

Mme. Glyon (sternly). What? How dare you say so? He has forgotten me as utterly as a lasting irritation and my memory allow him to do.

Princess. Well, you know, I mean—not fond of you *still*—fond of you *again.* Oh, don't look so angry? Do you know, he spoke so nicely about her—I mean you—I can't express myself properly; but indeed it is quite true. He says he feels he must have looked heartless and cowardly, and all that, just now when he talked to you, but that he isn't so one bit really; and he does so want you to do him justice.

Mme. Glyon (bitterly). Justice! You pleading to *me* for justice for *him!* My dear, I really think that even your teetotum of a mind should not have spun round quite so quickly. To defend him to me! I do not know whether it be the more ridicule or the more insult. Indeed, it is both!

Princess (with tears in her eyes). Oh Claire, I think him just as much of a wretch as ever I did. I don't spin round; I don't change—no, never—about you. But he can be very nice in manner when he is natural; and though you will not listen about it, he admires you—blindly—he is passionately anxious to have your good opinion.

Mme. Glyon. I dare say! Lord L'Estrange is sur feited by woman's adulation, and his pride is piqued by a person who is no one in the eyes of his world daring to be indifferent to him. His anxiety to please me was a caprice, as the other was!

Princess. Oh Claire, you are very hard! I can't see why you should not win him again and be happy.

Mme. Glyon. I suppose you think, as he does, that a woman of my birth should have no pride? Win him again! How can you speak so? He divorced me when I was the most innocent thing on earth, and——

Princess. No, he did not divorce you! He meant to come back in two years.

Mme. Glyon. Two years! He makes you believe that. He neither meant nor would have been likely to return. He separated himself from me because I offended his taste, got him laughed at by his friends, and committed social mistakes every time I moved or spoke. He said himself just now that his marriage was an incomprehensible act of absolute idiocy.

Princess. But if he had known *you* were *you*——

Mme. Glyon. No doubt I should have been once more odious and contemptible to him! He admires me, you say; yes, I believe he does; but what he admires is a woman who repulses him, who is famous, who has a talent that happens to be to his taste, and who he fancies has a past that is mysterious and not too creditable. His imagination and curiosity are at work, and his pride is stimulated and irritated; if he knew this moment that I am his wife, he would change in one instant. I should be a mere awkward, ignorant peasant once more in his sight; he would say once more what an unutterable fool he was twelve years ago. His fancy for me when I was a child was caprice, but it was passion too; his fancy for me now is only caprice *doublé* with curiosity and pique. I am not likely to be his dupe twice over.

Princess. You are dreadfully unforgiving. Do you know, if I were you, I should revenge myself, since you will not pardon him, in quite another way. I should encourage him, and I should refuse him. For I am certain he will ask you to marry him.

Mme. Glyon (*bitterly*). Surely not. Since his marriage twelve years ago was an idiocy, he would never, now that he is twelve years older, desire to make another that would be an equal imbecility! Remember the voice of society is the voice of God to him!

Princess.   But if he *did*—would you—would you
tell him the truth or refuse him?

Mme. Glyon.   The latter, certainly.   My life is
tranquil and altogether given to art; his is full of the
world and the world's friendships and flatteries; he has
no need of any affections, they are 'bad form,' and I—I
have no need of them either.   Art contents me, and
some time or other kindly death will come and I shall
forget that I have ever suffered.

Princess (with tears in her eyes).   And suffer
still.

Mme. Glyon.   Of course.   The utmost one gets
after a mortal wound is some dull drowsy lulling of the
pain from sheer habit of bearing with it, and the
familiarity of time.

   [*Servant enters and announces* Lady Cowes, Lady
      St. Asaph.   Mme. Glyon *goes out as they*
      approach.

Lady Cowes.   Dear Princess, we are so late and it
isn't your day, but we thought we must take a peep at
you, though we cannot stop an instant.   Lady St.
Asaph had something very especial to say to you—to
ask you.

Princess (aside).   I am sure it is to subscribe to a
church, or to do something spiteful on my visiting-list.
(*Aloud.*)   I shall be so charmed if I can be any use.
Yes?   What is it?   Do tell me, please?

Lady St. Asaph (dropping her voice).   Could you
—would you mind—pray do not think me too personal

—but would you tell me if Madame Glyon is really going to marry Aldred Dorian?

Princess. Mr. Dorian? No; I don't think so—I don't know. What made you think of it?

Lady St. Asaph. Oh, everyone is talking about it; they say it is definitely arranged, and it would be so very —very—*very*—VERY dreadful.

Princess (*sharply*). Dreadful? Why?

Lady St. Asaph. Oh, dear Princess, you see Aldred Dorian is a sort of cousin of ours—distant, but still a cousin—the sixteenth Lord St. Asaph married a Dorian of Deepdene. Of course he has always been very strange and odd, caring for nothing but painting, and throwing away all his chances; but still he *is* a cousin of ours and of heaps of other people too, and if you do know anything of this marriage, I do entreat you to tell me the truth.

Princess. I don't know anything of it; but if the thing were so, what would it matter? why would it be dreadful? You know that Madame Glyon is my guest and my friend.

Lady Cowes (*imploringly*). Oh, dear Princess, pray do not be quite too vexed with us. We remembered your affection for her, but for all that we resolved to come and ask you frankly to tell us the truth.

Lady St. Asaph. And beg you to stop this marriage without scandal; that is the great thing to do. Aldred Dorian is so headstrong; if there were any opposition, it would make him ten times more determined.

Princess. But why should I stop it? Mind, I don't know anything about it; but why should I try to stop it if I did?

Lady St. Asaph (lowering her voice). Dear Princess, you are very young, and you have a very warm heart, and you will let an old woman, who knows this wicked world better than you do, tell you something painful, that it is necessary you should know? You will allow me?

Princess. I never knew anyone wish to tell me anything unless it were painful! Yes; pray say it out. I am very inquisitive.

Lady Cowes. You know we can only have one motive: to save Dorian and to open your eyes.

Lady St. Asaph. And I feel that you ought to know it.

Princess. To know what? Oh, please be quick!

Lady St. Asaph. Well—that—well, I never can bear to say these things; for, after all, one cannot be sure, and one can never be too charitable—but still, sometimes it is one's duty—dear Princess, what *did* you know of Madame Glyon?

Princess. She was at the convent where I was.

Lady St. Asaph. Ah, quite so; but who was she?

Princess. Of very humble birth, I believe; she never disguises it; she is not ashamed of it.

Lady St. Asaph. Ah, I see; dear sweet creature,

your goodness and your innocence naturally lead you
to be too trustful; but indeed, if you will allow me
to advise you, you will make some excuse for bringing this lady's visit to you to a close. We know
for certain, on most unimpeachable authority,
that M. Glyon never existed. You will understand
me?

Princess (colouring). I really don't. I don't
care the least for M. Glyon; I love Claire.

Lady Cowes. Ah, dear Princess, that is so sweet
and unsuspecting! Of course you fall a prey——

Lady St. Asaph. It was Aldred Dorian's infatuation that led me to make inquiries at the proper
sources of information. You really do not seem to see
the matter in its true and very serious light. There
has never been a M. Glyon. The whole thing, name
and marriage and all, is false. She is a clever artist,
no doubt—at least, they say so; but she is quite—
quite—unfit for the honour of your affection and
protection. They told me in the very strictest confidence at the French Embassy——

Princess (rising and speaking quickly). Then
please, Lady St. Asaph, keep their confidence. You
must think the very worst of me if you like, but I will
not hear another word against Claire.

Lady Cowes. But she has an assumed name.

Lady St. Asaph. There never was a M. Glyon.

Lady Cowes. They say she has two millions worth
of diamonds; how did she get them?

Lady St. Asaph. Aldred Dorian will close society against him for ever if he marry her.

Lady Cowes. You know, everybody knows she does not paint her own pictures—she never did.

Lady St. Asaph. If you will only allow me, I can prove to you that you harbour a mere adventuress.

Princess. Oh, please don't make me quarrel with you ; I should be so sorry to have to do that ; but not a word more must you say. You are all wrong, entirely wrong ; and as for her marrying Aldred Dorian, she will no more marry him than I shall.

Lady St. Asaph. So positive an assurance from you is a great comfort, for you must know so much better than anyone else. But some day when you are calmer about it, I think I shall convince you that French artists with feigned names are very compromising guests.

Lady Cowes. Dear Princess, you have told me yourself that her husband was cruel to her.

Princess. So he was.

Lady Cowes and Lady St. Asaph (together). But if he never existed ?

Princess. He did—he does.

Lady Cowes and Lady St. Asaph (in chorus). Does ! Then she is not a widow ? She is separated ?

Princess (impatiently). If she be, at least Aldred Dorian is safe from her ! You will pardon me if I ask you to leave my friend's name in peace.

Lady St. Asaph (softly). If one only knew what

her name is! Oh, I am so quite too grieved that I have vexed you, but really I thought you ought to know what they say.

Princess. '*They say*' has killed many friendships and much happiness, but it won't kill mine and Claire's. Won't you have some tea? No? Oh, you have not vexed me. One is not vexed at what is not in the very least true.

Lady St. Asaph (with a sigh). How beautiful such confidence is! But, alas! dear Princess, when you are as old as I you will have learnt that there is no enemy so dangerous and so costly as belief in others! We shall meet to-night? You will be *en beauté*, I am sure, and I hear Rodrigues has done something marvellous for you in humming-birds and ivory satin. *Au revoir*—don't be angry, love!

Princess (left alone). Oh, the old cats! the horrid old cats! And I am quite sure I answered so badly; and I let them know that her husband was alive! Two millions worth of diamonds! Claire! who won't wear as much as a silver bangle, and spends all her money on the poor of Paris! Oh, the horrid old cats! Poking into everybody's cupboards, and if they see a cobweb declaring it's a skeleton! I haven't told any of them any stories yet, but I think—I shall begin. Intrusion ought to be answered by invention. If only Claire would declare herself!—but she never will. Of course, as she has had the strength to keep silent all these twelve years, she will go on doing so. Carlino! Carlino!

(*The* PRINCE *enters.*)   Will you tell me one thing, truthfully if you can?   Do people ever ask you questions about Claire's husband?

Prince.   Mia cara! I think they do, now you name it.

Princess.   And what do you answer?

Prince.   Mia cara, I know nothing of the gentleman, so what can I say?   She does not produce her husband, and I think you said he was dead; but whether he is dead, or in Russia, or in America, what does it matter?   She is a handsome woman, and might amuse herself very well if she chose.   I know two or three men who admire her greatly, only she has too much the air of the *nemo me impune lacessit.*

Princess.   You would like my female friends to be like yours, then?

Prince.   Amiability is always agreeable.   I should be so glad if you would remember that.

Princess.   I will try and remember it, and you must not blame me if you dislike the results of my remembrance.

Prince.   You mean some menace very profound, but I do not follow it.   And I do not think you will ever get out of your regrettable habit of making little scenes about everything—you like them too well.

Princess.   I detest them, but when you insult me——

Prince.   Ah, ah! what is coming but a scene? Rather instruct me what I am to say about the dead or the vanished husband of your friend. They do talk much about her just now!

Princess. Say she is an angel, and that he was most utterly unworthy.

Prince. Oh, *cara mia*, they would laugh at me for being in love with her. And as for being un-worthy, everyone knows that husbands are always that; there is not a pretty woman in Europe whose husband is not a brute—if you listen to her. I am convinced you tell Montelupo I am a monster.

Princess. Montelupo sees for himself that you outrage my feelings on every occasion.

Prince. And he consoles you for the outrage. Ah, yes, that is just as it should be. Only, Montelupo is a puppy—a *grullo*—an inanity—an absolute ass—you might choose better, more creditably.

Princess (aside). He has some decency left; he is jealous. Perhaps he will tire of that horrid woman yet! (*Aloud.*) I find Montelupo quite charming; he has so much tact, so much silent sympathy.

Prince. And recompenses himself for his silence by boasting with both lungs in the club!

Princess. And don't you boast, sometimes?

Prince (angrily). No, never. I am not a monkey, all grimace, like your *servo*; and I tell you now, once for all, that though you can divert yourself as you please, and have any number of young men about you that you like, it is a number that you must have, and not anyone in especial; for if I get laughed at about you, or hear my name dragged through the club, then, Signora Principessa———

Princess. Oh, then you mean you will stand up in your shirt with a big sabre? Very well. That will be very flattering to me. But the Duchess Danta will be very angry!

> [*She leaves the room with a little laugh, and the* PRINCE *stands disconcerted. He pours himself out a glass of kümmel at the tea-table, and says with a sigh,*

If she were not my wife, she would really be bewitching. As it is—*che seccatura!*

SCENE V.

Same room, five o'clock next day.

Present: L'ESTRANGE *and the* PRINCESS.

L'Estrange. Princess, in spite of your kind promises, which I am sure have been sustained by kind offices, Madame Glyon remains for ever on the defensive with me. What is the reason? Do not spare my vanity in answering me.

Princess. Well, I must tell you a secret if I am to answer you honestly.

L'Estrange. I will be worthy of your confidence.

Princess. Oh, it is not very much of one, only Claire would be angry if I spoke of it. You must know, then, that she and I were at the convent with—what did you call her the other day?—the poor young girl who had the misfortune to be your wife of a year.

L'Estrange. I understand. Madame Glyon remembers her, pities her, and so deems me a wretch?

Princess. Exactly. Of course you know it did make a terrible impression on all of us, and Claire being older than I, felt it more. I do not think anything you could ever say or do would change the impression that she has of you.

L'Estrange. She is very unjust; it is of no use to go over that old ground, yet it is strange that so serene a woman should show herself so implacable on a matter that can never have touched herself.

Princess. She was attached to your wife; pity is very strong in such a woman as Claire.

L'Estrange. She has none for me.

Princess. My dear Lord L'Estrange, she probably is as convinced as I am that you never can possibly be a subject for compassion.

L'Estrange. Be serious, dear Princess. Surely, by all I have said to you, you must believe that my admiration for your friend is so strong that it must be called by another word. Therefore, her coldness to me is more than painful; it is so distressing to me that I am a fool to linger on in Rome.

Princess. Oh, she is going back to Paris at *Mi-carême.* But, really and truly, with all this feeling for her, would you go so far as to commit another folly?

L'Estrange. You are her friend, and you would call it a folly?

Princess. Certainly; from the world's point of view, as your other marriage was. Claire is a famous woman, but she is not of high birth; she is not rich, and the ill nature of society has touched her. You know it is like London soot; it flies about by the merest accident, but if it smudges you, the smut makes you look foolish, though you be yourself white as snow.

L'Estrange. Princess, she is your friend, therefore you will believe that I would not insult either you or herself by a mere frivolous curiosity. Will you let me ask you then honestly—is she free to marry?

Princess. To marry you?

L'Estrange. Well, put it so—is she? There is a rumour, more than a rumour, that Glyon is not dead.

Princess. But would you marry her?

L'Estrange. Please answer my question first.

Princess. Then, yes; ten times over, yes; she can be your wife, if she wish it, with as clear a conscience as I am Carlino's. But do you wish it? That I doubt very much.

L'Estrange. I am beginning to wish it passionately. I gave her to understand me so, last night.

Princess. And what did she say?

L'Estrange. Nothing; we were interrupted; your rooms were so full.

Princess. But seriously—you do not seriously

mean that you are ready to give your title a second time to a woman without birth?

L'Estrange. If I be willing to dower your friend with all I possess, it is not you, Princess, who should quarrel with me. She has a grand genius, and I am sure a grand nature. They are worth sixteen quarterings. I am a conservative in some ways, but I have no prejudices.

Princess. I am sure you mean what you say now, or you think you do; but I am so afraid that—you are so very changeable——

L'Estrange. That is her idea. I am not so.

Princess. I mean, you know, that when you see a rare piece of Celadon or Crackling that charms you, you bid against everybody, and would ruin yourself to have it knocked down to you. But, then, when you have had it in your collection a little time, you begin to think—perhaps it is an imposture, perhaps it is not worth its money, perhaps somebody else has something like it, or something better; and then, little by little, little by little, you quite grow into disgust with the poor piece, and would like to put it out of your cabinets altogether, if you were only quite sure. Now, one woman you have already treated like the bit of Celadon; and, though you are so eager now to pay any price for another, I am afraid you would feel much the same to her in time, if you had your way. And Claire is not a mere piece of china who will let herself be broken like the other; she is a very sensitive and very proud woman.

L'Estrange. You have a poor impression of me; your friend has inoculated you with her opinions.

Princess. Can you deny that towards your china you do gradually grow from adoration to indifference, from indifference to doubt, from doubt to downright disgust?

L'Estrange. One always depreciates or over-estimates what is one's own. But your parallel is not quite true. I have pieces of Old Vienna, of Japanese, of Crackling, with which I have been satisfied for twenty years. It is only where there is a doubt that one grows whimsical and dissatisfied.

Princess. Well, Claire to you would be like the china that you do doubt about. If you won her, you would always be saying to yourself, What does the world think of her?

L'Estrange. You make me a poor creature.

Princess. No, no; only a connoisseur not easy with his *bibelôts* unless the whole of mankind be envying them. Envy is the mark that society scratches on the very best of everything, as they used to put double L's on the Bourbon Sèvres. Unless your Sèvres had the double L's, you would not care for it.

L'Estrange. You are so witty, Princess, that it is impossible to keep up with you, and I do not want wit to-day; I want sympathy.

Princess. Try and get it from Claire.

[MME. GLYON *enters, not seeing* L'ESTRANGE ; *she has a quantity of daffodils and narcissus in her hand. She speaks to the* PRINCESS.

Laura, these are lovelier than your camellias and azaleas. I will put them in your Venetian bowl (*sees* L'ESTRANGE). You here again, Lord L'Estrange? Good morning. Why must one say morning even while vespers are sounding?

L'Estrange. Dinner is the only meridian we recognise. I never knew why we have not called it supper. You have got those flowers in the Doria woods, I think?

Mme. Glyon. Yes, I have been there with Bébé.

Princess. Ah, my Bébé! I must go and see him. I hope you have not tired him. I am afraid he is getting to love you better than me.

Mme. Glyon. I shall be gone in ten days, and then Bébé will forget.

[*Exit the* PRINCESS. L'ESTRANGE *approaches* MME, GLYON *as she is arranging the daffodils.*

L'Estrange. Do you believe it is so easy for even Bébé to forget you?

Mme. Glyon. Yes, it is very easy. Bébé is a boy ; over his Easter eggs he will forget even what my face is like.

L'Estrange. I do not think even Bébé at his mature years will be so faithless. I wish you would have more true conception of the hold you take upon us. Most people have so far too much self-esteem.

You err in the very opposite fault of self-detraction and self-depreciation.

Mme. Glyon. No; I know where my strength lies and where my weakness does. I can force the world into admiration of my works, but I never yet could influence a living being. Some people are like that; their power of volition is expended on their art; in the facts of life they are weak, and write their names in water.

L'Estrange. You write yours in fire on men's memories. Will you let me say again what I said ill last night? Will you——

Mme. Glyon. Leave it unsaid; I will consider it unsaid. You spoke on a mere impulse—a whim of the moment. We all know such a whim cost you dear once.

L'Estrange. Can you never leave in oblivion that one folly? After all, it was no crime.

Mme. Glyon. I think it was one. I may be hypercritical.

L'Estrange. If it were, leave it in its grave.

Mme. Glyon. In her grave.

L'Estrange. You are most unjust. One moment you call my hapless marriage a whim, the next a crime. It cannot be both. If I be such a poor light piece of thistledown, I cannot seriously be loaded with responsibilities so weighty. I cannot see what that one action of my past can have to do with you.

Mme. Glyon. Nothing; only, I am quite well

aware that what you profess to feel for me is of no more worth, and will have no longer life, than what you felt for the gardener's daughter, of whom you made a countess.

L'Estrange. Good heavens! how shall I convince you? Can you compare yourself one instant, in your genius, your brilliancy, your fame, to that poor child whose mere physical loveliness, for an hour of summer-passion, made me lose my wits and brave the laughter of the world?

Mme. Glyon (looking at him sternly). There is not so very vast a difference. I am of the people. Your world, if it do not laugh at me, often slanders me. To love *me,* a man would need to be indifferent to comment and to innuendo; no coward before conventionality, and deaf as a marble wall to the envenomed buzz of chattering tongues. Lord L'Estrange, you are not such a man.

L'Estrange. I could become such—for you.

Mme. Glyon. You think so at this moment. I believe you to be sincere. But you deceive yourself. You never would resist the pressure of social opinion. You see me through your own eyes now, and do me more than justice; but, if I listened to you, soon—very soon—you would see me through the eyes of others, and little by little you would quarrel with yourself once more for having been a fool.

L'Estrange (bitterly). Ah! You can reason so ably and so coldly because I do not touch a fibre of your sympathies; I do not for a moment quicken a pulse of your heart! If you had the faintest feeling for me, you would not condemn me with such chilly logic.

Mme. Glyon (*looking down on the daffodils*). I am not insensible to the honour you do me, and I believe in the momentary sincerity of your assurances. But—that is all.

L'Estrange (*passionately*). What can I say to make you believe more?

Mme. Glyon. *Nothing* would make me believe in the duration of the fantasy that moves you this idle Carnival time, and will have left you, as my memory will have left Bébé, by Easter-day.

          [*She rings. A servant enters.*

Mme. Glyon (*to* SERVANT). Bring water for this bowl of flowers. Lord L'Estrange, why do you distress yourself and me? Go—go in peace; and when you awake out of this momentary madness, as you will do very soon, you will say to yourself, ' How nearly I committed a second folly because a woman's pictures had a *morbidezza* and a fancy in them that I liked!'

L'Estrange. You are cruel! You are unjust! You are utterly wrong!

Mme. Glyon. Here is Giovanni with the water. He understands English very well.

L'Estrange. But if I could convince you of the sincerity of my feelings—of their constancy—would there be anything on your side to forbid your listening to me?

Mme. Glyon. It is mere waste of time to discuss the impossible.

L'Estrange. At least do me the justice of a frank reply. Would you be free to grant me what I solicit?

Mme. Glyon. What do you mean?

L'Estrange. I mean in plain words—is Glyon dead?

Mme. Glyon (with embarrassment). Were there a shadow of claim on me from any other, you may be sure I would never have let you speak such words as you have done. But these questions are very idle. Lord L'Estrange, in plain words, since you ask for them, I refuse you.

L'Estrange. I will leave you. You will make my excuses to the Prince. [*Exit.*

   [*She completes the arrangement of the flowers and then dismisses the servant. Alone, she sinks into a seat and bursts into tears.*

He loves me now! And if I could keep up the comedy, he would love me, perhaps, always. I might marry him again, and he need never know the truth. But I would not win him by a lie—it would be too base. Maybe, even as far as I have gone is wrong; and yet it was such temptation to see his cold heart day by day warm and soften towards me, and his fastidious fancy find in me his ideal. And he is so dear to me—so dear! How could he not know that I resented so passionately because I loved so well! Maybe even now we might be happy—no, not if he knew the truth. I should lose all my charm for him ; he would be once more afraid of all my antecedents ; he would be once more seeing the peasant in my step, in my voice, in my habits ; he thinks me a muse, a goddess, *now*—but if he knew! He is so utterly the unconscious slave of his fancy, he is so entirely under the dominance of mere caprice, that when he learned that he was in love with his own wife he would be disenchanted, like a child who sees the fairy of a pantomime, stripped of her gossamer wings and golden crown, trudging through mud, in common everyday attire. He is entirely the creature of his fancy, as the child is. And I could not risk it again—the gradual disillusion, the impatience that only courtesy controlled, the fading away of tenderness into dissatisfaction, the changing of adoration into incessant criticism ; no, I could never bear them now. Better that we should for ever live apart. I have art ; he has the world. He will be happy ; in three months' time he will have forgotten my rejection. And yet, oh heaven ! how hard it is not to cry out to him—My love! my love!

SCENE VI.

Dorian's Studio.

Present : LADY COWES, LADY ST. ASAPH, *the* PRINCESS, IPSWICH, MONTELUPO.

Princess. Is Dorian really gone ?

Lady St. Asaph. Oh yes, to the Soudan. I am so thankful.

Princess. Oh dear, how can you be! All his delightful life in Rome to be broken up like this, and all these delicious things to be sold—it is too utterly vexing; and his Tuesday teas for us in Carnival were the very pleasantest things one had—how can you say you are thankful? and that delicious negro and the *niello* teapot!

Lady St. Asaph. Dear Princess, you know *why* I am thankful. A temporary break-up is very much better for him than a lifelong misfortune, and you can buy the teapot at the sale; the negro is gone with him to Africa.

Lady Cowes. And of course he will come back with another negro in a year or two, and begin to buy teapots again, and get tapestries together in a new studio. It was the very wisest thing he could do to go.

Ipswich. Is it true, Princess, that your handsome

friend sent him to the Soudan because she is trying it on with L'Estrange?

Lady Cowes. Everyone knows that, Lord Ipswich, except, perhaps, the Princess.

Princess (*hastily*). It is utterly false.

Lady Cowes and Lady St. Asaph (*together*). Oh, dear Princess!

Princess. Utterly false! If you must know, she refused to marry both Aldred Dorian and Lord L'Estrange. There! you make me say mean things— things I never ought to say—because you are so obstinate, so untrue, so unkind.

Lady St. Asaph (*angrily*). She certainly did not refuse Aldred Dorian. We talked to him—we are cousins—and he said how right we were, and determined to go to Africa.

Princess. As if Dorian was such a contemptible creature as to be talked to—talked over! Of course you don't believe me, but I know she refused him here in this very studio.

Lady Cowes. She told you so, I suppose?

Princess. No, she did not. Dorian told me himself. He was wretched. He will never be the same man or the same artist again——

Ipswich (*laughing*). And is L'Estrange wretched? On my word, I don't see it. He was buying brocades in the Ghetto this morning with all the zest imaginable.

Princess. His soul never rises above brocades and *bibelôts!* No, I don't mean that; he can be very nice, very charming, but it makes me angry to see how he does absorb himself in old rubbish. It is better than horses, though.

Lady St. Asaph. I thought you said he was in love with your friend? She certainly is entirely modern, as nobody ever heard of her till five years ago '

Princess. Oh, you mean till all Paris crowded to her great picture of the 'Gleaners.' Well, no artist can be heard of until something's exhibited.

Ipswich. Come, Princess, you don't mean seriously that she has thrown over L'Estrange?

Princess. I am very sorry I said it. I ought not to have said it; but as I have said it, I can't unsay it, and it is true.

Ipswich. Well—it beats me!—when his marriage twelve years ago was such a blunder.

Lady St. Asaph. There cannot be any question of anything half so innocent as even a stupid marriage. Madame Glyon's husband is alive—the Princess told us so the other day.

Princess. You quite misunderstood what I meant, and my friend is quite free to marry Lord L'Estrange if she choose to marry him.

Lady Cowes. Well, I think he had better ask a few questions in Paris first—the questions *you* should have asked, dear Princess!

Princess. I never do ask questions about my friends. I was born in a country-house on the St.

Lawrence, where nobody is supposed to know good manners, and I was taught that to sneak behind anybody's back, to pry about them, was a very vulgar sort of thing to do. But, in society, everybody does seem to me to be vulgar.

[LADY COWES *and* LADY ST. ASAPH *laugh slightly.*

Ipswich. Well, yes, society *is* a bit of a cad, there's no doubt about it; we do slang one another so awfully. Here's L'Estrange; come to look after the *niello* teapot, I'll be bound.

L'Estrange (salutes them and adds to LADY ST. ASAPH)—I cannot tell you how sorry I am about Dorian. Are these things really to be sold?

Ipswich. There! that's all he thinks about. He wants the teapot and the tapestries. To have one's friends really interested in one's disappearance or death, one must have got together a lot of good things in pots and pans and bed-curtains and old iron.

L'Estrange. Are they really to be sold?

Lady St. Asaph. Oh, yes; he does not mean to come back.

L'Estrange. He will come back. No one can stay away from Rome who once has cared for it.

Lady St. Asaph. But they are all to be sold; he has left all directions to Costa's judgment.

L'Estrange. He is great friends with Costa. I am so very sorry; few have so fine a mind as Dorian; few give one such genial companionship.

Princess. And such delightful Tuesday teas. How

we shall miss those Tuesdays with those solemn tapestries frowning at our frivolity!

Lady St. Asaph. We must be going homewards. Good-day, dear Princess; we shall meet at Madame Minghetti's. [*Exit with* LADY COWES *and* IPSWICH.

Princess. I have to wait here for Carlino. He wants to look over the things before any regular arrangement is made about them. It seems Dorian has some wonderful *trasferato* work in steel and silver.

L'Estrange. Yes; I know it: it is exquisite. I will see Costa at once, and try and buy everything as it stands, without letting a sale come on. Dorian is terribly mistaken to think of selling his things. One should never do that.

Princess. Lord L'Estrange, I said just now that you cared for nothing but brocades and *bric-à-brac.* It seemed a little harsh when I had said it, but you see it is true. You are feeling nothing for Aldred Dorian; you are only thinking of buying his things, just as Carlino is.

L'Estrange. Princess, I am thinking of buying them, it is true; but I am only thinking of it for this reason—that I want to keep the *atelier* together just as Dorian left it, so that when he comes back, as he will certainly do, he can have it all again if he please to have it; he will only need to hand me over my purchase-money. I do not like Dorian's things to be dispersed.

Princess. Oh—h—h! I beg your pardon, I did

misjudge you. But how can you go buying brocades at the Ghetto when you pretend to be miserable about Claire's indifference?

L'Estrange. L'un n'empêche pas l'autre. One's habits are a part of oneself; one puts them on as one puts one's boots on in the morning. Besides, you must remember I do not 'sorrow as those that have no hope.' I believe that Madame Glyon will come in time to do me justice, as you have now done in a lesser matter.

Princess. But she is going away.

L'Estrange. To Paris? Well, I usually spend the spring in Paris. I do not foresee any great obstacle in her return to Paris. If there were no greater——

Princess. And you really would make her your Countess?

L'Estrange. I would really make her my Countess, if you like that Court Circular form of expression. I prefer to say that I would make her my wife. It seems the warmer term.

Princess. Do you know, Lord L'Estrange, I am getting quite fond of you?

L'Estrange. I am too charmed.

Princess. I never thought you had so much feeling; and it isn't *only* evanescent, is it?

L'Estrange. As far as I know myself, it is not. It is of this that I want you to persuade your friend. She got rid of me yesterday by means of daffodils and a servant, and it is difficult for me to approach her again yet. She was so very cold. Indeed, she seems always disposed to resent as an impertinence the highest compliment that a man can pay to a woman.

Princess. Well, I have done all I can. But Claire has her own views—it is difficult to change them. I think you will do better not to worry her.

L'Estrange. Worry her! You certainly do treat one to rough facts, Princess. I suppose what you mean is that one must ride a waiting-race.

Princess. Yes, that is what I do mean. I quite understand your impatience. You are a very great person, and you have got a very high place, and you would give all you have to Claire, and you naturally expect your generosity to meet at least with gratitude. Only you see it is all spoilt in her eyes by the fact that you were equally generous to that poor peasant girl, and repented it.

L'Estrange. I think it hard that a long-past folly, which was after all a chivalrous folly, should for ever be quoted against me.

Princess. Perhaps it is hard, but it is good for you to taste a wholesome bitterness for once. You have been fed on honey. (*The* PRINCE *enters.*) Carlino, it is no use your fretting yourself over the *trasferato*; Lord L'Estrange is going to buy up everything by a private arrangement.

Prince. Is that so, *cara mia*?

L'Estrange. I am going to try and do it, at any rate. It is folly to break up this charming *atelier*. Dorian will certainly return.

Prince. When he has ceased to break his heart about La Glyon. Laura should send that lady back to Paris: she makes mischief here. There is Sant' Elmo now wild to marry her, and he is *bon prince* and enormously rich, and a handsome lad too; she will take him, I dare say.

Princess. No, she will not; you will not understand, Carlino. She does not want to marry—again.

Prince. Oh, yes; she is a muse, and all that, but she will take a very big thing when it comes to her. Dorian was not a very big thing; he was only a fairly nice thing. That was not enough for your friend. She is ambitious. One sees that in the way her head is poised. Now, Sant' Elmo is a grand marriage; you cannot have a grander—off a throne: Roman prince, Spanish duke, Hungarian margraf, and rich—ouf!—if I were only as rich!

Princess (low to L'ESTRANGE). Don't you feel as if you were at Christie's or the Drouot, bidding against Lord Dudley for a *vieux Vienne* cup?

L'Estrange. I did not need the stimulus.

Prince. Lord L'Estrange, shall we go together to the Via Margutta? If Costa refuse to let you purchase *en bloc*, I should ike to say a word to him about the *trasferato.*

L'Estrange. Certainly. The Princess comes with us?

Princess. No; I shall stay here till Claire comes, and then we are going very far out to some convent to see some Madonna of Mino's that no male eyes must profane.

[MME. GLYON *enters. The* PRINCE *and* L'ESTRANGE *bow to her and go out.*

Claire, he is going to buy all Dorian's things and keep them till Dorian comes back. Isn't it nice of him? Do you know, he *is* very nice when you understand him. I do—I do, indeed, think you are in error.

Mme. Glyon. I know that I have been in error when I came into this room. I allowed a noble nature like Dorian's to fasten its hopes on me, which he never would have done, if we had not, tacitly at any rate, led him to believe that my husband was not living. I can never forgive myself the wreck of Dorian's happy and noble life; but, if you will believe me, until he spoke of it here, I never dreamed of his feeling for me anything more than that sympathy which the same tastes and art beget.

Princess. And now Carlino says there is Sant' Elmo?

Mme. Glyon. Oh, that handsome boy will find many to console him. Dorian is very different—to him I have been guilty.

Princess. And I think you are—not altogether right to Lord L'Estrange.

Mme. Glyon. How can anyone in a false position be altogether right to anyone? A false position is like a wrong focus in photography; it distorts everything.

My motives in all I have done have been innocent
enough, but concealment always ends in some sin or
another.

Princess.   No, no—sin is too big a word—too ugly
a word; it does not suit you at all.   Your worse faults
are pride and over-sensitiveness; they are no very
grave ones.   But indeed, Claire, he does love you now,
not only with his fancy.   I cannot see why you should
not tell him.

Mme. Glyon.   He would be disenchanted in one
instant.   He is only captive by his imagination.
The other day he saw the cast of my foot at Story's
studio, and found it perfect; if he knew now that it
had ever gone in wooden shoes over the ploughed
fields, he would find at once that the ankle was too
thick or the instep too high.   Alas!   I know him so
well—so well!

Princess.   And you make him out a fool.

Mme. Glyon.   Oh, no; only a *dilettante* full of
caprice.

Princess.   Well, I think you wrong him.   I have
said so fifty times; and I never thought to live to say
so, either.   Would you let me try the experiment I
told you of the other day?   He ought at least to know
you live.   If you continue to reject him, he may turn
for solace to someone else; then he may want to marry
that someone else, and then you will have to tell
him, *coûte que coûte.*

Mme. Glyon.   Oh, no; I have kept silence twelve

years. I can very well keep it all my life. And you will never betray me ?

Princess. Never, unless you bid me. But I think you do very wrongly. You are of that sort of nature which self-sacrifice fascinates ; and because an act is a martyrdom, you cannot also imagine that it may be at the same time an error.

Mme. Glyon. Laura! you grow quite logical and subtle in your arguments ; I never knew you thought out things so much.

Princess. I think them out because I love you, and I see your whole life going to waste ; no, not to waste, because your works are fine, and you spend all your days doing good ; but barren of all happiness, of all sympathy, of all tenderness, and even, you know, subject to the rumours of lying tongues.

Mme. Glyon. That last does not matter.

Princess. Oh, no ; you are very proud, and falsehood cannot touch you ; but still it tells, somehow, when the world crowns you with one hand and scourges you with the other. Will you let me try my experiment—just try it ?

Mme. Glyon. It would be unwise, and it would be useless ; I am sure he would take his release so gladly on any terms.

Princess. That is what I will see if you will let me. Do think it over. Tell me to-night. I don't wish to persuade, but indeed—indeed, Claire—it is not fair to him to let him go on in ignorance, in a fool's paradise; and if he do know, and behaves unworthily, he will never force you to live with him—he is too truly a gentleman.

Mme. Glyon. He will have no wish, my dear, when once he knows, ever to see my face again. Try your experiment, as you call it; but if he would take his liberty *so*, remember, I will be dead to him for ever, though I hide myself in the uttermost ends of the earth.

Princess. That, of course. But if he be loyal to his forgotten wife, then you will pardon him?

[MME. GLYON *is silent.*

Princess. Silence is assent. Let us drive to the convent, and we will not speak another word. I have all my fibs to fabricate.

Mme. Glyon. He will accept.

Princess. He will refuse!　　　　　　　*[Exeunt.*

SCENE VII.

In the Cimontanara Grounds; on the stone seat of S. Filippo Neri are seated L'ESTRANGE *and the* PRINCESS; *facing them are the Campagna, Porta San Giovanni, the mountains of Albano.*

Princess. In this stone summer-house S. Philip, your namesake, preached to the giddy youths that loved him. Now I, who am very giddy, am going to preach to you. I asked you to come here because I am never sure of not being interrupted in my own house, and I have to tell you something very, very, very serious.

L'Estrange. I am sure you are my friend, Princess.

Princess. I am. But my friendship can be of little use to you. Now Claire does care for you—cares for you as you wish, but——

L'Estrange. Never mind the 'buts!' How can I thank you, Princess?

Princess. It will be a folly, you know. Another folly!

L'Estrange. I do not think so.

Princess. And you did not think so once of the other. Are you sure you will not change?

L'Estrange. I am certain that I shall not.

Princess. But if the world——

L'Estrange. The world will have no power over me.

Princess. It had much twelve years ago.

L'Estrange. Pray let the past alone. I want to live in the present. What you have told me this morning makes it as cloudless as the day is.

Princess. Wait! I have more to tell you.

L'Estrange. What else can matter? I am happy.

Princess. Ah, don't say so ; wait till you hear everything. Claire could have cared for you, but—— I feel frightened to go on, but——

L'Estrange (*growing pale*). Glyon is not dead?

Princess. It is not that. Maître Jules Desrosne,

the great French advocate, you know, is in Rome.   He
has come for the French Cardinals——.

L'Estrange.   What has that to do with me?

Princess.   Well, I don't know how to tell you, but
I must; and I could not, if there were not some consolation in it too; but Maître Desrosne has known me
from a child—he defended a case for my father against
the French Government—and as he heard the gossip of
Rome, which made out that Claire was going to marry
you next week, he told me to tell you something, which
he thought I might break to you better than he could,
as you have never known him.

L'Estrange.   Well?   Speak out, Princess.   What
is this terrible thing that a French lawyer knows?

Princess.   Oh, do not jest; pray do not jest.
Maître Desrosne is quite distressed for you; it is—it is,
that your first wife—I mean—the person you married,
you know—did not die.

L'Estrange.   What?

Princess.   Yes, that is it—that is what he says;
she is alive—he knows her very well; he has been her
counsel.

L'Estrange.   Good God!   Are you mad, or am I?

Princess.   Nobody is; oh, pray do not look so; you
frighten me.   You look as if I had turned you into
stone.

    [L'ESTRANGE *rises and moves about with his*
       face averted.

L'Estrange.   I will not frighten you, Princess.

Only give me one moment to get my breath—you have stunned me.

Princess (murmuring). I am so sorry! Desrosne could not tell you before, because he only knew it in confidence, as her adviser; she gave him permission now because she heard of your——

L'Estrange. But how can it be? She was drowned, and it was supposed her body was washed out by the underground waters to the Seine.

Princess. Oh, yes; that is quite true. I mean, it is quite true that she did throw herself into the moat, and meant to drown herself; but her father had come to the convent, begging to be taken on as gardener there for the sake of being near her; and Maître Desrosne tells me that her father rescued her from the water when she had sunk twice unseen—for it was twilight—and hid himself with her for some time, in the cottage of a forester who was his friend. She heard you thought her dead, and let it be so. She had friends amongst the convent girls; one of them she wrote to, and confided in, and asked how she could gain a livelihood. This girl was going back to her own country for the vacation, and as she loved your wife, took her with her to her own people. In that new land she maintained herself by teaching drawing; she would not be dependent on her friends, though they were rich. When they came to Europe, she, I believe, came with them. All this Maître Desrosne has known for years.

L'Estrange. Where is she now?

Princess. You do frighten me! Carlino's violence is not one half so terrible as your English quietude. Your eyes look as if you saw a ghost——

L'Estrange. I do see—many. Not dead, good God!—and I—hear it as the worst calamity that could befall me! Not dead! Not dead!

Princess. No; Maître Desrosne has known her seven years. He should have told you earlier.

L'Estrange. He should indeed.

Princess. But I suppose he could not. Lawyers are like confessors, and must keep the secrets told to them. Your wife has lived honourably, quite honourably.

L'Estrange. Ah!

Princess. She has maintained herself here, and in America.

L'Estrange. She has been in America?

Princess. So he says. You will wish to see her?

L'Estrange (with a shudder). In America! Do not talk of it! I will endeavour to do my duty.

Princess. But if she were so contrary to all your tastes and wishes then, will she be less so now? Twelve years passed in hard work does not give the bloom of Ninon, and you—you are not less fastidious now than then. What a future for you!

L'Estrange. Spare me! This advocate will give me means of proving all that he has said?

Princess. Oh, yes; he will, of course. I do not think, **though,** that she wants you to take her back.

[L'ESTRANGE *covers his eyes with his hand a moment.*

Princess. And I do know Claire cares for you.

L'Estrange. Spare me a little, Princess! Where is this Maître Desrosne? I must see him at once.

Princess. He stays at the Farnese Palace.

L'Estrange. You believe he speaks the truth?

Princess. He must! He is so great a person in the French Courts; he will be a judge whenever he pleases; he has your wife's letters with him. And—and—he said something else, Lord L'Estrange, which gave me courage to tell you this; if he had not said the good with the bad, I never could have dealt you such a blow; for you know I have got quite fond of you since you loved Claire.

L'Estrange. What good can there be?

Princess. Well, it seems that when she returned to France, years ago, your wife went to him with an introduction from a French bishop, and told him her position, and asked him as to the legality of her marriage, of which she had become doubtful. Now, Maître Desrosne told me——

L'Estrange. What?

Princess. Well, that the marriage is not a perfectly legal one—not perfectly; that there are loopholes by which you could get free—some omission of some trifle, some blunder in the date of your wife's birth through the stupidity of her own people—no fault of yours—

but you attended too much to the religious ceremony and not enough to the civil one.   He would explain it better, but his strong opinion is that you can break the marriage; annul it, if you please; he is sure that both France and England will set you free.   If he had not said that, I never should have summoned courage to tell you, knowing as I do, too, that Claire's happiness is at stake.

[L'ESTRANGE *looks at her in silence.*

Princess.   How you do look!   Indeed, indeed, Maître Desrosne said so, and you can see himself any day you like; he stays a month at the Palazzo Farnese.   He had gone into the question years ago for your wife *au grand secret,* and he is one of the very greatest lawyers in all France.   He never would give an opinion lightly.

[L'ESTRANGE *is still silent.*

Princess.   Do say something!   You frighten me!   Perhaps I should have told you the good news first.   You don't look now one bit more glad.

L'Estrange (rising and standing facing her).   Princess, I do not know what you take me for; that this poor creature lives is most terrible to me, that I do not deny.   I am no saint, as was S. Philip Neri.   But, if you believe I could take advantage of a legal quibble to cast shame upon a woman who in her youth trusted me,—well! you have known me very little, though we have spent so many pleasant hours together.

Princess.   But heavens and earth!   I thought you loved Claire?

L'Estrange. You know well that I do love her most dearly, but I cannot stoop to dishonour even for her: the very basest sort of dishonour, too! Just heavens! to hire men of law to hound down in the dust a hapless soul who gave herself to me in all good faith and innocence! Can you think I would deny her rights, whatever they may cost me, merely because some forgotten minutiæ of men's trumpery laws have lost them to her?

Princess. You refuse to free yourself?

L'Estrange. At such a price I must refuse, or be a scoundrel. My life will be most wretched if all you say is true; but, at least, it will not be foul with perfidy and cowardice.

Princess. Ah! ah! there *are* depths in you to be stirred! I was right. And now——. Well—well—perhaps, you know, you will not be so *very* wretched after all. The afternoon may be brighter than the dawn was.   [*She rises and moves away.*

MME. GLYON *advances slowly from behind the stone summer-house and the bay and arbutus that grow about it. She holds out her hands.*

Philip! I forgive you. Will you forgive me, or will you despise me?

L'Estrange. Great God! How could I be so blind?

IN PITTI

A SCENE

(FOUNDED ON FACT)

DRAMATIS PERSONÆ.

SIR OSCAR BERESFORD, *An English Gentleman.*
DOROTHY CLAREMONT, *A Tapestry Painter.*

IN PITTI.

SCENE : *The Sale degli Arazzi in Palazzo Pitti.*

TIME : *An April morning : twelve o'clock.*

Sir Oscar Beresford. Mind you let me out at one.

*Custodian. Al toccò — al toccò ! — non dubiti,
signore !*

Sir Oscar. Why on earth do you lock one in ?

Custodian (shrugs his shoulder). M-a-h !

Sir Oscar. Of course I know you only obey orders ;
but it is an utterly idiotic regulation, and devilish un-
complimentary to one's appearance.

Custodian (shrugs, and bows, and smiles.) M-a-h !

Sir Oscar. Suppose one fell ill?—had a fit? It
is awfully stupid this lock and key business. You
know very well one couldn't get an order to paint here,
unless one were pretty honest.

Custodian (shrugs, smiles, spreads out his hands).
M-a-h !

Sir Oscar. Well, if it must be, it must be. Thanks ;
you may go,

> [CUSTODIAN *retires and locks the door on the out-
> side; his steps die away in the distance.* SIR
> OSCAR *goes to open a window.*

Dorothy Claremont (seated painting with her back to him, looks around, and speaks). You must not do that ; they will turn you out.

Sir Oscar. Why?

Dorothy. Why? No one knows, except that Italy just now is in love with red tape, and ties up her tiniest parcels with it. She thinks it an emblem of freedom.

Sir Oscar. But it is such a warm morning, and by noon it will be terrible.

Dorothy. You are a stranger, I see, or you would not expect such simple reasons to have any weight.

Sir Oscar. And you really mean the windows are never opened ?

Dorothy. Never. At least not by such profane hands as ours. Besides, Italians never see the necessity for open windows. In winter if open they would let in the wind ; in summer if open they would let in the sun. Such a trifle as air does not count.

Sir Oscar. Good heavens !

Dorothy. Would you kindly stand a little aside ? You take off the light.

Sir Oscar. A thousand pardons ! Excuse me, you are copying this tapestry ?

Dorothy. This sofa. I have an order for the sofa and all the chairs.

Sir Oscar (aside). An order ! She looks like a princess out in a cotton frock for a freak. (*Aloud.*) How much that painted imitation tapestry is the fashion, isn't it? It must be a great bore to do, though; at least, I should think so. Myself, I hate copying.

Dorothy (*coldly*). Probably you do not need to do it.

Sir Oscar. Oh, yes, indeed—at least—no, I do not need to do it—but I want to have rooms just like these built down at my place in Dorsetshire; and as I can draw a little, I thought I would design their decorations and take the scale of their proportions myself, Don't you think it better to do things oneself as far as one can?

Dorothy (*briefly*). No doubt.

Sir Oscar (*thinks*). How chilly she is all in a moment! I dare say she is vexing herself about having talked so familiarly to me. What a pretty girl it is! and all that bright short hair of her own is charming. She is copying that sofa as if her life depended on it. Perhaps her bread does depend on it, poor child! I will go into the next room and take my measurements. When I come back she may have thawed again. Who on earth can her people be that let her come out and be locked up all alone? I am sure she is English. No other than an English girl would dare be all alone with the face of Venus on her shoulders. There is something absurdly wrong, now, in a pretty child like that having to paint linen for her bread, whilst here am I, who could very well earn my own living if I were pushed to it, bothered with more land and more money than I know what to do with. I must say Fate is a very silly person; she always gorges her fat chickens and starves her lean ones. (*Goes into the next room and remains there ten minutes; then returns.*) This is the finest room, don't you think?

Dorothy (*coldly*). By no means. There are others far finer. Take the Sala degli Stucchi.

Sir Oscar. Oh, yes; but that is not what I want. It is superb; but all that snow-white immensity would not suit a dusky English country-house. These carvings, these sombre tapestries, this solemn gold, will suit it down to the ground. Do you—do you—know England at all? I think I cannot be mistaken in claiming you as a *compatriote*?

Dorothy (*coldly*). Yes; I am English by descent.

Sir Oscar. But you live in Italy?

Dorothy. I live in Italy.

Sir Oscar (*to himself*). I am sure she thinks me a confoundedly impudent fellow. May not one talk in these old galleries? Art surely is a very good chaperon. She has got shy all in a second. Did I say anything insolent? Surely not. I had better sketch a little, perhaps, or she will think I cannot. (*For twenty minutes measures proportions and draws outlines; stealthily glances from time to time at the tapestry painter.*) How steady she is over that linen and her bottles of dyes! She never raises her head. How well-shaped it is, and all those loose boyish curls are charming. I should say she would be tall if she stood up.

How can I get her to talk? How very thoughtful of
them when they lock one in to give one such consolation! (*Aloud.*) Pardon me, I think the sun is touching your work. I will move the shutter a little.
(*Moves it; she does not speak.*) Isn't that better? It
grows excruciatingly warm ; and to think those duffers
keep the windows shut! (*She does not answer; he
walks about, and pauses behind her.*) How very
beautiful all this Gobelin is! What a charming landscape this upon your sofa!—a perfect picture in itself.

Dorothy (*coldly*). It is not in very good taste *on* a
sofa.

Sir Oscar. Oh, you are hypercritical! You are
right, of course, æsthetically. One ought not to lean
one's shoulders against a seashore, a sky, and a cart.

Dorothy (*coldly*). There are the Dolce pictures
and much fine furniture in the other rooms of this
suite.

Sir Oscar. I am afraid I bother you by drawing
here. You want me to go away ?

Dorothy (*with significance*). Oh—if you draw—
you have as much right here as I.

Sir Oscar (*conscious of reproof*). But I am drawing! Only if you would permit me to talk just now
and then—I can always work so much better when
talking.

Dorothy. I cannot.

Sir Oscar (*sensible of a snub, retires to his seat
and draws diligently in profound silence*). What a

dear little girl!   How she gives it to one!   To be sure she does not know anything about me.   Perhaps it is bad form to try and draw out a woman whilst one's unknown oneself.   How can I tell her my name, I wonder?   I won't lose sight of her.   She is too charming for anything.   I must wait a little before I try.

> *[Draws carefully for an hour, but draws the profile of his companion instead of the proportions and decorations of the room.   She is engrossed in her own work.*

Sir Oscar (to himself).   There! with a few washes of colour, what a perfect head that will be!   And she has not an idea of what I have done.   It is a very delicate profile ; she must have good blood in her.   Women always are kind to me ; I don't see why she should be so uncivil.   I suppose it puts a woman's back up to be seen here by all the idiots that dawdle through their Murray—stared at, pestered, and worried all day long.   I will leave her alone till the time comes to go, and then—— (*Aloud.*)   Pray forgive me if I venture to disturb you before I go ; it is now one o'clock ; the man will come for me.   Might I be permitted to ask—did I hear you rightly ?—did you really say you were copying these tapestries for—for— any one ?

Dorothy.   For the tradesman who has ordered them —yes.

Sir Oscar.   Then might I ask a very great favour indeed of you ?   Might I beg you to paint me a suite of this furniture ?   As I said, I am going to have some rooms in my own house decorated like these, with some tapestries that I found in Flanders, and if you would have the infinite goodness——

Dorothy. There is no question of goodness—I copy for any one who employs me.

Sir Oscar (disconcerted). Ah, exactly—but, still, you know, it will be a very great favour for me if you will permit me to be classed amongst your——

Dorothy. Patrons. When I have finished this set I shall be happy to begin other pieces for you. It is my trade.

Sir Oscar. Pray do not call it a trade!

Dorothy. You cannot call it an art.

Sir Oscar. But indeed it is, as you do it. You have made me very happy. May I see you again to-morrow?

Dorothy. I am always here. But there is nothing to see me for, if you will give your orders now, and tell me where to send the pieces when finished.

Sir Oscar. Here is my card. I am staying in Florence at the Hotel dell' Arno; but the paintings of course will be sent to Rivaux, my own place. We had one wing burnt down last autumn; and, as I must re-build it, I thought I would make it a *replica* of this part of the Pitti.

Dorothy (glancing at his card). Since you are rich enough to do that, you should not have imitation tapestries on your sofas and chairs, when you have real ones on the walls. Go to the Royal works at Windsor. They say their tapestries are beautiful.

Sir Oscar. Oh, thanks; but I want you to do me these identical chairs.

Dorothy. As you please. If you will write your directions, I will attend to them as soon as this commission is finished.

Sir Oscar (*to himself*). Clearly she wants to get rid of me. (*Aloud.*) Where may I send them?

Dorothy. You might leave them on that table.

Sir Oscar. I shall return to-morrow. I will bring them. I suppose the man won't forget to unlock the door?

Dorothy. Probably not. I was once forgotten until sunset.

Sir Oscar (*sotto voce*). I wish I might be to-day if you were forgotten too! What a cool young lady it is! She knows who I am now, but it don't seem to make any difference. (*Looks at his watch.*) By Jove, it is half-past one! Pardon me—how late do you stay here?

Dorothy. Till four.

Sir Oscar. Without eating anything?

Dorothy. I breakfasted before I came out.

Sir Oscar. So did I. Still, when it gets on to luncheon time—not that I care much what I eat, but one must have something.

Dorothy. Yes; humanity is very badly organised.

Sir Oscar. We should lose a good deal of enjoyment though, if we didn't eat.

Dorothy. You think so? To me it seems such a waste of time.

Sir Oscar. Not more than the stoker's; the train couldn't get on without coals. But I suppose at your age you think yourself able to live upon air?

Dorothy (to herself). What business has he with my age? And he is not so very old himself either.

Sir Oscar. Might I be favoured with your address, in case—in case—anything should prevent my coming back here to-morrow?

Dorothy. Certainly. My name is Claremont, and I live at the Colombaia, Viale di Petrarca.

Sir Oscar (writes it down). So many thanks! The Dovecot—what a pretty idea! And are there any other doves beside you in it?

Dorothy (coldly). I live with my mother. It is a poor place. *We* are poor.

Sir Oscar (tempted to say that with such a face as hers any one is rich enough, but refraining). But does not your mother feel uneasy about you when you are so long away?

Dorothy. Oh, no; she knows I am strong and well.

Sir Oscar (thinks). Is it absolute innocence, or admirable acting? I'll be shot if I can tell! The girl must be conscious of her own pretty face. (*Aloud.*) It's quite awfully hot, don't you think? I really must open that window and call somebody. They have certainly forgotten us.

Dorothy (uneasily). It is very odd. They must come in a minute or two. Every one must be gone from the galleries.

Dorothy (*aloud*). The *custode* has certainly forgotten you.

Sir Oscar (*gallantly*). Very fortunate for *me*.

Dorothy. What, when you have had no luncheon! I have two buns here; but I am afraid those will scarcely console you.

Sir Oscar. Indeed, I am perfectly happy. One can lunch any day, but it isn't every day that one can enjoy the happiness of being——

Dorothy. Locked up! Well, certainly you will have full time to complete your designs.

Sir Oscar. Who taught you to snub people so mercilessly?

Dorothy. Strangers—who suppose that because I am copying in the palace I may be addressed without any ceremony. and am here only to amuse them.

Sir Oscar (*colouring*). Oh, come; that is very severe! I assure you, my dear young lady, I never dreamed of being impertinent; I wouldn't be so for worlds; nobody could be to you——

Dorothy. I shall be more convinced of that if you will kindly allow me to continue my work in silence.

Sir Oscar. Oh, of course! I beg your pardon (*goes again into the next room and begins to draw*). What a severe little kitten it is! Perhaps she is right, though. It is not altogether good form to bother these people who are pinned to their easels here; they must be mobbed and stared at day after day till they naturally show fight. That man decidedly has forgotten me. If the little girl would let one talk to her it wouldn't matter, but making architectural sketches all alone on an empty stomach is not enlivening. I suppose I ought to have tipped the fellow beforehand. This is one of the lands of backsheesh. How pluckily the child holds on at her work! She makes one ashamed. To think I have never done anything I did not like all my life long, and that pretty child there has to slave away in a stifling room to make a few pounds at an age when she ought to be doing nothing but lawn-tennis, garden parties, and cotillions. If one only might speak to her! —but it will seem such awful bad form after that snub direct.

[*Hesitates, then sits down again to his plans; an hour passes: four o'clock strikes.*

Sir Oscar (taking out his watch). Yes, four, as I live. Well, now we shall get out. I think I may say a word. She is putting up her calicoes. (*Aloud.*) I suppose we shall be let out soon, shall we not? How fearfully warm it is! Are you not very tired? Do you never get a headache or anything?

Dorothy (rising). Yes, I often get a headache in the heat of the rooms. The *custode* will be here in a moment. The people all leave the galleries at four.

Sir Oscar. May I not come and see your studio? I am sure you must have quantities of pretty things to show me? (*Opens the window and shouts half-a-dozen times; there are echoes but no answers*). Certainly that row of mine ought to wake up the ghost of

Lucca Pitti himself. The courtyard is absolutely empty and mute, and every window round it hermetically closed.

Dorothy. It is an inner court, quite a secluded one; I am afraid nobody will hear you. Something must have happened!

Sir Oscar. Oh, no; the fellow has only had an extra dose of garlic and blue wine, and has gone to sleep somewhere. He'll be sure to come as you said just now. Pray don't mind, and do eat one of your buns.

Dorothy. I do not want to eat, thanks; I am very thirsty. That air is pleasant.

Sir Oscar. Yes, we'll keep the window open, though you hint that the tortures of the Inquisition would follow.

Dorothy. It is the rule for no one to touch them.

Sir Oscar. And do you always follow rules?

Dorothy. Yes; I think one ought, else what use is it for them to be made?

Sir Oscar. Well, none that I ever could see, that is why I make a point of breaking them.

Dorothy. I suppose that is all very well for a man.

Sir Oscar. Why, what an old-fashioned little lady you are! you are not a bit emancipated, you are quite *arriérée.* Women want all the fun and all the frolic nowadays. They don't care to have a day out unless they break down every fence in the country.

Dorothy. I do not understand your metaphors.

Sir Oscar. Well, you know, I mean they like all

their birds to be rocketers, and they like to put all their money on dark horses, and they like the spot stroke in billiards, and they'll always win by a fluke if they can—you know what I mean.

Dorothy.   I really do not.

Sir Oscar.   Well, I mean women never run straight if they can help it.

Dorothy (coldly).   Your experience must have been unfortunate.

Sir Oscar (smiling).   It's a good deal longer than yours, anyhow; you'll allow that.   I ought to beg your pardon for uttering such a beastly cynical sentiment; I am sure I didn't mean it.   If women do get off the line, it's because men shunt them there.

Dorothy.   It is ten minutes past five; the man is late.

Sir Oscar.   One can't make him hear?

Dorothy.   Quite impossible.   There is nothing for it but patience.

Sir Oscar.   An admirable quality wholly missing from my character.

Dorothy.   Especially   when   you   have   had   no luncheon!

Sir Oscar.   Oh, that does not matter; you know when one is out grouse-shooting or deer-stalking one goes a whole day on cold tea.   Do you really come here every morning?

Dorothy.   Here, or some similar place, wherever there are tapestries or frescoes to be copied.   You seem to have forgotten—it is my trade, I am only a copyist.

Sir Oscar. But do you do nothing original?

Dorothy. Can the mill-horse run about where he likes? I never even dare to think of anything original; I should have no sale for it.

Sir Oscar. It makes me sad to hear you say that; I fancy you would like to be sketching birds, and flowers, and trees, out in the air, wouldn't you? It must be such drudgery imitating all these faded figures. I am sorry now that I ventured to ask you to paint these chairs for me.

Dorothy. Pray do not be so. I shall be happy to execute the work.

Sir Oscar. I think you said your name is Claremont?

Dorothy (coldly). I did say so.

Sir Oscar. I wonder if you are any relation of a man I was much attached to once: he was my tutor at Eton, a magnificent scholar and a true gentleman. What became of him I never knew. I am ashamed to say I forgot all about him when I went into the Guards; one grows so brutally selfish in the world. He was called Tom Claremont; he had been a Balliol Scholar——

Dorothy. I think you speak of my father.

Sir Oscar (with great animation). You don't mean it! Well, you are like him, now I think of it. Is he—is he—living?

Dorothy. No; he died many years ago. He had been obliged to come to Italy for his health. He married here. I know he was once a tutor at Eton.

Sir Oscar (with feeling). My dear little lady, don't snub me any more; I can assure you I loved Tom Claremont as much as a boy can love anything; any grain of sense or decency I have in me I owe to him, to say nothing of any Greek and Latin. You are the daughter of a very noble fellow. He deserved a better fate than to die in a foreign land and leave his child to work for her living.

Dorothy. He had always worked for his own, I believe. He always told me to rely on myself. He said poverty mattered little, but independence was the bread of life.

Sir Oscar. Oh, he was always a very proud fellow —if he had been less so he might have been a head master or a bishop before now; but he could never eat that humble pie which is the only food that makes a man climb like a beanstalk. I was only a boy—a very graceless tiresome boy—but I was devoutly attached to him. You do not seem to believe me?

Dorothy (hesitates). You did not care to learn what became of him!

Sir Oscar. My dear child—I beg your pardon—I mean you don't understand what the world is when a young fellow is just launched into it, with money enough and birth enough for everybody to come buzzing about him like bees. There is no room left for old friendships. The whole year is a galop *ventre à terre.* Everybody flatters you; everybody tempts you; everybody invites you; you think everybody feminine is an

angel, and every man Jack of them a good fellow. You
are like a colt in a clover field—you don't know that
the pace will tell on you and that you may come a
cropper before you've done, though you are first favourite. Myself, I went straight from Eton into the First
Life, and—and—and I enjoyed myself; I did no end of
follies; I spent a great deal of money—I bought my
experience, in a word—and bought it pretty dear.
Well, all this don't interest you, I know: only I want
you to understand how it was that I came not to know
anything about Tom Claremont. One never does know
anything about one's tutors. But, on my honour, I very
often thought of him. He had had great ideas of what
I might do, and I had disappointed him greatly by
going into the Service—no doubt he thought much
better of me than I deserved, for he expected all kinds
of great things. I had a sort of reluctance to see him
when, after all, I had just fallen into the ruck with the
others, and done nothing on earth except amuse myself;
and so, you see, the time slipped away and I never met
him again; and now you say that he died years ago,
and that you are his daughter?

Dorothy (the tears in her eyes). Yes, he died some
years ago; he died at Camaldoli one summer.

Sir Oscar (earnestly). When one of my big livings
came vacant, I wrote and offered it to him. I was just
of age then. He thanked me, but he would not take
it. He had some scruples about preaching what he
did not believe. He was not orthodox; he was some-

thing much better. I ought to have gone and offered
it to him. I shall never forgive myself.

Dorothy. He would not have taken it. He thought
the whole system of the Church of England wrong. He
used to say that the beneficed clergyman was worse
than the fat monk, for the monk at least gave no
dinner-parties and had no liveried servants.

Sir Oscar. How like him! I can hear him say it.
Yes, he was one of the few men who lived up to their
principles. What did old Hildebrand write? 'Dilexi
justitiam, et odivi iniquitatem, propterea morior in
exsilio.'

Dorothy. I am prouder of him, so.

Sir Oscar. Quite justly. To have the courage of
one's opinions and to suffer for them is the grandest
thing a man can do. It is not my way: but I can
admire it.

Dorothy. Have you no opinions? I suppose you
hardly lack the courage?

Sir Oscar. Perhaps I lack both—I don't know.
You see there is nothing to try me; I have always done
what I wished to do; and when you are an idle Colonel
of Life Guards, nobody expects you to have any 'views.'

Dorothy (with interest). The Life Guards! Did
you go to Egypt?

Sir Oscar. Oh, yes—Kassassin and Cairo, and all
the rest of it. It was over too soon; that was the worst
of it. If only Arabi had destroyed the Canal we should
have had a great deal more fun; we might have been

there now. To be sure (*lowering his voice*) I should not have had the happiness of meeting dear Tom Claremont's charming daughter.

Dorothy (*brusquely*). Please do not pay me compliments. Remember I cannot get away from them.

Sir Oscar. I beg your pardon for the hundredth time; and it wasn't a compliment. Did your father teach you to draw?

Dorothy. No; but he encouraged me to draw and to study in the galleries. He thought I should be able to support myself. He knew he could only leave us a hundred and fifty pounds a year in English money.

Sir Oscar. Good heavens! what one **gives** for **a** weight-carrier.

Dorothy. A weight-carrier?

Sir Oscar. A horse that can carry twelve stone over plough. I forget you are not used to the English we talk at home. Claremont, I am sure, reared you on Shakspeare and Ford and Marlowe?

Dorothy. Why do you talk that other English?

Sir Oscar. I don't know why. In the world one gets a sort of jargon. It is the same thing in French; what we say on the Boulevards and in the Cercles would sound like high Dutch to Voltaire or Marmontel or Madame de Sévigné. Fashion always has its *patois*. You know it is a law to itself.

Dorothy. I know nothing about it. Fashion and I have never been introduced to each other.

Sir Oscar (*thinks*). And yet what a charming

creature you would look if one handed you over to Wörth, and put five rows of pearls round your throat, and gave you tan gloves up to your elbow, and a big fan with sapphires in the handle?—you would take to it in five seconds. You have the *éternel féminin* in you though you work away so bravely with your dyes and your varnishes at that ugly coarse cloth. What an amusement it would be to teach you everything—to show you your own powers, to make you understand all there is in yourself—and one must never try to do it, because you are Tom Claremont's daughter! If one could hurt his daughter one would deserve hanging without court-martial. (*Aloud.*) Might I ask—you spoke of your mother—did my old friend marry an Italian?

Dorothy. My mother is a German; she was Countess Hedenige von Brander. She met my father in Rome. Her own people have refused to know her since her marriage; they leave us quite to ourselves. She is blind.

Sir Oscar. Blind! Good heavens, my poor child! what have you done to Fate that you should be so persecuted?

Dorothy. Fate might be much more cruel. I have my blessings. My mother is not at all unhappy. She is of the sweetest temper. She has a beautiful voice and sings beautifully. If she could be reconciled to her own people she would desire nothing more; but they are very hard of heart. They thought the marriage beneath her because my father was not noble and was poor; but if you knew him you knew that he was worthy of an empress.

Sir Oscar. Most surely. (*Thinks to himself.*) So that is where you get your blond curls and your little air of hauteur. You are a German aristocrat at bottom, though you have Claremont's brown eyes, and Claremont's simple good sense. You are really very interesting; and how innocently you accept me for your father's friend, though for aught you could know I might be only telling you a heap of falsehoods!

Dorothy (*restlessly*). Is it not very strange this *custode* does not come? He left me here once until six; but then it was only myself—now that he knows you are here.

Sir Oscar. I ought to have refreshed his memory with five francs. But if you are not in a hurry I am not; if he had come at the regulation hour I should never have found out you were Claremont's daughter. Now you will let me call on you, won't you?

Dorothy (*hesitating*). Yes—I suppose—I don't know—I will ask my mother. She does not wish people to call: she dislikes new acquaintances.

Sir Oscar (*sotto voce*). Afraid of the hawks for her dove—one can understand; and she can't see what's going on, poor soul. But I shan't do the child any harm; I should always feel Tom Claremont's ghost after me.

Dorothy (*uneasily*). What time is it? Perhaps my watch has stopped.

Sir Oscar. Mine's half-past six, but it may be too fast; I haven't listened to the town clocks lately. Do tell me more about your father. Did he suffer greatly? Ah! how sad that is! Where did you say he died? At Camaldoli? Where is Camaldoli?

Dorothy. It is a monastery in the hills which has been changed into an hotel; it stands in the midst of pine forests. The physicians ordered him to go to Davos Platz; but we could not afford to move so far. He was so patient, so quiet; it seems only yesterday— please do not speak of it——

Sir Oscar. If only he had accepted my living! It is the living of Rivaux—my own place. I should have seen you as a little child; you would have had all an English child's playtime—archery, lawn-tennis, pony-riding, boating; Rivaux would please you, I think. It's an old Stuart place buried in very deep woods; you can ride thirty miles on turf. I used to call it beastly dull, but of late I've got fond of it; after the glare and scorch of Egypt last year it looked so cool and green and pleasant I was glad to see it again.

Dorothy. If I had a place like that I should never leave it.

Sir Oscar. Well, you know, I think it was much better for the country when people didn't leave their places. In the last century it was a mere handful of people who could afford Court life in London or in Paris, and the country-houses in England and the châteaux in France benefited proportionately; the territorial nobility and gentry lived in their own county or their own province all their lives. Now we've changed all that; even the little bits of folks think they must have their town season, and never go near their places except when they have a house-party at Easter, or for the shooting in autumn. They play right into the hands of the Socialists; it is ridiculous that heaps of great houses and great parks should all be monopolised by people who are scarcely in them six whole weeks out of the year.

Dorothy. Why are you in Florence in April?

Sir Oscar. Well, because I have the disease of the time; the French call it *pérégrinomanie*. Besides, you know, a man alone—if I were married I would live more than half my time at Rivaux. As it is, I'm a good deal there.

Dorothy. But if you are a soldier?

Sir Oscar. Oh, yes, I am in the First Life; but that doesn't tie one much. I did go to Egypt; I would go anywhere else if they sent us anywhere else; but they don't. Sometimes I think your father was right. I ought not to have gone into the Life Guards; I might have studied, and that sort of thing; instead, I let all my best years slip away in that idle London life which makes one good for nothing else.

Dorothy. Have you no relatives at all?—no mother or sisters?

Sir Oscar. My mother died long ago; I have two sisters; entirely fine ladies; they don't care a hang about me, nor I a rap about them; they are larky women, both of them, more than I like.

Dorothy. That is the English which is not Shakespeare's. What does it mean?

Sir Oscar. It is hardly worth while to tell you. I only meant to say that my sisters both married whilst I was at Eton, and there is no sort of sympathy between us. Oh, I have lots of relations; about five hundred; but I see as little of them as possible; they are always wanting something—my county borough, or my lord-lieutenancy, or my tenants' votes, or a hundred guineas for a charity; they are always wanting something, if it's only to be asked to dine at Hurlingham.

Dorothy. You are honey, and the flies eat you.

Sir Oscar. Oh, I assure you, I am not honey; I can be as bitter as gall sometimes, especially if I feel people want to get over me.

Dorothy. To get over? That means—— ?

Sir Oscar. Well, in our language, it means cheat one, use one for their own purposes.

Dorothy. Is it not just as easy to say 'cheat' as 'get over'?

Sir Oscar. I suppose it would be. That slipshod language is a habit—a bad habit, like smoking cigarettes. I hope you don't smoke, do you?

Dorothy. I! Smoke! I——!

Sir Oscar. How dreadfully scandalised you looked! I was sure you didn't. If you knew how sick one gets of seeing the women smoke, and making believe they like it, and spoiling their lips and their breath!

Dorothy.   I did not know women ever smoked. In what country do they?

Sir Oscar.   In that very queer country which you happily have never traversed—Society. If you had smoked, however, I have some cigarettes with me, and it might have made you feel less hungry.

Dorothy.   Thanks, I am not hungry, I have eaten my buns. But you must want your dinner terribly, Colonel—Sir Oscar—I am not sure what you are called?

Sir Oscar.   My men call me the first; society the second. You can call me whatever you like, so long as you don't call me *de trop* or impertinent. You did think me impertinent, didn't you?

Dorothy.   Yes, a little. You see, when one is working, as I am, one is so much at the mercy of those who pass through; and my mother is always so anxious that I should speak to no strangers. I cannot help answering now and then, because they ask me questions about my work or about the pictures, and sometimes they are very kind and agreeable—sometimes they are rude.

Sir Oscar.   I was in the latter category, but I shall never be so again. Your mother is quite right; you are much too—young—to speak to people you see in these places that are open to the public.

Dorothy (gaily).   But when one works for the public!

Sir Oscar. I can't believe you do. I mean, you know, it seems awfully wrong that you should need to work hard, whilst here am I——

Dorothy. What has that to do with it? There is nothing wrong about it. That is the sort of thing the Communists say; but an English gentleman——

Sir Oscar. May feel ashamed of himself, mayn't he? I mean, you know, that to see a little lady of your years, and your—your appearance—shutting herself up all day and toiling away for her mother, makes one's own selfish, idle, self-indulgent life seem the most hateful thing under the sun.

Dorothy. I do not see it at all. I am not the least bit of a radical. I am sure it is all these inequalities which make life picturesque; if it were all a dead level, there would be no hills to climb, no valleys to repose in; I think it delightful that there should be people rich enough and happy enough to enjoy themselves all their lives long. If I were living near Rivaux, I should be the better for Rivaux every time I walked through it; I should not want to own it. To hear the birds sing, to see the primroses come out——

Sir Oscar (*admiringly*). What a philosopher you are! I recognise Claremont's spirit in that admirable unselfishness, in that absolute absence of envy; he was always like that. He came to Rivaux once in my father's time, and I remember that he enjoyed it just in your spirit; he said he made it his own through his eyes. Are you his only child?

Dorothy. Yes. He taught me all I know. Were I only more like him!

Sir Oscar. I think you are very like him. Perhaps the best gift of all he gave you has been that of his cheerful content and sweet ungrudging justice to all men. It is such a rare quality in private as in public life; no doubt it is so rare because it is only possible to the highest natures.

Dorothy. How well you understood him!

Sir Oscar. Perhaps I understand him better by my memories of him than I did when I was a lad, too eager to enjoy myself to care much for anything else. If I had followed his example and his counsels, I should have been a very different man and a much more useful one in my generation.

Dorothy. You have been fighting in Egypt.

Sir Oscar. Is that useful? Well, anybody could have done what I did—lost three chargers and hunted down a few poor beasts of fellahs. I made some sketches certainly, but they're not worth much. Those marvellous sunsets, and great white moons—one could not reproduce them if one were Turner himself.

Dorothy (in awe). Did you really *kill* an Egyptian?

Sir Oscar. I really did—three or four, I believe. One was there to do it, you know. I would rather they had been Germans or Russians. It seems a little too like mowing down grass.

Dorothy. I suppose it had to be done, as you say; but it is horrible—to see any one sit there—drawing—

and to think that they have killed others a few months ago; you cannot fancy how terrible it seems! It frightens me——

Sir Oscar (smiling). Desdemona was frightened, but she liked it. Women always do like it.

Dorothy. I do not like it.

Sir Oscar. Oh, yes, you do. You are not quite so sincere as usual when you say you don't.

Dorothy (colouring). Perhaps—I do not know—yes, perhaps in a way I like it. It seems wonderful to think you have killed men last year and would not hurt me; but still it is terrible to think of——

Sir Oscar. Precisely; it was terrible to Desdemona.

Dorothy. Desdemona!

Sir Oscar. Yes; you remember she loved him for the perils he had passed, and I dare say a little also for the damage he had done.

Dorothy (hurriedly). I don't see—I mean——How very strange it is that the *custode* does not come! the light seems growing less; it will soon be dusk.

Sir Oscar (cheerfully). Of course the old fellow will come when night falls. They are sure to shut the palace up carefully. Do you know that I am beginning to believe in fate?

Dorothy. Indeed? Because an Italian doorkeeper has forgotten his keys?

Sir Oscar. Well, yes, and for other things. Oddly enough, I hated coming into Italy. I had got together a nice lot of people for Easter down at my place; and after that I meant to spend May in Paris; I like Paris immensely, and my horses are running there; but an old friend of mine telegraphed to me that he was dying in Rome. He had set his heart on seeing me, meant to make me guardian to his boy, and all that; a nice sort of guardian, you will say; but, however, he'd got that idea in his head, and he was down with typhoid, and the boy all alone with him; so I went. He didn't die, not a bit of it; and he's going home next week. But he would have died, I am sure, if I'd stayed in London, out of the very perversity of things. So as he got well and I found myself in Italy I stopped a few days here on my way back just to see the pictures and things, and I thought I'd take a sketch of the Arazzi rooms for Rivaux, for I recollected them; and so—and so, you see—you know now why I begin to believe in fate.

Dorothy. I really do not. You say your friend would have died if you had stayed at home; so there can't be any fate at all—only a rigmarole contradictory set of chances.

Sir Oscar. That is very unkind; I only meant that things go like that. As I set off to see him die, he didn't die; if I had stayed at home, he would have died inevitably, so that I should have been full of self-reproach all the rest of my days. I believe in fate, though you refuse to see its hand.

Dorothy. I cannot see anything except a natural sequence of circumstances.

Sir Oscar. Well, but why is it that one 'sequence

of circumstances' leaves a man just where he was before, and another alters everything and brings him
across somebody who changes the face of things for
him ?

Dorothy (with a little embarrassment). A *custode*,
for instance, who keeps one without luncheon and makes
one late for dinner! Well, it is to be hoped he is not
met with every day. You must be very hungry, Sir
Oscar.

Sir Oscar. I am, I grant; but it don't matter; we
were awfully hungry at times in Egypt. The cook was
all there, but the food wasn't. Here we are like those
poor brutes that the Chinese kill by hanging them up
in a cage in sight of a meat-shop. There is food all
round us in Florence, but we can't get at it. There is
a kind of scent of dinner in the air, isn't there ?

Dorothy. I hardly perceive it. Do you hear the
nightingales in Boboli ?

Sir Oscar. Ah! you see that is the difference between our ages. Sunset to you suggests nightingales,
and to me dinner.

Dorothy. But you must hear the nightingales.
Listen !

Sir Oscar. Very pretty. Where are they ?

Dorothy. In Boboli, the gardens yonder. Are your
gardens at Rivaux equal to ours, with their dark ilexes
and their moss-grown marbles ?

Sir Oscar. They are another sort of garden altogether. Italian gardens are meant for moonlight

nights and Romeo and Juliet, and perhaps a dagger glistening somewhere under the white lilies; ours are made rather for sunny afternoons and lawn-tennis, and tea in Worcester cups, and Kate Greenaway's little girls, and all kinds of cigars. There is an old Dutch garden though at Rivaux, very prim and shady, and full of sweet-scented flowers, which might please you, and where you would sit under clipped walls of box and read old Herrick. Do you think you will come to England this year?

Dorothy. This year! we never go there or anywhere. I have never even seen England. I was born here.

Sir Oscar. Florence has been always a fortunate city! I should be so glad if you and your mother would come to Rivaux. I have lots of ladies who honour me there.

Dorothy (laughs a little). Fancy me in my grey gown amongst a number of grand people. Do you know I have never been to a party of any kind in all my life, nor to any theatre, even though we are in the land of *Mimi*?

Sir Oscar. How delightful! How I should like to be the first to drive you down the Champs Elysées at the *retour du Bois*, or take you on a Saturday to Hurlingham or Ranelagh, and to the opera afterwards! I wonder if it would strike you as bewilderingly enchanting or preposterously absurd! Sometimes the whole thing seems to me the hugest farce under the sun.

Dorothy. Listen! (*the nightingales sing louder in the gardens on the other side of the court below*).

Sir Oscar. The last nightingales I heard were at Marlow. We had sailed down the river and dined; they chaffed me about going out to Egypt, said I and my charger should sink overhead down in the sand, like the Master of Ravenswood, you know. What trash we all talked; and when we were a minute silent there was the shouting of the birds—for they do shout, you know—and little Nessie Hamilton vowed that Nilsson wasn't a patch on them. (*Is silent thinking.*) What a beast I am to speak of Nessie Hamilton to her—to be sure it don't hurt her, she don't know what brutes we were at Marlow that night while the nightingales sang on through it all just outside the windows. How pretty she looks! the little grey frock is enchanting, it makes her look as if she had dressed up as a boy-monk for a freak. These dusky rooms with all their tapestries, and just that fair curly hair in the midst of them, and the birds trilling away outside—it's much better than Marlow; it's a scene out of some old drama of Massinger or Ford. How reverent she looks as she listens; she has the face of a girl at prayer. I should like her to think of me in her prayers. Somehow one fancies it would do one good, if there be really anything better than this life.

[*The big bell of S. Maria dei Fiori rings for the Ave Maria.*

Dorothy (*rising with agitation*). That is the

Venti tre! and they do not come!   What shall I do?
Whatever will my mother think?   Can we make no
one hear?

Sir Oscar.   Won't the nightingales console you?

Dorothy.   Oh, pray do not make a jest of it!   Only
think how wretched my mother will be, expecting me
hour after hour—I am never later than five—and
nobody is with her but our stupid Teresina; and they
do not dream I am here, because I went out to paint in
the Spanish cloister and came here instead because the
church was shut up.   Oh, cannot you make them hear?
Do call—shout out—as if you were telling the Life
Guards to charge!

Sir Oscar.   I will do my very best.   I do shout a
good deal, especially on a field-day, and still more
when my yacht's shipping heavy seas and the skipper's
a duffer; here goes.

   [*Leans out of the window and halloos; there is
      no response save from an echo.*

Dorothy (in despair).   No one hears!   Oh, how
terrible it is!   What ever can I do?

Sir Oscar.   I fear there is nothing to be done.   I
would get down the wall somehow or another, but
these confounded French windows—French windows
in an Italian palace!—are too narrow for me to
squeeze through them; you see, unluckily, I'm the
big Life-guardsman of *Punch's* pictures.   If I only
knew what to do!   I'm afraid I must bore you
horribly.

Dorothy. Oh, no! you are so kind, and I am so selfish. I forget how you must want your dinner.

Sir Oscar. That is a minor ill; I have been hungry ere now and have survived it. What concerns me is the worry for yourself and your mother at home. Of course it will end all right; we are not shut up here to endure the fate of the Ugolini; somebody will come some time; but meantime you must be beginning to hate the sight of me.

Dorothy (*naïvely*). No, indeed, you have made me forget the time; you have been very kind. I should feel much more frightened if I were alone.

Sir Oscar (*to himself*). How sweetly she says that! and not an idea of any suspicion of me. Good heavens! what capital Nessie Hamilton, or any of them, would have made out of this as a 'situation.' What affected fears, what nasty modesties, what suggestive attitudes they would have got out of it! This child only thinks that her mother is crying at home, and that I want my dinner. (*He makes the tour of the three apartments which are open, and returns.*) I have tried to force each of the doors, but they defy me. There is no exit of any sort possible. What can I do? You know the place. Command me. I will do the possible and the impossible.

Dorothy (*growing pale*). I think there is nothing you can do, as you can make no one hear. It is quite inexplicable. The man must have drunk too, much and gone to sleep—and it is nearly dark.

Sir Oscar. How these nightingales do go on; their little voices penetrate where mine is lost—the superior power of sweetness over volume. It looks darker here than it is outside, because of all these tapestries. To think you have had nothing to eat all day!

Dorothy. I do not mind that; I often eat nothing all day. Would you like to smoke? I think you said you had cigars.

Sir Oscar. No, thanks; I don't care about it. It would only bother you.

Dorothy. Indeed, no; I do not mind. You say if you smoke you feel less hungry.

Sir Oscar. Well, I'll go and light up in the next room to show you how I appreciate your kindness. (*He goes and smokes and reflects.*) On my honour, if there be such a thing as love at first sight, I am in love! After all, what could one find better than Tom Claremont's daughter? He was the finest fellow that ever lived; beggared himself for sake of being honest to his Church and loyal to his opinions; he was a scholar and a gentleman, every inch of him. If I've anything decent in me, it is to Claremont that I owe it. I was a horrid little spoilt bumptious ass when I went to him, and he made a man of me. If I fell away from his teachings afterwards it was nobody's fault but my own. She's infinitely charming, she is so utterly innocent, and yet you can see she could hold her own very bravely. What a pretty voice too! and what a complexion, like a roseleaf! After all, Piver can't give them anything that looks like the real thing. I wonder what she would say if she were told I thought of her seriously—box my ears, I fancy. It sounds awfully ridiculous, when I've been afraid of being caught by women ever since I was twenty, and when I've seen her just a few hours ago in these rooms; but I think one might do worse. I'd always an idea of finding somebody out of the common run; I'm dead sick of all our women, they are so terribly alike; and then, one knows those girls would marry the devil himself if he made good settlements. Now, this one I believe would go on painting linen to the end of her days rather than sell herself. What immense fun it would be to show her the world; I am sure she's got it in her to enjoy herself; shut up with a blind mother, and forced to drudge in galleries for her livelihood, she must be like a bird in a cage. If one had her with one, and just took her to Paris, and gave Wörth *carte blanche*, what a picture she'd be in a month! and it would do one good to hear her laugh; yet I think she'd hate it all, and like to get to the greenery and the roses down at Rivaux—at least, I fancy so. I fancy she'd always like the country best, and perhaps she'd like riding, she's the figure that ought to ride well. Good heavens! to be tied down here in the heat, painting saints and goddesses and landscapes on cloth for a lot of dealers and Yankees! It is atrocious! Andromeda and the rock was nothing to it. And so brave and so quiet and

so grateful as she is about it! and only thinking of her
mother, never a bit of herself. It seems a shame to
make love to her shut up alone with me as she is, it
would only frighten her; and it's growing dark as
pitch. It will be very horrid for her; one must not
say anything that would scare her; it would be too
unfair. (*He throws the end of the cigarette in a corner,
and looks around the room.*) If only one could find
a bit of light it would comfort her; it's odious for her,
poor child, to be alone with a stranger like this. If
she weren't so unsuspicious she would think I'd bribed
the *custode*. (*Sees on a marble console an end of wax
candle; takes it and goes to her.*) Here's an atom of
wax candle; I found it in that inner room. I'll try and
light it, though I've only fusees, and stick it in one
of those candelabra; it will be better than nothing.
Perhaps they will see a light in those windows, and
come up, some of them. There! A feeble illumina-
tion, but still it will serve to keep ghosts away. If
they imprison people here they ought to leave a lamp
or two and something in the cupboard to eat. Pray
don't be alarmed at—at—about anything, Miss Claremont. I'll go in the farthest room, if you like, and you
can pile the furniture between us——

Dorothy (*simply*). Why should I do that? I
should be more alarmed if I were alone. I am a little
—just a little—afraid of being in the dark. My father
was always angry with me for being so; he said it
was to distrust Nature, to limit the power of God; of

course it is if one reason about it; but one can't always reason; at least, I can't.

Sir Oscar. No pretty woman ever should! Don't be angry with me. It slipped out unawares. You see, it was such a natural reply to you. (*Thinks to himself.*) You are adorable! It never enters your head that I might be a brute to you. On my soul, I will be the lion to your Una. I don't think I've led a very decent life; but no old woman could be more careful of you than I will be. Only there will be the mischief to pay if we do stay here all night and the gossips get hold of my name in the morning. They will damn you, poor child, for all the rest of your days. The world don't believe in Una. What a blackguard world it is! (*Aloud.*) Hark at your nightingales! Did your father ever recite to you Ford's '*Lutist and Nightingale?*' I almost think it is the finest poem in the English language.

Dorothy. It is very beautiful—I know it by heart. Only there is one fault in all the poets when they write of nightingales. They speak of *her* as sad. Now, it is *he* who is most joyous.

Sir Oscar. To be sure; you are quite right. That blunder comes from Ædon! Hark at them! What a flood of song! What rivalry!

Dorothy. Do they sing like that in England?

Sir Oscar. I think not.

Dorothy. Perhaps in England they cannot see their notes; there are no fireflies to light them! (*She meets his glance, and colours and looks away.*) Tell me all about Egypt; that will pass the time. I am so fond of stories; my father used to tell me so many.

Sir Oscar. Ah, I haven't your father's talent. I've talked what you call bad English so many years that I've lost all power of speaking in the sort of language you like. I can tell you what I saw myself, but I'm afraid I shall tell it ill. The thing that hurt me most was the death of poor Black Douglas, my best horse; I bred him myself at Rivaux six years ago; an Arab stabbed him, in a thicket of reeds, and he carried me five miles home, to camp, with the knife sticking in him, and then dropped.

> [*He tells her about Egypt for half an hour; the bells sound half-past eight; it grows dark outside; the candle burns low.*

Sir Oscar (aloud). That fellow hasn't twenty minutes more life in him; perhaps there are some other bits of wax somewhere. Kassassin, do you say? Oh, no, it wasn't anything wonderful; it was a *mêlée*; we cut and thrust and charged and recharged, but we didn't know very well what we were doing. It is always so with us English, you know; we go into the thing as if it were polo, and we get out of it, God knows how. I wish we could get out of this for your sake; you begin to look so tired. It's quite shocking for you to have gone all day on those two buns, and not even a drop of water.

Dorothy. If I could let my mother know I am

safe! She will imagine every dreadful accident under the sun, and they will never think to come here—at least, I fear not.

Sir Oscar. Perhaps they may, later on; I always fancied there was nothing money couldn't do for one, but this is certainly a facer. (*He thinks.*) I should like to tell her all I think of her; but I suppose it would be brutal when she is shut up like this; it might frighten her, she wouldn't understand. On my honour, I never felt so inclined to marry a woman before! but she might be frightened or angry; she can't get away from me; it won't do to embarrass her. It's likely enough we shan't get out till morning; it will be awfully cruel for her. What a tale they'd make of it in the clubs if it were to get wind; I suppose they'd chaff me and call me Scipio for the rest of my days.

Dorothy (*with distress*). How can they possibly treat me like this!—they know me so well, I come here so continually. Of course it is not like the galleries, which they must close; but still they ought to shut up the palace at sunset.

Sir Oscar. They have forgotten this particular corner of it. Pray don't fret; if I could get them to come by breaking my neck I assure you I wouldn't hesitate a minute; but when I can't get out of any one of the windows!—there are moments, and these are one of them, in which one feels that it may occasionally be better to be a midge than a giant.

Dorothy. If you could get out of the windows you could do nothing; they are an immense height.

Sir Oscar. I would chance it for your sake.

Dorothy (smiling). Or—to dine?

Sir Oscar. That is very cruel. Have I shown any remembrance that I have not dined? Indeed, after that cigarette which you so kindly allowed me, I am quite refreshed body and spirit. But that you should not even have a glass of water distresses me infinitely.

Dorothy (the tears coming to her eyes). Oh, all that does not matter in the least. It is to think how unhappy my poor mother must be! And you know everything is so much worse to those who are blind. They feel they can do nothing.

Sir Oscar (moves restlessly). Pray, pray, don't cry. I never can stand seeing a woman cry. I know it's awful for you, and one feels such a fool not to be able to do something. Perhaps I could smash the door if I put my shoulder to it. Shall I try?

Dorothy. No, I think you could not move it; these doors are so strong; and they would put you in prison afterwards.

Sir Oscar. I would chance that. If it won't frighten you I'll try if I can't smash the panels in; I'm about as strong as most men. I see nothing else for it. Here goes!

Dorothy. Oh! pray don't; you may hurt yourself, and they will be so angry.

Sir Oscar (smiling). My dear, I'm more likely to

hurt the wall. The worst of it is, that these things
they made in the dark ages are so confoundedly well
made that they'd almost resist artillery. If it were a
door in my house in London, we'd send it flying into
splinters in two seconds. Stand out of the way and
let me have a try before the candle goes out; you won't
mind my taking my coat off? Why, how pale you are!
Do you think the thing will tumble on me like the
gates of Gaza? Pray don't be frightened. I thought
you were such a cool courageous little lady. I assure
you the only damage done will be to these very handsome panels, and money will repair that. Now, see
here, I am going to try. If I fail, you will be no worse
off; if I succeed, you can run away as soon as the
door's down, and they'll never know that you have been
shut up here with me, don't you see? (*Thinks.*) What
an innocent it is! She don't dream that people might
say horrid things! Here is the real innocence—Una's
innocence—too pure even to imagine evil, and knowing
no fear. I always wished to find that sort of thing, but
I thought it was like the four-leaved shamrock! (*Aloud.*)
Will you please stand out of the way and hold that
candle while I try? Here goes!

> [*Puts his shoulder to the door; heaves and
> pushes vainly for ten minutes; pauses to
> take breath.*

Dorothy (*with clasped hands*). Oh! pray do not
try to do it, you will hurt yourself; you must be
bruised and strained already; and if you did knock it

down they would put you in the Bargello. You know this is the king's palace !

Sir Oscar (laughing). They won't behead me; perhaps they'll behead the *custode.* Don't think I'm going to give in; I haven't got safe out of Egypt only to go down before a wooden door. (*He tries again; and sends the panels flying in splinters.*) There! I knew I should beat the confounded thing. Now you are free, my bonny bird. Will you run down the stairs and leave me here, or do you prefer that I should go and call them ?

Dorothy. Oh, how strong you are ! How beautiful to be as strong as that !

Sir Oscar (smiling). Hercules always wins by a head with you ladies. That unhappy door! it is only good to split up for matches; but I know all the Royal household; they'll make it right. Why, you are paler than you were before ! What is the matter ?

Dorothy (gathering up her colours and brushes). I am only so glad, and it seems so wonderful to be as strong as you are ! You rent the door as I should paper.

Sir Oscar. Not quite; it took me fifteen minutes. Don't be in such a tremendous hurry. I—I—want to ask you something.

Dorothy. I cannot wait a moment, indeed I cannot. I shall run all the way home. It must be nearly nine o'clock. Think of mamma !

Sir Oscar. Yes; but I want a word, just a word,

with you first before anyone comes upstairs. They must have heard that row down below. Do wait one second; you can run off afterwards as soon as you please; but I must say it if I die for it. Half a day like this counts more than half a year, don't you think so? I don't know what you feel about me; I can't hope that you feel anything; but what I feel is just this—you please me more than any woman that ever lived. Will you come and live at Rivaux? By George, there is the candle gone out! well, it served our time. My dear, don't be frightened; give me your hand; we will feel our way downstairs. But before we go out do answer me.

Dorothy (agitated). It is quite dark!

Sir Oscar. It is quite dark; but the nightingales find their tongues in the darkness, and so can you.

Dorothy. We must speak to the *custode.*

Sir Oscar. We must certainly speak to the *custode* —at least, I will, and forcibly—but first please speak to me. Of course you know very little about me, but your mother shall know everything. All you have to do, my dear, is to tell me you don't dislike me'

Dorothy. Dislike you?

Sir Oscar. May I take you home?

Dorothy (in a whisper). If you wish.

ROMANCE AND REALISM

I WILL not give the names of the persons concerned in the following story, but I vouch for its absolute truth. Indeed, the little drama has been acted within a stone's throw of my gates. A cantatrice of obscure position had a lover in a Genoese gentleman, who not only had many claims on her fidelity by reason of his devotion to her, but also by the education which he had had her given when a poor girl, and the liberality which he had shown to her family ; nevertheless, *telle est la femme*, she betrayed this generous lover, and carried on an intrigue with a young noble of the neighbour-hood, a youth much younger than herself and very rich. For some time the Genoese gentleman, only able to visit her at intervals in the Tuscan village where she lived, was without much difficulty deceived ; and when he did see the young noble, was assured that he was a relation of his *dama*. At last, however, his suspicions were fully aroused ; instead of going back to Genoa he one day unexpectedly returned, and had full proofs of the worthlessness of his siren. Furious to be thus *canzonato* by a creature whom he had too in-genuously adored, he pursued his rival to his villa, and, failing to provoke him to a duel, swore that he would kill him. The Carabineers intervening, he found himself deprived of his just vengeance, and, in the madness of his despair and agony, shot himself by the river's side, while his faithless mistress jeered at him from her open window in the lovely stillness of the moonlit September eve. This was but a few nights ago; he is not dead, but still lies in great peril in a cottage near where he fell. The sympathy of the whole rural population is with this man, who at least knew how to love and how to avenge dishonour. The village populace were with trouble prevented from lynching his worthless *dama*; and the veteran Brigadier of the Guard wept like a child at the fate of this *vittima d'amore*. This is only one out of a thousand tragedies which yearly occur in this, the home of Romeo and Giulietta, where love is not a dead letter. Why are not those who can love and suffer thus as deserving of portrayal in fiction as the epicene beings who know no woes but a passing hysteria of conscience or a disillusion before the melting of a foggy and impalpable ideal? Because passion has never touched with its fire and its glory the prim life of the æsthetic prig. or the rotund Philistine, it is not for that reason perished off the face of the earth. It exists in the same force and the same fervour as in the days of Othello and Stradella; and, I confess, seems to me much more fitly a subject for the novelist or the dramatist than the fictitious 'realism' of the spineless commonplace. After all, there is no more vivid reality than love. The Genoese lover lying here now shot through the chest by his own hand, because his generous faith has been deceived by a heartless mistress, is every whit as ' real ' as the British prig going to his æsthetic afternoon teas or the British Philistine driving in an omnibus; therefore his story or its similitude presented in fiction would be as legitimate a centre of interest as Anthony Trollope's gossiping bishops or Henry James's heroines perplexed by a plethora or a paucity of proposals. The Tuscan villagers sorrowing by his bedside see nothing strange or unusual in a man of twenty-five years old giving up his life for love; but were it embodied in a romance that were printed and published, the English reviewer would find his history ' sensational ' or pronounce it impossible. I remember when George Lawrence was told that the end of ' Sword and Gown ' was improbable, he answered, 'Improbable! Oh, very likely; only, you see, it was true.'

The *éternellement vrai* is as real as the *infiniment petit*. It may be well that there should exist painters of the latter as it may be well that there should exist carvers of cherry-stones, and men who give ten years of their existence to the production of a ladybird in ivory. But the Vatican Hermes is as ' real ' as the Japanese netzké, and the dome of St. Peter's is as real as the gasometer of East London; and I presume that the fact can hardly be disputed if I even assert that the passion flower is as real as the potato! I have, I believe, sometimes been accused of writing 'fairy stories'; but is not life itself very often a fairy story, if too often, alas! one in which the evil genius preponderates, and the wishing cap is foolishly used by the unwise? To some of us, at least, a dreary and insipid story of an uneventful and unimpassioned life seems much more 'unreal' (i.e., unlike our own experiences) than the more romantic narrative conceived by the wildest fancy. To many of us—to myself, I confess, among the number—the world seems a marvellous union of tragedy and comedy, which run side by side like twin children; like a 'web of Tyrian looms' with the gold threads crossing and recrossing on the dusky purple of its intricate meshes. But there are, no doubt, a number of good and tiresome people to whom it seems only a Quaker mute, a suit of homespun, a length of huckaback; they judge by what they have known themselves. How is one to persuade them that their knowledge is not the measure of the world? The amorous, magnificent, heroic life of Skobeleff would, no doubt, seem incredible to the London *littérateur* with his prim domesticities bound up in a duodecimo suburban villa, papered by Morris, or the rural clergyman solemnly pacing his treadmill of weekly monotonies; but Michael Skobeleff was just as 'real' as are the modern Puff and Wormwood going up and down in their underground railway trains, or the Reverend Crawleys surrounded with their olive branches in muddy midland villages.

At this moment, fighting for the French flag at Tonquin, is a young man, the fame of whose *nom de plume* (were I to give it here) would be at once recognised as that of one of the great masters of French fiction; this gallant sailor is also a great musician and an admirable artist, and he may very likely die in a barbarous country (as Henri Rivière died), burying with him his genius, his youth, and his marvellous and multitudinous powers. Well, is not this man every whit as 'real' as Mr. Precisian Dulle, passing his life between a Civil Service desk and a house in South Kensington, or Mr. Smalle Joker, penning his blameless fiction, which ' never brings a blush on the cheek,' &c., with his six daughters playing lawn-tennis in his back garden, and his physical and mental vision limited to the chimney pots ?

No doubt, all the world over character creates circumstance ; and the tortoise is not to blame if it cannot leap, only it need not disbelieve in the greyhound and the horse. No doubt ' adventures are to the adventurous ' in the most extended sense of the word ; and romantic and brilliant lives will not fall to the lot of the dull and the mediocre. But such lives exist, nevertheless, and it is not true that a pale uniformity extends like a pall over the whole of the human race. Every one, certainly, is not beautiful, but there are very beautiful people ; and it is legitimate to describe beauty in fiction as it is legitimate to depict it in painting or reproduce it in sculpture.

x

Every one does not possess a great or beautiful house, but many people do. Why is not the palace as fit a subject for description as the hovel, or the 'commodious dwelling' of advertising agents? A friend of mine never gives a reception without having 1,500f. worth of wax candles lighted in his room ; is he not as 'real' as Jones or Brown whose housemaid lights his single gasalier? A little while ago I said to a well-known diplomatist, who is also a great virtuoso and a great artist, and who has also a most romantic personal history, 'If you were "put in a book," as people say, nobody would believe in you.' Let me beg to be distinctly understood; I do not object to realism in fiction; what I object to is the limitation of realism in fiction to what is commonplace, tedious, and bald—to the habit, in a word, of insisting that the potato is real and that the passion-flower is not. A novel is not necessarily any the more like real life because it is a story about nothing, leading to nowhere, which might meander on through half a century for any climax that it ever reaches. It is not correct to call this kind of writing miniature painting; the miniature may represent the hero as well as the infant, the court beauty as well as the white-coiffed peasant; on its few inches of ivory the miniature has borne the mature features of Napoleon as well as the baby face of the Roi de Rome. This pseudo-realistic literature, on the contrary, is rather similar to those small Dutch carvings in bone, which somewhat clumsily imitate the Japanese netzkés in ivory. When a novel is vapid, tedious, without any originality of circumstance or of character, and incapable of issuing out of one dead level of commonplace, it is very easy to praise it as 'natural,' but it does not in the least follow that it is so. The realistic novels of France are very fine of their kind, because they are not afraid to grapple with vice and depravity in its worst form; but the realistic novel of English or English-writing authors is no more real than the faded daguerreotypes of our grandmothers, where all the features are blurred into one indistinct brown cloud of shadow. I cannot suppose that my own experiences can be wholly exceptional ones, yet I have known very handsome people, I have known very fine characters, I have also known some very wicked ones, and I have also known many circumstances so romantic that were they described in fiction, they would be ridiculed as exaggerated and impossible; in real life there are coincidences so startling, mysteries so singular, destinies so strange, that no wise novelist could venture to portray them for fear of making his work appear too *bizarre* and too melodramatic. That 'truth is stranger than fiction' is found at every turn in the world. The sunset on the Alps is as 'real' as a Dutch cheese on a wooden platter; but the painter of the former will always be considered an idealist and the painter of the latter a realist. Again, if there be one thing more than another that is the most conspicuous note of our century, it is the number of great fortunes which are possessed in it; the extreme luxury and splendour of life in general, the self-indulgence and feverishness of society, the grace and ennui of existence. To describe great riches in a novel is surely therefore as legitimate as to describe middle-class competence, or the harshness of absolute poverty; the former has quite as much effect on the times as the latter, and infinitely more effect on the manners. Dunrobin or Belvoir, Chénonçeaux, or the Trostberg, is surely as 'real' as Westbourne Grove and Clapham, as Belleville or the crowded Trattnerhof; therefore, why is not a great house, similar to any one of the many great houses that exist in Europe, as legitimate a *venue* for the action of a romance, as a doctor's house in a square or a grocer's villa in the *banlieue*?

A lecturer in the north of England, lecturing on my novels, remarked with *naïveté* and incredulity on the number of residences assigned in 'Moths' to Prince Zouroff. Now, had the lecturer taken the trouble to inquire of anyone conversant with the world, he would have learned that most great persons of all nationalities have three or four different residences at the least, and that a Russian noble is invariably extravagant in these matters. Indeed, is it ever possible to over-colour in fiction the expenditure and self-indulgence of what we call society in this day? The influences of the Second Empire are still with us all over Europe, but in English literature this is neither accurately traced nor truthfully acknowledged. The world is not exclusively composed

of the English middle class, varied with a few American
young ladies. Would it not be well if lecturers or
reviewers, before calling everything which seems strange
to themselves unreal or unnatural, were visited with a
wholesome doubt as to whether it might not be their
own experiences which were limited? Allow me to
conclude with a repetition of a passage which I wrote
some years ago, and which is pertinent to this subject:—

' When the soldier dies at his post, unhonoured and
unpitied, and out of sheer duty, is that unreal because
it is noble? When the sister of charity hides her
youth and her sex under a grey shroud, and gives up
her whole life to woe and solitude, to sickness and pain,
is that unreal because it is wonderful? A man paints
a spluttering candle, a greasy cloth, a mouldy cheese, a
pewter can; "How real!" they cry. If he paints the
spirituality of dawn, the light of the summer sea, the
flame of arctic lights, of tropic woods, they are called
unreal, though they exist no less than the candle and
cloth, the cheese and the can. Ruy Blas is now con-
demned as unreal because the lovers kill themselves;
the realists forget that there are lovers still to whom
that death would be possible, would be preferable, to
low intrigue and yet more lowering falsehood. They
can only see the mouldy cheese, they cannot see the
sunrise glory. All that is heroic, all that is sublime,
impersonal, or glorious, is derided as unreal. It is a
dreary creed. It will make a dreary world. Is not

my Venetian glass with its iridescent hues of opal as
real every whit as your pot of pewter? Yet the time
is coming when every one, morally and mentally at
least, will be allowed no other than a pewter pot to
drink out of, under pain of being " writ down an ass "
—or worse.   It is a dreary prospect.'

I put these words into the lips of Corrèze ; and, by-
the-by, will anyone be good enough to tell me why
Corrèze has been considered an ' impossible ' character
in a century which has known Mario, Marchese di
Candia, and seen the women of Paris mad for a smile
from Capoul?

LONDON · PRINTED BY
SPOTTISWOODE AND CO., NEW·STREET SQUARE
AND PARLIAMENT STREET

CHATTO & WINDUS'S
LIST OF BOOKS.

About.—The Fellah : An Egyptian Novel. By EDMOND ABOUT. Translated by Sir RANDAL ROBERTS. Post 8vo, illustrated boards, 2s. ; cloth limp, 2s. 6d.

Adams (W. Davenport), Works by :

A Dictionary of the Drama. Being a comprehensive Guide to the Plays, Playwrights, Players. and Playhouses of the United Kingdom and America, from the Earliest to the Present Times. Crown 8vo, half-bound, 12s. 6d. [*Preparing.*

Latter-Day Lyrics. Edited by W. DAVENPORT ADAMS. Post 8vo, cloth limp, 2s. 6d.

Quips and Quiddities. Selected by W. DAVENPORT ADAMS. Post 8vo, cloth limp, 2s. 6d.

Advertising, A History of, from the Earliest Times. Illustrated by Anecdotes, Curious Specimens, and Notices of Successful Advertisers. By HENRY SAMPSON. Crown 8vo, with Coloured Frontispiece and Illustrations, cloth gilt, 7s. 6d.

Agony Column (The) of "The Times," from 1800 to 1870. Edited, with an Introduction, by ALICE CLAY. Post 8vo, cloth limp, 2s. 6d.

Aïde (Hamilton), Works by :

Carr of Carrlyon. Post 8vo, illustrated boards, 2s.

Confidences. Post 8vo, illustrated boards, 2s.

Alexander (Mrs.) NOVELS by :
Post 8vo, illustrated boards, 2s. ; crown 8vo, cloth extra, 3s. 6d. each.

Maid, Wife, or Widow ? A Romance.

Valerie's Fate.

Allen (Grant), Works by :
Crown 8vo, cloth extra, 6s. each.

The Evolutionist at Large. Second Edition, revised.

Vignettes from Nature.

Colin Clout's Calendar.

Strange Stories. With a Frontispiece by GEORGE DU MAURIER.

Architectural Styles, A Handbook of. Translated from the German of A. ROSENGARTEN, by W. COLLETT-SANDARS. Crown 8vo, cloth extra, with 639 Illustrations, 7s. 6d.

Art (The) of Amusing : A Collection of Graceful Arts, Games, Tricks, Puzzles, and Charades. By FRANK BELLEW. With 300 Illustrations. Cr. 8vo, cloth extra, 4s. 6d.

Artemus Ward :

Artemus Ward's Works: The Works of CHARLES FARRER BROWNE, better known as ARTEMUS WARD. With Portrait and Facsimile. Crown 8vo, cloth extra, 7s. 6d.

Artemus Ward's Lecture on the Mormons. With 32 Illustrations Edited, with Preface, by EDWARD P HINGSTON. Crown 8vo, 6d.

The Genial Showman: Life and Adventures of Artemus Ward. By EDWARD P HINGSTON. With a Frontispiece. Cr. 8vo, cl. extra, 3s. 6d

Ashton (John), Works by:

A History of the Chap-Books of the Eighteenth Century. With nearly 400 Illusts., engraved in facsimile of the originals. Cr. 8vo, cl. ex., 7s. 6d.

Social Life in the Reign of Queen Anne. From Original Sources. With nearly 100 Illusts. Cr. 8vo, cl. ex., 7s. 6d.

Humour, Wit, and Satire of the Seventeenth Century. With nearly 100 Illusts. Cr. 8vo, cl. extra, 7s. 6d.

English Caricature and Satire on Napoleon the First. 120 Illusts. from Originals. Two Vols., demy 8vo, 28s.

Bacteria.—A Synopsis of the Bacteria and Yeast Fungi and Allied Species. By W. B. Grove, B.A. With 87 Illusts. Crown 8vo, cl. extra, 3s. 6d.

Balzac's "Comedie Humaine" and its Author. With Translations by H. H. Walker. Post 8vo, cl. limp, 2s. 6d.

Bankers, A Handbook of Lon- don; together with Lists of Bankers from 1677. By F. G. Hilton Price. Crown 8vo, cloth extra, 7s. 6d.

Bardsley (Rev. C.W.), Works by:

English Surnames: Their Sources and Significations. Third Ed., revised. Cr. 8vo, cl. extra, 7s. 6d.

Curiosities of Puritan Nomenclature. Crown 8vo, cloth extra, 7s. 6d.

Bartholomew Fair, Memoirs of. By Henry Morley. With 100 Illusts. Crown 8vo, cloth extra, 7s. 6d.

Basil, Novels by:

A Drawn Game. Cr. 8vo., cl. ex., 3s. 6d.

The Wearing of the Green. Three Vols., crown 8vo, 31s. 6d.

Beaconsfield, Lord: A Biogra- phy. By T. P O'Connor, M.P. Sixth Edit., New Preface. Cr. 8vo, cl. ex. 7s. 6d.

Beauchamp. — Grantley Grange: A Novel. By Shelsley Beauchamp. Post 8vo, illust. bds., 2s.

Beautiful Pictures by British Artists: A Gathering of Favourites from our Picture Galleries. In Two Series. All engraved on Steel in the highest style of Art. Edited, with Notices of the Artists, by Sydney Armytage, M.A. Imperial 4to, cloth extra, gilt and gilt edges, 21s. per Vol.

Bechstein. — As Pretty as Seven, and other German Stories. Collected by Ludwig Bechstein. With Additional Tales by the Brothers Grimm, and 100 Illusts. by Richter. Small 4to, green and gold, 6s. 6d.; gilt edges, 7s. 6d.

Beerbohm. — Wanderings in Patagonia; or, Life among the Ostrich Hunters. By Julius Beerbohm. With Illusts. Crown 8vo, cloth extra, 3s. 6d.

Belgravia for 1885. One Shilling Monthly, Illustrated by P. Macnab. — A Strange Voyage, by W. Clark Russell, is begun in the January Number, and will be continued throughout the year. This Number contains also the Opening Chapters of a New Story by Cecil Power, Author of "Philistia," entitled Babylon.

*** *Now ready, the Volume for* November, 1884, *to* February, 1885, *cloth extra, gilt edges,* 7s. 6d.; *Cases for binding Vols.,* 2s. *each.*

Belgravia Holiday Number. With Stories by F. W. Robinson, Justin H. McCarthy, B. Montgomerie Ranking, and others. Demy 8vo, with Illusts., 1s. [*July.*

Bennett (W.C., LL.D.), Works by:

A Ballad History of England. Post 8vo, cloth limp, 2s.

Songs for Sailors. Post 8vo, cloth limp, 2s.

Besant (Walter) and James Rice, Novels by. Post 8vo, illust. boards, 2s. each; cloth limp, 2s. 6d. each; or cr. 8vo, cl. extra, 3s. 6d. each.

Ready-Money Mortiboy.
With Harp and Crown.
This Son of Vulcan.
My Little Girl.
The Case of Mr. Lucraft.
The Golden Butterfly.
By Celia's Arbour.
The Monks of Thelema.
'Twas in Trafalgar's Bay.
The Seamy Side.
The Ten Years' Tenant.
The Chaplain of the Fleet.

Besant (Walter), Novels by:

Crown 8vo, cloth extra, 3s. 6d. each; post 8vo, illust. boards, 2s. each; cloth limp, 2s. 6d. each.

All Sorts and Conditions of Men: An Impossible Story. With Illustrations by Fred. Barnard.

The Captains' Room, &c. With Frontispiece by E. J. Wheeler.

All in a Garden Fair. With 6 Illusts. by H. Furniss.

Dorothy Forster. New and Cheaper Edition. With Illustrations by Chas. Green. Cr. 8vo, cloth extra, 3s. 6d.

Uncle Jack, and other Stories. Crown 8vo, cloth extra, 6s.

The Art of Fiction. Demy 8vo, 1s.

Betham-Edwards (M.), Novels by. Crown 8vo, cloth extra, 3s. 6d. each.; post 8vo, illust. bds., 2s. each.

Felicia. | Kitty.

Bewick (Thos.) and his Pupils. By AUSTIN DOBSON. With 95 Illustrations. Square 8vo, cloth extra, 10s. 6d.

Birthday Books :—

The Starry Heavens: A Poetical Birthday Book. Square 8vo, handsomely bound in cloth, 2s. 6d.

Birthday Flowers: Their Language and Legends. By W. J. GORDON. Beautifully Illustrated in Colours by VIOLA BOUGHTON. In illuminated cover, crown 4to, 6s.

The Lowell Birthday Book. With Illusts., small 8vo, cloth extra, 4s. 6d.

Blackburn's (Henry) Art Handbooks. Demy 8vo, Illustrated, uniform in size for binding.

Academy Notes, separate years, from 1875 to 1884, each 1s.

Academy Notes, 1885. With 142 Illustrations. 1s.

Academy Notes, 1875-79. Complete in One Vol., with nearly 600 Illusts. in Facsimile. Demy 8vo, cloth limp, 6s.

Academy Notes, 1880-84. Complete in One Volume, with about 700 Facsimile Illustrations. Cloth limp, 6s.

Grosvenor Notes, 1877. 6d.

Grosvenor Notes, separate years, from 1878 to 1884, each 1s.

Grosvenor Notes, 1885. With 75 Illustrations. 1s.

Grosvenor Notes, 1877-82. With upwards of 300 Illustrations. Demy 8vo, cloth limp, 6s.

Pictures at South Kensington. With 70 Illustrations. 1s.

The English Pictures at the National Gallery. 114 Illustrations. 1s.

The Old Masters at the National Gallery. 128 Illustrations. 1s. 6d.

A Complete Illustrated Catalogue to the National Gallery. With Notes by H. BLACKBURN, and 242 Illusts. Demy 8vo, cloth limp, 3s.

Illustrated Catalogue of the Luxembourg Gallery. Containing about 250 Reproductions after the Original Drawings of the Artists. Edited by F. G. DUMAS. Demy 8vo, 3s. 6d.

The Paris Salon, 1884. With over 300 Illusts. Edited by F. G. DUMAS. Demy 8vo, 3s.

The Paris Salon, 1885. With about 300 Facsimile Sketches. Edited by F. G. DUMAS. Demy 8vo, 3s.

ART HANDBOOKS, *continued—*

The Art Annual, 1883-4. Edited by F. G. DUMAS. With 300 full-page Illustrations. Demy 8vo, 5s.

Boccaccio's Decameron ; or, Ten Days' Entertainment. Translated into English, with an Introduction by THOMAS WRIGHT, F.S.A. With Portrait, and STOTHARD'S beautiful Copperplates. Cr. 8vo, cloth extra, gilt, 7s. 6d.

Blake (William): Etchings from his Works. By W. B. SCOTT. With descriptive Text. Folio, half-bound boards, India Proofs, 21s.

Bowers'(G.) Hunting Sketches:

Canters in Crampshire. Oblong 4to, half-bound boards, 21s.

Leaves from a Hunting Journal Coloured in facsimile of the originals Oblong 4to, half-bound, 21s.

Boyle (Frederick), Works by:

Camp Notes: Stories of Sport and Adventure in Asia, Africa, and America. Crown 8vo, cloth extra 3s. 6d.; post 8vo, illustrated bds., 2s

Savage Life. Crown 8vo, cloth extra 3s. 6d. ; post 8vo, illustrated bds., 2s

Chronicles of No-Man's Land Crown 8vo, cloth extra, 6s.; post 8vo, illust. boards, 2s.

Brand's Observations on Popular Antiquities, chiefly Illustrating the Origin of our Vulgar Customs, Ceremonies, and Superstitions. With the Additions of Sir HENRY ELLIS. Crown 8vo, cloth extra, gilt, with numerous Illustrations, 7s. 6d.

Bret Harte, Works by :

Bret Harte's Collected Works. Arranged and Revised by the Author. Complete in Five Vols., crown 8vo, cloth extra, 6s. each.

Vol. I. COMPLETE POETICAL AND DRAMATIC WORKS. With Steel Portrait, and Introduction by Author.

Vol. II. EARLIER PAPERS—LUCK OF ROARING CAMP, and other Sketches —BOHEMIAN PAPERS — SPANISH AND AMERICAN LEGENDS.

Vol. III. TALES OF THE ARGONAUTS —EASTERN SKETCHES.

Vol. IV. GABRIEL CONROY.

Vol. V. STORIES — CONDENSED NOVELS, &c.

The Select Works of Bret Harte, in Prose and Poetry. With Introductory Essay by J. M. BELLEW, Portrait of the Author, and 50 Illustrations. Crown 8vo, cloth extra, 7s. 6d.

Gabriel Conroy: A Novel. Post 8vo, illustrated boards, 2s.

Bret Harte's Works, *continued*—

An Heiress of Red Dog, and other Stories. Post 8vo, illustrated boards, 2s. ; cloth limp, 2s. 6d.

The Twins of Table Mountain. Fcap. 8vo, picture cover, 1s. ; crown 8vo, cloth extra, 3s. 6d.

Luck of Roaring Camp, and other Sketches. Post 8vo, illust. bds., 2s.

Jeff Briggs's Love Story. Fcap. 8vo, picture cover, 1s. ; cloth extra, 2s. 6d.

Flip. Post 8vo, illustrated boards, 2s. ; cloth limp, 2s. 6d.

Californian Stories (including THE TWINS OF TABLE MOUNTAIN, JEFF BRIGGS'S LOVE STORY, &c.) Post 8vo, illustrated boards, 2s.

Brewer (Rev. Dr.), Works by :

The Reader's Handbook of Allusions, References, Plots, and Stories. Fourth Edition, revised throughout, with a New Appendix, containing a COMPLETE ENGLISH BIBLIOGRAPHY. Cr. 8vo, 1,400 pp., cloth extra, 7s. 6d.

Authors and their Works, with the Dates: Being the Appendices to "The Reader's Handbook," separately printed. Cr. 8vo, cloth limp, 2s.

A Dictionary of Miracles: Imitative, Realistic, and Dogmatic. Crown 8vo, cloth extra, 7s. 6d. ; half-bound, 9s.

Brewster (Sir David), Works by:

More Worlds than One: The Creed of the Philosopher and the Hope of the Christian. With Plates. Post 8vo, cloth extra, 4s. 6d.

The Martyrs of Science: Lives of GALILEO, TYCHO BRAHE, and KEPLER. With Portraits. Post 8vo, cloth extra, 4s. 6d.

Letters on Natural Magic. A New Edition, with numerous Illustrations, and Chapters on the Being and Faculties of Man, and Additional Phenomena of Natural Magic, by J. A. SMITH. Post 8vo, cloth extra, 4s. 6d.

Brillat-Savarin.—Gastronomy

as a Fine Art. By BRILLAT-SAVARIN. Translated by R. E. ANDERSON, M.A. Post 8vo, cloth limp, 2s. 6d.

Burnett (Mrs.), Novels by :

Surly Tim, and other Stories. Post 8vo, illustrated boards, 2s.

Kathleen Mavourneen. Fcap. 8vo, picture cover, 1s.

Lindsay's Luck. Fcap. 8vo, picture cover, 1s.

Pretty Polly Pemberton. Fcap. 8vo, picture cover, 1s.

Buchanan's (Robert) Works :

Ballads of Life, Love, and Humour. With a Frontispiece by ARTHUR HUGHES. Crown 8vo, cloth extra, 6s.

Selected Poems of Robert Buchanan. With Frontispiece by T. DALZIEL. Crown 8vo, cloth extra, 6s.

Undertones. Cr. 8vo, cloth extra, 6s

London Poems. Cr. 8vo, cl. extra, 6s.

The Book of Orm. Cr. 8vo, cl. ex., 6s

White Rose and Red: A Love Story. Crown 8vo, cloth extra, 6s.

Idylls and Legends of Inverburn. Crown 8vo, cloth extra, 6s.

St. Abe and his Seven Wives: A Tale of Salt Lake City. With a Frontispiece by A. B. HOUGHTON. Crown 8vo, cloth extra, 5s.

Robert Buchanan's Complete Poetical Works. With Steel-plate Portrait. Crown 8vo, cloth extra, 7s. 6d.

The Hebrid Isles: Wanderings in the Land of Lorne and the Outer Hebrides. With Frontispiece by W. SMALL. Crown 8vo, cloth extra, 6s.

A Poet's Sketch-Book: Selections from the Prose Writings of ROBERT BUCHANAN. Crown 8vo, cl. extra, 6s.

The Shadow of the Sword: A Romance. Crown 8vo, cloth extra, 3s. 6d. ; post 8vo, illust. boards, 2s.

A Child of Nature: A Romance. With a Frontispiece. Crown 8vo, cloth extra, 3s. 6d. ; post 8vo, illust. bds., 2s.

God and the Man: A Romance. With Illustrations by FRED. BARNARD. Crown 8vo, cloth extra, 3s. 6d. ; post 8vo, illustrated boards, 2s.

The Martyrdom of Madeline: A Romance. With Frontispiece by A. W. COOPER. Cr. 8vo, cloth extra, 3s. 6d.; post 8vo, illustrated boards, 2s.

Love Me for Ever. With a Frontispiece by P. MACNAB. Crown 8vo, cloth extra, 3s. 6d. ; post 8vo, illustrated boards, 2s.

Annan Water: A Romance. Crown 8vo, cloth extra, 3s. 6d. ; post 8vo, illust. boards, 2s.

The New Abelard: A Romance. Crown 8vo, cloth extra, 3s. 6d. ; post 8vo, illust. boards, 2s.

Foxglove Manor: A Novel. Crown 8vo, cloth extra, 3s. 6d.

Matt: A Romance. Crown 8vo, cloth extra, 3s. 6d.

Burton (Robert) :

The Anatomy of Melancholy. A New Edition, complete, corrected and enriched by Translations of the Classical Extracts. Demy 8vo, cloth extra, 7s. 6d.

Melancholy Anatomised: Being an Abridgment, for popular use, of BURTON'S ANATOMY OF MELANCHOLY. Post 8vo, cloth limp, 2s. 6d.

Burton (Captain), Works by:

To the Gold Coast for Gold: A Personal Narrative. By RICHARD F. BURTON and VERNEY LOVETT CAMERON. With Maps and Frontispiece. Two Vols., crown 8vo, cloth extra, 21s.

The Book of the Sword: Being a History of the Sword and its Use in all Countries, from the Earliest Times. By RICHARD F. BURTON. With over 400 Illustrations. Square 8vo, cloth extra, 32s.

Bunyan's Pilgrim's Progress.
Edited by Rev. T. SCOTT. With 17 Steel Plates by STOTHARD, engraved by GOODALL, and numerous Woodcuts. Crown 8vo, cloth extra, gilt, 7s. 6d.

Byron (Lord):

Byron's Letters and Journals. With Notices of his Life. By THOMAS MOORE. A Reprint of the Original Edition, newly revised, with Twelve full-page Plates. Crown 8vo, cloth extra, gilt, 7s. 6d.

Byron's Don Juan. Complete in One Vol., post 8vo, cloth limp, 2s.

Cameron (Commander) and
Captain Burton.—To the Gold Coast for Gold. A Personal Narrative. By RICHARD F. BURTON and VERNEY LOVETT CAMERON. With Frontispiece and Maps. Two Vols., crown 8vo, cloth extra, 21s.

Cameron (Mrs. H. Lovett),
Novels by:
Crown 8vo, cloth extra, 3s. 6d. each; post 8vo, illustrated boards, 2s. each.
Juliet's Guardian.
Deceivers Ever.

Campbell.—White and Black:
Travels in the United States. By Sir GEORGE CAMPBELL, M.P. Demy 8vo, cloth extra, 14s.

Carlyle (Thomas):

Thomas Carlyle: Letters and Recollections. By MONCURE D. CONWAY, M.A. Crown 8vo, cloth extra, with Illustrations, 6s.

On the Choice of Books. By THOMAS CARLYLE. With a Life of the Author by R. H. SHEPHERD. New and Revised Edition, post 8vo, cloth extra, Illustrated, 1s. 6d.

The Correspondence of Thomas Carlyle and Ralph Waldo Emerson, 1834 to 1872. Edited by CHARLES ELIOT NORTON. With Portraits. Two Vols., crown 8vo, cloth extra, 24s.

Chapman's (George) Works:
Vol. I. contains the Plays complete, including the doubtful ones. Vol. II., the Poems and Minor Translations, with an Introductory Essay by ALGERNON CHARLES SWINBURNE. Vol. III., the Translations of the Iliad and Odyssey. Three Vols., crown 8vo, cloth extra, 18s.; or separately, 6s. each.

Chatto & Jackson.—A Treatise
on Wood Engraving, Historical and Practical. By WM. ANDREW CHATTO and JOHN JACKSON. With an Additional Chapter by HENRY G. BOHN; and 450 fine Illustrations. A Reprint of the last Revised Edition. Large 4to, half-bound, 28s.

Chaucer:
Chaucer for Children: A Golden Key. By Mrs. H. R. HAWEIS. With Eight Coloured Pictures and numerous Woodcuts by the Author. New Ed., small 4to, cloth extra, 6s.
Chaucer for Schools. By Mrs. H. R. HAWEIS. Demy 8vo, cloth limp, 2s. 6d.

Clodd. — Myths and Dreams.
By EDWARD CLODD, F.R.A.S., Author of "The Childhood of Religions," &c. Crown 8vo, cloth extra, 5s.

City (The) of Dream: A Poem.
Fcap. 8vo, cloth extra, 6s. [*In the press.*

Cobban.—The Cure of Souls:
A Story. By J. MACLAREN COBBAN. Post 8vo, illustrated boards, 2s.

Collins (C. Allston).—The Bar
Sinister: A Story. By C ALLSTON COLLINS. Post 8vo, illustrated bds., 2s.

Collins (Mortimer & Frances),
Novels by:
Sweet and Twenty. Post 8vo, illustrated boards, 2s.
Frances. Post 8vo, illust. bds., 2s.
Blacksmith and Scholar. Post 8vo, illustrated boards, 2s.; crown 8vo, cloth extra, 3s. 6d.
The Village Comedy. Post 8vo, illust. boards, 2s.; cr. 8vo, cloth extra, 3s. 6d.
You Play Me False. Post 8vo, illust. boards, 2s.; cr. 8vo, cloth extra, 3s. 6d.

Collins (Mortimer), Novels by:
Sweet Anne Page. Post 8vo, illustrated boards, 2s.; crown 8vo, cloth extra, 3s. 6d.
Transmigration. Post 8vo, illust. bds., 2s.; crown 8vo, cloth extra, 3s. 6d.
From Midnight to Midnight. Post 8vo, illustrated boards, 2s.; crown 8vo, cloth extra, 3s. 6d.
A Fight with Fortune. Post 8vo, illustrated boards, 2s.

Collins (Wilkie), Novels by.

Each post 8vo, illustrated boards, 2s; cloth limp, 2s. 6d.; or crown 8vo, cloth extra, Illustrated, **3s. 6d.**

Antonina. Illust. by A. CONCANEN.

Basil. Illustrated by Sir JOHN GILBERT and J. MAHONEY.

Hide and Seek. Illustrated by Sir JOHN GILBERT and J. MAHONEY.

The Dead Secret. Illustrated by Sir JOHN GILBERT and A. CONCANEN.

Queen of Hearts. Illustrated by Sir JOHN GILBERT and A. CONCANEN.

My Miscellanies. With Illustrations by A. CONCANEN, and a Steel-plate Portrait of WILKIE COLLINS.

The Woman in White. With Illustrations by Sir JOHN GILBERT and F. A. FRASER.

The Moonstone. With Illustrations by G. DU MAURIER and F. A. FRASER.

Man and Wife. Illust. by W. SMALL.

Poor Miss Finch. Illustrated by G. DU MAURIER and EDWARD HUGHES.

Miss or Mrs.? With Illustrations by S. L. FILDES and HENRY WOODS.

The New Magdalen. Illustrated by G. DU MAURIER and C. S. RANDS.

The Frozen Deep. Illustrated by G. DU MAURIER and J. MAHONEY.

The Law and the Lady. Illustrated by S. L. FILDES and SYDNEY HALL.

The Two Destinies.

The Haunted Hotel. Illustrated by ARTHUR HOPKINS.

The Fallen Leaves.

Jezebel's Daughter.

The Black Robe.

Heart and Science: A Story of the Present Time.

"I Say No." Crown 8vo, cloth extra, 3s. 6d.   [*Shortly.*

Colman's Humorous Works:

"Broad Grins," "My Nightgown and Slippers," and other Humorous Works, Prose and Poetical, of GEORGE COLMAN. With Life by G. B. BUCKSTONE, and Frontispiece by HOGARTH. Crown 8vo, cloth extra, gilt, **7s. 6d.**

Convalescent Cookery: A

Family Handbook. By CATHERINE RYAN. Crown 8vo, 1s.; cloth, 1s.6d.

Conway (Moncure D.), Works by:

Demonology and Devil-Lore. Two Vols., royal 8vo, with 65 Illusts., 28s.

A Necklace of Stories. Illustrated by W. J. HENNESSY. Square 8vo, cloth extra, 6s.

The Wandering Jew. Crown 8vo, cloth extra, 6s.

Thomas Carlyle: Letters and Recollections. With Illustrations. Crown 8vo, cloth extra, 6s.

Cook (Dutton), Works by:

Hours with the Players. With a Steel Plate Frontispiece. New and Cheaper Edit., cr. 8vo, cloth extra, 6s.

Nights at the Play: A View of the English Stage. New and Cheaper Edition. Crown 8vo, cloth extra, 6s.

Leo: A Novel. Post 8vo, illustrated boards, 2s.

Paul Foster's Daughter. Post 8vo, illustrated boards, 2s.; crown 8vo, cloth extra, 3s. 6d.

Copyright. — A Handbook of

English and Foreign Copyright in Literary and Dramatic Works. By SIDNEY JERROLD, of the Middle Temple, Esq., Barrister-at-Law. Post 8vo, cloth limp, 2s. 6d.

Cornwall.—Popular Romances

of the West of England; or, The Drolls, Traditions, and Superstitions of Old Cornwall. Collected and Edited by ROBERT HUNT, F.R.S. New and Revised Edition, with Additions, and Two Steel-plate Illustrations by GEORGE CRUIKSHANK. Crown 8vo, cloth extra, **7s. 6d.**

Creasy.—Memoirs of Eminent

Etonians: with Notices of the Early History of Eton College. By Sir EDWARD CREASY, Author of "The Fifteen Decisive Battles of the World." Crown 8vo, cloth extra, gilt, with 13 Portraits, **7s. 6d.**

Cruikshank (George):

The Comic Almanack. Complete in TWO SERIES: The FIRST from 1835 to 1843; the SECOND from 1844 to 1853. A Gathering of the BEST HUMOUR of THACKERAY, HOOD, MAYHEW, ALBERT SMITH, A'BECKETT, ROBERT BROUGH, &c. With 2,000 Woodcuts and Steel Engravings by CRUIKSHANK, HINE, LANDELLS, &c. Crown 8vo, cloth gilt, two very thick volumes, 7s. 6d. each.

CRUIKSHANK (G.), *continued*—

The Life of George Cruikshank. By BLANCHARD JERROLD, Author of "The Life of Napoleon III.," &c. With 84 Illustrations. New and Cheaper Edition, enlarged, with Additional Plates, and a very carefully compiled Bibliography. Crown 8vo, cloth extra, 7s. 6d.

Robinson Crusoe. A beautiful reproduction of Major's Edition, with 37 Woodcuts and Two Steel Plates by GEORGE CRUIKSHANK, choicely printed. Crown 8vo, cloth extra, 7s. 6d. A few Large-Paper copies, printed on hand-made paper, with India proofs of the Illustrations, 36s.

Cussans.—Handbook of Heraldry; with Instructions for Tracing Pedigrees and Deciphering Ancient MSS., &c. By JOHN E. CUSSANS. Entirely New and Revised Edition, illustrated with over 400 Woodcuts and Coloured Plates. Crown 8vo, cloth extra, 7s. 6d.

Cyples.—Hearts of Gold: A Novel. By WILLIAM CYPLES. Crown 8vo, cloth extra, 3s. 6d.; post 8vo, illustrated boards, 2s.

Daniel. — Merrie England in the Olden Time. By GEORGE DANIEL. With Illustrations by ROBT. CRUIKSHANK. Crown 8vo, cloth extra, 3s. 6d.

Daudet.—Port Salvation; or, The Evangelist. By ALPHONSE DAUDET. Translated by C. HARRY MELTZER. With Portrait of the Author. Crown 8vo, cloth extra, 3s. 6d.; post 8vo, illust. boards, 2s.

Davenant. — What shall my Son be? Hints for Parents on the Choice of a Profession or Trade for their Sons. By FRANCIS DAVENANT, M.A. Post 8vo, cloth limp, 2s. 6d.

Davies (Dr. N. E.), Works by:
One Thousand Medical Maxims. Crown 8vo, 1s.; cloth, 1s. 6d.
Nursery Hints: A Mother's Guide. Crown 8vo, 1s.; cloth, 1s. 6d.
Aids to Long Life. Crown 8vo, 2s.; cloth limp, 2s. 6d.

Davies' (Sir John) Complete
Poetical Works, including Psalms I. to L. in Verse, and other hitherto Unpublished MSS., for the first time Collected and Edited, with Memorial-Introduction and Notes, by the Rev. A. B. GROSART, D.D. Two Vols., crown 8vo, cloth boards 12s.

De Maistre.—A Journey Round
My Room. By XAVIER DE MAISTRE. Translated by HENRY ATTWELL. Post 8vo, cloth limp, 2s. 6d.

De Mille.—A Castle in Spain.
A Novel. By JAMES DE MILLE. With a Frontispiece. Crown 8vo, cloth extra, 3s. 6d.; post 8vo, illust. bds., 2s.

Derwent (Leith), Novels by:
Crown 8vo, cloth extra, 3s. 6d.; post 8vo, illustrated boards, 2s.
Our Lady of Tears.
Circe's Lovers.

Dickens (Charles), Novels by:
Post 8vo, illustrated boards, 2s. each.

Sketches by Boz.	Nicholas Nickleby.
Pickwick Papers.	Oliver Twist.

The Speeches of Charles Dickens. (*Mayfair Library.*) Post 8vo, cloth limp, 2s. 6d.

The Speeches of Charles Dickens, 1841-1870. With a New Bibliography, revised and enlarged. Edited and Prefaced by RICHARD HERNE SHEPHERD. Crown 8vo, cloth extra, 6s.

About England with Dickens. By ALFRED RIMMER. With 57 Illustrations by C. A. VANDERHOOF, ALFRED RIMMER, and others. Sq. 8vo, cloth extra, 10s. 6d.

Dictionaries:
A Dictionary of Miracles: Imitative, Realistic, and Dogmatic. By the Rev. E. C. BREWER, LL.D. Crown 8vo, cloth extra, 7s. 6d.; hf.-bound, 9s.
The Reader's Handbook of Allusions, References, Plots, and Stories. By the Rev. E. C. BREWER, LL.D. Fourth Edition, revised throughout, with a New Appendix, containing a Complete English Bibliography. Crown 8vo, 1,400 pages, cloth extra, 7s. 6d.
Authors and their Works, with the Dates. Being the Appendices to "The Reader's Handbook," separately printed. By the Rev. E. C. BREWER, LL.D. Crown 8vo, cloth limp, 2s.
Familiar Allusions: A Handbook of Miscellaneous Information; including the Names of Celebrated Statues, Paintings, Palaces, Country Seats, Ruins, Churches, Ships, Streets, Clubs, Natural Curiosities, and the like. By WM. A. WHEELER and CHARLES G. WHEELER. Demy 8vo, cloth extra, 7s. 6d.
Short Sayings of Great Men. With Historical and Explanatory Notes. By SAMUEL A. BENT, M.A. Demy 8vo. cloth extra 7s. 6d.

DICTIONARIES, *continued—*

A Dictionary of the Drama: Being a comprehensive Guide to the Plays, Playwrights, Players, and Playhouses of the United Kingdom and America, from the Earliest to the Present Times. By W. DAVENPORT ADAMS. A thick volume, crown 8vo, half-bound, 12s. 6d.   *[In preparation.*

The Slang Dictionary: Etymological, Historical, and Anecdotal. Crown 8vo, cloth extra, 6s. 6d.

Women of the Day: A Biographical Dictionary. By FRANCES HAYS. Cr. 8vo, cloth extra, 5s.

Words, Facts, and Phrases: A Dictionary of Curious, Quaint, and Out-of-the-Way Matters. By ELIEZER EDWARDS. New and Cheaper Issue. Cr. 8vo, cl. ex., 7s. 6d. ; hf.-bd., 9s.

Diderot.—The Paradox of Acting. Translated, with Annotations, from Diderot's "Le Paradoxe sur le Comédien," by WALTER HERRIES POLLOCK. With a Preface by HENRY IRVING. Cr. 8vo, in parchment, 4s. 6d.

Dobson (W. T.), Works by :

Literary Frivolities, Fancies, Follies, and Frolics. Post 8vo, cl., lp., 2s. 6d.

Poetical Ingenuities and Eccentricities. Post 8vo, cloth limp, 2s. 6d.

Doran. — Memories of our Great Towns; with Anecdotic Gleanings concerning their Worthies and their Oddities. By Dr. JOHN DORAN, F.S.A. With 38 Illustrations. New and Cheaper Ed., cr. 8vo, cl. ex., 7s. 6d.

Drama, A Dictionary of the. Being a comprehensive Guide to the Plays, Playwrights, Players, and Playhouses of the United Kingdom and America, from the Earliest to the Present Times. By W. DAVENPORT ADAMS. (Uniform with BREWER'S "Reader's Handbook.") Crown 8vo, half-bound, 12s. 6d.   *[In preparation.*

Dramatists, The Old. Cr. 8vo, cl. ex., Vignette Portraits, 6s. per Vol.

Ben Jonson's Works. With Notes Critical and Explanatory, and a Biographical Memoir by WM. GIFFORD. Edit. by Col. CUNNINGHAM. 3 Vols.

Chapman's Works. Complete in Three Vols. Vol. I. contains the Plays complete, including doubtful ones; Vol. II., Poems and Minor Translations, with Introductory Essay by A. C. SWINBURNE; Vol. III., Translations of the Iliad and Odyssey.

Marlowe's Works. Including his Translations. Edited, with Notes and Introduction, by Col. CUNNINGHAM. One Vol.

DRAMATISTS, THE OLD, *continued—*

Massinger's Plays. From the Text of WILLIAM GIFFORD. Edited by Col. CUNNINGHAM. One Vol.

Dyer. — The Folk - Lore of Plants. By T. F. THISELTON DYER, M.A., &c. Crown 8vo, cloth extra, 7s. 6d.   *[In preparation.*

Early English Poets. Edited, with Introductions and Annotations, by Rev. A. B. GROSART, D.D. Crown 8vo, cloth boards, 6s. per Volume.

Fletcher's (Giles, B.D.) Complete Poems. One Vol.

Davies' (Sir John) Complete Poetical Works. Two Vols.

Herrick's (Robert) Complete Collected Poems. Three Vols.

Sidney's (Sir Philip) Complete Poetical Works. Three Vols.

Herbert (Lord) of Cherbury's Poems. Edited, with Introduction, by J. CHURTON COLLINS. Crown 8vo, parchment, 8s.

Edwardes (Mrs. A.), Novels by:

A Point of Honour. Post 8vo, illustrated boards, 2s.

Archie Lovell. Post 8vo, illust. bds., 2s. ; crown 8vo, cloth extra, 3s. 6d.

Eggleston.—Roxy: A Novel. By EDWARD EGGLESTON. Post 8vo, illust. boards, 2s. ; cr. 8vo, cloth extra, 3s. 6d.

Emanuel.—On Diamonds and Precious Stones: their History, Value, and Properties ; with Simple Tests for ascertaining their Reality. By HARRY EMANUEL, F.R.G.S. With numerous Illustrations, tinted and plain. Crown 8vo, cloth extra, gilt, 6s.

Englishman's House, The : A Practical Guide to all interested in Selecting or Building a House, with full Estimates of Cost, Quantities, &c. By C. J. RICHARDSON. Third Edition. Nearly 600 Illusts. Cr. 8vo, cl. ex., 7s. 6d.

Ewald (Alex. Charles, F.S.A.), Works by:

Stories from the State Papers. With an Autotype Facsimile. Crown 8vo, cloth extra, 6s.

The Life and Times of Prince Charles Stuart, Count of Albany, commonly called the Young Pretender. From the State Papers and other Sources. New and Cheaper Edition, with a Portrait, crown 8vo, cloth extra, 7s. 6d.

Studies Re-studied: Historical Sketches from Original Sources. Demy 8vo, cloth extra, 12s.

Eyes, The.—How to Use our Eyes, and How to Preserve Them. By JOHN BROWNING, F.R.A.S., &c. With 52 Illustrations. 1s ; cloth, 1s. 6d.

Fairholt.—Tobacco: Its His-tory and Associations; with an Account of the Plant and its Manufacture, and its Modes of Use in all Ages and Countries. By F. W. FAIRHOLT, F.S.A. With Coloured Frontispiece and upwards of 100 Illustrations by the Author. Cr. 8vo. cl ex., 6s.

Familiar Allusions: A Hand-book of Miscellaneous Information; including the Names of Celebrated Statues, Paintings, Palaces, Country Seats, Ruins, Churches, Ships, Streets, Clubs, Natural Curiosities, and the like. By WILLIAM A. WHEELER, Author of " Noted Names of Fiction ;" and CHARLES G. WHEELER. Demy 8vo, cloth extra, 7s. 6d.

Faraday (Michael), Works by :
The Chemical History of a Candle: Lectures delivered before a Juvenile Audience at the Royal Institution. Edited by WILLIAM CROOKES, F.C.S. Post 8vo, cloth extra, with numerous Illustrations, 4s. 6d.
On the Various Forces of Nature, and their Relations to each other: Lectures delivered before a Juvenile Audience at the Royal Institution. Edited by WILLIAM CROOKES, F.C.S. Post 8vo, cloth extra, with numerous Illustrations, 4s. 6d.

Farrer. — Military Manners and Customs. By J. A. FARRER, Author of "Primitive Manners and Customs," &c. Crown 8vo, cloth extra, 6s.

Fin-Bec. — The Cupboard Papers : Observations on the Art of Living and Dining. By FIN-BEC. Post 8vo, cloth limp, 2s. 6d.

Fitzgerald (Percy), Works by :
The Recreations of a Literary Man ; or, Does Writing Pay? With Recollections of some Literary Men, and a View of a Literary Man's Working Life. Cr. 8vo, cloth extra, 6s.
The World Behind the Scenes. Crown 8vo, cloth extra, 3s. 6d.
Little Essays: Passages from the Letters of CHARLES LAMB. Post 8vo, cloth limp, 2s. 6d.

Post 8vo, illustrated boards, 2s. each.
Bella Donna. | Never Forgotten.
The Second Mrs. Tillotson.
Polly.
Seventy-five Brooke Street.
The Lady of Brantome.

Fletcher's (Giles, B.D.) Com-plete Poems: Christ's Victorie in Heaven, Christ's Victorie on Earth, Christ's Triumph over Death, and Minor Poems. With Memorial-Introduction and Notes by the Rev. A. B. GROSART, D.D. Cr. 8vo, cloth bds., 6s.

Fonblanque.—Filthy Lucre : A Novel. By ALBANY DE FONBLANQUE. Post 8vo, illustrated boards, 2s.

Francillon (R. E.), Novels by :
Crown 8vo, cloth extra, 3s. 6d. each ; post 8vo, illust. boards, 2s. each.
Olympia. | Queen Cophetua.
One by One. | A Real Queen.
Esther's Glove. Fcap. 8vo, picture cover, 1s.

French Literature, History of. By HENRY VAN LAUN. Complete in 3 Vols., demy 8vo. cl. bds., 7s. 6d. each.

Frere.—Pandurang Hari ; or, Memoirs of a Hindoo. With a Preface by Sir H. BARTLE FRERE, G.C.S.I., &c. Crown 8vo, cloth extra, 3s. 6d. ; post 8vo, illustrated boards, 2s.

Friswell.—One of Two: A Novel. By HAIN FRISWELL. Post 8vo, illustrated boards, 2s.

Frost (Thomas), Works by :
Crown 8vo, cloth extra, 3s. 6d. each.
Circus Life and Circus Celebrities.
The Lives of the Conjurers.
The Old Showmen and the Old London Fairs.

Fry.—Royal Guide to the Lon-don Charities, 1885-6. By HERBERT FRY. Showing their Name, Date of Foundation, Objects, Income, Officials, &c. Published Annually. Crown 8vo, cloth, 1s. 6d.   [*Shortly.*

Gardening Books:
A Year's Work in Garden and Greenhouse : Practical Advice to Amateur Gardeners as to the Management of the Flower, Fruit, and Frame Garden. By GEORGE GLENNY. Post 8vo, 1s. : cloth, 1s. 6d.
Our Kitchen Garden: The Plants we Grow, and How we Cook Them. By TOM JERROLD. Post 8vo, 1s. ; cloth limp, 1s. 6d.
Household Horticulture: A Gossip about Flowers. By TOM and JANE JERROLD. Illustrated. Post 8vo, 1s. : cloth limp, 1s. 6d.
The Garden that Paid the Rent. By TOM JERROLD. Fcap. 8vo, illustrated cover, 1s. ; cloth limp, 1s. 6d.
My Garden Wild, and What I Grew there. By F. G. HEATH. Crown 8vo, cloth extra, 5s. ; gilt edges, 6s.

Garrett.—The Capel Girls: A Novel. By EDWARD GARRETT. Post 8vo, illust. bds., 2s.; cr. 8vo, cl. ex., 3s. 6d.

Gentleman's Magazine (The) for 1885. One Shilling Monthly. A New Serial Story, entitled "The Unforeseen," by ALICE O'HANLON, begins in the JANUARY Number. "Science Notes," by W. MATTIEU WILLIAMS, F.R.A.S., and "Table Talk," by SYLVANUS URBAN, are also continued monthly.

*** Now ready, the Volume for JULY to DECEMBER, 1884, cloth extra, price 8s. 6d.; Cases for binding, 2s. each.*

German Popular Stories. Collected by the Brothers GRIMM, and Translated by EDGAR TAYLOR. Edited, with an Introduction, by JOHN RUSKIN. With 22 Illustrations on Steel by GEORGE CRUIKSHANK. Square 8vo, cloth extra, 6s. 6d.; gilt edges, 7s. 6d.

Gibbon (Charles), Novels by:
Crown 8vo, cloth extra, 3s. 6d. each; post 8vo, illustrated boards, 2s. each.

Robin Gray.	In Pastures Green
For Lack of Gold.	Braes of Yarrow.
What will the World Say?	The Flower of the Forest.
In Honour Bound.	A Heart's Problem.
In Love and War.	
For the King.	The Golden Shaft.
Queen of the Meadow.	Of High Degree.

Post 8vo, illustrated boards, 2s.
The Dead Heart.

Crown 8vo, cloth extra, 3s. 6d. each.
Fancy Free. | Loving a Dream.

By Mead and Stream. Three Vols., crown 8vo, 31s. 6d.
A Hard Knot. Three Vols., crown 8vo, 31s. 6d.
Heart's Delight. Three Vols., crown 8vo, 31s. 6d. [In the press.

Gilbert (William), Novels by:
Post 8vo, illustrated boards, 2s. each.
Dr. Austin's Guests.
The Wizard of the Mountain.
James Duke, Costermonger.

Gilbert (W. S.), Original Plays by: In Two Series, each complete in itself, price 2s. 6d. each.
The FIRST SERIES contains—The Wicked World—Pygmalion and Galatea—Charity—The Princess—The Palace of Truth—Trial by Jury.
The SECOND SERIES contains—Broken Hearts—Engaged—Sweethearts—Gretchen—Dan'l Druce—Tom Cobb—H.M.S. Pinafore—The Sorcerer—The Pirates of Penzance.

Glenny.—A Year's Work in Garden and Greenhouse: Practical Advice to Amateur Gardeners as to the Management of the Flower, Fruit, and Frame Garden. By GEORGE GLENNY. Post 8vo, 1s.; cloth, 1s. 6d.

Godwin.—Lives of the Necromancers. By WILLIAM GODWIN. Post 8vo, cloth limp, 2s.

Golden Library, The:
Square 16mo (Tauchnitz size), cloth limp, 2s. per volume.
Bayard Taylor's Diversions of the Echo Club.
Bennett's (Dr. W. C.) Ballad History of England.
Bennett's (Dr.) Songs for Sailors.
Byron's Don Juan.
Godwin's (William) Lives of the Necromancers.
Holmes's Autocrat of the Breakfast Table. With an Introduction by G. A. SALA.
Holmes's Professor at the Breakfast Table.
Hood's Whims and Oddities. Complete. All the original Illustrations.
Irving's (Washington) Tales of a Traveller.
Irving's (Washington) Tales of the Alhambra.
Jesse's (Edward) Scenes and Occupations of a Country Life.
Lamb's Essays of Elia. Both Series Complete in One Vol.
Leigh Hunt's Essays: A Tale for a Chimney Corner, and other Pieces. With Portrait, and Introduction by EDMUND OLLIER.
Mallory's (Sir Thomas) Mort d'Arthur: The Stories of King Arthur and of the Knights of the Round Table. Edited by B. MONTGOMERIE RANKING.
Pascal's Provincial Letters. A New Translation, with Historical Introduction and Notes, by T. M'CRIE, D.D.
Pope's Poetical Works. Complete.
Rochefoucauld's Maxims and Moral Reflections. With Notes, and Introductory Essay by SAINTE-BEUVE.
St. Pierre's Paul and Virginia, and The Indian Cottage. Edited, with Life, by the Rev. E. CLARKE.
Shelley's Early Poems, and Queen Mab. With Essay by LEIGH HUNT.
Shelley's Later Poems: Laon and Cythna, &c.
Shelley's Posthumous Poems, the Shelley Papers, &c.

Golden Library, The, *continued—*
Shelley's Prose Works, including A Refutation of Deism, Zastrozzi, St. Irvyne, &c.
White's Natural History of Selborne. Edited, with Additions, by THOMAS BROWN, F.L.S.

Golden Treasury of Thought,
The: An ENCYCLOPÆDIA OF QUOTATIONS from Writers of all Times and Countries. Selected and Edited by THEODORE TAYLOR. Crown 8vo, cloth gilt and gilt edges, 7s. 6d.

Gordon Cumming (C. F.), Works by:
In the Hebrides. With Autotype Facsimile and numerous full-page Illustrations. Demy 8vo, cloth extra, 8s. 6d.
In the Himalayas and on the Indian Plains. With numerous Illustrations. Demy 8vo, cloth extra, 8s. 6d.
Via Cornwall to Egypt. With a Photogravure Frontispiece. Demy 8vo, cloth extra, 7s. 6d.

Graham. — The Professor's
Wife: A Story. By LEONARD GRAHAM. Fcap. 8vo, picture cover, 1s.; cloth extra, 2s. 6d.

Greeks and Romans, The Life
of the, Described from Antique Monuments. By ERNST GUHL and W. KONER. Translated from the Third German Edition, and Edited by Dr. F. HUEFFER. With 545 Illustrations. New and Cheaper Edition, demy 8vo, cloth extra, 7s. 6d.

Greenwood (James), Works by:
The Wilds of London. Crown 8vo, cloth extra, 3s. 6d.
Low-Life Deeps: An Account of the Strange Fish to be Found There. Crown 8vo, cloth extra, 3s. 6d.
Dick Temple: A Novel. Post 8vo, illustrated boards, 2s.

Guyot.—The Earth and Man;
or, Physical Geography in its relation to the History of Mankind. By ARNOLD GUYOT. With Additions by Professors AGASSIZ, PIERCE, and GRAY; 12 Maps and Engravings on Steel, some Coloured, and copious Index. Crown 8vo, cloth extra, gilt, 4s. 6d.

Hair (The): Its Treatment in
Health, Weakness, and Disease. Translated from the German of Dr. J. PINCUS. Crown 8vo, 1s.; cloth, 1s. 6d.

Hake (Dr. Thomas Gordon),
Poems by:
Maiden Ecstasy. Small 4to, cloth extra, 8s.

Hake's (Dr. T. G.) Poems, *continued—*
New Symbols. Cr. 8vo, cloth extra, 6s.
Legends of the Morrow. Crown 8vo, cloth extra, 6s.
The Serpent Play. Crown 8vo, cloth extra, 6s.

Hall.—Sketches of Irish Character. By Mrs. S. C. HALL. With numerous Illustrations on Steel and Wood by MACLISE, GILBERT, HARVEY, and G. CRUIKSHANK. Medium 8vo, cloth extra, gilt, 7s. 6d.

Hall Caine.—The Shadow of a
Crime: A Novel. By HALL CAINE. Cr. 8vo, cloth extra, 3s. 6d.

Halliday.—Every-day Papers.
By ANDREW HALLIDAY. Post 8vo, illustrated boards, 2s.

Handwriting, The Philosophy
of. With over 100 Facsimiles and Explanatory Text. By DON FELIX DE SALAMANCA. Post 8vo, cl. limp, 2s. 6d.

Hanky-Panky: A Collection of
Very Easy Tricks, Very Difficult Tricks, White Magic, Sleight of Hand, &c. Edited by W. H. CREMER. With 200 Illusts. Crown 8vo, cloth extra, 4s. 6d.

Hardy (Lady Duffus). — Paul
Wynter's Sacrifice: A Story. By Lady DUFFUS HARDY. Post 8vo, illust. boards, 2s.

Hardy (Thomas).—Under the
Greenwood Tree. By THOMAS HARDY, Author of "Far from the Madding Crowd." Crown 8vo, cloth extra, 3s. 6d.; post 8vo, illustrated bds., 2s.

Haweis (Mrs. H. R.), Works by:
The Art of Dress. With numerous Illustrations. Small 8vo, illustrated cover, 1s.; cloth limp, 1s. 6d.
The Art of Beauty. New and Cheaper Edition. Crown 8vo, cloth extra, with Coloured Frontispiece and Illustrations, 6s.
The Art of Decoration. Square 8vo, handsomely bound and profusely Illustrated, 10s. 6d.
Chaucer for Children: A Golden Key. With Eight Coloured Pictures and numerous Woodcuts. New Edition, small 4to, cloth extra, 6s.
Chaucer for Schools. Demy 8vo, cloth limp, 2s. 6d.

Haweis (Rev. H. R.).—American
Humorists. Including WASHINGTON IRVING, OLIVER WENDELL HOLMES, JAMES RUSSELL LOWELL, ARTEMUS WARD, MARK TWAIN, and BRET HARTE. By the Rev. H. R. HAWEIS, M.A. Crown 8vo, cloth extra, 6s.

Hawthorne (Julian), Novels by.
Crown 8vo, cloth extra, 3s. 6d. each ; post 8vo, illustrated boards, 2s. each.

Garth.	Sebastian Strome.
Ellice Quentin.	Dust.

Prince Saroni's Wife.
Fortune's Fool.
Beatrix Randolph.

Mrs. Gainsborough's Diamonds. Fcap. 8vo, illustrated cover, 1s. ; cloth extra, 2s. 6d.

Miss Cadogna. Crown 8vo, cloth extra, 3s. 6d. each.

IMPORTANT NEW BIOGRAPHY.

Hawthorne (Nathaniel) and his Wife. By JULIAN HAWTHORNE. With 6 Steel-plate Portraits. Two Vols., crown 8vo, cloth extra, 24s.

[Twenty-five copies of an *Edition de Luxe*, printed on the best hand-made paper, large 8vo size, and with India proofs of the Illustrations, are reserved for sale in England, price 48s. per set. Immediate application should be made by anyone desiring a copy of this special and very limited Edition.]

Hays.—Women of the Day : A Biographical Dictionary of Notable Contemporaries. By FRANCES HAYS. Crown 8vo, cloth extra, 5s.

Heath (F. G.). — My Garden Wild, and What I Grew There. By FRANCIS GEORGE HEATH, Author of "The Fern World," &c. Crown 8vo, cl. ex., 5s. ; cl. gilt, gilt edges, 6s.

Helps (Sir Arthur), Works by :
Animals and their Masters. Post 8vo, cloth limp, 2s. 6d.

Social Pressure. Post 8vo, cloth limp, 2s. 6d.

Ivan de Biron : A Novel. Crown 8vo, cloth extra, 3s. 6d. ; post 8vo, illustrated boards, 2s.

Heptalogia (The); or, The Seven against Sense. A Cap with Seven Bells. Cr. 8vo, cloth extra, 6s.

Herbert.—The Poems of Lord Herbert of Cherbury. Edited, with Introduction, by J. CHURTON COLLINS. Crown 8vo, bound in parchment, 8s.

Herrick's (Robert) Hesperides, Noble Numbers, and Complete Collected Poems. With Memorial-Introduction and Notes by the Rev. A. B. GROSART, D.D., Steel Portrait, Index of First Lines, and Glossarial Index, &c. Three Vols., crown 8vo, cloth, 18s.

Hesse - Wartegg (Chevalier Ernst von), Works by :
Tunis : The Land and the People. With 22 Illustrations. Crown 8vo, cloth extra, 3s. 6d.

The New South-West : Travelling Sketches from Kansas, New Mexico, Arizona, and Northern Mexico. With 100 fine Illustrations and Three Maps. Demy 8vo, cloth extra, 14s. [*In preparation.*

Hindley (Charles), Works by :
Crown 8vo, cloth extra, 3s. 6d. each.

Tavern Anecdotes and Sayings : Including the Origin of Signs, and Reminiscences connected with Taverns, Coffee Houses, Clubs, &c. With Illustrations.

The Life and Adventures of a Cheap Jack. By One of the Fraternity. Edited by CHARLES HINDLEY.

Hoey.—The Lover's Creed. By Mrs. CASHEL HOEY. With 12 Illustrations by P MACNAB. Three Vols., crown 8vo, 31s. 6d.

Holmes (O. Wendell), Works by :

The Autocrat of the Breakfast-Table. Illustrated by J. GORDON THOMSON. Post 8vo, cloth limp, 2s. 6d. ; another Edition in smaller type, with an Introduction by G. A. SALA. Post 8vo, cloth limp, 2s.

The Professor at the Breakfast-Table ; with the Story of Iris. Post 8vo, cloth limp, 2s.

Holmes. — The Science of Voice Production and Voice Preservation: A Popular Manual for the Use of Speakers and Singers. By GORDON HOLMES, M.D. With Illustrations. Crown 8vo, 1s. ; cloth, 1s. 6d.

Hood (Thomas) :

Hood's Choice Works, in Prose and Verse. Including the Cream of the Comic Annuals. With Life of the Author, Portrait, and 200 Illustrations. Crown 8vo, cloth extra, 7s. 6d.

Hood's Whims and Oddities. Complete. With all the original Illustrations. Post 8vo, cloth limp, 2s.

Hood (Tom), Works by :

From Nowhere to the North Pole : A Noah's Arkæological Narrative. With 25 Illustrations by W. BRUNTON and E. C. BARNES. Square crown 8vo, cloth extra, gilt edges, 6s.

A Golden Heart : A Novel. Post 8vo, illustrated boards, 2s.

Hook's (Theodore) Choice Humorous Works, including his Ludicrous Adventures, Bons Mots, Puns and Hoaxes. With a New Life of the Author, Portraits, Facsimiles, and Illusts. Cr. 8vo, cl. extra, gilt, 7s. 6d.

Hooper.—The House of Raby: A Novel. By Mrs. GEORGE HOOPER. Post 8vo, illustrated boards, 2s.

Horne.—Orion: An Epic Poem, in Three Books. By RICHARD HENGIST HORNE. With Photographic Portrait from a Medallion by SUMMERS. Tenth Edition, crown 8vo, cloth extra, 7s.

Howell.—Conflicts of Capital and Labour, Historically and Economically considered: Being a History and Review of the Trade Unions of Great Britain, showing their Origin, Progress, Constitution, and Objects, in their Political, Social, Economical, and Industrial Aspects. By GEORGE HOWELL. Cr. 8vo, cloth extra, 7s. 6d.

Hugo. — The Hunchback of Notre Dame. By VICTOR HUGO. Post 8vo, illustrated boards, 2s.

Hunt.—Essays by Leigh Hunt. A Tale for a Chimney Corner, and other Pieces. With Portrait and Introduction by EDMUND OLLIER. Post 8vo, cloth limp, 2s.

Hunt (Mrs. Alfred), Novels by: Crown 8vo, cloth extra, 3s. 6d. each; post 8vo, illustrated boards, 2s. each.

> Thornicroft's Model.
> The Leaden Casket.
> Self-Condemned.

Ingelow.—Fated to be Free: A Novel. By JEAN INGELOW. Crown 8vo, cloth extra, 3s. 6d.; post 8vo, illustrated boards, 2s.

Irish Wit and Humour, Songs of. Collected and Edited by A. PERCEVAL GRAVES. Post 8vo, cl. limp, 2s. 6d.

Irving (Washington), Works by: Post 8vo, cloth limp, 2s. each.
Tales of a Traveller.
Tales of the Alhambra.

Janvier.—Practical Keramics for Students. By CATHERINE A. JANVIER. Crown 8vo, cloth extra, 6s.

Jay (Harriett), Novels by. Each crown 8vo, cloth extra, 3s. 6d.; or post 8vo, illustrated boards, 2s.
> The Dark Colleen.
> The Queen of Connaught.

Jefferies (Richard), Works by:
Nature near London. Crown 8vo, cloth extra, 6s.
The Life of the Fields. Crown 8vo, cloth extra, 6s.

Jennings (H. J.), Works by:
Curiosities of Criticism. Post 8vo, cloth limp, 2s. 6d.
Lord Tennyson: A Biographical Sketch. With a Photograph-Portrait. Crown 8vo, cloth extra, 6s.

Jennings (Hargrave). — The Rosicrucians: Their Rites and Mysteries. With Chapters on the Ancient Fire and Serpent Worshippers. By HARGRAVE JENNINGS. With Five full-page Plates and upwards of 300 Illustrations. A New Edition, crown 8vo, cloth extra, 7s. 6d.

Jerrold (Tom), Works by:
The Garden that Paid the Rent. By TOM JERROLD. Fcap. 8vo, illustrated cover, 1s.; cloth limp, 1s. 6d.
Household Horticulture: A Gossip about Flowers. By TOM and JANE JERROLD. Illustrated. Post 8vo, 1s.; cloth, 1s. 6d.
Our Kitchen Garden: The Plants we Grow, and How we Cook Them. By TOM JERROLD. Post 8vo, 1s.; cloth limp, 1s. 6d.

Jesse.—Scenes and Occupations of a Country Life. By EDWARD JESSE. Post 8vo, cloth limp, 2s.

Jones (Wm., F.S.A.), Works by:
Finger-Ring Lore: Historical, Legendary, and Anecdotal. With over 200 Illusts. Cr. 8vo, cl. extra, 7s. 6d.
Credulities, Past and Present; including the Sea and Seamen, Miners, Talismans, Word and Letter Divination, Exorcising and Blessing of Animals, Birds, Eggs, Luck, &c. With an Etched Frontispiece. Crown 8vo, cloth extra, 7s. 6d.
Crowns and Coronations: A History of Regalia in all Times and Countries. With One Hundred Illustrations. Cr. 8vo, cloth extra, 7s. 6d.

Jonson's (Ben) Works. With Notes Critical and Explanatory, and a Biographical Memoir by WILLIAM GIFFORD. Edited by Colonel CUNNINGHAM. Three Vols., crown 8vo, cloth extra, 18s.; or separately, 6s. each.

Josephus, The Complete Works of. Translated by WHISTON. Containing both "The Antiquities of the Jews" and "The Wars of the Jews." Two Vols., 8vo, with 52 Illustrations and Maps, cloth extra, gilt, 14s.

Kavanagh.—The Pearl Fountain, and other Fairy Stories. By BRIDGET and JULIA KAVANAGH. With Thirty Illustrations by J. MOYR SMITH. Small 8vo, cloth gilt, 6s.

Kempt.—Pencil and Palette: Chapters on Art and Artists. By ROBERT KEMPT. Post 8vo, cloth limp, 2s. 6d.

Kingsley (Henry), Novels by: Each crown 8vo, cloth extra, 3s. 6d.; or post 8vo, illustrated boards, 2s.

Oakshott Castle. | Number Seventeen

Knight.—The Patient's Vade Mecum: How to get most Benefit from Medical Advice. By WILLIAM KNIGHT, M.R.C.S., and EDWARD KNIGHT, L.R.C.P. Crown 8vo, 1s.; cloth, 1s. 6d.

Lamb (Charles):
Mary and Charles Lamb: Their Poems, Letters, and Remains. With Reminiscences and Notes by W. CAREW HAZLITT. With HANCOCK's Portrait of the Essayist, Facsimiles of the Title-pages of the rare First Editions of Lamb's and Coleridge's Works, and numerous Illustrations. Crown 8vo, cloth extra, 10s. 6d.

Lamb's Complete Works, in Prose and Verse, reprinted from the Original Editions, with many Pieces hitherto unpublished. Edited, with Notes and Introduction, by R. H. SHEPHERD. With Two Portraits and Facsimile of Page of the "Essay on Roast Pig." Cr. 8vo, cloth extra, 7s. 6d.

The Essays of Elia. Complete Edition. Post 8vo, cloth extra, 2s.

Poetry for Children, and Prince Dorus. By CHARLES LAMB. Carefully reprinted from unique copies. Small 8vo, cloth extra, 5s.

Little Essays: Sketches and Characters. By CHARLES LAMB. Selected from his Letters by PERCY FITZGERALD. Post 8vo, cloth limp, 2s. 6d.

Lane's Arabian Nights, &c.:
The Thousand and One Nights: commonly called, in England, "THE ARABIAN NIGHTS' ENTERTAINMENTS." A New Translation from the Arabic, with copious Notes, by EDWARD WILLIAM LANE. Illustrated by many hundred Engravings on Wood, from Original Designs by WM. HARVEY. A New Edition, from a Copy annotated by the Translator, edited by his Nephew, EDWARD STANLEY POOLE. With a Preface by STANLEY LANE-POOLE. Three Vols., demy 8vo, cloth extra, 7s. 6d. each.

LANE'S ARABIAN NIGHTS, *continued*—
Arabian Society in the Middle Ages: Studies from "The Thousand and One Nights." By EDWARD WILLIAM LANE, Author of "The Modern Egyptians," &c. Edited by STANLEY LANE-POOLE. Cr. 8vo, cloth extra, 6s.

Lares and Penates; or, The Background of Life. By FLORENCE CADDY. Crown 8vo, cloth extra, 6s.

Larwood (Jacob), Works by:
The Story of the London Parks. With Illustrations. Crown 8vo, cloth extra, 3s. 6d.

Clerical Anecdotes. Post 8vo, cloth limp, 2s. 6d.

Forensic Anecdotes Post 8vo, cloth limp, 2s. 6d.

Theatrical Anecdotes. Post 8vo, cloth limp, 2s. 6d.

Leigh (Henry S.), Works by:
Carols of Cockayne. With numerous Illustrations. Post 8vo, cloth limp, 2s. 6d.

Jeux d'Esprit. Collected and Edited by HENRY S. LEIGH. Post 8vo, cloth limp, 2s. 6d.

Life in London; or, The History of Jerry Hawthorn and Corinthian Tom. With the whole of CRUIKSHANK's Illustrations, in Colours, after the Originals. Crown 8vo, cloth extra, 7s. 6d.

Linton (E. Lynn), Works by:
Post 8vo, cloth limp, 2s. 6d. each.
Witch Stories.
The True Story of Joshua Davidson.
Ourselves: Essays on Women.

Crown 8vo, cloth extra, 3s. 6d. each; post 8vo, illustrated boards, 2s. each.
Patricia Kemball.
The Atonement of Leam Dundas.
The World Well Lost.
Under which Lord?
With a Silken Thread.
The Rebel of the Family.
"My Love!"
Ione.

Locks and Keys.—On the Development and Distribution of Primitive Locks and Keys. By Lieut.-Gen. PITT-RIVERS, F.R.S. With numerous Illustrations. Demy 4to, half Roxburghe, 16s.

Longfellow:

Longfellow's Complete Prose Works. Including "Outre Mer," "Hyperion," "Kavanagh," "The Poets and Poetry of Europe," and "Driftwood." With Portrait and Illustrations by VALENTINE BROMLEY. Crown 8vo, cloth extra, 7s. 6d.

Longfellow's Poetical Works. Carefully Reprinted from the Original Editions. With numerous fine Illustrations on Steel and Wood. Crown 8vo, cloth extra, 7s. 6d.

Long Life, Aids to: A Medical, Dietetic, and General Guide in Health and Disease. By N. E. DAVIES, L.R.C.P. Crown 8vo, 2s; cloth limp, 2s. 6d.

Lucy.—Gideon Fleyce: A Novel. By HENRY W. LUCY. Crown 8vo, cl. extra, 3s. 6d.; post 8vo, illust. bds., 2s.

Lusiad (The) of Camoens. Translated into English Spenserian Verse by ROBERT FFRENCH DUFF. Demy 8vo, with Fourteen full-page Plates, cloth boards, 18s.

McCarthy (Justin, M.P.), Works by:

A History of Our Own Times, from the Accession of Queen Victoria to the General Election of 1880. Four Vols. demy 8vo, cloth extra, 12s. each.—Also a POPULAR EDITION, in Four Vols. cr. 8vo, cl. extra, 6s. each.

A Short History of Our Own Times. One Vol., crown 8vo, cloth extra, 6s.

History of the Four Georges. Four Vols. demy 8vo, cloth extra, 12s. each. [Vol. I. *now ready.*

Crown 8vo, cloth extra, 3s. 6d. each; post 8vo, illustrated boards, 2s. each.
Dear Lady Disdain.
The Waterdale Neighbours.
My Enemy's Daughter.
A Fair Saxon.
Linley Rochford
Miss Misanthrope.
Donna Quixote.
The Comet of a Season.
Maid of Athens.

McCarthy (Justin H., M.P.), Works by:

An Outline of the History of Ireland, from the Earliest Times to the Present Day. Cr. 8vo, 1s.; cloth, 1s. 6d.

England under Gladstone. Crown 8vo, cloth extra, 6s.

MacDonald (George, LL.D.), Works by:

The Princess and Curdie. With 11 Illustrations by JAMES ALLEN. Small crown 8vo, cloth extra, 5s.

Gutta-Percha Willie, the Working Genius. With 9 Illustrations by ARTHUR HUGHES. Square 8vo, cloth extra, 3s. 6d.

Paul Faber, Surgeon. With a Frontispiece by J. E. MILLAIS. Crown 8vo, cloth extra, 3s. 6d.; post 8vo, illustrated boards, 2s.

Thomas Wingfold, Curate. With a Frontispiece by C. J. STANILAND. Crown 8vo, cloth extra, 3s. 6d.; post 8vo, illustrated boards, 2s.

Macdonell.—Quaker Cousins: A Novel. By AGNES MACDONELL. Crown 8vo, cloth extra, 3s. 6d.; post 8vo, illustrated boards, 2s.

Macgregor. — Pastimes and Players. Notes on Popular Games. By ROBERT MACGREGOR. Post 8vo, cloth limp, 2s. 6d.

Maclise Portrait-Gallery (The) of Illustrious Literary Characters; with Memoirs—Biographical, Critical, Bibliographical, and Anecdotal—illustrative of the Literature of the former half of the Present Century. By WILLIAM BATES, B.A. With 85 Portraits printed on an India Tint. Crown 8vo, cloth extra, 7s. 6d.

Macquoid (Mrs.), Works by:

In the Ardennes. With 50 fine Illustrations by THOMAS R. MACQUOID. Square 8vo, cloth extra, 10s. 6d.

Pictures and Legends from Normandy and Brittany. With numerous Illustrations by THOMAS R. MACQUOID. Square 8vo, cloth gilt, 10s. 6d.

Through Normandy. With 90 Illustrations by T. R. MACQUOID. Square 8vo, cloth extra, 7s. 6d.

Through Brittany. With numerous Illustrations by T. R. MACQUOID. Square 8vo, cloth extra, 7s. 6d.

About Yorkshire. With 67 Illustrations by T. R. MACQUOID, Engraved by SWAIN. Square 8vo, cloth extra, 10s. 6d.

The Evil Eye, and other Stories. Crown 8vo, cloth extra, 3s. 6d.; post 8vo, illustrated boards, 2s.

Lost Rose, and other Stories. Crown 8vo, cloth extra, 3s. 6d.; post 8vo, illustrated boards, 2s.

Mackay.—Interludes and Undertones: or, Music at Twilight. By CHARLES MACKAY, LL.D. Crown 8vo, cloth extra, **6s.**

Magic Lantern (The), and its Management: including Full Practical Directions for producing the Limelight, making Oxygen Gas, and preparing Lantern Slides. By T. C. HEPWORTH. With 10 Illustrations. Crown 8vo, **1s.** ; cloth, **1s. 6d.**

Magician's Own Book (The): Performances with Cups and Balls, Eggs, Hats, Handkerchiefs, &c. All from actual Experience. Edited by W. H. CREMER. With 200 Illustrations. Crown 8vo, cloth extra, **4s. 6d.**

Magic No Mystery: Tricks with Cards, Dice, Balls, &c., with fully descriptive Directions; the Art of Secret Writing; Training of Performing Animals, &c. With Coloured Frontispiece and many Illustrations. Crown 8vo, cloth extra, **4s. 6d.**

Magna Charta. An exact Facsimile of the Original in the British Museum, printed on fine plate paper, 3 feet by 2 feet, with Arms and Seals emblazoned in Gold and Colours. Price **5s.**

Mallock (W. H.), Works by: The New Republic; or, Culture, Faith and Philosophy in an English Country House. Post 8vo, cloth limp, **2s. 6d.** ; Cheap Edition, illustrated boards, **2s.**
The New Paul and Virginia; or, Positivism on an Island. Post 8vo, cloth limp, **2s. 6d.**
Poems. Small 4to, bound in parchment, **8s.**
Is Life worth Living? Crown 8vo, cloth extra, **6s.**

Mallory's (Sir Thomas) Mort d'Arthur: The Stories of King Arthur and of the Knights of the Round Table. Edited by B. MONTGOMERIE RANKING. Post 8vo, cloth limp, **2s.**

Marlowe's Works. Including his Translations. Edited, with Notes and Introduction, by Col. CUNNINGHAM. Crown 8vo, cloth extra, **6s.**

Marryat (Florence), Novels by: Crown 8vo, cloth extra, **3s. 6d.** each; or, post 8vo, illustrated boards, **2s.**
  Open! Sesame!
  Written in Fire.

Post 8vo, illustrated boards, **2s.** each.
  A Harvest of Wild Oats.
  A Little Stepson.
  Fighting the Air.

Masterman.—Half a Dozen Daughters: A Novel. By J. MASTERMAN. Post 8vo, illustrated boards, **2s.**

Mark Twain, Works by: The Choice Works of Mark Twain. Revised and Corrected throughout by the Author. With Life, Portrait, and numerous Illustrations. Crown 8vo, cloth extra, **7s. 6d.**
The Adventures of Tom Sawyer. With 111 Illustrations. Crown 8vo, cloth extra, **7s. 6d.**
⁎ Also a Cheap Edition, post 8vo, illustrated boards, **2s.**
An Idle Excursion, and other Sketches. Post 8vo, illustrated boards, **2s.**
The Prince and the Pauper. With nearly 200 Illustrations. Crown 8vo, cloth extra, **7s. 6d.**
The Innocents Abroad; or, The New Pilgrim's Progress: Being some Account of the Steamship "Quaker City's" Pleasure Excursion to Europe and the Holy Land. With 234 Illustrations. Crown 8vo, cloth extra, **7s. 6d.** CHEAP EDITION (under the title of "MARK TWAIN'S PLEASURE TRIP"), post 8vo, illust. boards, **2s.**
Roughing It, and The Innocents at Home. With 200 Illustrations by F. A. FRASER. Crown 8vo, cloth extra, **7s. 6d.**
The Gilded Age. By MARK TWAIN and CHARLES DUDLEY WARNER. With 212 Illustrations by T. COPPIN. Crown 8vo, cloth extra, **7s. 6d.**
A Tramp Abroad. With 314 Illustrations. Crown 8vo, cloth extra, **7s. 6d.** ; Post 8vo, illustrated boards, **2s.**
The Stolen White Elephant, &c. Crown 8vo, cloth extra, **6s.** ; post 8vo, illustrated boards, **2s.**
Life on the Mississippi. With about 300 Original Illustrations. Crown 8vo, cloth extra, **7s. 6d.**
The Adventures of Huckleberry Finn. With 174 Illustrations by E. W. KEMBLE. Crown 8vo, cloth extra, **7s. 6d.**

Massinger's Plays. From the Text of WILLIAM GIFFORD. Edited by Col. CUNNINGHAM. Crown 8vo, cloth extra, **6s.**

Mayhew.—London Characters and the Humorous Side of London Life. By HENRY MAYHEW. With numerous Illustrations. Crown 8vo, cloth extra, **3s. 6d.**

Mayfair Library, The: Post 8vo, cloth limp, **2s. 6d.** per Volume.
A Journey Round My Room. By XAVIER DE MAISTRE. Translated by HENRY ATTWELL.
Latter-Day Lyrics. Edited by W. DAVENPORT ADAMS.

MAYFAIR LIBRARY, *continued—*

Quips and Quiddities. Selected by W. DAVENPORT ADAMS.

The Agony Column of "The Times," from 1800 to 1870. Edited, with an Introduction, by ALICE CLAY.

Balzac's "Comedie Humaine" and its Author. With Translations by H. H. WALKER.

Melancholy Anatomised: A Popular Abridgment of "Burton's Anatomy of Melancholy."

Gastronomy as a Fine Art. By BRILLAT-SAVARIN.

The Speeches of Charles Dickens.

Literary Frivolities, Fancies, Follies, and Frolics. By W. T. DOBSON.

Poetical Ingenuities and Eccentricities. Selected and Edited by W. T. DOBSON.

The Cupboard Papers. By FIN-BEC.

Original Plays by W. S. GILBERT. FIRST SERIES. Containing: The Wicked World — Pygmalion and Galatea—Charity — The Princess—The Palace of Truth—Trial by Jury.

Original Plays by W. S. GILBERT. SECOND SERIES. Containing: Broken Hearts — Engaged — Sweethearts—Gretchen—Dan'l Druce—Tom Cobb—H.M.S. Pinafore — The Sorcerer —The Pirates of Penzance.

Songs of Irish Wit and Humour. Collected and Edited by A. PERCEVAL GRAVES.

Animals and their Masters. By Sir ARTHUR HELPS.

Social Pressure. By Sir A. HELPS.

Curiosities of Criticism. By HENRY J. JENNINGS.

The Autocrat of the Breakfast-Table. By OLIVER WENDELL HOLMES. Illustrated by J. GORDON THOMSON.

Pencil and Palette. By ROBERT KEMPT.

Little Essays: Sketches and Characters. By CHAS. LAMB. Selected from his Letters by PERCY FITZGERALD.

Clerical Anecdotes. By JACOB LARWOOD.

Forensic Anecdotes; or, Humour and Curiosities of the Law and Men of Law. By JACOB LARWOOD.

Theatrical Anecdotes. By JACOB LARWOOD.

Carols of Cockayne. By HENRY S. LEIGH.

Jeux d'Esprit. Edited by HENRY S. LEIGH.

True History of Joshua Davidson. By E. LYNN LINTON.

Witch Stories. By E. LYNN LINTON.

Ourselves: Essays on Women. By E. LYNN LINTON.

Pastimes and Players. By ROBERT MACGREGOR.

MAYFAIR LIBRARY, *continued—*

The New Paul and Virginia. By W. H. MALLOCK. [LOCK.

The New Republic. By W. H. MAL-

Puck on Pegasus. By H. CHOLMONDE-LEY-PENNELL.

Pegasus Re-Saddled. By H. CHOLMONDELEY-PENNELL. Illustrated by GEORGE DU MAURIER.

Muses of Mayfair. Edited by H. CHOLMONDELEY-PENNELL.

Thoreau: His Life and Aims. By H. A. PAGE.

Puniana. By the Hon. HUGH ROWLEY.

More Puniana. By the Hon. HUGH ROWLEY.

The Philosophy of Handwriting. By DON FELIX DE SALAMANCA.

By Stream and Sea. By WILLIAM SENIOR. [THORNBURY.

Old Stories Retold. By WALTER

Leaves from a Naturalist's Note-Book. By Dr. ANDREW WILSON.

Medicine, Family.—One Thousand Medical Maxims and Surgical Hints, for Infancy, Adult Life, Middle Age, and Old Age. By N. E. DAVIES, L.R.C.P. Lond. Cr. 8vo, 1s.; cl., 1s. 6d.

Merry Circle (The): A Book of New Intellectual Games and Amusements. By CLARA BELLEW. With numerous Illustrations. Crown 8vo, cloth extra, 4s. 6d.

Mexican Mustang (On a). Through Texas, from the Gulf to the Rio Grande. A New Book of American Humour. By ALEX. E. SWEET and J. ARMOY KNOX, Editors of "Texas Siftings." 265 Illusts. Cr. 8vo, cloth extra, 7s. 6d.

Middlemass (Jean), Novels by:

Touch and Go. Crown 8vo, cloth extra, 3s. 6d.; post 8vo, illust. bds., 2s.

Mr. Dorillion. Post 8vo, illust. bds., 2s.

Miller. — Physiology for the Young; or, The House of Life: Human Physiology, with its application to the Preservation of Health. For use in Classes and Popular Reading. With numerous Illustrations. By Mrs. F. FENWICK MILLER. Small 8vo, cloth limp, 2s. 6d.

Milton (J. L.), Works by:

The Hygiene of the Skin. A Concise Set of Rules for the Management of the Skin; with Directions for Diet, Wines, Soaps, Baths, &c. Small 8vo, 1s.; cloth extra, 1s. 6d.

The Bath in Diseases of the Skin. Small 8vo, 1s.; cloth extra, 1s. 6d.

The Laws of Life, and their Relation to Diseases of the Skin. Small 8vo, 1s.; cloth extra, 1s. 6d.

Moncrieff. — The Abdication; or, Time Tries All. An Historical Drama. By W. D. SCOTT-MONCRIEFF. With Seven Etchings by JOHN PETTIE, R.A., W. Q. ORCHARDSON, R.A., J. MACWHIRTER, A.R.A., COLIN HUNTER, R. MACBETH, and TOM GRAHAM. Large 4to, bound in buckram, 21s.

Murray (D. Christie), Novels by. Crown 8vo, cloth extra, 3s. 6d. each; post 8vo, illustrated boards, 2s. each.
A Life's Atonement.
A Model Father.
Joseph's Coat.
Coals of Fire.
By the Gate of the Sea.
Val Strange.
Hearts.

Crown 8vo, cloth extra, 3s. 6d. each.
The Way of the World.
A Bit of Human Nature.

North Italian Folk. By Mrs. COMYNS CARR. Illust. by RANDOLPH CALDECOTT. Square 8vo, cloth extra, 7s. 6d.

Number Nip (Stories about), the Spirit of the Giant Mountains. Retold for Children by WALTER GRAHAME. With Illustrations by J. MOYR SMITH. Post 8vo, cloth extra, 5s.

Nursery Hints: A Mother's Guide in Health and Disease. By N. E. DAVIES, L.R.C.P. Crown 8vo, 1s.; cloth, 1s. 6d.

Oliphant. — Whiteladies: A Novel. With Illustrations by ARTHUR HOPKINS and HENRY WOODS. Crown 8vo, cloth extra, 3s. 6d.; post 8vo, illustrated boards, 2s.

O'Connor.—Lord Beaconsfield A Biography. By T. P. O'CONNOR, M.P. Sixth Edition, with a New Preface, bringing the work down to the Death of Lord Beaconsfield. Crown 8vo, cloth extra, 7s. 6d.

O'Reilly.—Phœbe's Fortunes: A Novel. With Illustrations by HENRY TUCK. Post 8vo, illustrated boards, 2s.

O'Shaughnessy (Arth.), Works by:
Songs of a Worker. Fcap. 8vo, cloth extra, 7s. 6d.
Music and Moonlight. Fcap. 8vo, cloth extra, 7s. 6d.
Lays of France. Crown 8vo, cloth extra, 10s. 6d.

Ouida, Novels by. Crown 8vo, cloth extra, 5s. each; post 8vo, illustrated boards, 2s. each.

Held in Bondage.	Pascarel.
Strathmore.	Signa.
Chandos.	In a Winter City
Under Two Flags.	Ariadne.
Cecil Castlemaine's Gage.	Friendship.
	Moths.
Idalia.	Pipistrello.
Tricotrin.	A Village Commune.
Puck.	
Folle Farine.	Bimbi.
TwoLittleWooden Shoes.	In Maremma.
	Wanda.
A Dog of Flanders.	Frescoes.

Bimbi: PRESENTATION EDITION. Sq. 8vo, cloth gilt, cinnamon edges, 7s. 6d.

Princess Napraxine. New and Cheaper Edition. Crown 8vo, cloth extra, 5s.

Wisdom, Wit, and Pathos. Selected from the Works of OUIDA by F. SYDNEY MORRIS. Small crown 8vo, cloth extra, 5s.

Page (H. A.), Works by:
Thoreau: His Life and Aims: A Study. With a Portrait. Post 8vo, cloth limp, 2s. 6d.
Lights on the Way: Some Tales within a Tale. By the late J. H. ALEXANDER, B.A. Edited by H. A. PAGE Crown 8vo, cloth extra, 6s.

Pascal's Provincial Letters. A New Translation, with Historical Introduction and Notes, by T. M'CRIE, D.D. Post 8vo, cloth limp, 2s.

Patient's (The) Vade Mecum: How to get most Benefit from Medical Advice. By WILLIAM KNIGHT, M.R.C.S., and EDWARD KNIGHT, L.R.C.P. Crown 8vo, 1s.; cloth, 1s. 6d.

Paul Ferroll:
Post 8vo, illustrated boards, 2s. each.
Paul Ferroll: A Novel.
Why Paul Ferroll Killed his Wife.

Paul.—Gentle and Simple. By MARGARET AGNES PAUL. With a Frontispiece by HELEN PATERSON. Cr. 8vo, cloth extra, 3s. 6d.; post 8vo, illustrated boards, 2s.

Payn (James), Novels by.
Crown 8vo, cloth extra, 3s. 6d. each;
post 8vo, illustrated boards, 2s. each.
Lost Sir Massingberd.
The Best of Husbands.
Walter's Word.
Halves. | Fallen Fortunes.
What He Cost Her.
Less Black than we're Painted.
By Proxy. | High Spirits.
Under One Roof. | Carlyon's Year.
A Confidential Agent.
Some Private Views.
A Grape from a Thorn.
For Cash Only. | From Exile.

Post 8vo, illustrated boards, 2s. each.
A Perfect Treasure.
Bentinck's Tutor.
Murphy's Master.
A County Family.
At Her Mercy.
A Woman's Vengeance.
Cecil's Tryst.
The Clyffards of Clyffe.
The Family Scapegrace
The Foster Brothers.
Found Dead.
Gwendoline's Harvest.
Humorous Stories.
Like Father, Like Son.
A Marine Residence.
Married Beneath Him.
Mirk Abbey.
Not Wooed, but Won.
Two Hundred Pounds Reward.
Kit: A Memory.
The Canon's Ward.

In Peril and Privation: A Book for
Boys.   With numerous Illustrations. Crown 8vo, 6s.   [*Preparing.*

Pennell (H. Cholmondeley),
Works by: Post 8vo, cloth limp,
2s. 6d. each.
Puck on Pegasus. With Illustrations.
The Muses of Mayfair.   Vers de
Société, Selected and Edited by H.
C. Pennell.
Pegasus Re-Saddled. With Ten full-
page Illusts. by G. Du Maurier.

Phelps.—Beyond the Gates.
By Elizabeth Stuart Phelps,
Author of "The Gates Ajar." Crown
8vo, cloth extra, 2s. 6d.

Pirkis (Mrs. C. L.) Novels by:
Trooping with Crows. Fcap. 8vo
picture cover, 1s.
Lady Lovelace. Three Vols., cr. 8vo,
31s. 6d.

Planche (J. R.), Works by:
The Cyclopædia of Costume; or,
A Dictionary of Dress—Regal, Ec-
clesiastical, Civil, and Military—from
the Earliest Period in England to the
Reign of George the Third. Including Notices of Contemporaneous
Fashions on the Continent, and a
General History of the Costumes of
the Principal Countries of Europe.
Two Vols., demy 4to, half morocco
profusely Illustrated with Coloured
and Plain Plates and Woodcuts,
£7 7s. The Vols. may also be had
separately (each complete in itself)
at £3 13s. 6d. each : Vol. I. The
Dictionary. Vol. II. A General
History of Costume in Europe.
The Pursuivant of Arms; or, Her-
aldry Founded upon Facts. With
Coloured Frontispiece and 200 Illus-
trations. Cr. 8vo, cloth extra, 7s. 6d.
Songs and Poems, from 1819 to 1879.
Edited, with an Introduction, by his
Daughter, Mrs. Mackarness. Crown
8vo, cloth extra, 6s.

Play-time: Sayings and Doings
of Baby-land. By E. Stanford. Large
4to, handsomely printed in Colours, 5s.

Plutarch's Lives of Illustrious
Men.   Translated from the Greek,
with Notes Critical and Historical, and
a Life of Plutarch, by John and
William Langhorne. Two Vols.,
8vo, cloth extra, with Portraits, 10s. 6d.

Poe (Edgar Allan):—
The Choice Works, in Prose and
Poetry, of Edgar Allan Poe. With
an Introductory Essay by Charles
Baudelaire, Portrait and Fac-
similes. Crown 8vo, cl. extra, 7s. 6d.
The Mystery of Marie Roget, and
other Stories. Post 8vo, illust. bds., 2s.

Pope's Poetical Works. Complete in One Vol. Post 8vo, cl. limp, 2s.

Power.—Philistia: A Novel. By
Cecil Power. Three Vols., cr. 8vo,
31s. 6d.

Price (E. C.), Novels by:
Crown 8vo, cloth extra, 3s. 6d.; post
8vo, illustrated boards, 2s.
Valentina. | The Foreigners.
Mrs. Lancaster's Rival.

Gerald. Three Vols., cr. 8vo, 31s. 6d.

Proctor (Richd. A.), Works by :

Flowers of the Sky. With 55 Illusts. Small crown 8vo, cloth extra, 4s. 6d.

Easy Star Lessons. With Star Maps for Every Night in the Year, Drawings of the Constellations, &c. Crown 8vo, cloth extra, 6s.

Familiar Science Studies. Crown 8vo, cloth extra, 7s. 6d.

Rough Ways made Smooth: A Series of Familiar Essays on Scientific Subjects. Cr. 8vo, cloth extra, 6s.

Our Place among Infinities: A Series of Essays contrasting our Little Abode in Space and Time with the Infinities Around us. Crown 8vo, cloth extra, 6s.

The Expanse of Heaven: A Series of Essays on the Wonders of the Firmament. Cr. 8vo, cloth extra, 6s.

Saturn and its System. New and Revised Edition, with 13 Steel Plates. Demy 8vo, cloth extra, 10s. 6d.

The Great Pyramid: Observatory, Tomb, and Temple. With Illustrations. Crown 8vo, cloth extra, 6s.

Mysteries of Time and Space. With Illusts. Cr. 8vo, cloth extra, 7s. 6d.

The Universe of Suns, and other Science Gleanings. With numerous Illusts. Cr. 8vo, cloth extra, 7s. 6d.

Wages and Wants of Science Workers. Crown 8vo, 1s. 6d.

Pyrotechnist's Treasury (The);

or, Complete Art of Making Fireworks. By THOMAS KENTISH. With numerous Illustrations. Cr. 8vo, cl. extra, 4s. 6d.

Rabelais' Works.

Faithfully Translated from the French, with variorum Notes, and numerous characteristic Illustrations by GUSTAVE DORÉ. Crown 8vo, cloth extra, 7s. 6d.

Rambosson.—Popular Astronomy.

By J. RAMBOSSON, Laureate of the Institute of France. Translated by C. B. PITMAN. Crown 8vo, cloth gilt, with numerous Illustrations, and a beautifully executed Chart of Spectra, 7s. 6d.

Reader's Handbook (The) of

Allusions, References, Plots, and Stories. By the Rev. Dr. BREWER. Fourth Edition, revised throughout, with a New Appendix, containing a COMPLETE ENGLISH BIBLIOGRAPHY. Cr. 8vo, 1,400 pages, cloth extra, 7s. 6d.

Richardson. — A Ministry of

Health, and other Papers. By BENJAMIN WARD RICHARDSON, M.D., &c. Crown 8vo, cloth extra, 6s.

Reade (Charles, D.C.L.), Novels

by. Post 8vo, illust., bds., 2s. each ; or cr. 8vo, cl. ex., illust..3s. 6d. each.

Peg Woffington. Illustrated by S. L. FILDES, A.R.A.

Christie Johnstone. Illustrated by WILLIAM SMALL.

It Is Never Too Late to Mend. Illustrated by G. J. PINWELL.

The Course of True Love Never did run Smooth. Illustrated by HELEN PATERSON

The Autobiography of a Thief; Jack of all Trades; and James Lambert. Illustrated by MATT STRETCH.

Love me Little, Love me Long. Illustrated by M. ELLEN EDWARDS.

The Double Marriage. Illust. by Sir JOHN GILBERT, R.A., and C. KEENE.

The Cloister and the Hearth. Illustrated by CHARLES KEENE.

Hard Cash. Illust. by F. W. LAWSON.

Griffith Gaunt. Illustrated by S. L. FILDES, A.R.A., and WM. SMALL.

Foul Play. Illust. by DU MAURIER.

Put Yourself in His Place. Illustrated by ROBERT BARNES.

A Terrible Temptation. Illustrated by EDW. HUGHES and A. W. COOPER.

The Wandering Heir. Illustrated by H. PATERSON, S. L. FILDES, A.R.A., C. GREEN, and H WOODS, A.R.A.

A Simpleton. Illustrated by KATE CRAUFORD.

A Woman-Hater. Illustrated by THOS. COULDERY.

Readiana. With a Steel-plate Portrait of CHARLES READE.

Singleheart and Doubleface: A Matter-of-fact Romance. Illustrated by P. MACNAB.

Good Stories of Men and other Animals. Illustrated by E. A. ABBEY, PERCY MACQUOID, and JOSEPH NASH.

The Jilt, and other Stories. Illustrated by JOSEPH NASH.

Riddell (Mrs. J. H.), Novels by:

Crown 8vo, cloth extra, 3s. 6d. each ; post 8vo, illustrated boards, 2s. each.

Her Mother's Darling.

The Prince of Wales's Garden Party.

Weird Stories.

The Uninhabited House.

Fairy Water.

Rimmer (Alfred), Works by :

Our Old Country Towns. With over 50 Illusts. Sq. 8vo, cloth gilt, 10s. 6d.

Rambles Round Eton and Harrow. 50 Illusts. Sq. 8vo, cloth gilt, 10s. 6d.

About England with Dickens. With 58 Illusts. by ALFRED RIMMER and C. A. VANDERHOOF. Sq. 8vo, cl. gilt, 10s. 6d

Robinson (F. W.), Novels by:

Crown 8vo, cloth extra, 3s. 6d. ; post 8vo, illustrated boards, 2s.

Women are Strange.
The Hands of Justice.

Robinson (Phil), Works by:

The Poets' Birds. Crown 8vo, cloth extra, 7s. 6d.
The Poets' Beasts. Crown 8vo, cloth extra, 7s. 6d.

Robinson Crusoe: A beautiful

reproduction of Major's Edition, with 37 Woodcuts and Two Steel Plates by GEORGE CRUIKSHANK, choicely printed. Crown 8vo, cloth extra, 7s. 6d. A few Large-Paper copies, printed on hand-made paper, with India proofs of the Illustrations, price 36s.

Rochefoucauld's Maxims and

Moral Reflections. With Notes, and an Introductory Essay by SAINTE-BEUVE. Post 8vo, cloth limp, 2s.

Roll of Battle Abbey, The ; or,

A List of the Principal Warriors who came over from Normandy with William the Conqueror, and Settled in this Country, A.D. 1066-7. With the principal Arms emblazoned in Gold and Colours. Handsomely printed, 5s.

Rowley (Hon. Hugh), Works by:

Post 8vo, cloth limp, 2s. 6d. each.

Puniana: Riddles and Jokes. With numerous Illustrations.

More Puniana. Profusely Illustrated.

Russell (W. Clark), Works by:

Round the Galley-Fire. Crown 8vo, cloth extra, 6s. ; post 8vo, illustrated boards, 2s.
On the Fo'k'sle Head: A Collection of Yarns and Sea Descriptions. Crown 8vo, cloth extra, 6s.

Sala.—Gaslight and Daylight.

By GEORGE AUGUSTUS SALA. Post 8vo, illustrated boards, 2s.

Sanson.—Seven Generations

of Executioners: Memoirs of the Sanson Family (1688 to 1847). Edited by HENRY SANSON. Cr. 8vo, cl. ex. 3s. 6d.

Saunders (John), Novels by:

Crown 8vo, cloth extra, 3s. 6d. each ; post 8vo, illustrated boards, 2s. each.

Bound to the Wheel.
One Against the World.
Guy Waterman.
The Lion in the Path.
The Two Dreamers.

Saunders (Katharine), Novels by :

Crown 8vo, cloth extra, 3s. 6d. each; post 8vo, illustrated boards, 2s. each.
Joan Merryweather.
Margaret and Elizabeth.
Gideon's Rock.
The High Mills.

Crown 8vo, cloth extra, 3s. 6d. each.
Heart Salvage. | Sebastian.

Science Gossip: An Illustrated

Medium of Interchange for Students and Lovers of Nature. Edited by J. E. TAYLOR, F.L.S., &c. Devoted to Geology, Botany, Physiology, Chemistry, Zoology, Microscopy, Telescopy, Physiography, &c. Price 4d. Monthly ; or 5s. per year, post free. Each Number contains a Coloured Plate and numerous Woodcuts. Vols. I. to XIV. may be had at 7s. 6d. each ; and Vols. XV. to XX. (1884), at 5s. each. Cases for Binding, 1s. 6d. each.

Scott's (Sir Walter) Marmion.

An entirely New Edition of this famous and popular Poem, with over 100 new Illustrations by leading Artists. Elegantly and appropriately bound, small 4to, cloth extra, 16s.

[The immediate success of "The Lady of the Lake," published in 1882, has encouraged Messrs. CHATTO and WINDUS to bring out a Companion Edition of this not less popular and famous poem. Produced in the same form, and with the same careful and elaborate style of illustration, regardless of cost, Mr. Anthony's skilful supervision is sufficient guarantee that the work is elegant and tasteful as well as correct.]

"Secret Out" Series, The

Crown 8vo, cloth extra, profusely Illustrated, 4s. 6d. each.

The Secret Out: One Thousand Tricks with Cards, and other Recreations; with Entertaining Experiments in Drawing-room or "White Magic." By W. H. CREMER. 300 Engravings.

The Pyrotechnist's Treasury; or, Complete Art of Making Fireworks. By THOMAS KENTISH. With numerous Illustrations.

The Art of Amusing: A Collection of Graceful Arts, Games, Tricks, Puzzles, and Charades. By FRANK BELLEW. With 300 Illustrations.

Hanky-Panky: Very Easy Tricks, Very Difficult Tricks, White Magic, Sleight of Hand. Edited by W. H. CREMER. With 200 Illustrations.

SECRET OUT " SERIES, *continued*—

The Merry Circle: A Book of New Intellectual Games and Amusements. By CLARA BELLEW. With many Illustrations.

Magician's Own Book: Performances with Cups and Balls, Eggs, Hats, Handkerchiefs, &c. All from actual Experience. Edited by W. H. CREMER. 200 Illustrations.

Magic No Mystery: Tricks with Cards, Dice, Balls, &c., with fully descriptive Directions; the Art of Secret Writing; Training of Performing Animals, &c. With Coloured Frontis. and many Illusts.

Senior (William). Works by :

Travel and Trout in the Antipodes. Crown 8vo, cloth extra, 6s.

By Stream and Sea. Post 8vo, cloth limp, 2s. 6d.

Seven Sagas (The) of Prehistoric Man. By JAMES H. STODDART, Author of " The Village Life." Crown 8vo, cloth extra, 6s.

Shakespeare :

The First Folio Shakespeare.—MR. WILLIAM SHAKESPEARE'S Comedies, Histories, and Tragedies. Published according to the true Originall Copies. London, Printed by ISAAC IAGGARD and ED. BLOUNT. 1623.—A Reproduction of the extremely rare original, in reduced facsimile, by a photographic process—ensuring the strictest accuracy in every detail. Small 8vo, half-Roxburghe, 7s. 6d.

The Lansdowne Shakespeare. Beautifully printed in red and black, in small but very clear type. With engraved facsimile of DROESHOUT'S Portrait. Post 8vo, cloth extra, 7s. 6d.

Shakespeare for Children: Tales from Shakespeare. By CHARLES and MARY LAMB. With numerous Illustrations, coloured and plain, by J. MOYR SMITH. Cr. 4to, cl. gilt, 6s.

The Handbook of Shakespeare Music. Being an Account of 350 Pieces of Music, set to Words taken from the Plays and Poems of Shakespeare, the compositions ranging from the Elizabethan Age to the Present Time. By ALFRED ROFFE. 4to, half-Roxburghe, 7s.

A Study of Shakespeare. By ALGERNON CHARLES SWINBURNE. Crown 8vo, cloth extra, 8s.

The Dramatic Works of Shakespeare: The Text of the First Edition, carefully reprinted. Eight Vols., demy 8vo, cloth boards, 40s.

*** Only 250 Sets have been printed, each one numbered. The volumes will not be sold separately.

Shelley's Complete Works, in Four Vols., post 8vo, cloth limp, 8s.; or separately, 2s. each. Vol. I. contains his Early Poems, Queen Mab, &c., with an Introduction by LEIGH HUNT; Vol. II., his Later Poems, Laon and Cythna, &c.; Vol. III., Posthumous Poems, the Shelley Papers, &c.; Vol. IV., his Prose Works, including A Refutation of Deism, Zastrozzi, St. Irvyne, &c.

Sheridan :—

Sheridan's Complete Works, with Life and Anecdotes. Including his Dramatic Writings, printed from the Original Editions, his Works in Prose and Poetry, Translations, Speeches, Jokes, Puns, &c. With a Collection of Sheridaniana. Crown 8vo, cloth extra, gilt, with 10 full-page Tinted Illustrations, 7s. 6d.

Sheridan's Comedies: The Rivals, and The School for Scandal. Edited, with an Introduction and Notes to each Play, and a Biographical Sketch of Sheridan, by BRANDER MATTHEWS. With Decorative Vignettes and 10 full-page Illusts. Demy 8vo, half-parchment, 12s. 6d.

Short Sayings of Great Men. With Historical and Explanatory Notes by SAMUEL A. BENT, M.A. Demy 8vo, cloth extra, 7s. 6d.

Sidney's (Sir Philip) Complete Poetical Works, including all those in " Arcadia." With Portrait, Memorial-Introduction, Notes, &c., by the Rev. A. B. GROSART, D.D. Three Vols., crown 8vo, cloth boards, 18s.

Signboards : Their History. With Anecdotes of Famous Taverns and Remarkable Characters. By JACOB LARWOOD and JOHN CAMDEN HOTTEN. Crown 8vo, cloth extra, with 100 Illustrations, 7s. 6d.

Sims (George R.), Works by :

How the Poor Live. With 60 Illusts. by FRED. BARNARD. Large 4to, 1s.

Rogues and Vagabonds. Post 8vo, illustrated boards, 2s.

Sketchley.—A Match in the Dark. By ARTHUR SKETCHLEY. Post 8vo, illustrated boards, 2s.

Slang Dictionary, The : Etymological, Historical, and Anecdotal. Crown 8vo, cloth extra, gilt, 6s. 6d.

Smith (J. Moyr), Works by :

The Prince of Argolis: A Story of the Old Greek Fairy Time. By J. MOYR SMITH. Small 8vo, cloth extra, with 130 Illustrations, 3s. 6d.

SMITH'S (J. MOYR) WORKS, *continued—*

Tales of Old Thule. Collected and Illustrated by J. MOYR SMITH. Cr. 8vo, cloth gilt, profusely Illust., 6s.

The Wooing of the Water Witch: A Northern Oddity. By EVAN DAL-DORNE. Illustrated by J. MOYR SMITH. Small 8vo, cloth extra, 6s.

Society in London. By a FOREIGN RESIDENT. Fourth Edition. Crown 8vo, cloth extra, 6s.

Spalding.—Elizabethan Demon-ology: An Essay in Illustration of the Belief in the Existence of Devils, and the Powers possessed by Them. By T. ALFRED SPALDING, LL.B. Crown 8vo, cloth extra, 5s.

Spanish Legendary Tales. By S. G. E. MIDDLEMORE, Author of "Round a Posado Fire." Crown 8vo, cloth extra, 6s. [*In the press.*

Speight. — The Mysteries of Heron Dyke. By T. W. SPEIGHT. With a Frontispiece by M. ELLEN EDWARDS. Crown 8vo, cloth extra, 3s. 6d. ; post 8vo, illustrated boards, 2s.

Spenser for Children. By M. H. TOWRY. With Illustrations by WALTER J. MORGAN. Crown 4to, with Coloured Illustrations, cloth gilt, 6s.

Staunton.—Laws and Practice of Chess; Together with an Analysis of the Openings, and a Treatise on End Games. By HOWARD STAUNTON. Edited by ROBERT B. WORMALD. New Edition, small cr. 8vo, cloth extra, 5s.

Sterndale.—The Afghan Knife: A Novel. By ROBERT ARMITAGE STERN-DALE. Cr. 8vo, cloth extra, 3s. 6d.; post 8vo, illustrated boards, 2s.

Stevenson (R. Louis), Works by:

Travels with a Donkey In the Cevennes. Frontispiece by WALTER CRANE. Post 8vo, cloth limp, 2s. 6d.

An Inland Voyage. With Front. by W. CRANE. Post 8vo, cl. lp., 2s. 6d.

Virginibus Puerisque, and other Papers. Crown 8vo, cloth extra, 6s.

Familiar Studies of Men and Books. Crown 8vo, cloth extra, 6s.

New Arabian Nights. Crown 8vo, cl. extra, 6s.; post 8vo, illust. bds., 2s.

The Silverado Squatters. With Frontispiece. Cr. 8vo, cloth extra, 6s.

Prince Otto: A Romance. Crown 8vo, cloth extra, 6s. [*In preparation.*

St. John.—A Levantine Family. By BAYLE ST. JOHN. Post 8vo, illus-trated boards, 2s.

Stoddard.—Summer Cruising In the South Seas. By CHARLES WARREN STODDARD. Illust. by WALLIS MACKAY. Crown 8vo, cl. extra, 3s 6d.

St. Pierre.—Paul and Virginia, and The Indian Cottage. By BER-NARDIN ST. PIERRE. Edited, with Life, by Rev. E. CLARKE. Post 8vo, cl. lp., 2s.

Stories from Foreign Novel-ists. With Notices of their Lives and Writings. By HELEN and ALICE ZIM-MERN; and a Frontispiece. Crown 8vo, cloth extra, 3s. 6d.

Strutt's Sports and Pastimes of the People of England; including the Rural and Domestic Recreations, May Games, Mummeries, Shows, Pro-cessions, Pageants, and Pompous Spectacles, from the Earliest Period to the Present Time. With 140 Illus-trations. Edited by WILLIAM HONE. Crown 8vo, cloth extra, 7s. 6d.

Suburban Homes (The) of London: A Residential Guide to Favourite London Localities, their Society, Celebrities, and Associations. With Notes on their Rental, Rates, and House Accommodation. With Map of Suburban London. Cr. 8vo, cl. ex., 7s. 6d.

Swift's Choice Works, in Prose and Verse. With Memoir, Portrait, and Facsimiles of the Maps in the Original Edition of "Gulliver's Travels." Cr. 8vo, cloth extra, 7s. 6d.

Swinburne (Algernon C.), Works by:

The Queen Mother and Rosamond. Fcap. 8vo, 5s.

Atalanta In Calydon. Crown 8vo, 6s.

Chastelard. A Tragedy. Cr. 8vo, 7s.

Poems and Ballads. FIRST SERIES. Fcap. 8vo, 9s. Also in crown 8vo, at same price.

Poems and Ballads. SECOND SERIES. Fcap. 8vo, 9s. Cr. 8vo, same price.

Notes on Poems and Reviews. 8vo, 1s.

William Blake: A Critical Essay. With Facsimile Paintings. Demy 8vo, 16s.

Songs before Sunrise. Cr. 8vo, 10s. 6d.

Bothwell: A Tragedy. Cr. 8vo, 12s. 6d.

George Chapman: An Essay. Crown 8vo, 7s.

Songs of Two Nations. Cr. 8vo, 6s.

Essays and Studies. Crown 8vo, 12s.

Erechtheus: A Tragedy. Cr. 8vo, 6s.

Note of an English Republican on the Muscovite Crusade. 8vo, 1s.

A Note on Charlotte Bronte. Crown 8vo, 6s.

A Study of Shakespeare. Cr. 8vo, 8s.

Songs of the Springtides. Cr. 8vo, 6s.

Studies In Song. Crown 8vo, 7s.

SWINBURNE (ALGERNON C.) WORKS, *con.*
Mary Stuart : A Tragedy. Cr. 8vo, 8s.
Tristram of Lyonesse, and other
Poems. Crown 8vo, 9s.
A Century of Roundels. Small 4to,
cloth extra, 8s.
A Midsummer Holiday, and other
Poems. Crown 8vo, cloth extra, 7s.
Marino Faliero : A Tragedy. Crown
8vo, cloth extra, 6s.

Symonds.—Wine, Women and
Song : Mediæval Latin Students'
Songs. Now first translated into Eng-
lish Verse, with an Essay by J. AD-
DINGTON SYMONDS. Small 8vo, parch-
ment, 6s.

Syntax's (Dr.) Three Tours :
In Search of the Picturesque, in Search
of Consolation, and in Search of a
Wife. With the whole of ROWLAND-
SON's droll page Illustrations in Colours
and a Life of the Author by J. C.
HOTTEN. Med. 8vo, cloth extra, 7s. 6d.

Taine's History of English
Literature. Translated by HENRY
VAN LAUN. Four Vols., small 8vo,
cloth boards, 30s.—POPULAR EDITION,
Two Vols., crown 8vo, cloth extra, 15s.

Taylor (Dr. J. E., F.L.S.), Works
by :
The Sagacity and Morality of
Plants : A Sketch of the Life and
Conduct of the Vegetable Kingdom.
With Coloured Frontispiece and 100
Illusts. Crown 8vo, cl. extra, 7s. 6d.
Our Common British Fossils, and
Where to Find Them. With nu-
merous Illustrations. Crown 8vo,
cloth extra, 7s. 6d.

Taylor's (Bayard) Diversions
of the Echo Club : Burlesques of
Modern Writers. Post 8vo, cl. limp, 2s.

Taylor's (Tom) Historical
Dramas : "Clancarty," "Jeanne
Darc," "'Twixt Axe and Crown,"
"The Fool's Revenge," "Arkwright's
Wife," "Anne Boleyn," "Plot and
Passion." One Vol., crown 8vo, cloth
extra, 7s. 6d.
*** The Plays may also be had sepa-
rately, at 1s. each.

Tennyson (Lord) : A Biogra-
phical Sketch. By H. J. JENNINGS.
With a Photograph-Portrait. Crown
8vo, cloth extra, 6s.

Thackerayana : Notes and Anec-
dotes. Illustrated by Hundreds of
Sketches by WILLIAM MAKEPEACE
THACKERAY, depicting Humorous
Incidents in his School-life, and
Favourite Characters in the books of
his every-day reading. With Coloured
Frontispiece. Cr. 8vo, cl. extra, 7s. 6d.

Thomas (Bertha), Novels by.
Crown 8vo, cloth extra, 3s. 6d. each
post 8vo, illustrated boards, 2s. each.
Cressida.
Proud Maisie
The Violin-Player.

Thomas (M.).—A Fight for Life :
A Novel. By W. MOY THOMAS. Post
8vo, illustrated boards, 2s.

Thomson's Seasons and Castle
of Indolence. With a Biographical
and Critical Introduction by ALLAN
CUNNINGHAM, and over 50 fine Illustrations on Steel and Wood. Crown 8vo,
cloth extra, gilt edges, 7s. 6d.

Thornbury (Walter), Works by
Haunted London. Edited by ED-
WARD WALFORD, M.A. With Illus-
trations by F. W. FAIRHOLT, F.S.A.
Crown 8vo, cloth extra, 7s. 6d.
The Life and Correspondence of
J. M. W. Turner. Founded upon
Letters and Papers furnished by his
Friends and fellow Academicians.
With numerous Illusts. in Colours,
facsimiled from Turner's Original
Drawings. Cr. 8vo, cl. extra, 7s. 6d.
Old Stories Re-told. Post 8vo, cloth
limp, 2s. 6d.
Tales for the Marines. Post 8vo,
illustrated boards, 2s.

Timbs (John), Works by :
The History of Clubs and Club Life
in London. With Anecdotes of its
Famous Coffee-houses, Hostelries,
and Taverns. With numerous Illus-
trations. Cr. 8vo, cloth extra, 7s. 6d.
English Eccentrics and Eccen-
tricities : Stories of Wealth and
Fashion, Delusions, Impostures, and
Fanatic Missions, Strange Sights
and Sporting Scenes, Eccentric
Artists, Theatrical Folks, Men of
Letters, &c. With nearly 50 Illusts.
Crown 8vo, cloth extra, 7s. 6d.

Torrens. — The Marquess
Wellesley, Architect of Empire. An
Historic Portrait. By W. M. TOR-
RENS, M.P. Demy 8vo, cloth extra, 14s.

Trollope (Anthony), Novels by :
Crown 8vo, cloth extra, 3s. 6d. each
post 8vo, illustrated boards, 2s. each.
The Way We Live Now.
The American Senator.
Kept in the Dark.
Frau Frohmann.
Marion Fay.
Mr. Scarborough's Family.
The Land-Leaguers.

Post 8vo, illustrated boards, 2s. each.
The Golden Lion of Granpere.
John Caldigate.

Trollope (Frances E.), Novels by
Crown 8vo, cloth extra, 3s. 6d.; post 8vo, illustrated boards, 2s.
> Like Ships upon the Sea.
> Mabel's Progress.
> Anne Furness.

Trollope (T. A.).—Diamond Cut Diamond, and other Stories. By T. Adolphus Trollope. Cr. 8vo, cl. ex., 3s. 6d.; post 8vo, illust. boards, 2s.

Trowbridge.—Farnell's Folly: A Novel. By J. T. Trowbridge. Two Vols., crown 8vo, 12s.

Turgenieff (Ivan), &c. Stories from Foreign Novelists. Post 8vo, illustrated boards, 2s.

Tytler (Sarah), Novels by:
Crown 8vo, cloth extra, 3s. 6d. each; post 8vo, illustrated boards, 2s. each.
> What She Came Through.
> The Bride's Pass.

> Saint Mungo's City. Crown 8vo, cloth extra, 3s. 6d.
> Beauty and the Beast. Three Vols., crown 8vo, 31s. 6d.

Tytler (C. C. Fraser-). — Mistress Judith: A Novel. By C. C. Fraser-Tytler. Cr. 8vo, cloth extra, 3s. 6d.; post 8vo, illust. boards, 2s.

Van Laun.—History of French Literature. By Henry Van Laun. Complete in Three Vols., demy 8vo, cloth boards, 7s. 6d. each.

Villari. — A Double Bond: A Story. By Linda Villari. Fcap. 8vo, picture cover, 1s.

Walcott.— Church Work and Life in English Minsters; and the English Student's Monasticon. By the Rev. Mackenzie E. C. Walcott, B.D. Two Vols., crown 8vo, cloth extra, with Map and Ground-Plans, 14s.

Walford (Edw., M.A.), Works by:
The County Families of the United Kingdom. Containing Notices of the Descent, Birth, Marriage, Education, &c., of more than 12,000 distinguished Heads of Families, their Heirs Apparent or Presumptive, the Offices they hold or have held, their Town and Country Addresses, Clubs, &c. Twenty-fifth Annual Edition, for 1885, cloth, full gilt, 50s.

The Shilling Peerage (1885). Containing an Alphabetical List of the House of Lords, Dates of Creation, Lists of Scotch and Irish Peers, Addresses, &c. 32mo, cloth, 1s. Published annually.

Walford's (Edw., M.A.) Works, con.—
The Shilling Baronetage (1885). Containing an Alphabetical List of the Baronets of the United Kingdom, short Biographical Notices, Dates of Creation, Addresses, &c. 32mo, cloth, 1s. Published annually.

The Shilling Knightage (1885). Containing an Alphabetical List of the Knights of the United Kingdom, short Biographical Notices, Dates of Creation, Addresses, &c. 32mo, cloth, 1s. Published annually.

The Shilling House of Commons (1885). Containing a List of all the Members of the British Parliament, their Town and Country Addresses, &c. 32mo, cloth, 1s. Published annually.

The Complete Peerage, Baronetage, Knightage, and House of Commons (1885). In One Volume, royal 32mo, cloth extra, gilt edges, 5s. Published annually.

Haunted London. By Walter Thornbury. Edited by Edward Walford, M.A. With Illustrations by F. W. Fairholt, F.S.A. Crown 8vo, cloth extra, 7s. 6d.

Walton and Cotton's Complete Angler; or, The Contemplative Man's Recreation; being a Discourse of Rivers, Fishponds, Fish and Fishing, written by Izaak Walton; and Instructions how to Angle for a Trout or Grayling in a clear Stream, by Charles Cotton. With Original Memoirs and Notes by Sir Harris Nicolas, and 61 Copperplate Illustrations. Large crown 8vo, cloth antique, 7s. 6d.

Wanderer's Library, The:
Crown 8vo, cloth extra, 3s. 6d. each.
Wanderings in Patagonia; or, Life among the Ostrich Hunters. By Julius Beerbohm. Illustrated.
Camp Notes: Stories of Sport and Adventure in Asia, Africa, and America. By Frederick Boyle.
Savage Life. By Frederick Boyle.
Merrie England in the Olden Time. By George Daniel. With Illustrations by Robt. Cruikshank.
Circus Life and Circus Celebrities. By Thomas Frost.
The Lives of the Conjurers. By Thomas Frost.
The Old Showmen and the Old London Fairs. By Thomas Frost.
Low-Life Deeps. An Account of the Strange Fish to be found there. By James Greenwood.
The Wilds of London. By James Greenwood.
Tunis: The Land and the People. By the Chevalier de Hesse-Wartegg. With 22 Illustrations.

Wanderer's Library, The, *continued—*

The Life and Adventures of a Cheap Jack. By One of the Fraternity. Edited by Charles Hindley.

The World Behind the Scenes. By Percy Fitzgerald.

Tavern Anecdotes and Sayings: Including the Origin of Signs, and Reminiscences connected with Taverns, Coffee Houses, Clubs, &c. By Charles Hindley. With Illusts.

The Genial Showman: Life and Adventures of Artemus Ward. By E. P. Hingston. With a Frontispiece.

The Story of the London Parks. By Jacob Larwood. With Illusts.

London Characters. By Henry Mayhew. Illustrated.

Seven Generations of Executioners: Memoirs of the Sanson Family (1688 to 1847). Edited by Henry Sanson.

Summer Cruising in the South Seas. By C. Warren Stoddard. Illustrated by Wallis Mackay.

Warner.—A Roundabout Journey. By Charles Dudley Warner, Author of "My Summer in a Garden." Crown 8vo, cloth extra, **6s.**

Warrants, &c. :—

Warrant to Execute Charles I. An exact Facsimile, with the Fifty-nine Signatures, and corresponding Seals. Carefully printed on paper to imitate the Original, 22 in. by 14 in. Price **2s.**

Warrant to Execute Mary Queen of Scots. An exact Facsimile, including the Signature of Queen Elizabeth, and a Facsimile of the Great Seal. Beautifully printed on paper to imitate the Original MS. Price **2s.**

Magna Charta. An exact Facsimile of the Original Document in the British Museum, printed on fine plate paper, nearly 3 feet long by 2 feet wide, with the Arms and Seals emblazoned in Gold and Colours. Price **5s.**

The Roll of Battle Abbey; or, A List of the Principal Warriors who came over from Normandy with William the Conqueror, and Settled in this Country, A.D. 1066-7. With the principal Arms emblazoned in Gold and Colours. Price **5s.**

Weather, How to Foretell the, with the Pocket Spectroscope. By F. W. Cory, M.R.C.S. Eng., F.R.Met. Soc., &c. With 10 Illustrations. Crown 8vo, **1s.** ; cloth, **1s. 6d.**

Westropp.—Handbook of Pottery and Porcelain; or, History of those Arts from the Earliest Period. By Hodder M. Westropp. With numerous Illustrations, and a List of Marks. Crown 8vo, cloth limp, **4s. 6d.**

Whistler v. Ruskin: Art and Art Critics. By J. A. Macneill Whistler. 7th Edition, sq. 8vo, **1s.**

White's Natural History of Selborne. Edited, with Additions, by Thomas Brown, F.L.S. Post 8vo, cloth limp, **2s.**

Williams (W. Mattieu, F.R.A.S.), Works by:

Science Notes. See the Gentleman's Magazine. **1s.** Monthly.

Science in Short Chapters. Crown 8vo, cloth extra, **7s. 6d.**

A Simple Treatise on Heat. Crown 8vo, cloth limp, with Illusts., **2s. 6d.**

The Chemistry of Cookery. Crown 8vo, cloth extra, **6s.**

Wilson (Dr. Andrew, F.R.S.E.), Works by:

Chapters on Evolution: A Popular History of the Darwinian and Allied Theories of Development. Second Edition. Crown 8vo, cloth extra, with 259 Illustrations, **7s. 6d.**

Leaves from a Naturalist's Notebook. Post 8vo, cloth limp, **2s. 6d.**

Leisure-Time Studies, chiefly Biological. Third Edition, with a New Preface. Crown 8vo, cloth extra, with Illustrations, **6s.**

Winter (J. S.), Stories by : Crown 8vo, cloth extra, **3s. 6d.** each. post 8vo, illustrated boards, **2s.** each.

Cavalry Life. | Regimental Legends.

Women of the Day: A Biographical Dictionary of Notable Contemporaries. By Frances Hays. Crown 8vo, cloth extra, **5s.**

Wood.—Sabina: A Novel. By Lady Wood. Post 8vo, illust. bds., **2s.**

Words, Facts, and Phrases : A Dictionary of Curious, Quaint, and Out-of-the-Way Matters. By Eliezer Edwards. New and cheaper issue, cr. 8vo, cl. ex., **7s. 6d.** ; half-bound, **9s.**

Wright (Thomas), Works by :

Caricature History of the Georges. (The House of Hanover.) With 400 Pictures, Caricatures, Squibs, Broadsides, Window Pictures, &c. Crown 8vo, cloth extra, **7s. 6d.**

History of Caricature and of the Grotesque in Art, Literature, Sculpture, and Painting. Profusely Illustrated by F. W. Fairholt, F.S.A. Large post 8vo, cl. ex., **7s. 6d.**

Yates (Edmund), Novels by : Post 8vo, illustrated boards, **2s.** each.

Castaway. | The Forlorn Hope. Land at Last.

NOVELS BY THE BEST AUTHORS.

WILKIE COLLINS'S NEW NOVEL.

"I Say No." By WILKIE COLLINS. Three Vols., crown 8vo.

Mrs. CASHEL HOEY'S NEW NOVEL.

The Lover's Creed. By Mrs. CASHEL HOEY, Author of "The Blossoming of an Aloe," &c. With 12 Illustrations by P. MACNAB. Three Vols., cr. 8vo.

SARAH TYTLER'S NEW NOVEL.

Beauty and the Beast. By SARAH TYTLER, Author of "The Bride's Pass," "Saint Mungo's City," "Citoyenne Jacqueline," &c. Three Vols., cr. 8vo.

NEW NOVELS BY CHAS. GIBBON.

By Mead and Stream. By CHARLES GIBBON, Author of "Robin Gray," "The Golden Shaft," "Queen of the Meadow," &c. Three Vols., cr. 8vo.

A Hard Knot. By CHARLES GIBBON. Three Vols., crown 8vo.

Heart's Delight. By CHARLES GIBBON. Three Vols., crown 8vo. [*Shortly.*

NEW NOVEL BY CECIL POWER.

Philistia. By CECIL POWER. Three Vols., crown 8vo.

NEW NOVEL BY THE AUTHOR OF "VALENTINA."

Gerald. By ELEANOR C. PRICE. Three Vols., crown 8vo.

BASIL'S NEW NOVEL.

"The Wearing of the Green." By BASIL, Author of "Love the Debt," "A Drawn Game," &c. Three Vols., crown 8vo.

NEW NOVEL BY J. T. TROW-BRIDGE.

Farnell's Folly. Two Vols., crown 8vo, 12s.

Mrs. PIRKIS' NEW NOVEL.

Lady Lovelace. By C. L. PIRKIS, Author of "A Very Opal." Three Vols., crown 8vo.

THE PICCADILLY NOVELS.

Popular Stories by the Best Authors. LIBRARY EDITIONS, many Illustrated, crown 8vo, cloth extra, 3s. 6d. each.

BY MRS. ALEXANDER.

Maid, Wife, or Widow?

BY BASIL.

A Drawn Game.

BY W. BESANT & JAMES RICE.

Ready-Money Mortiboy.
My Little Girl.
The Case of Mr. Lucraft.
This Son of Vulcan.
With Harp and Crown.
The Golden Butterfly.
By Celia's Arbour.
The Monks of Thelema.
'Twas in Trafalgar's Bay.
The Seamy Side.
The Ten Years' Tenant.
The Chaplain of the Fleet.
Dorothy Forster.

BY WALTER BESANT.

All Sorts and Conditions of Men.
The Captains' Room.
All in a Garden Fair.
Dorothy Forster.

BY ROBERT BUCHANAN.

A Child of Nature.
God and the Man.
The Shadow of the Sword.
The Martyrdom of Madeline.
Love Me for Ever.
Annan Water. | The New Abelard.
Matt. | Foxglove Manor.

BY MRS. H. LOVETT CAMERON.

Deceivers Ever. | Juliet's Guardian.

BY MORTIMER COLLINS.

Sweet Anne Page.
Transmigration.
From Midnight to Midnight.

MORTIMER & FRANCES COLLINS.

Blacksmith and Scholar.
The Village Comedy.
You Play me False.

BY WILKIE COLLINS.

Antonina. | New Magdalen.
Basil. | The Frozen Deep.
Hide and Seek. | The Law and the
The Dead Secret. | Lady.
Queen of Hearts. | The Two Destinies
My Miscellanies. | Haunted Hotel.
Woman in White. | The Fallen Leaves
The Moonstone. | Jezebel's Daughter
Man and Wife. | The Black Robe.
Poor Miss Finch. | Heart and Science
Miss or Mrs.?

BY DUTTON COOK.

Paul Foster's Daughter.

BY WILLIAM CYPLES.

Hearts of Gold.

BY ALPHONSE DAUDET.

Port Salvation.

BY JAMES DE MILLE.

A Castle in Spain.

Piccadilly Novels, *continued*—
  BY J. LEITH DERWENT.
Our Lady of Tears. | Circe's Lovers.
  BY M. BETHAM-EDWARDS.
Felicia. | Kitty.
  BY MRS. ANNIE EDWARDES.
Archie Lovell.
  BY R. E. FRANCILLON.
Olympia. | One by One.
Queen Cophetua. | A Real Queen.
  Prefaced by Sir BARTLE FRERE.
Pandurang Hari.
  BY EDWARD GARRETT.
The Capel Girls.
  BY CHARLES GIBBON.
Robin Gray. | For Lack of Gold.
In Love and War.
What will the World Say?
For the King.
In Honour Bound.
Queen of the Meadow.
In Pastures Green.
The Flower of the Forest.
A Heart's Problem.
The Braes of Yarrow.
The Golden Shaft.
Of High Degree.
Fancy Free. | Loving a Dream.
  BY HALL CAINE.
The Shadow of a Crime.
  BY THOMAS HARDY.
Under the Greenwood Tree.
  BY JULIAN HAWTHORNE.
Garth.
Ellice Quentin.
Sebastian Strome.
Prince Saroni's Wife.
Dust. | Fortune's Fool.
Beatrix Randolph.
Miss Cadogna.
  BY SIR A. HELPS.
Ivan de Biron.
  BY MRS. ALFRED HUNT.
Thornicroft's Model
The Leaden Casket.
Self-Condemned.
  BY JEAN INGELOW.
Fated to be Free.
  BY HARRIETT JAY.
The Queen of Connaught
The Dark Colleen.
  BY HENRY KINGSLEY.
Number Seventeen.
Oakshott Castle

Piccadilly Novels, *continued*—
  BY E. LYNN LINTON.
Patricia Kemball.
Atonement of Leam Dundas.
The World Well Lost.
Under which Lord?
With a Silken Thread.
The Rebel of the Family
"My Love!" | Ione.
  BY HENRY W. LUCY.
Gideon Fleyce.
  BY JUSTIN McCARTHY, M.P.
The Waterdale Neighbours.
My Enemy's Daughter.
Linley Rochford. | A Fair Saxon.
Dear Lady Disdain.
Miss Misanthrope.
Donna Quixote.
The Comet of a Season.
Maid of Athens.
  BY GEORGE MAC DONALD, LL.D.
Paul Faber, Surgeon.
Thomas Wingfold, Curate.
  BY MRS. MACDONELL.
Quaker Cousins.
  BY KATHARINE S. MACQUOID.
Lost Rose | The Evil Eye.
  BY FLORENCE MARRYAT.
Open! Sesame! | Written in Fire.
  BY JEAN MIDDLEMASS.
Touch and Go.
  BY D. CHRISTIE MURRAY.
Life's Atonement. | Coals of Fire.
Joseph's Coat. | Val Strange.
A Model Father. | Hearts.
By the Gate of the Sea
The Way of the World.
A Bit of Human Nature.
  BY MRS. OLIPHANT.
Whiteladies.
  BY MARGARET A. PAUL.
Gentle and Simple.
  BY JAMES PAYN.
Lost Sir Massing- | Carlyon's Year.
  berd. | A Confidentia
Best of Husbands | Agent.
Fallen Fortunes. | From Exile.
Halves. | A Grape from a
Walter's Word. | Thorn.
What He Cost Her | For Cash Only.
Less Black than | Some Private
  We're Painted. | Views.
By Proxy. | Kit: A Memory.
High Spirits. | The Canon's
Under One Roof. | Ward.
  BY E. C. PRICE.
Valentina. | The Foreigners.
Mrs. Lancaster's Rival.

PICCADILLY NOVELS, *continued—*
BY CHARLES READE, D.C.L.
It Is Never Too Late to Mend.
Hard Cash. | Peg Woffington.
Christie Johnstone.
Griffith Gaunt. | Foul Play.
The Double Marriage.
Love Me Little, Love Me Long.
The Cloister and the Hearth.
The Course of True Love.
The Autobiography of a Thief.
Put Yourself in His Place.
A Terrible Temptation.
The Wandering Heir. | A Simpleton.
A Woman-Hater. | Readiana.
Singleheart and Doubleface.
The Jilt. [male.
Good Stories of Men and other Ani-
BY MRS. J. H. RIDDELL.
Her Mother's Darling.
Prince of Wales's Garden-Party.
Weird Stories.
BY F. W. ROBINSON.
Women are Strange.
The Hands of Justice.
BY JOHN SAUNDERS.
Bound to the Wheel.
Guy Waterman. | Two Dreamers.
One Against the World.
The Lion in the Path.
BY KATHARINE SAUNDERS.
Joan Merryweather.
Margaret and Elizabeth.
Gideon's Rock. | Heart Salvage.
The High Mills. | Sebastian.

PICCADILLY NOVELS, *continued—*
BY T. W. SPEIGHT.
The Mysteries of Heron Dyke.
BY R. A. STERNDALE.
The Afghan Knife.
BY BERTHA THOMAS.
Proud Maisie. | Cressida.
The Violin-Player.
BY ANTHONY TROLLOPE.
The Way we Live Now.
The American Senator
Frau Frohmann. | Marion Fay.
Kept in the Dark.
Mr. Scarborough's Family.
The Land-Leaguers.
BY FRANCES E. TROLLOPE.
Like Ships upon the Sea.
Anne Furness.
Mabel's Progress.
BY T. A. TROLLOPE.
Diamond Cut Diamond
By IVAN TURGENIEFF and Others.
Stories from Foreign Novelists.
BY SARAH TYTLER.
What She Came Through.
The Bride's Pass.
Saint Mungo's City.
BY C. C. FRASER-TYTLER.
Mistress Judith.
BY J. S. WINTER.
Cavalry Life.
Regimental Legends.

CHEAP EDITIONS OF POPULAR NOVELS.
Post 8vo, illustrated boards, 2s. each.

BY EDMOND ABOUT.
The Fellah.
BY HAMILTON AÏDÉ.
Carr of Carrlyon. | Confidences
BY MRS. ALEXANDER.
Maid, Wife, or Widow?
Valerie's Fate.
BY SHELSLEY BEAUCHAMP.
Grantley Grange.
BY W. BESANT & JAMES RICE
Ready-Money Mortiboy.
With Harp and Crown.
This Son of Vulcan. | My Little Girl.
The Case of Mr. Lucraft.
The Golden Butterfly.
By Celia's Arbour.
The Monks of Thelema.

By BESANT AND RICE, *continued—*
'Twas in Trafalgar's Bay.
The Seamy Side.
The Ten Years' Tenant.
The Chaplain of the Fleet.
BY WALTER BESANT.
All Sorts and Conditions of Men.
The Captains' Room.
All in a Garden Fair.
BY FREDERICK BOYLE.
Camp Notes. | Savage Life.
Chronicles of No-man's Land.
BY BRET HARTE.
An Heiress of Red Dog.
The Luck of Roaring Camp.
Californian Stories.
Gabriel Conroy. | Flip.

CHEAP POPULAR NOVELS, *continued—*
BY ROBERT BUCHANAN.

The Shadow of the Sword.	TheMartyrdomof Madeline.
A Child of Nature.	Annan Water.
God and the Man.	The New Abelard.
Love Me for Ever.	

BY MRS. BURNETT.
Surly Tim.

BY MRS. LOVETT CAMERON.

Deceivers Ever.	Juliet's Guardian.

BY MACLAREN COBBAN.
The Cure of Souls.

BY C. ALLSTON COLLINS.
The Bar Sinister.

BY WILKIE COLLINS.

Antonina.	The New Magdalen.
Basil.	
Hide and Seek.	The Frozen Deep.
The Dead Secret.	Law and the Lady.
Queen of Hearts.	TheTwo Destinies
My Miscellanies.	Haunted Hotel.
Woman In White.	TheFallen Leaves.
The Moonstone.	Jezebel'sDaughter
Man and Wife.	The Black Robe.
Poor Miss Finch.	Heart and Science
Miss or Mrs. ?	

BY MORTIMER COLLINS.

Sweet Anne Page.	From Midnight to Midnight.
Transmigration.	
A Fight with Fortune.	

MORTIMER & FRANCES COLLINS.

Sweet and Twenty.	Frances.
Blacksmith and Scholar.	
The Village Comedy.	
You Play me False.	

BY DUTTON COOK.

Leo.	Paul Foster's Daughter.

BY WILLIAM CYPLES.
Hearts of Gold.

BY ALPHONSE DAUDET.
The Evangelist; or, Port Salvation.

BY DE MILLE.
A Castle In Spain.

BY J. LEITH DERWENT.

Our Lady of Tears.	Circe's Lovers.

BY CHARLES DICKENS.

Sketches by Boz.	Oliver Twist.
Pickwick Papers.	Nicholas Nickleby

BY MRS. ANNIE EDWARDES.

A Point of Honour.	Archie Lovell.

BY M. BETHAM-EDWARDS.

Felicia.	Kitty.

BY EDWARD EGGLESTON.
Roxy.

CHEAP POPULAR NOVELS, *continued—*
BY PERCY FITZGERALD.

Bella Donna.	Never Forgotten.
The Second Mrs. Tillotson.	
Polly.	
Seventy-five Brooke Street.	
The Lady of Brantome.	

BY ALBANY DE FONBLANQUE.
Filthy Lucre.

BY R. E. FRANCILLON.

Olympia.	Queen Cophetua.
One by One.	A Real Queen.

Prefaced by Sir H. BARTLE FRERE.
Pandurang Harl.

BY HAIN FRISWELL.
One of Two.

BY EDWARD GARRETT
The Capel Girls.

BY CHARLES GIBBON.

Robin Gray.	Queen of the Meadow.
For Lack of Gold.	
What will the World Say ?	The Flower of the Forest.
In Honour Bound.	A Heart's Problem
The Dead Heart.	The Braes of Yarrow.
In Love and War.	
For the King.	The Golden Shaft.
In Pastures Green	Of High Degree.

BY WILLIAM GILBERT.
Dr. Austin's Guests.
The Wizard of the Mountain.
James Duke.

BY JAMES GREENWOOD.
Dick Temple.

BY ANDREW HALLIDAY.
Every-Day Papers.

BY LADY DUFFUS HARDY
Paul Wynter's Sacrifice.

BY THOMAS HARDY.
Under the Greenwood Tree.

BY JULIAN HAWTHORNE.

Garth.	Sebastian Strome
Ellice Quentin.	Dust.
Prince Saroni's Wife.	
Fortune's Fool.	
Beatrix Randolph.	

BY SIR ARTHUR HELPS.
Ivan de Biron.

BY TOM HOOD.
A Golden Heart.

BY MRS. GEORGE HOOPER.
The House of Raby.

BY VICTOR HUGO.
The Hunchback of Notre Dame.

CHEAP POPULAR NOVELS, *continued—*
By CHARLES READE, *continued.*

Griffith Gaunt.
Put Yourself in His Place.
The Double Marriage.
Love Me Little, Love Me Long.
Foul Play.
The Cloister and the Hearth.
The Course of True Love.
Autobiography of a Thief.
A Terrible Temptation.
The Wandering Heir.
A Simpleton. | A Woman-Hater.
Readiana. | The Jilt.
Singleheart and Doubleface.
Good Stories of Men and other Animals.

BY MRS. J. H. RIDDELL.
Her Mother's Darling.
Prince of Wales's Garden Party.
Weird Stories.
The Uninhabited House.
Fairy Water.

BY F. W. ROBINSON.
Women are Strange.
The Hands of Justice.

BY W. CLARK RUSSELL.
Round the Galley Fire.

BY BAYLE ST. JOHN.
A Levantine Family.

BY GEORGE AUGUSTUS SALA.
Gaslight and Daylight.

BY JOHN SAUNDERS.
Bound to the Wheel.
One Against the World.
Guy Waterman.
The Lion in the Path.
Two Dreamers.

BY KATHARINE SAUNDERS.
Joan Merryweather.
Margaret and Elizabeth.
Gideon's Rock.
The High Mills.

BY GEORGE R. SIMS.
Rogues and Vagabonds.

BY ARTHUR SKETCHLEY.
A Match in the Dark.

BY T. W. SPEIGHT.
The Mysteries of Heron Dyke.

BY R. A. STERNDALE.
The Afghan Knife.

BY R. LOUIS STEVENSON.
New Arabian Nights.

BY BERTHA THOMAS.
Cressida. | Proud Maisie.
The Violin-Player.

BY W. MOY THOMAS.
A Fight for Life.

BY WALTER THORNBURY.
Tales for the Marines.

CHEAP POPULAR NOVELS, *continued—*
BY T. ADOLPHUS TROLLOPE.
Diamond Cut Diamond.

BY ANTHONY TROLLOPE.
The Way We Live Now.
The American Senator.
Frau Frohmann.
Marion Fay.
Kept in the Dark.
Mr. Scarborough's Family.
The Land-Leaguers.
The Golden Lion of Granpere.
John Caldigate.

By FRANCES ELEANOR TROLLOPE
Like Ships upon the Sea.
Anne Furness.
Mabel's Progress.

BY IVAN TURGENIEFF, &c.
Stories from Foreign Novelists.

BY MARK TWAIN.
Tom Sawyer.
An Idle Excursion.
A Pleasure Trip on the Continent of Europe.
A Tramp Abroad.
The Stolen White Elephant.

BY C. C. FRASER-TYTLER.
Mistress Judith.

BY SARAH TYTLER.
What She Came Through.
The Bride's Pass.

BY J. S. WINTER.
Cavalry Life. | Regimental Legends.

BY LADY WOOD.
Sabina.

BY EDMUND YATES.
Castaway. | The Forlorn Hope.
Land at Last.

ANONYMOUS
Paul Ferroll.
Why Paul Ferroll Killed his Wife.

Fcap. 8vo, picture covers, 1s. each.
Jeff Briggs's Love Story. By BRET HARTE.
The Twins of Table Mountain. By BRET HARTE.
Mrs. Gainsborough's Diamonds. By JULIAN HAWTHORNE.
Kathleen Mavourneen. By Author of "That Lass o' Lowrie's."
Lindsay's Luck. By the Author of "That Lass o' Lowrie's."
Pretty Polly Pemberton. By the Author of "That Lass o' Lowrie's."
Trooping with Crows. By Mrs. PIRKIS.
The Professor's Wife. By LEONARD GRAHAM.
A Double Bond. By LINDA VILLARI.
Esther's Glove. By R. E. FRANCILLON.
The Garden that Paid the Rent. By TOM JERROLD.